DON'T JUDGE A BOOK BY ITS HOVER

WITCHY EXPO SERVICES MYSTERIES BOOK 1

AMY MCNULTY

Crimson Fox
PUBLISHING

Nimue Toothaker had mastered her Non-Repetitive Charms Course at the age of six. She'd broken the record for flying all around the circumference of Cauldron Cove—home to a thousand witches and warlocks, and frequent host to scores of human guests—at just age fourteen on a hand-me-down broomstick.

What she couldn't handle, even at the age of forty, was typing on one of those human smartphones.

Scold gone well? Like new Roomba?

"What the freckle are you attempting to type there, Nimue?" Gowdie perched on his witch's shoulder, his familiar form of a blue-

scaled miniature dragon allowing him to wrap his spiny tail around her neck like a prickly scarf.

Nimue grit her teeth and tried again. But for all that was good in the world, the dratted thing would not cooperate. "School. Going. Well," she said. As she typed the words and input a space, they transformed on their own. "Like. New. Roomie?" Her voice grew more irritated with each word.

"Who's Naomi?" Gowdie asked in her head, reading the text.

"New. Roomie!" Nimue shouted. "Argh!" She tossed the phone atop her flowery purple comforter. "What nonsense wicked charm are these humans concocting, changing my words like that?"

Gowdie lifted the scale above his sparkling blue eye into an arch. *"It's called AutoCorrect, I believe. So the hip kids tell me."*

"And what hip kids do *you* speak to?" Nimue asked. Though a familiar understood anyone who spoke to them, their responses were only heard telepathically in their witch's or warlock's head—or in another familiar's mind. Magic users could

2

think their sides of conversations back to them, too, but Nimue was at the point where shouting her frustration out loud was doing her some good.

Gowdie arched his scaly back like a cat, digging his taloned feet into Nimue's shoulder for better balance. *"All the young humans love me."* Barely keeping his balance, he lifted a back foot and scratched behind one cat-like ear. *"I'm like a superstar at conventions."*

He was right about that. As her grandmother's assistant, Nimue hardly had time to sit back and enjoy any of Witchy Expo Services's conventions from a guest's perspective, but when she did wander out onto the con floor, all the humans looked her way. It was usually because of the little blue dragon riding on her shoulder or flying in lazy, swooping circles overhead. Familiars were amorphous at birth until they found one form they liked, and then they stuck to it. Gowdie was one of the few who'd insisted on becoming a mythical creature.

"Well, it should be *AutoIncorrect,*" Nimue said as her phone started vibrating.

"That's a Greg joke," said Gowdie, referring to Nimue's human ex-husband.

"It most definitely is *not!*" she protested. But she bit her lip. He was right. Greg had a very "dad" sense of humor, as their daughter called it.

Willow had loved it as a kid, but now he made her groan every time.

She didn't want her daughter to groan at her, too. Willow was only just about to leave her testy teenage years behind her.

"The phone's ringing now," Gowdie pointed out to her.

"Yes, I know." She crossed the room and picked it up, her finger hovering over the green button below the smiling picture of her nineteen-year-old daughter. She pushed it.

The phone kept ringing, its irritating crescendo repetitive and incessant.

Gowdie pointed a dragon talon down toward the screen. *"You have to swipe it."*

Nimue's eyes bulged. "Why in the world can I not just *push* it?"

"Swipe," said Gowdie, mimicking the

movement in the air over the phone. *"Swipe it. Swipe—"*

"I know to swipe it!"

"And the call ended." Gowdie put his foot back on Nimue's shoulder, the two of them just staring down at the screen indicating Willow's missed call.

Mom. A text message from Willow popped up. *Just checking in. I don't under-stand your message, but I'm fine.*

Sighing, Nimue tossed the phone back on the bed, pulled her smooth, cherrywood wand out of its holster on her belt, and cast her single use of the Communication Charm for the day. "Hi, sweet pea," she said as a shimmering image of Willow hovered into view.

"Mom!" Willow jumped in place. Her long, black hair, so much like her mother's —minus the occasional wisp of gray—was pulled into a messy bun atop her head, and she had on a baggy gray sweatshirt and black jersey pants that made her ashen complexion pop even paler. She was seated at her dorm room desk, chopsticks with dangling ramen noodles halfway to her mouth.

Gasping, she put the round cup down on her desk. "I told you not to Communication Charm me at human school!"

Nimue winced and slid her wand back into its holster. "I know that, dear, and I'll definitely never do so out of the blue—"

"This was *definitely* out of the blue," said Willow, rolling her wide, blue eyes that also resembled her mother's. There was almost nothing about her that favored her father, except, perhaps, and Nimue knew Willow would find this embarrassing, their snorting laugh.

"But I texted first, and you called me—" Nimue started.

"Yeah. That's *why* you have the human phone. To contact me like Daddy would." She tucked a stray hair behind her ear, refusing to look straight ahead at the hovering image of her mother in front of her.

"I'm sorry," Nimue said, digging her nails into her palm at the mention of how she'd failed to stack up to her daughter's father.

Nimue had done the human world. She'd tried to fit in.

She'd moved back twelve years ago and taken Willow with her during weekdays for half the years and weekends on the other half. Greg lived just outside of Cauldron Cove in the nearest human town, Huntsville. But *nearest* human town hadn't been near enough for Nimue.

There was a different kind of life on offer here at home.

Something Willow, child of witch and human man, knew too well.

Her daughter sighed as she rapped a white ruler against her desk. "You're lucky Veronica isn't here to see you."

Veronica. New roommate? Now Nimue felt like she was getting somewhere.

"So you're liking the human roommate?" Nimue asked hopefully.

Willow smiled, her defenses melting. "She's great! I mean, I miss Cassie, but I was serious when I said I wanted to commit to half a human world education and half a witch one." She shrugged. "I like both sides of myself, you know?"

Behind her on the bottom bunk of a rather small twin-sized bed, Reoch, a seemingly innocuous white beagle puppy, lifted his head and stared at the floating Communication Charm projection. Willow turned and spoke to him, having heard her familiar's voice in her head.

"Of course I'll never leave all of my witch life behind," said Willow, going over to the bed to give Reoch a scratch under her chin. The human college had granted Willow an exemption to their no-animals-on-campus rule so she could have a familiar with her. It was impossible to go more than a few minutes without being within a few feet of one's familiar, so both Nimue and Greg had fought hard to make sure the admissions office understood their daughter's needs if they hoped to have her study there.

Reoch was hardly truly an "animal" regardless.

"Are you keeping your wand with you?" Nimue asked. "At all times?"

Willow shook her head. "Yes, Mom."

"I don't see a holster for it on that outfit."

Willow *tsked* and walked over to her desk, holding up the white ruler. It *was* a familiar color. "I charm it into this when I'm heading to class. Don't want humans to notice it and ask me to do tricks."

Willow's wand. The one thing standing between her having access to magic and being entirely helpless like a human in the face of an emergency and she'd disguised it as *a ruler*. Most witches and warlocks never changed their wands' shapes like that. Who needed common human tools when spells would do? But it was certainly possible.

Admittedly, Nimue had turned hers into a bookmark once when she couldn't find where hers had slipped off to and the doorbell had rung.

She couldn't exactly chastise Willow for keeping hers hidden as a human object.

"So," Willow said, sliding her disguised wand under a textbook's cover, "next time you need me and it's not a day we've arranged for a Communication Charm, you'll text instead?"

"I tried to text you, honey. I'm just all thumbs." Nimue wriggled her hands in front of her to demonstrate.

Willow shook her head, but the corner of

her lips was cracking into a smile. "You lived in the human world for eight years, Mom. How come you still bumble around every little unique aspect of it?"

"Phones were *not* that sophisticated when I was your age!" Nimue protested. "Your father and I could text, but we had an *actual* little keyboard to type on, for one thing. And forget browsing the online network with one!"

"The Internet," Willow corrected.

"The Internet." Nimue knew that. It was mostly Soren—*ugh, Ren*—who handled the human marketing efforts, but the Internet was a huge part of that.

Other witches and warlocks weren't impressed by Witchy Expo Services's magical convention offerings. Which made humans—who were always eager to experience magic firsthand—the sole clientele.

"Okay, Mom," said Willow, picking up her ramen cup and helping herself to another mouthful. "You're hopeless. I get it," she said with a full mouth.

Gowdie chuckled, the sound like a little

tittering chirp that Nimue knew even Willow could hear.

Nimue frowned, though, her focus on something else entirely. "Tell me you're eating better than that most days—"

"*Mom.*" Willow put her cup down. "I'm a grown-up. I know witch lifespans can make you lose sight of that—"

"I know that! I left Cauldron Cove at twenty myself! All by myself!"

Willow nodded politely, like she'd heard the story a thousand times before. Because she had. Gregory Taylor had attended a Health & Wellness Seminar at the Cauldron Cove Convention Center and Nimue had been helping her grandmother out as part of her witch studies, just like Willow herself had done for the school year before this one.

Nimue had fallen in love with the tall, broad human, and he'd come back and gifted her a BlackBerry phone—not edible, as Nimue had sadly soon figured out. They'd texted and called, but mostly called, and she'd even used up her daily Communication Charm to chat on occasion. The witch world had been far head of the human world when it came to face-to-face long-distance chatting, though Nimue knew Willow and her dad could do that now, too, with these overly complicated smartphones.

Greg had asked her to marry him and she hadn't looked back.

Until a few years later when that was all she'd been able to do.

Now, at least, both Greg and she were happier. And they got along great, both for Willow's sake and because they enjoyed each other's company as long-time friends. On occasion. Greg had human wife Jenna now, and they were often traveling.

And Nimue had Witchy Expo Services.

"Well, my point is, please let me make my own junk-food mistakes, okay?" Willow picked up her cup and drank it back like a cup of hot coffee.

Nimue briefly closed her eyes and took a breath, letting her baby's mistake go.

As far as mistakes went, that was nothing. Willow was a good kid.

A good adult.

A good daughter.

"So," said Willow, slapping her empty

cup on the desk in front of her. "Dorm life recap. Daddy and Jenna left early this morning, and it didn't take us too long to unload everything yesterday." Willow stood and gestured around the room. Nimue recognized the plush silverback gorilla Willow had wanted from the Huntsville Zoo at age three, which she had loved to pieces—literal patchwork tufts of fur—but had never wanted to fix with magic. Reoch was curled up beside it on the bed's pillow. Other bits of Willow's childhood were wedged into the small, concrete space, the dismal gray walls spiced up with posters, including one of a witch's cottage in a forest alight with sparkling fireflies. It was a depiction of the founder of Cauldron Cove's home, complete with the giant black iron cauldron the original Bessa Toothaker had kept beside her cottage—and had eventually melted with a brew right into the very ground to form the magic sustaining the town.

Nimue smiled at Cauldron Cove's inclusion in her daughter's new little home for herself.

"Mom, are you *crying*?"

Nimue realized she was. She laughed and wiped a tear away as Gowdie gently dabbed her other cheek with the softer-membrane tip of his tail. "I'm happy for you, darling."

Willow beamed. "Thank you. Classes start tomorrow, but I'm already making friends. Veronica invited me to a party tonight at her boyfriend's fraternity."

Nimue opened her mouth to protest but bit her tongue.

Willow chuckled. "No worries. I said *no*. I want to be well rested for tomorrow."

"Chip off the old block, that one," Gowdie said into Nimue's head. *"Responsible to a fault."*

"And far more adaptable and smarter," added Nimue.

"What was that?" Willow asked, stroking Reoch's furry head.

"Just complimenting my lovely, intelligent daughter to Gowdie," Nimue said, tickling her dragon familiar under his chin. He purred into the touch, nuzzling the top of Nimue's head.

Willow reddened and sat down beside

her own familiar. "Well, thank you, Mom. I have you and Daddy and Jenna to look up to. Good role models."

If Nimue could have reached through the charm's projection to hug her daughter, she would have. She was just so perfectly sweet.

Which was why she had to trust that she'd be okay out there, a year in the human world, hundreds of miles from both her homes. She was far from the only witch or warlock to mingle with humans, and she knew not to draw too much attention to her magic powers. It'd be different if she set up a business, got licensed through the International Magic Guild. But that wasn't necessary if she just wanted to sample everyday human life.

"Say *hi* to Great-Grandma for me," said Willow. Most people didn't intimately know their great-grandmothers like Willow did, but being a witch had its perks. Bernadette Toothaker was town founder Bessa's daughter and was two hundred and ninety years old.

"She sends her love," Nimue assured

her. "And apparently, she wants us all to come in this evening because she has some big news."

"Oh?" Willow's eyes sparkled. "Sounds intriguing."

"I'm sure it's just her getting her ducks in a row before Bookshop Con next week," Nimue said, doing a quick onceover in the mirror to make sure she was ready to go.

"Hmm, I wonder," said Willow.

Nimue stopped and stared at her daughter. "You know something."

Willow shrugged. "Great-Grandma may have said something to me last week after I finished my summer stint with Witchy ExS." People behind the scenes often abbreviated Witchy Expo Services that way.

"Such as?"

Gowdie grumbled. *"She's no snitch."*

"I'm no snitch," Willow said almost at the same time Gowdie did.

Well, that didn't fill Nimue with a well of confidence. She held her arm out for Gowdie to climb down and stared him in the eye, too.

He broke under her glare and immediately started licking the thin membranes of his wings with his barbed tongue, ideal for grooming. *"Familiars talk,"* he said, and familiars could communicate with one another, that was true.

But as for what they'd said… Nimue would just have to wait until she got to work to find out.

CHAPTER TWO

September brought mild breezes and stepid temperatures to Cauldron Cove, Lake Salem offering a cooling effect on the early Midwest fall weather. Of course, there were witches and warlocks on weather duty, too. Nature's whims were important, but if a client paid extra for good weather for their convention, they received it.

Winter sports enthusiasts got a kick out of being able to ski down Hemlock Hill even during summer events.

Bookshop Con and fall weather went together just fine, so the weather witches would only need to be on the lookout for disruptive weather as the week approached.

Nimue found the crisp, mild air of early evening refreshing as she flew along the lane to the convention center, Gowdie flapping his wings at her side.

She waved at short, pink-haired Sylvie Palmer closing up her Sylvie's Sweets Bakery early on Sunday evening. Nimue worked with her husband, Herne, at Witchy ExS.

But tourism, mostly brought in via the conventions, really benefited the entire town. Some con-goers loved just walking the cobblestone streets of Cauldron Cove, no cars allowed outside of the town's giant parking lot at the outskirts leading to the highway. Special flying carriages were made available to all not up for the walk, powered by three flying broomsticks.

Nimue waved at Klaus Fowler, driving one of those carriages full of tourists right past her down the lane.

"Good evening," the elder warlock said, tipping his chauffer's hat as both Nimue and his carriage came to a stop.

"Evening," she responded, watching the tourists whisper amongst each other as the children in the carriage noticed Gowdie flying overhead.

Klaus's familiar, which took the form of a bright yellow mouse, rode on the tip of one of the broomsticks' brushes and probably hadn't caused quite a ruckus.

"Morph headed over to the center an hour ago," said Klaus while they waited for the dangling lantern light to glow green and indicate they were allowed to cross. Broomsticks and carriages flew past in the other directions, but it was Sunday, and even tourists tended to prefer a quiet evening at the local hotel, so traffic was fairly light.

"Am I late?" Nimue asked, a sudden rise of panic filling a pit in her stomach.

"Of course not." Klaus winked and the floating lantern glowed green. "Morpheus just thinks he has to always be early." He took off, taking a right toward the small, sandy beach this side of Lake Salem.

He was right about that. Morpheus Fowler was particular to a fault when it came to convention setup and cleanup. He'd probably been at the convention center for most of the weekend, prepping for

Bookshop Con, which was set to start the following Tuesday and last through next weekend.

The general public tended to prefer cons from Thursday or Friday through Sunday, but there were plenty of industry events that managed to attract professionals on business trips throughout the week.

There was hardly more than a few days between most cons for the witches and warlocks of Witchy ExS to rest, but they always managed to schedule smaller events between the larger ones, which occurred about once a month.

Still, Bernadette Toothaker insisted on some time between cons. Even with magic, cleanup and setup took some time. And "a witch or warlock needs a life outside of work, too," Nimue's grandma had always said.

Nimue had once believed that wholeheartedly. Now with her empty nest, she struggled to find much else to do. She got up, went to work, went home, read, took a bath, went to sleep. Rinse and repeat.

At the end of the lane, the Cauldron

Cove Convention Center—sometimes called "the Bessa"—rose higher and higher into Nimue's sight.

Her breath caught at the way the setting sun reflected off of its rows and rows of glassy windows. The trees that had once surrounded Bessa Toothaker's home had grown to act as pillars to the four-story structure that covered several football fields' worth of horizontal space. Between sleek, modern windows and metal beam reinforcements, the witchy woods that had once stood on these grounds grew up and around the building—even inside the building. Above the structure, thousands of glittering candle-lit lanterns grew brighter as the sun dimmed.

Electricity was available—and well-used—inside the building, of course, but sometimes the clientele just appreciated those little touches.

"I smell a cat," said Gowdie in Nimue's head, and he flapped nearer. *"Or should I say a rat?"*

Nimue doubted familiars smelled anything at all like the real creatures whose forms they borrowed, but she didn't have a familiar's nose.

Still, Gowdie had a knack for detecting—

Just as Nimue passed Southern Hotel, Cauldron Cove's seven-story hotel with a skywalk—a literal path across an invisible platform in the sky—to the neighboring convention center, the revolving front door burst open and out flew a warlock on a sleek, black broomstick.

Nimue let out a little yelp and course-corrected her own flight path, managing to keep her grip with an abrupt evasive ma-neuver. She hadn't broken speed records for nothing.

Records the warlock beside her had then broken just a few years later.

"Ren," Nimue said through gritted teeth, nodding courteously at the warlock.

Gowdie flew directly above her, his eyes drawn to Ren's familiar, which took the form of a black-and-orange cat.

Balfour stuck her little pink nose in the air, sitting on the broomstick between Ren's hands and legs with her back straight and her tail curled, for all the world pretending she wasn't the least bit in danger of losing her balance.

"I just told her, 'Nice evening,'" muttered Gowdie into Nimue's head.

Nimue knew the other familiar would have heard that. But the stuck-up feline gave no indication she had.

"It's Soren," said the warlock as they both pulled their broomsticks onto the employee landing balcony on the Bessa's second story, around the back. There was a similar bay for guests flown directly to the convention center on the ground floor on the side closer to the street.

Nimue hopped off her broomstick—cherrywood to match her wand—and took a look at her co-worker slash rival.

It *was* Soren Southern at the moment. Wavy, blond hair, hanging messily down over his brow. Rounded cheekbones leading to dark brown eyes mostly hidden under hair. A jagged scar from his left ear and to the corner of his mouth. Tall, and a bit on the thin side, though he wasn't too bony. Ren and Soren shared a similar appearance, but there were little differences. Most of all was the way the forty-two-year-old warlock carried himself.

Soren always seemed a bit hunched over, like a shy child being dragged out from the comfort of his room to perform a piano solo in the middle of his parents' party. If he pulled out his black wand, he'd fail to carry it with any menace.

The meeker version of the warlock spent far less time at the surface. No doubt as overwhelmed by Ren's personality as everyone else was.

Well, mostly just Nimue, it seemed.

"Could have fooled me," Nimue said as they walked inside and to the employee break room. "The way you almost ran me over." To the left was a balcony that overlooked the sprawling convention center below, currently abuzz with the setup of numerous booths. To the right, a line of rooms and offices, the biggest of which was the break room. Gowdie took his perch on his witch's shoulder as Soren held out an arm for Balfour to sit on like some kind of hunting hawk. The cat never changed personalities. Always haughty.

"I'm sorry," Soren said, his deep voice cracking a bit as he stumbled to apologize. "I didn't want to be late."

"I get it." Nimue held the door for him since his appendages were busy with his broomstick and cat. "No problem. Just remember that's a busy street most days."

"Right. Yes. Of course." Soren thanked her and shuffled inside, heading straight for his locker. It detected its owner—or it'd open for anyone who ranked higher than him on the team, she supposed, if one needed to get inside to grab something he'd left behind on a vacation or sick day—and opened at his approach so he could stuff his broomstick inside.

Four locker doors down, Nimue's did the same, and she dropped her broomstick inside, pulling out the lanyard and badge listing her credentials.

Nimue Toothaker. Assistant to Head Witch General Manager.

Balfour hopped from Soren's arm and up to the top of the lockers, prowling along the length of them and giving Nimue a stern look as she passed overhead. Soren brushed some twigs off of his tweed coat before placing his own lanyard over his head.

Soren Southern. Activities and Event Planner, Marketing Coordinator.

"Messing with plant life again?" Nimue asked. She couldn't help herself. She liked Soren. She used to like Soren, anyway. They'd grown up together. He'd been a sweet boy. Once.

Soren followed her line of sight to the back of his jacket. She reached over to pick a burr from his corduroy elbow patch.

"Don't tell Ren," he hissed, his pallid face flushing red.

"You don't have to worry about *me.*" Nimue nudged her head to Balfour, who still prowled along the tops of the lockers.

She'd tell him. She'd been born with Soren, but she preferred Ren clearly.

Soren sighed. "He doesn't like when I lose track of time. He doesn't like when we're late."

"Well, you're not late." Nimue closed

her locker door. "And it's none of his concern what you do when you're in charge."

Soren's mouth quirked into a wicked smile, his wild bangs slipping just enough to reveal his sparkling, dark eyes.

Nimue felt her heart skip a beat. Yes, she'd liked Soren very much indeed. Long ago.

Balfour let out a little trill and jumped, perhaps warning Soren in advance. Or he was just used to it. He caught her in his arms without so much as a moment of delay.

"I had to rush home to clean up," Soren explained. He lived at the hotel, which was owned by his parents. He'd moved back there twenty years ago now, shortly after Nimue had left for Huntsville. After the accident.

Balfour perched up against his chest, her front paws resting on his shoulder as her assessing eyes focused on Gowdie atop Nimue. Gowdie flapped his wings and Balfour rolled her eyes, focusing behind Soren instead.

"She just told me I need to do a better job of

warning you! About dangers on the road! Dangers her *warlock caused!"*

Nimue scratched him under his chin. "Hush, it's okay."

What was done was done. If it had been *Ren* who'd plowed into her, though…

The door leading to the hallway burst open and Tituba Jonesdochter, Witchy ExS Convention and Catering Operations Manager, all-around great witch, and Nimue's lifelong best friend, strode in, her own oaken broomstick in hand. Graves, her neon green frog familiar, hopped along behind her at her feet.

He didn't relish being carried, but he often got underfoot that way, particularly in crowds.

Tituba shook her hair and her weave of brown-and-golden braids clacked against her dark brown cheek. It was hard to pinpoint whether she had longer legs or a longer torso. She was just tall and slender, her pale yellow peasant dress longer than Nimue's red dress of a similar variety to accommodate her length.

Witches didn't have uniforms, but they

often gravitated toward the same things. Plus, the clientele expected it, the whole "witch look" when on duty.

Even if there weren't any guests due to be here today, Nimue pulled her red witch's hat out of her locker and placed it on her head just as Tituba put her matching yellow conical hat on top of hers.

"Evening, Nimue, Soren." Tituba didn't often mix up Soren and Ren. Though, to be fair, Nimue had only done so because she couldn't stand looking at Ren if she could help it.

Balfour's tail twitched as she took in Graves's bouncing form. Soren didn't notice as the cat leaped from his arms to the floor.

"Evening," Nimue responded. "Willow sends her love." She had, in a text after their Communication Charm chat. Nimue hadn't bothered to respond or the AutoCorrect may have unleashed more gibberish on her daughter.

"How's she liking human school?" Tituba asked as her locker door shut.

"Loves it so far," Nimue said. "But *school* hasn't actually started. Just the socializing."

Tituba nudged her with her upper arm. "Well, that's half the fun of the experience, if you ask me."

Nimue and Tituba shared a wide smile. Neither had gone to human school, but they'd gotten up to a few hijinks in Cauldron Cove at that age before Nimue had gone off to make a new life with Greg in Huntsville.

Gowdie flapped his wings and jumped off of Nimue's shoulder, dive-bombing the slinking cat at everyone's feet.

"No! Balfour!" said Soren, brushing past the witches to grab hold of Balfour around the torso.

Unhurt but acting as if more than her pride had been wounded, Balfour licked her paw erratically as she curled up in Soren's arms once more.

Gowdie took hold of Graves in one gentle talon grip and dropped him into Tituba's hand.

"That cat was going to munch on Graves!" Gowdie shouted into Nimue's mind before settling on top of the lockers. *"She doesn't*

even need to eat!" He glared at Balfour, who hissed up at him.

"'*Only one little leg*,'" Gowdie translated for the cat familiar. "'*He could grow it back*.'" He *tsked*.

Soren flushed red. "Sorry," he mumbled to Tituba and he shuffled away before she could respond, out of the break room.

Tituba was cooing at her frog, who breathed deeply, his little chest expanding and collapsing quickly, as though he'd just run a marathon. He calmed down a bit as she stroked his little belly. "Nasty old kitty, huh?"

Gowdie flew over and perched on Nimue's shoulder. "*You'd think that feline could at least be nice when her master is.*"

"Oh, but someone's got to keep up the mean streak," Nimue said.

Used to hearing only half of conversations when it came to other witches' familiars—if anything was spoken aloud at all—Tituba just offered her friend a smile, no doubt finding it easy to guess what was said.

"We better get going." Tituba wove her

arm through her friend's. "Bernadette only begins the meetings when we're all there."

Together, they headed down the long hallway in the Bessa's offices, no sign of Soren ahead. They were almost at the door when Zelena Varlett, Convention Security Manager, and her husband, Linden, Director of Guest Services, approached from the tele-portation pad at the end of the hall, which flashed brown.

"Good evening, ladies," said Linden. With wiry, gray hair and thick Coke-bottle glasses, Linden was every bit the picture of an absentminded professor. But he was as sharp as a tack and as soft as a cushion, which the shy Dyer, his rose-colored chin-chilla-shaped familiar currently weaving around his ankles, seemed to love about her warlock.

"Evening," said Nimue and Tituba as one.

Zelena crossed her arms and sent them a suspicious look, as if wondering if them speaking in unison was the first part of a charm with which she was unfamiliar. "Any idea why Bernadette wants to see us so late?" she asked, clipped, her voice alto and sonorous. She was taller than her husband, broad at the shoulders, with brown-and-gray hair in a low bun. Her familiar, Messenger, a black sloth, hung around her neck unremarked upon like some kind of fur stole.

"Nope," said Nimue because she knew she'd be the one most likely to know what her grandmother had in store for them. Not just because they were family, but because she was her assistant. Had been almost ten years, since not too long after returning to Cauldron Cove full-time.

Zelena *harrumphed* and headed inside, not bothering to hold the door for anyone.

Linden chuckled and held the door for the two other witches. "She was trying to rest today after last night's long shift," he said by way of explanation.

Nimue and Tituba thanked him and waited for him to follow them inside before they filed through the reception area, past the hat rack Gowdie often perched on as well as a series of couches beside Nimue's reception desk, and up to Bernadette's office door. Everyone else had already gone inside.

"I doubt she'd be in a better mood even when well-rested," Nimue muttered. *At least around me.*

Zelena Varlett, granddaughter of town founder Bessa's best friend slash nemesis, Gala Varlett, wasn't keen on nepotism. Bernadette may have won her over in the sixty years Zelena had been a part of Witchy ExS, but Nimue had yet to do so.

She doubted she ever would.

Nimue got the door this time, and everyone stepped in.

Morpheus and Herne were already inside, the former a short and squat man with clipped, dark hair and a pale complexion, the latter a tall and lanky dark-skinned man with a clean-shaven head. Beside Herne was Zelena and on the other side of Zelena…

Was Ren. Not Soren.

His hair was slicked back as if the warlock just produced hair pomade out of thin air when he changed. His nose was upturned, his cheeks now a touch sallow. His jaw clenched so tightly as he stared straight forward that the scar on his left cheek practically popped into relief.

Balfour had strewn herself rather languidly around his shoulders like a boa.

"You're. Late," said Ren, his deep voice firm and brooking no argument.

An hourglass on Bernadette's desk flipped over on its own, indicating the change of hour. It had been perma-charmed to complete its task until the end of time.

"Looks like we're just in time," Nimue said.

Ren sent her a glowering stare. "Professionals should always be early." Frowning, he examined a piece of leaf Soren had failed to remove from his jacket at his wrist. He picked it off between two pinched fingers.

"Professionals ought to have an impeccable appearance, too," Nimue said, sending silent apologies to Soren. She'd never have criticized *him* for such a thing, even if he'd shown up with half a hedge bush stuck upon his person.

"All right, enough of this." Bernadette Toothaker's voice—a cheery soprano, at odds with the elderly witch's firm appearance—put an end to the conversation as her desk chair spun around. It'd been facing the vast Lake Salem view.

Bernadette, Cauldron Cove's oldest and most renowned living witch, stared down the few core employees she'd gathered in her office late in the day on a Sunday between conventions. She had all gray hair, which she tied off to one side in a low ponytail. Her bright blue eyes resembled Nimue's, though hers had crow's feet, lending them more weight. If she were human, she'd pass for a spry eighty, but she had just started to age into her current appearance in the last several decades or so.

"I hope the two of you can learn to keep the sniping to a minimum from now on," Bernadette said, steepling her fingers together as she leaned her elbows on the immaculately uncluttered giant mushroom-shaped desk before her. The wall without windows, the one covered in convention industry awards and books stacked evenly on a wide bookcase, was flawlessly tidy as well. As her assistant, Nimue made sure of such things. She'd even brought some of her favorite books from home just to even out the shelves. Bernadette sometimes found disorder distracting.

"Because tonight," the head of Witchy Expo Services said, "I'm announcing my retirement."

Zelena gasped loudest of all, slapping her mouth with a blemished hand, but everyone mumbled their surprise.

Naismith, Bernadette's golden songbird familiar, chirped out a song as he fluttered overhead his witch.

Nimue felt as if the floor had been ripped out from underneath her. "But, Grandma, you can't retire!" she said, almost forgetting Bernadette's rule to address her by her name when on the clock.

Bernadette arched an eyebrow but leaned her mouth onto her steepled fingers. "I've worked this job a hundred and twelve years."

"And you could work a hundred and twelve more!" protested Zelena. That wasn't true. No witch had lived longer than three hundred and fifty. But Zelena clearly wasn't thinking, her sloth familiar's jaw dropping slowly, centimeter by arduous centimeter, clearly sharing her witch's feelings.

"No, I cannot," Bernadette said. "I've given enough of my life to this organization. And I'm ready to appoint my successor."

Ren straightened at that, Balfour leaping smoothly into the crux of his arm and stiffening her own back.

Gowdie's talons dug into Nimue's shoulder, but she didn't cry out. She was too enraptured in watching her grandmother, awaiting the news that would affect her career for decades—perhaps more than a century—to come.

"Soren Southern," Bernadette said, referring to him by his full, legal name regardless of which warlock personality was at the helm at the moment. Ren's wicked smile went wide as he tugged at the lapel of his tweed coat. "You and my granddaughter, Nimue Toothaker. The both of you will be Co-Head General Managers of Witchy Expo Services."

Ren's smile fell.

Nimue's heart plummeted.

She hadn't even thought to *want* the job, let alone expect it.

But if Ren Southern thought he was going to lord over her by being Head Warlock General Manager alone, she'd step up to the plate.

She'd do whatever it took to make sure Witchy Expo Services continued to succeed by following in her grandmother's footsteps.

CHAPTER THREE

"That's preposterous!" Ren shouted. "She's *an assistant* and she's worked here half the time I have—"

Nimue bristled. "You have eight extra years on me. In a witch or warlock's life, that's not a lot. Not to mention, it was *Soren* for a lot of your time here."

Ren's face purpled, but Zelena put a hand on his shoulder. There were faint, white lines amidst the slight tan of her skin on the back of that hand. It looked like a cat had scratched her and the lines had never really healed. "Nepotism," she said under her breath.

But Nimue heard her.

"Prove her wrong," Gowdie said in her mind. He rubbed the top of his head against Nimue's cheek, jostling the brim of her witch's hat. *"Success is the best revenge."*

"Work together or you'll *both* be out of a job," Bernadette said simply. The room went quiet and Bernadette got to her feet. "So if you'll excuse me, I don't like a lot of fuss. I'll leave you to it."

Ren's usually stony face blanched. "You're retiring *now*? Before Bookshop Con?"

"No time like the present." Bernadette pulled her walnut-wood wand out of her holster at her waist and cast a Collection Charm. The personal effects decorating her desk and in its drawers flew out and gathered above her head. Naismith flittered amongst the collection of framed photos and snacks and well-worn magic books.

"But guests will begin arriving tomorrow night!" Ren protested.

"What's the matter?" Tituba crossed her arms. "You don't think you can handle the pressure?"

Ren scowled as Bernadette reached a

hand out and her knotted elm broomstick flew via the ongoing Collection Charm over from the corner into her waiting grip.

"You know where to reach me if you have any questions." She stopped at the door and looked over her shoulder at each of the gathered witches and warlocks in turn. "But don't have any questions." She exited the room, her floating personal items and her familiar following behind her over-head, leaving an awkward gathering of magic users all staring at one another.

Ren *harrumphed* and strode after Bernadette, Balfour trotting at his heels, her tail straight up in the air.

"Congrats!" Tituba scooped Nimue into a hug, Graves jumping up to settle on the top of the yellow hat's brim.

Linden clapped his white-gloved hands behind her. "Congratulations, Nimue. Well earned."

Zelena snorted and brushed past them to the door. "Well, *some of us* have to make sure this won't turn out to be a disaster." She glared at Nimue and Gowdie offered her a little hiss with a pop of flame. Messenger the sloth slowly reached a single toe in Gowdie's direction, but before anything could come of the confrontation, Zelena's eyes narrowed and she left the room.

Nimue patted her familiar's head. "Enough, Gowdie. We have to all get along."

He closed his jaw, a little bit of smoke escaping from between his teeth. *"Sorry."*

"Well, if you're in charge now, I have to run some booth assignments past you," said Herne, after both he and Morpheus had offered their congratulations. Morpheus and Linden started up a conversation, their voices traveling down the empty hallway as they exited the manager's office and reception room.

"Ri-Right," said Nimue, straightening her back. She dealt with these kinds of things all the time. She just usually ran any big decisions past her grandmother.

Her grandmother. Retired. And she'd picked Nimue to take her place—well, half her place anyway.

Nimue's stomach fluttered with a mix of giddiness and nervousness and anticipation.

"I should get checking on some orders," said Tituba as Herne tapped the perma-charm crystal he, like everyone else on staff, wore on a black strap on his wrist. The action brought up the witch network and the screen he wanted to show Nimue. The witch network was similar to humanity's Internet—and could connect to that when necessary, for business purposes—but there were a few more tricks to it than that and it required a perma-charm crystal wrist band and witch or warlock blood for access. It was easier for Nimue to intuitively use.

Tituba nudged her best friend. "You can do this. You've already been doing it for years." Her voice lowered. "Don't let any naysayers stop you."

"Thanks," said Nimue. Her neck flushed. Gowdie tapped a tip of his wing membrane to Graves's extended foot in a sort of high-five and Tituba went on her way.

That was Witchy ExS in a nutshell. If any of them were as shocked as Nimue felt at her grandmother's sudden retirement, no one had much time to show it.

No retirement party for her grand-mother, either.

There was too much work to do.

And Witchy ExS was a well-oiled machine at this point. How much of a wrench could Bernadette Toothaker's absence throw into it?

Nimue was lost in thought as she and Herne consulted on how best to place exhibitors after some last-minute changes to layout, while Gowdie scrambled around the office with Ten Ham, Herne's zebra-striped familiar piglet.

Before long, the door to the reception area burst open and in flew a collection of flying items. A sleek, black stapler and a box of staples. A tape dispenser. Many black clips and several shiny black clipboards. A handful of books, all bound in identical crimson leather.

A single photograph in a small frame that Nimue recognized to be Lydia, Soren's wife.

Soren was a widower and had lost her two decades before.

Balfour strode in and leaped up onto the

mushroom desk, then onto the back of the leather chair behind it.

Ren followed, his wand at the ready. He froze when he spotted Nimue and Herne consulting over a projection of the up-coming exhibit map.

"I'll thank you to take your assistant business elsewhere," he snapped, then before anyone could reply, he cast a Transformation Charm on Bernadette's mushroom desk. It transformed into a sleek, shiny black rectangular desk. Streamlined. Unnatural.

"*Excuse me*," Nimue said, casting her own Transformation Charm so that the desk went right back to being mushroom-shaped, just as Ren's belongings all settled into place.

Ren scowled as he sat behind it.

Nimue let out a small chuckle. He *did* look ridiculous behind the mushroom desk.

He folded his hands on top of the spongy surface. "I'm so glad this amuses you. I can just change it back tomorrow."

Charms were like that. Each witch and warlock could cast any spell they'd learned once a day. But it took until the next sunrise for the magic used in the charm to recharge inside their bodies. That was when friends came in handy, if they weren't using theirs. Without another witch or warlock willing to perform the charm nearby, if they needed something done more than once, they had to get creative, think of Non-Repetitive Charms similar in nature. Or create a perma-charm crystal to do the job for them.

"And I can change it right back," Nimue protested.

Herne ran a hand behind his bald head as Ten Ham trotted over on cloven feet. "Thanks, Nim. I'll go input your suggestions."

"Wait," said Ren just as Herne reached the door, about to wave the witch network projection of the booth assignments away. "Let me see."

"I took care of it." Nimue tapped her foot on the sleek, mossy-like carpet beneath her feet. Gowdie took to the air and landed on her shoulder.

"Are you going to let him just take over the

office?" he asked, his second eyelids blinking and narrowing his reptile-like eyes into slits.

There was that, too. Nimue had been so caught up in him changing her grandmother's office décor—which she was rather partial to—that she'd forgotten Ren had no right to just barge in here.

She slipped in front of Herne and slammed her hands on the desk. It was spongy, and the thud was muffled. "Herne and I took care of it. *You* never deal with booth placement."

"But I have to keep an eye on everything now, don't I?" Ren held his hand out to signal Herne to approach.

Herne hesitated in the doorway, no doubt eager to input the solution Nimue had offered him.

"It's fine," she said to him. "Go ahead and give us a minute."

Herne scrambled to leave, Ten Ham kicking the door closed with her back feet behind her.

Ren and Nimue stared one another down, Ren not the least bit intimidated by Nimue towering over him.

In fact, he smirked and sat back in the General Manager's chair, and Nimue realized that he actually had the advantage. Though seated, he was in the place of power.

Balfour purred and rubbed the top of her head against Ren's greasy, slicked-back hair.

"This is *our* office now," Nimue said.

Ren gestured around him. "There's hardly room for two."

Nimue looked around. There *was* room if they shifted furniture around a bit, but... Not a lot of it. And Nimue wouldn't relish being in such close proximity to Ren for much of the day regardless.

Ren opened a drawer in the desk and started riffling through it. "You have a desk out there."

There *was* more room in the reception area. And all of her stuff was there, just where she liked it.

But...

"I'm not your assistant!"

Ren scoffed as he pulled a stack of papers out of the drawer and tossed it on the desk. "I wouldn't want you in the position anyway."

Nimue's heart sunk. So if only Ren had been named General Manager alone, would he have fired her from her position?

Was *that* why her grandmother had offered her the co-manager title? Because she'd known her job had been in peril otherwise?

"Duplication Charm!" Nimue said, waving her wand at the manager's desk.

Another one appeared perpendicular to it, and Nimue cast a Collection Charm to gather her belongings from her desk in the other room.

Gowdie took to the air, soaring around in circles.

"What are you doing?" Ren looked dumbfounded as Nimue's items flew into the room.

She stood behind her desk and started sorting her things. "We're co-managers," she said simply. She was missing a chair. Only she'd already cast her Duplication Charm for the day.

Sighing, she left the room and took hold

of her desk chair, wheeling it back into the Head Manager's office as her personal items flew overhead.

Ren watched her, bemused, as she rolled it into place and sat down.

Gowdie tried to perch on the back of the chair, but there wasn't as much room as there was on Bernadette's old chair. He didn't look quite so poised and balanced as Balfour did across the room.

"I'm setting up my desk," said Nimue. She realized with a start she'd duplicated all of the contents of the other desk, too.

On the corner in the sleek, black frame, was the smiling Lydia Southern, her strawberry-red curls popping out from under her pink witch's hat, a swath of freckles across her nose. She was nuzzling her familiar, a purple chipmunk Nimue remembered to be frenetic and flighty, far more than even her bubbly, sunny witch.

Wincing, she waved her wand at the copied picture, sending it across the room to Ren's desk with a Hover Charm as she settled her own photos from her previous desk in its place. Willow as a toddler, her nose covered in cookie dough. Tituba and Nimue as teens, riding their brooms. Nimue, pre-teen Willow, and Nimue's parents on vacation at a resort. Willow's human high school graduation photo.

Ren took the extra photo of his—or Soren's, really—wife as it flew toward him and slipped it inside a top desk drawer, pulling out a book and opening it as seamlessly as if that were what he'd meant to do all along. Balfour watched, letting out a soft little mew as she gazed over Ren's shoulder to see Lydia and her familiar.

Nimue swallowed, the awkwardness in the air palpable. Though her view was of Bernadette's bookcase instead of the door when anyone approached, if she spun around, she could still see out over Lake Salem.

He might have settled in first, but she was still here and his equal.

"We *will* need an assistant, though," Nimue said, remembering everything she'd done in her previous job. She'd been her grandmother's right-hand woman, even more than Ren, who'd hovered by incessantly with suggestions and questions. "I'm thinking Cassie—"

"Cassie," said Ren at almost the exact same time.

They looked at one another. Blinked. Then Ren bent the corner of the open page of his book before shutting it closed, causing Nimue to wince. She didn't like creasing a book's paper like that, even if it was some work-related industry title and not a beloved fiction classic.

"So it's decided," he said, putting the book to the side of his desk and staring down at the stack of papers he then dragged in front of him.

Nimue realized she'd replicated that stack, too. An outline of the upcoming Bookshop Con agreement and the pro-posal… put together by Nimue herself, as Bernadette's assistant.

"Settled," said Nimue, re-reading the top page.

Perhaps, since they both wished whole-heartedly for Witchy ExS's success, they'd work well enough together, after all.

CHAPTER FOUR

"We don't work well together *at all!*" Nimue muttered between sips of her Grandma Prue's cider hot chocolate. "He's so rude. He won't take *any* of my suggestions! He won't even let me fully explain them!" She bobbed her head wildly, doing her best impression of Ren with a stick up his behind. "'We cannot make sweeping changes so late in the game. All changes are subject to the Bookshop Owner's League's approval.' It wasn't like I was making *sweeping* changes! I have ideas!" She downed the last of her hot chocolate. "Like this interactive Book Scene Booth. How cool would that be? You *think* of a scene from your favorite book, a witch taps a perma-charm crystal special made, and the person gets to live out the scene in an illusion! But *no*! 'Too ambitious,' Ren said. 'Too *whimsical*. Not to mention potentially dangerous.' *How is that dangerous, I ask!*"

Across from her, Prue chuckled. At two hundred and sixty, she was definitely starting to show some of her elder age, but she was still a beauty. Her black-and-white curly hair stuck out voluminously from her head, and her pale brown complexion was weathered, the hands clutching her cup of hot chocolate a bit bony. She wore free-flowing, baggy clothes: a wrinkled, long skirt; a blouse; and a vest all in earth tones. An array of necklaces, bracelets, and rings clanked every time she moved.

"Well, I suppose there's getting lost in a good book and there's *getting lost in a literal book*, for one thing. Sounds like he's a good match for you," she said, taking a sip. At Nimue's slack jaw, she chuckled. "As a business partner."

"No, no, and no." Nimue clutched her empty mug with both hands and watched as Gowdie flew around the room, letting Prue's golden lovebird, Dunlop, flitter after him. "I told him Grandma surprised clients *all the time*, that that was responsible for so much of the positive reception Witchy Expo Services gets, but he insisted it was *too risky. Ugh.*"

"He's not wrong," Prue said, raising her brows as she took another sip. "Spontaneity comes with risk."

Nimue pinched her lips and glowered at her Grandma Prue. Bernadette had had her only child, Rowena, with her first spouse, a warlock who'd died a hundred and five years in the past, but Grandma Prue was the only other grandparent on that side Nimue had ever known. Her father's parents traveled a lot, like her own did, so it was always Bernadette and Prue's cottage in the woods at Cauldron Cove's edge that Nimue called her second home.

"Is she still complaining?" muttered Bernadette as she poked her head into the kitchen where Nimue and Prue sat. Naismith, her lovebird, fluttered in behind her and went straight for Dunlop, the two twittering and dancing around one another until they settled on a perch together over the fire, nuzzling cheek to cheek.

Gowdie flapped over to a rocking chair before the hearth, yawning and curling up like a cat.

Nimue chuckled to herself at the reminder that he wouldn't appreciate the comparison. He and Balfour had gotten along today about as well as she and Ren had.

"Grandma, how could you spring that surprise on me?" Nimue asked as Bernadette sat down between her and Prue. "Did *Willow* know?"

Bernadette chuckled. "Maybe. But she agreed that if you'd been given any warning, you might have tried to talk me out of it."

Nimue scowled. "I wouldn't have. I'm proud to take on Witchy Expo Services. Even if I still feel a little out of my depth."

"I meant, you'd try to talk me out of making you co-manager. With Soren."

"Soren's fine," Nimue said bitterly. "But

you know Ren usually rears his ugly head when he's at work."

"Well, *Ren* brings all of the calm and rational thought I think Witchy ExS needs to succeed."

"*I'm* calm!" Nimue shouted, slapping the table and belying her own point. "I'm rational!"

Bernadette and Prue exchanged a look and then both burst out into a laugh.

"Oh, ha ha," Nimue muttered, feeling her face flush.

Prue reached across the table to take hold of Nimue's hand. "Nimue, my dear, you're smart and full of amazing ideas. You work hard—maybe even a little *too* hard." She looked pointedly to Bernadette, as if making a comparison. "You'll bring the big-picture ideas. Ren will rein you in when those ideas get too wild. And the both of you will work hard to ensure each convention's success."

"If you say so." Nimue frowned but squeezed her grandma's hand. "I just… I just wish he'd listen to me. We agreed to hire Cassie as our assistant—she accepted, by the way—and from then on, it was just an evening of bickering."

"Well, the bickering will have to end. You'll have to find a way to work together. Divvy up tasks, one of you spend more time on the floor—whatever it takes." Bernadette's mouth went grim. "More than just a successful, fulfilling career is at stake."

There was that, too.

The magic seeped into the soil beneath Cauldron Cove did a lot of wonderful things for the town. It kept the town protected, enhanced a witch's or warlock's magic, and helped the town thrive. But the convention center, over Bessa Toothaker's melted cauldron, was the key.

The conventions held there kept the magic in the town fed.

Conventions had to be held often, no more than a week between events. The happiness of the guests fed into the cauldron's magic, the more the better.

A convention couldn't be stopped once it'd started, either, not until it reached its natural end. That had happened just once, many decades ago, and Bernadette had only just managed to save the town from utter destruction.

The disappointment and distress of the con-goers had been that potent, that dangerous for the cauldron feeding off the energy above.

"I know," said Nimue, swallowing hard. Witchy ExS had never been so close to shutting down a convention in her lifetime.

But it had never been run without Bernadette Toothaker at the helm, either.

"Bookshop Con is a walk in the park," said Bernadette, fluffing her hand in the air. "The perfect first con for you and Ren. Most of the setup's already completed."

Tomorrow they'd put on the finishing touches and start welcoming the guests who'd chosen to arrive a day before the convention officially began. Nimue's grandmother was right. It was one of their annual conventions, officially intended for bookshop owners and publishers interested in selling to them but also attracting so many ravenous readers, it may as well have just been a celebration of reading in general. Readers met authors. Authors signed and talked about books. Booksellers sold books and reader goodies, bought stock wholesale, and discussed tips and tricks with others in the industry. There really wasn't a lot of pressure.

And Nimue was a bookworm, too. She usually found time to sneak off during Bookshop Con to meet a few new and favorite authors. But this year, she'd be too busy.

She straightened her back, reminding herself to consider the convention from a new angle. All that mattered was the convention's success.

Even if that meant she had to acquiesce on occasion to Ren Southern.

"Maybe you should use a Calming Charm every morning before work," Prue suggested, stretching her arms above her. "That and yoga keep me limber."

"I did. Well, about an hour into sharing an office with that warlock, I excused myself to the bathroom and I did." Nimue practically squeezed the mug with both hands. "My irritation apparently was strong enough to break through. Maybe I needed a double dose."

"Bern?" Prue asked. "I already used mine for today."

"It's fine." Nimue took a deep breath and leaned back in the hardbacked kitchen chair. "It's better not to get too calm, anyway. A sharp mind doesn't like calm." She tapped her temple, a gleeful thought that perhaps Ren was *too* calm. He kept it all bottled up inside, often only letting his feelings leak through onto his face.

Soren managed to show emotions. For the most part, anyway.

But Ren, *superior* Ren, didn't have a good handle on his emotions, despite what he seemed to think.

"Nimue is as sharp as a tack and calm most of the time besides," Bernadette said. "It's just one or two people who seem to rub her the wrong way."

Two? Nimue got along just fine with Greg. She really did. Her foot bounced under the table, her mind suppressing memories of the shouting matches they'd had when she'd told him she hadn't been happy in the human world.

Humans didn't feel comfortable living in the witch world, so what choice had they had? Visiting, sure. But spend too long in one of the witch towns like Cauldron Cove, and… The magic in the ground seeping out and into the air started really wearing down the human mind.

But that took years and years of exposure.

"Bit like her mom that way." Prue nodded.

That was a surprise. Outside of their appearances, Rowena and Nimue Toothaker really seemed to share so little in common.

"Oh, speaking of Rowena, she sent this for you." Bernadette got up from the table and shuffled toward the cottage's mudroom. "As a congrats."

"Did *everyone* but me know in advance what you were up to?" Nimue *tsked*.

Prue smiled and stood, collecting her and Nimue's empty mugs. "Truth be told, she was a little afraid you'd talk her out of retiring, too."

"I would not!" Nimue said softly. But then she thought about it. Maybe she would have. She'd at least have pressed her grandmother to be sure she was certain first or to stay a bit longer to lend a helping hand.

Right now, it was only her desire to prove to Ren Southern that she had what it took to lead Witchy ExS that was really fueling her confidence.

Bernadette returned to the room as Prue performed a Cleaning Charm and got to work making all of the dishes stacked in the kitchen sink sparkle. She handed Nimue a box, wrapped in paper parcel.

It was postmarked from the Philippines.

"How long have they been in Manila?" Nimue asked, removing the paper with her hands.

Gowdie's ear perked up as the lovebirds chirped a little song, as bright and cheery as if it were morning instead of quite late on a Sunday night.

"A few months," Bernadette said. She kept better track of where Nimue's parents traveled than their daughter did. They'd stayed put in Cauldron Cove for virtually all of her childhood, but her mother had never had much interest in running the family business, so they hopped off from one location to the next around the world, a witch and warlock for hire for the right price—or for the right person.

Her parents were generous to those in need like that.

Inside was a small, wooden box. At first, Nimue didn't recognize it to be a jewelry box, perfect for a necklace.

Inside was an iridescent chain, with a series of charms. A broomstick, a dragon, a puppy, two lovebirds, and two bats.

"A charm for everyone in the family," Nimue said, running her fingers over the black bats she knew to represent Rowena and Prospero Toothaker—warlocks often took a witch's family name when they married into it—and their familiar bats, Sampson and Stout.

"Congrats, dear!" called Rowena's and Prospero's voices from inside the box. A Recording Charm. "We're so proud of you," said Rowena.

"We can't wait to visit soon and see your hard work in action!" added Prospero.

Nimue teared up a little and Bernadette took the box from her, offering to affix the clasp in place at the base of Nimue's neck.

"You've got this, Nim," Bernadette said. "I wouldn't have given you the job if I didn't believe that."

"And here I thought you'd just given it to me because Ren would have fired me otherwise."

Bernadette laughed, her eyes twinkling. "He'd never be able to handle Witchy ExS without you. He knows that."

"Well, his own lips told me otherwise."

Prue arched a brow as she leaned back against the kitchen sink. "His lips? Do you often pay attention to those still?"

Nimue flushed and Gowdie, picking up on her distress, flew over and landed in Nimue's lap. She scratched him behind the ears. "Ancient history," she mumbled. "And besides, that was Soren."

Her first boyfriend. When they'd both been just wee little pre-teens. It had felt so *real,* so important back then, though they hadn't even kissed. But now that she had a kid of her own, she couldn't imagine Willow finding the right person when she'd been just a child.

"Soren is still Soren," said Bernadette, shuffling beside Prue and slipping a hand on her wife's back. "His wife's death may have changed him, may have invited that restless warlock spirit to take over on occasion—but Soren's still in there."

"I know," Nimue said softly. But she knew herself, too. She worked, she read, she spent what little down time she had with family and friends.

Romance outside of a novel's pages was the last thing on her mind.

And she definitely didn't intend on dating a co-worker.

Some things were best left buried and forgotten.

CHAPTER FIVE

"Merga, wait! Did Herne update you on the PuffinHouse booth placement?" Nimue trotted down the exhibition hall aisle to where Merga, a witch a little older than Willow, was using an Assemble Charm to put a large publisher booth together. Witchy ExS offered setup services for individual exhibitors if requested, and PuffinHouse had sent a rather detailed schematic of what they wanted placed where.

"He said 12F." Merga frowned. The snow-pale redheaded witch dressed in all black—black dress pants, a black blouse, and a black witch's hat—flailed her wand helplessly as the charm continued to build everything in the wrong place. Spandemager, her red miniature llama familiar, nudged some of the PuffinHouse boxes off of the delivery cart and toward the booth with his nose.

Nimue knew what Merga was worried about. She only had the one Assemble Charm to use per day and everything had to be ready by tonight, when vendors, exhibitors, and guests started arriving.

"It *was* 12F, but last night, he told me about the extra payment they sent to get an edge row placement. 12A now." Nimue tapped her perma-charm wrist crystal to bring up her witch network projected screen and Cassie scrambled to do the same to hers behind her.

"Yes, 12A," said Cassie, another young witch with an eye for detail. Her wrinkle-free green pencil skirt and blazer popped against her dark sepia complexion, her sharp, green witch's hat at a perfect angle over her short, gold waves. On her shoulder rode Laveau, her green ferret familiar. "We moved Delgado Books to take its place, also rearranging previous aisle space devoted to AccuPress Printing. They'd emailed last week to request space amongst the vendors instead of upfront among the publishers and booksellers."

Merga bit her lip and cut the Assemble Charm short. "Well, no one told me. And now I'm out my Assemble Charm for the day."

"Let me," said Cassie, dismissing her witch network projection screen, pulling out her pale brown wand from its holster at her hip, and waving it toward PuffinHouse's half-opened boxes.

"Thank you, Cassie," Nimue said. "And don't sweat it, Merga. Must have just been a slipup in communication." On Nimue's first full-time day as General Manager. Co-General Manager. "Merga, check with Herne and make sure you get the updated floor layout."

Merga nodded and with her familiar trotting behind her, headed for the nearest transportation portal, which glowed a dull white until Merga and Spandemager stepped inside. It flashed red, indicating she'd opted to move to the red portal, in the Staff-Only hallway on the second floor, where all of the offices were located.

A red light flashed on Cassie's perma-charm wrist crystal and she tapped it to bring up a message, barely stopping her wand's movements as it glided in the air in time with the Assemble Charm. "Miss Toothaker, it's Mr. Southern."

"'Nimue' is fine, Cassie. You practically spent every other weekend at my house growing up. I think we're beyond 'Miss Toothaker.'"

Cassie offered a pained smile but didn't correct herself. Nimue knew instantly why Ren liked the young witch so much. Her attention to detail, her propriety, and her devotion to the task at hand. "He wants to know why there are books floating in the skylight over the lobby." She chuckled nervously.

"They're there because I told him they would be." Nimue clutched her wand tightly in her hand and summoned Gowdie down from his laps above the Bessa's showroom floor.

"Should I go with you?" Cassie asked, not offering an opinion one way or another. Cassie had helped her charm the extra books from the Head Manager's office into the lobby just an hour earlier that morning, then watched her use the item storage perma-charm crystal to send them all flying. Nimue had told Ren that was one of her ideas the night before, and he'd dismissed it as "an unnecessary waste of magic" and "a potential hazard to boot," but Nimue had gone ahead with it anyway.

How could anyone not walk into that lobby and be overcome with whimsy?

"No, you finish here," Nimue said, fingering the broomstick charm on her parents' gifted necklace at her clavicle. "I'll deal with him."

Not bothering to use any of the teleportation devices set up along the way, Nimue took her time to get to the lobby, taking in the witches and warlocks at work in bringing Bookshop Con together. Some booths were already assembled, witches and warlocks setting out books and displays and adding the little finishing touches requested

—like one bookshop booth that had a sparkling rainbow over it and another that offered passersby a place to rest and sample books in floating chairs. *That* posed a danger more than floating books, surely, but Ren hadn't said anything about that exhibitor's request.

Nimue hadn't quite reached the lobby before she'd spotted Zelena and Ren just beyond the entryway, where staff would check for guest badges once the convention opened. An alcove behind Zelena, down the hall and around the corner from the reception desk, housed the item storage check-in station, where guests could request their belongings to be safely stored in the air. A perma-charm crystal sent anything small enough that touched it flying upward, and a witch or warlock only needed to tap the device with their wand to get the item in question to come back down. A must when applying a Hover Charm more than once per day would be impossible for a single staff member.

The crystal was perma-charm crafted by Nimue's grandmother. Perma-charms required potions imbued into a crystalized form. Each perma-charm took a skilled witch, rare ingredients, and a lot of time to create, but they were well worth it if it meant a witch or warlock not wasting their daily use of a charm to cast a frequently-used spell. Witchy ExS's item storage crystal was one of Bernadette's first contributions to the convention center. It was a convention staple at this point.

Nimue had just expanded on the idea and used the crystal to shoot a bunch of books—most of the contents of Bernadette's bookshelf, actually—up over the lobby entryway.

"A hazard, to be sure." Zelena's deep, husky voice carried across the wide, virtually empty space as Nimue pulled up behind Ren.

"Let me guess," Nimue said. "My hovering books idea?"

Gowdie massaged her shoulder, lifting one front foot and then another as he stared down Ren's cat. Balfour was trotting across the table that housed the crystal, mere inches from being sent floating upward herself.

Ren turned on his heel, his slicked-back hair offering Nimue no hope of reasoning with him. He crinkled his nose. "We discussed your… *idea*. I rejected it."

"I don't need your approval," Nimue protested.

"But when it comes to guest safety, you sure need mine." Zelena put her hands on her hips, Messenger the sloth dangling from her neck and slowly, slowly turning her head. Zelena had put a miniature black witch's hat on her. Sometimes Nimue was startled to see signs of Zelena having any semblance of a softer side.

"It's no different than item storage." Nimue pointed at the floating item storage alcove behind the table. Currently, only a set of keys was floating there—either a test of the crystal or hopefully not something left behind after the last convention that hadn't then been funneled to lost and found—but her point stood.

"Actually, it's entirely different." Ren pointed up to the alcove. "We restrict access down this corridor so no one is caught beneath the floating items, and there's a staff member here at all times once the convention has begun to handle any issues."

Nimue bit her lip. She didn't want to admit he had a point. "There are many staff members in the lobby at all times!"

Ren clutched his hands behind his waist, thrusting his shoulders back. "And their jobs aren't specifically to pay attention to the volumes of Shakespeare floating over their heads."

"Brontë," Nimue protested. In addition to the encyclopedias and witches' history books and everything else that had been on the shelf, she'd shot one of her own books, a much-loved copy of *Jane Eyre* she'd brought to work to even out Bernadette's shelf, up there.

Ren's lips thinned. "Of course. Brontë."

He said it in such a way that Nimue couldn't quite tell if it was an insult or a compliment. Or just an observation.

Nimue tossed her hands out to either side and Gowdie glided into the air above her. "It's fun. Whimsical." She narrowed her eyes at Ren and Zelena, feeling the united force against her. "Don't you appreciate a little whimsy once in a while?"

Ren's eyebrow arched and Zelena patted Messenger's head, as if to cover the witch's hat she'd put on her and prove Nimue wrong.

Nimue scoffed. "When has Bernadette's item storage crystal *ever* malfunctioned and sent something floating down without a wand calling it back?"

"So that's how you did it?" Ren asked. "Using the item storage crystal?"

"Well, I couldn't rightly perform the Hover Charm on that many books all at once..." She decided not to let Ren know Cassie had helped her.

Ren scowled. "I didn't shoot down your idea because I'm not a fan of *whimsy*. It's—"

A pop of cracking fire and a piercing screech drew their attention. Gowdie hovered beside the floating keys, directing a little funnel of fire downward at Balfour, who had launched herself upward, presumably by touching the crystal, which still glowed a dim, yellowish white. She flailed at Gowdie but didn't have the command of the air that Gowdie did, as the dragon snickered and flapped his wings, doing loops around the floundering cat with her claws and paws flexed to their max.

"Balfour!"

"Gowdie!"

Ren and Nimue shouted at their familiars at almost the exact same moment.

Gowdie stuck his snout in the air and floated back down to Nimue's shoulder. *"She started it,"* he protested in Nimue's mind.

"Hush," she said as Ren pulled out his smooth, black wand and smacked it against the crystal. Balfour came floating downward, slowly, right into Ren's arms. She licked herself, her back toes stuck out and stretched, refusing to look Ren in the eye.

Nimue wondered what, if anything, Balfour had to say to Ren to excuse her behavior.

"If anything goes wrong, you can't stop the con," Zelena said abruptly.

Nimue ignored the familiars' kerfuffle and snapped back to the moment. "Of course I know that! Nothing is going to happen with the floating books."

"It's fine," said Ren curtly. "Leave the books be."

Zelena and Nimue craned their heads toward him as one. It was hard to say which seemed more surprised.

"We don't have time for petty arguments," he said, stroking his cat. "There's still so much to be done—"

An incomprehensible shout echoed out around the corner leading to the lobby.

With a crackle of static, Linden's face hovered at Zelena's shoulder. He was using his Communication Charm for the day. The hair on Nimue's neck prickled, wondering what the emergency could be.

"Zelena, security needed near lobby door." Linden was all-business speaking to his wife.

Zelena, Ren, and Nimue exchanged a look and nodded, their argument behind them as they funneled through the badge check station and toward the Bessa's front doors.

CHAPTER SIX

I n the wide, well-lit space of the lobby, what sounded like the flapping of wings proved to actually be the pages of hardcover books, languidly floating from end to end of the lobby.

Nimue had pictured guests looking up and seeing what she did. A flock of books brought to life, hovering overhead in greeting.

A sense of wonder. *Welcome to a world of books.*

Instead, there was a shouting group gathered near Linden's information and concierge desk, with one woman pointing a finger hard against a man's chest.

"You dare accuse me of *buying off judges*?" The woman wasn't familiar to Nimue at first. She was dowdy, wearing a baggy, wrinkled tan skirt and an oversized green cardigan, over which a long necklace dangled wildly, a circular gold band as its pendant. Her tempestuous, wavy, red-orange hair was held back just slightly at the temple with a bright green headband and her wide, pale brown eyes stared out from behind large, oversized glasses. Her creamy skin was splotchy with spots of eczema.

Rona Brynhild!

Reclusive cozy mystery author. Award-winning mystery author. Nimue had known she'd been pegged to make a rare appearance at one of the bookshops' booths, but it was still strange to see the author of books like the Miss Elwes's Cheery Mysteries Series out from her deep-woods cabin.

"It's called the Super Chilling Award! How in the blazes are your books *chilling*?"

Nimue recognized the man being poked with Rona's spindly finger, too. No stranger to the convention space—or any bookstore or convention signing—was Sherman Abbott, international bestseller spy thriller author.

She hadn't known the two were even acquainted with one another beyond often popping up on the mystery bestseller lists at the same time. They were both on the lists most of the time, actually.

Linden had come out from behind his desk and was attempting to direct Rona away from Sherman.

"Don't touch me!" Rona screeched as Linden's gloved hand gripped her upper arm. This, despite what she'd just been doing to Sherman herself. "And keep that mangy creature away from me."

Dyer the chinchilla had climbed down Linden's arm in her halting, rodent way. Rona whipped her hand out of Linden's grip and reached for her carpeted bag.

Zelena jogged ahead, holding out her wand. "What's the problem here?"

Ren winced beside Nimue, and Nimue realized a lot was riding on Rona Brynhild making a rare appearance at Bookshop Con in Cauldron Cove this year. Pre-registration numbers had reached capacity shortly after they'd made the announcement. As the former head of marketing, Ren had explained it all to Bernadette, how he and a human bookshop owner named Nicola Nash had managed to convince Rona to attend at Nicola's booth, how Nicola herself had been key to the arrangement.

Bernadette had never asked how Ren had known this Nicola and how the two of them had convinced the prolific mystery author. She'd just acknowledged the job well done.

Now that was about to blow up in his face if Rona left.

"Ms. Brynhild," Ren said, stepping between Zelena and his guest. "May I ask what the issue is?"

A woman from the small crowd gathered around the kerfuffle stepped forward. She looked to be about forty, with shiny, black hair in a sharp, angled bob. She was short but wore stiletto high heels that brought her up to Ren's shoulders. They seemed just a touch too fancy for the khaki pants and oversized white sweater and blouse that completed her ensemble.

"Rona, please—" the woman started.

Rona swirled on the woman in heels. "Don't 'Rona' me! No one warned me Sherman Abbott would be at this convention."

"All of our guests are publicized," said Ren, folding his hands in front of him.

Rona's eyes narrowed. "I don't pay attention to such things! My agent sends me everything I need to know and what I need to know, apparently, is this hack of a writer—"

"*Excuse me*?" Sherman bristled.

"Has been riling his fans up on these social message boards, accusing me of *bribing* the judges to win last year's Super Chilling Award!"

Gowdie tapped a wing against Nimue's head. *"Your boy Ren seems to be in hot water."*

He can handle it, said Nimue in her mind back to him. *He's the one who got her to come here.* She frowned. A glean of perspiration dotted Ren's brow and his jaw twitched. He *was* feeling nervous, as Gowdie had observed.

"What my fans say has nothing to do

with me." Sherman straightened his suitcoat as he stood beside his large rolling suitcase. He was dressed to the nines, his thinning silver hair smoothed back and affixed tightly in place. His thin mustache aged him somewhat, as did his overly tanned complexion, which seemed responsible for more than a few wrinkles around his mouth and neck. Nimue wondered if the author bio pics she'd seen of him had all been taken a decade or two ago or if the humans in charge of his publicity had used some of their computer tricks to smooth out all the signs of aging.

"You can tell them to knock it off!" shouted Rona. Ren hovered between her and Sherman, and Zelena stood closer to Sherman, along with Linden.

"I most certainly will not," said Sherman. "I don't interact with fans in such an uncouth manner."

"That's not what *I* hear!" shouted Rona.

"Baseless rumors, I assure you."

Nimue and Gowdie exchanged a look. *"Do I want to know what they're talking about?"*

Only if it's going to affect our con, thought Nimue back to him.

"Mr. Abbott," she said, speaking loud enough to be heard. "If Linden can please see to it that you have everything you need?"

Sherman bent down to grab the handle of his rolling suitcase, as well as a dry cleaning bag. "That's all I was *trying* to have the poor chap do before this wild woman came up from behind me and started screaming at me."

"'Wild woman'?" Rona screeched even louder. "You said yourself in an interview that *some* mystery authors don't even manage to make their books scary and yet they win Super Chilling Awards anyway!"

Sherman refused to look at her, draping the dry cleaning bag over his arm precisely. "Which is entirely true."

"I knew you were talking about me!"

"I didn't name names."

"You said, and I quote, 'We live in a world of magic, with witches and warlocks available to cast a spell for virtually anybody.'" Rona's face was growing red and

Nimue bristled at the description of a witch or warlock's duty—they were always discerning, the freelance ones, and the rest of them were too preoccupied with their own lives to bother selling charms to 'virtually anybody.' "'Which I make sure to weave into the mysteries of my books. Yet *some authors* pretend that worlds without magic exist and make it so average humans kill average humans with only the tools available to them. Poison in the wine. A rock to the back of the head. How dreary.'" Rona stomped her foot. "Those are two methods killers have used in Miss Elwes's Cheery Mysteries!"

"Oh? Are they?" Sherman cracked a smile. "I don't have a lot of time to read magic-less mysteries."

"It's *cozy human-only world* mysteries! And it's a legit genre! That I happen to be on top of!"

That much was true. Nimue had only read a couple of Rona Brynhild's books because the unrealistic portrayal of a world without magic, though quirky and enjoyable, just hadn't been her cup of tea.

It was something hundreds of thousands —perhaps millions—of other readers cared to disagree with her on, and that was fine.

Nimue didn't believe in genre snobbery amongst readers.

"Ms. Brynhild, if I may escort you to the Southern Hotel," Ren said. "Operated by my parents. I will be sure you get first-class treatment."

Rona frowned, her hand still shaking at her side, but she nodded at Ren. "Just keep that man away from me. And wait until my agent hears about this!"

Nimue wondered what a literary agent could do about any of this, but she kept her mouth shut.

"Allow me." Ren took Rona's carpeted bag from her and she seemed to perk up at the first-class treatment. A person who humbled even Ren Southern. "Nicola, if you'll join us?" Ren said to the short woman in heels. So that was the bookshop owner Ren knew somehow who'd convinced the reclusive Rona Brynhild to show her face.

The three left out the front door of the lobby to the sidewalk, Ren probably opting to avoid the skywalk and teleportation pad so they didn't have to brush past Sherman on their way to either place.

"Well," said Nimue, turning to Linden. She jumped in place as she noticed a red welt behind his glasses, a small cut where the frames must have dug into the skin. Dyer the chinchilla sat on his head, licking the wound.

"Linden, did Rona Brynhild do that to you?" Nimue realized with a start that Rona had gotten rather wild when she'd tugged her arm out of Linden's grip.

Linden put a hand to his temple. It came back with the smallest dot of blood. "So she did." He chuckled. "Don't get too close to an angry author."

"Lin... What have I told you? You don't work in security. Stop putting yourself in volatile situations like that." Zelena's hard features softened as she cast a Healing Charm on her husband with a wave of her wand. "Or if you must, at least whip out some defense magic."

"Witchy Expo Services Guest Services

staff *never* relies on magic among humans when elbow grease will do."

Sherman's jaw dropped slightly, his eyes widening. "I still can't get over it," he said, his voice tinged with awe. "Every time I see one of you casting magic."

A flutter of pride bubbled in Nimue's stomach, but it was cut short remembering the quote Rona had attributed to him—and the plot of most of his thrillers.

Witches and warlocks like her parents didn't cast spells for wicked people at any price.

"Excuse me?" A man from the surrounding crowd stepped up, looking at Linden, seemingly fascinated by Zelena's healing magic, too.

"Yes, sir?" Linden asked, all business and straightening his gloves. He didn't even react to his wife putting her wand away.

"I was just wondering… If I know you? You look familiar."

Linden was all smiles. "Have you been to a convention at the Bessa before?"

"Well, yes…" The man looked over his shoulder at a woman Nimue presumed to be his wife beside him. "We came for a Home Adornment Expo a few years back. Looking for interesting shelving ware for our bookshop."

"I've been here sixty years," Linden said. He didn't look a day over fifty, so Nimue could see the guests were taken aback. "So I would venture you *have* seen me before."

"Mr. Abbott," Nimue said smoothly, gesturing to the floating platform that took guests up to the skywalk. "I take it you're booked at the Southern Hotel, too?"

"I didn't know there was any other option in town." There wasn't, really. Short of local witches and warlocks opening up their doors to guests. An especially fluttery book swept by about a dozen feet above them, hovering overhead while it did a flashy pirouette. "Stunning. A reader's fairy land."

Nimue felt her guard softening around this man.

"I think it best we allow Ms. Brynhild a chance to check in," suggested Linden, going back around the concierge desk.

"I think we should kick her out." Zelena

crossed her arms and Messenger the sloth slowly nodded. "She's a security threat."

"Oh, don't worry on my account." Sherman fluffed off her suggestion. "There's plenty of room for both of us in this opulent convention center."

Zelena frowned and looked to Nimue, then to Linden, who was busy fussing with providing Sherman his VIP badge and gift bag.

Rona had attacked one of their own, too.

"Ren wouldn't be happy," Nimue explained, and she knew it was true. "Too many tickets sold for the chance to see her."

Zelena huffed. "Well, it was my job to offer you my professional opinion, and I did." She turned on her heel. "Don't blame me if you regret letting a security threat stay as *guest of honor*." She headed back to the main showroom floor.

Nimue took a step back and assessed the lobby. There were still four others who'd witnessed the altercation.

"Hi," she said, approaching the group. "Please let me apologize on behalf of Witchy Expo Services. I'm Nimue Toothaker, one of

the Head Witch General Managers." She extended her hand in turn to the three women
and one man who remained. "And this"—
she gestured at her familiar, as it was clear
he was getting the lion's share of the
group's attention—"is Gowdie, my
familiar."

Two of the women whispered to one another and laughed, their faces crinkling as
they cooed in Gowdie's direction.

He puffed up, showing off his little
broad chest proudly and stretching out his
wings behind Nimue's head.

"Nimue?" the eldest woman present
asked. She had black-and-gray hair in a
page cut and was all around a bit unremark-
able, though her bright brown eyes glistened beautifully from behind her pale
brown complexion. "Not Bernadette?"

The man beside her, the one who'd said
Linden had looked familiar, put an arm
around her. "Bernadette welcomed us on
the phone last week when we told her we
were thinking of booking last minute." He
was tall and broad, slightly darker-skinned
than his wife or partner, with thick, curly

black hair and a trimmed beard that was mostly silver. "Delgado Books. From New York?"

"I think I remember you…" Nimue said. Being Bernadette's assistant felt like a lifetime ago now.

"Penny and Virgil Delgado," the woman explained.

"Ah! Yes, we have a great placement for your booth this year." Nimue smiled. "And thank you for supporting Witchy ExS. Bernadette has retired. I'm her granddaughter."

"Oh, that's a shame," said another of the women there. She was dark-skinned and wearing a bright, orange hourglass dress. Her figure, along with her frizzy, black hair and orange eyeshadow, made her as stunning as a model. "She spoke to me directly when booking me for the con and I was planning to thank her for her kind attentions. Lola Jackson."

Nimue's eyes bugged out. *The* Lola Jackson! How could she not have recognized her! Her romances hit bestseller lists with every release—and since she was indie, she managed to put out at least six books a year. It was a wonder she had time to travel to any convention.

Bernadette must have pulled some strings to get her to show up.

"Well, she's still in town," Nimue said. "I bet she'll show up once the con is up and running, just to see how things go."

A book swooped down and then hovered overhead, causing the five of them—even Nimue—to cry out and duck, though it wasn't ever in any danger of hitting them.

The third woman, a thin, small woman with a smooth, tawny complexion and ultra-straight black hair, laughed. "Con-goers are going to love that."

Nimue felt her chest swell. "Shawna Higgins?" she ventured.

YA author. Her first series had been turned into a movie franchise a while back. The first couple had made hundreds of millions, though the last had kind of stuttered at the box office, the pacing of one book stretched into two movies—the second of which had been cancelled in pre-production—adding to a waning interest in the franchise. Her books still sold decently, but Hollywood hadn't come knocking again.

"Yup." Shawna winced and tucked a strand of hair behind her ear, as if she'd been called out and had to apologize.

Lola wrapped an arm around her. "We came together. Met at a con a few years back. Now we're best friends."

Shawna beamed. "But that con didn't have hovering books."

Virgil nudged his wife and pointed up above him. "What do you think, Pen? Should we pay a witch to make our books float at the bookshop, too?"

"I don't know." Penny shirked as one did another swooping loop. "I'd be afraid they'd fall on my head."

"Hey, don't judge a book by its hover." Virgil winked. "They look to be perfectly well-mannered books."

Nimue chuckled. The books would stay up there until a witch or warlock tapped their wand against the crystal and summoned them back. Unless the crystal itself was broken. But perma-charms were far sturdier than the average glass.

Sherman nodded his head at the book-shop owners. "Virgil, Penny, I shall see you anon." He and Linden walked away from the concierge.

"Yes, tomorrow! Thank you!" Penny cried.

"Sherman is signing at our booth." Virgil stuck his chest out, as if it were something of which he was quite proud.

Penny glanced at Shawna and Lola beside her. "Any chance you two might sign some of your books at our booth?"

The authors exchanged a look. "Well, we have panels and bookshops we're already doing signings at," said Lola. "But give us a nudge before you go and we can sign some to take back to your store."

Shawna nodded her agreement.

"I don't get authors," Gowdie said in Nimue's mind. *"Some are reclusive, and some are all out there, soaking up the limelight."*

It takes all kinds, Nimue thought to her familiar, giving him a tickle under his chin. He flew up, gliding, darting around and through all of the flying books overhead.

Shawna gasped and reached out toward him. "I want a baby dragon."

Lola sighed dreamily. "I want a grown-up dragon. Shifter. Boyfriend."

The two giggled again.

Shifter romance was a popular romance genre, though shifters didn't exist in real life. Authors were full of all sorts of imaginative ideas. Humans who turned into animals. Humans who lived without ever knowing magic was real.

Linden made his way back to the concierge desk and invited Lola and Shawna over to get their badges. Sherman could be seen walking outside on the skywalk in the air.

"You're hosting Sherman?" Nimue asked the Delgados.

The couple nodded.

"Well, it was sort of last minute," Penny said. "His agent called us up, said he'd seen we had a booth at Bookshop Con, and we jumped at the chance to host him."

Nimue tapped a finger to her lips. She'd never been in charge of memorizing all of the guests or anything, but she did remember Sherman Abbott's name on the roster the past few days. Perhaps he'd been a recent addition. If she'd ever been interested in reading more of his books, she might have cared more.

But he often painted a witch or warlock as the villain, or at least among the killer's helpers. That personally didn't sit right with Nimue, though she understood the appeal dark magic may have had to some readers.

"But I tell you one thing, if it had been Rona Brynhild's agent, we would have told her to forget it," added Virgil.

Nimue's interest was piqued. "Oh?"

Penny nodded. "Not even for a million dollars."

Nimue blinked slowly. Rona was clearly not a delight to deal with, but they'd pass up the opportunity to host one of the world's best-selling authors? She outsold Sherman Abbott, too, at nearly every opportunity.

"That woman just isn't nice." Virgil's lips thinned.

"I almost panicked when I saw her here," Penny said. "I mean, I knew she was coming, but I hoped we'd never run into her. But she didn't seem to recognize us."

"You know her?" Nimue asked. Linden was escorting Shawna and Lola to the sky-walk platform now, Gowdie riding a book like a surfboard and chirping out his delight.

Virgil squeezed his wife's shoulder. "Best not to badmouth her. Word spreads fast in the industry." He guided his wife to the concierge desk, waiting for Linden's return.

A red flash of light projected from Nimue's perma-charm wrist crystal and she swiped it to bring up her projected witch network screen. A message from Cassie awaited, asking where she was and what she needed to help with next.

"It was nice meeting you," Nimue said to the Delgados, a tiny part of her hoping they might elaborate on what had gone down with them and Rona.

Had she been wrong not to press for the reclusive author's expulsion from the event?

Penny offered her a flittering smile. "You, too, Nimue. See you around."

"See you around," Nimue echoed.

Well, word supposedly spread fast in the book world. If there was anything Nimue needed to know that might affect the operation of Bookshop Con, she was sure she'd find out soon enough.

CHAPTER SEVEN

"What do you think for the healthier option? Ants on a log or carrots and hummus?" Tituba tapped her wand to her lips in front of the ConSuite table.

"Hummus," Nimue answered. "Celery, too, is fine. But too many humans have peanut allergies. I'd rather not have a Medic Witch at the ready on hand."

"Ah, point taken." Tituba scribbled a note on her wrist crystal's projection of the witch network. "Speaking of, did Ren tell you about his idea? To hire a human doctor or nurse to man the first aid station along with the medical witches?"

"No." Nimue frowned. Ren was off

somewhere overseeing the final incoming shipment of books and other items to go into the individual booths, and he'd taken Cassie with him. "Did he hire someone for Bookshop Con?"

Tituba shook her head. "Not enough time. Bernadette sort of liked the idea—someone with knowledge of human medicine, who could always perform their tasks even if the medical witches expended all of their relevant charms for the day—but she found the likelihood of that happening to be too low. Any passerby witch could lend a hand with medical charms in a pinch anyway. Besides, most first aid calls are just for, like, exhaustion. Easy enough to fix."

Gowdie had Graves on his back and was flying the little frog familiar overhead up and down around the ConSuite. Nimue watched them, her heart lightening at the sight of their jubilant expressions, some of the tension of the day lifting from her shoulders.

"But I think I agree with Ren. A human expert on hand to treat humans could prove invaluable. Especially since the nearest human hospital takes a while to get to."

Tituba nudged her friend, her elbow coming up to just about Nimue's shoulder. "Is this Nimue Toothaker? Agreeing with Ren Southern on something?"

"All right, all right." Nimue suppressed a smile and rubbed her arm. "But I guess it might not hurt to tell him that I like the idea. Though I don't know why he never ran it by me."

"Too focused on *this* con, I'd wager."

The teleportation portal nearby flickered orange and Zelena stepped through. She grunted when she caught sight of Nimue with Tituba. "Staff's ready for dinner in the break room," she said to the taller witch.

Tituba nodded. "You coming?" she asked Nimue.

Nimue's stomach rumbled. "I thought I should be on hand for the welcome dinner for the guests of honor at the hotel instead." Her grandmother always had been. Nimue had gone a few times, but Ren had always been there, too. That, and Tituba's cooking offered in the break room here, had been reason enough to grab a bite from the break room instead of getting all fancy for some single-pea-on-a-plate type cuisine served at the Southern family's ritzy hotel restaurant.

Zelena frowned. "I suppose I should update you, too. As far as Brynhild goes, she's retreated to her room all afternoon. She's going to take dinner in there. Con security is keeping an eye on the situation."

"'Situation'?" Nimue laughed nervously as Tituba raised a questioning eyebrow. She hadn't thought it important to tell her friend about the kerfuffle in the lobby. "An argument between two authors is hardly a *situation*."

"When one of the authors is poking those bruising fingers of hers at all manner of chests, I take note." Zelena stiffened her body, as if ready to be called into action. "And I'd advise a Head Witch General Manager worth her salt to do the same."

She walked out through the front door of the ConSuite and Tituba dismissed her witch network screen.

"She's exaggerating," Nimue said with a chuckle. "There was a little argument between some rival authors who arrived at con check-in at the same time earlier."

Gowdie landed on the long, empty buffet table and Graves hopped off his back and to Tituba's open palm.

"Zelena may rub most people the wrong way, but she's good at her job," said Tituba. "If she says to keep an eye on things, I'd keep an eye on things."

Nimue sighed, wilting under Tituba's assessing glare. "Fine," she said. Perhaps she'd been especially keen to dismiss Zelena's concerns because Zelena, on the whole, was so quick to dismiss Nimue entirely. "I'll try to keep the rival authors apart."

Pulling out her wand, she did a Makeover Charm, extending it outward to cover Gowdie, too. With a twirl, she showed off her new look: red, ankle-length, hourglass dress, no witch hat, and her hair smoothed back into a lower bun. Her regular clothes would appear again by sunrise, when a witch's magic reset. Gowdie, wearing a matching red bowtie, took his place on her shoulder.

"Nice," said Tituba, whistling. "You'll knock 'em dead."

Nimue chuckled. "I hope not. Or I'll wish Ren had gotten his human doctor hired in time for this con. It's our guests of honor's time to shine."

"Well, there's nothing wrong with shining a little bit yourself from your corner overseeing it all." Tituba walked with Nimue toward the ConSuite's teleportation pad. "Especially since you don't get out enough when not working."

"Look who's talking!" Nimue rolled her eyes. "I know you're not interested in romance—"

"For myself," Tituba said. That was true enough. She loved reading romance novels, but she was aro ace.

"But," said Nimue, undeterred, "you haven't taken a day off in months."

"And you know that because you've been here working Witchy ExS yourself every single day you can." Tituba's voice was nearly drowned out by Graves's croaks as he settled into place for the teleportation on the brim of Tituba's hat. "Ever since

Willow went off to college, your work addiction has only gotten worse."

"Well, *you* could go visit Atlantes in the human world for once instead of him always coming here."

"My brother and his family enjoy coming to most of the conventions." Tituba shrugged. "If they're open to the public, the kids look forward to them. They love playing around in Cauldron Cove."

None of Atlantes's children had inherited the magic necessary to become witches and warlocks themselves. When witches married humans, they passed the gene along. When warlocks did, the magic line cut off with them. But for most people, love was more important than any magic family line. Even if that meant that the Jonesdochter line was in danger of being at an end.

"Well, I love seeing them, too," Nimue admitted. There was little like the joy of a child in a world of wonder to remind Nimue that their work was, in its own way, important to those even beyond their home's borders. And the magic produced by Witchy ExS fed into Cauldron Cove itself, making each convention's success particularly important to local witches and warlocks.

"I'll make sure they swing by to say *hi*," Tituba said. "Not sure when they'll get here." They lived in Huntsville, so it wasn't much of a commute to the parking area at the edge of town. But between work and school, they often weren't able to show up until the weekends of a con.

Tituba gave Nimue a little salute and stepped through the teleportation pad, the white glow changing to blue. Once it flickered back to white, Nimue held her destination at the forefront of her mind—the Southern Hotel lobby, the only transportation pad set up in the neighboring hotel, for those less inclined to use the skywalk—and vanished through.

The Southern Hotel lobby wanted to have its cake and eat it, too. Or at least the minds behind its décor did.

To the left of the teleportation pad, just beside the pad that launched those to the skywalk who were willing to walk to the Bessa, was a wide, open space with glistening white floors opposite a giant, crystal chandelier. It sparkled bright light over sleek, modern tables and chairs beside a dimly lit bar with golden stools around a gold-and-black countertop, as well as a few scattered small tables. To Nimue's right, the forest theme that worked its way into much of Cauldron Cove's décor had overtaken the space, which had far less overhead light but was plenty lit by the floating balls of light meant to invoke something like a firefly effect. An overgrown tree root acted as the concierge desk. It connected to an oak tree that grew all the way up through the top of the hotel, its bushy boughs visibly poking out over the roof.

"Miss Toothaker," said the warlock behind the front desk as Nimue passed by, her wedge heels echoing out against the polished floor. Probably around Willow's age, he was a tall, young man with long, voluminous hair and a dark complexion whom

Nimue had seen around town on occasion. A little lizard stuck its tongue out from the top of the desk. It had to be his familiar. "Mr. Southern told me to expect you. He's gone ahead and started the guest of honor dinner in the banquet hall."

Nimue stopped short, her footsteps echoing outward. "He's *what?*"

Gowdie took to the air from her shoulder, scouting ahead as far as he could fly from her on her behalf.

The young man in his shiny, blue uniform suit shirked at her stare.

"Miss Tooth—Nimue!" Cassie's familiar voice, followed by clopping heels, drew Nimue's attention from the forest-path-like hallway out into the lobby. "Mr. Southern wanted me to see if you'd arrived yet."

Her stern lips turned into a slight smile as she spared a glance at the man behind the counter. "Thank you, Fidelity. I'll take it from here."

"Yes, of course, Cas—Miss Cabot." He grinned back. Nimue would have thought she'd been imagining things, but Cassie's green ferret slipped off his witch's shoulders to offer cheek rubs to Fidelity's lizard on the concierge desk before hopping back into place, all business on Cassie's shoulder once more.

Nimue hustled after Cassie, Gowdie shooting out from down the dark hallway to sit on her shoulder again. "Did he start the dinner without me? It was supposed to start at seven."

"They're already eating in there," Gowdie reported in Nimue's mind.

Nimue frowned. She was ten minutes early. Or she was *supposed to be*.

"Miss Brynhild had second thoughts about enjoying dinner in her room," Cassie explained, as if that would also explain why Ren had started the dinner without his co-manager. "She *is* the main draw for Bookshop Con, after all. So we reached out to the other guests to tell them to come early." The other guests. But not Nimue. "Mr. Abbott refused our offer of providing *him* with a dinner in his room, even though Mr. Southern offered the finest the hotel has to offer, free of charge, and well, Mr. Varlett is keeping him distracted until seven with the hopes that Miss Brynhild will be finished by then."

"And Sherman Abbott won't notice the fact that everyone present is on dessert when he arrives?" Nimue asked, flabbergasted.

"He's aware he's going to be late. He expressed an interest in seeing the behind-the-scenes of Witchy Expo Services earlier, and Mr. Southern had Mr. Varlett, as Director of Guest Services, undertake the duties of showing him around."

Nimue gritted her teeth as they turned the corner and the open door of the banquet hall at hallways' end beckoned them. No guest of a con had ever been given a *tour* of "behind-the-scenes" efforts before. She hoped Linden knew to keep trade secrets to a minimum. There were other witches and warlocks out there who'd started offering events similar to Witchy ExS's. None could match the scale so far, but there was a reason why Bernadette had never indulged any of these other covens' requests for a friendly industry expo at Cauldron Cove's own convention center.

"Why didn't *you* keep me informed?" Nimue snapped. Ren, she could almost see wanting to hog the glory of this plan, or presuming Nimue wasn't up to the task of juggling two important guests whose paths oughtn't ever meet. But Cassie was a friend of her daughter's. Nimue had recommended her for the job as much as Ren had.

The fur on Laveau, Cassie's ferret, went stiff.

"I've been busy," said Cassie. "But I apologize. I should have at least sent a message." If not by Communication Charm, then by witch network, certainly. A flash of red would have alerted Nimue to the message.

"Make sure you do in the future," Nimue said. Gowdie let out a little puff of smoke to accentuate her point. "I'm supposed to be Ren's *co*-manager."

Caught out, Cassie wrinkled her nose. "Mr. Southern worried you might not agree with his—"

"That doesn't give him the right to just go ahead and do whatever he wants behind my back." Nimue winced. Like she had done with the floating books display. But so what? That was less consequential than shutting a partner out of an important dinner—and showing a *guest* behind the scenes of Witchy ExS.

Nimue shot out in front of Cassie, arriving inside the banquet hall before her.

The warmly lit banquet hall shared more of the stark, modern décor Nimue knew the elder Mr. Southern was fond of, red carpeting and red-backed sleek chairs around tables covered in bright white tablecloths.

Nimue recognized Lola and Shawna, the two author best friends, seated with a few unfamiliar faces. Nimue could make her rounds around the room to introduce herself later. They all had coffees and desserts in front of them already.

Virgil and Penny, bookstore owners, were dining with some unfamiliar faces, though Nimue was sure one of them might have been Professor Wayne Gomez, a prolific non-fiction author of history. The man was laughing at something Penny said, gesticulating wildly with bony hands in response.

At the head table was Rona Brynhild herself, next to Nicola, the bookstore owner hosting Rona for the event, and Ren. Beside Ren was an empty seat without a dish in front of it that ought to have belonged to Nimue.

She strode past the few tables of guests, sidling up beside one of the hotel staff gathering plates, complete with a large slug familiar that started eating up the crumbs on Ren's plate, and stood straight in front of Ren on the other side of the table.

She stared him down. Gowdie took flight, flapping his wings and settling down at the top of the empty high-backed chair, shooting daggers downward. Balfour, wherever she was at Ren's feet, responded with a hiss.

Ren didn't flinch under her glare. "Nimue, so nice of you to join us." He gestured to Rona, who was digging into a piece of dark chocolate cake with relish. "You missed Rona's story about what inspired her latest mystery."

Rona gave Nimue a onceover, her lips

pinched, as if deciding what to make of the witch.

Looking around at how the others had dressed, well, Nimue didn't feel *overdressed*, per se. But Rona herself was still wearing the same wrinkly Bohemian getup she'd arrived in, her hair somehow even messier.

"She researched real murders," said Nicola from Rona's other side. She gazed at the mystery author beside her, clearly enraptured, her own dessert just picked at. "And imagined what it would have been like if there hadn't been witch and warlock consulting detectives to solve them, didn't you, Rona?"

"Yes." Rona spoke with her mouth still full of cake. "It takes a good, *human* sleuth to figure things out." She took a sip of wine and decided to ignore Nimue entirely after that.

Nimue bristled despite herself, finding her sympathies lying with Sherman Abbott the more time she spent around Rona, and she wasn't particularly a fan of Sherman, either. Though at least he didn't pretend witches and wizards didn't *exist* in his novels.

Not that there was anything wrong with creativity. She hadn't particularly cared about authors writing all-human worlds before meeting Rona.

Now she wondered if Rona's creativity was rooted in some kind of *deeper* dislike of witches and warlocks. Though what she was doing in Cauldron Cove of all places, then…

Nimue clenched her jaw and walked around the table, sitting in front of Gowdie in the empty chair.

"Would you like chicken or fish?" the slug-familiar warlock waiter asked, as if it were totally normal for a member of the dinner party to come so much later.

Nimue's stomach growled. She wished she could skip the dinner entirely. "Fish," she said, clearing her throat. Once the waiter left, she grabbed her napkin and laid it over her lap for lack of something better to do.

"So, Ren," said Nicola, picking up her fork and getting back to work on her cake, "despite how long we've known each other, I guess I never got around to asking before. What kind of books do you read?"

How long they've known each other? Nimue wondered.

Rona also seemed to perk up at the prospect of finding out what kind of books he read.

Ren didn't seem to pick up on Rona's interest. "Non-fiction, mostly."

Rona's jaw worked overtime to finish off her cake as she tossed her fork down to the plate with a clatter. "Non-fiction dulls the mind."

Ren raised an eyebrow but didn't comment. Nimue took a sip from her lukewarm water that had been poured probably an hour before.

Then, with Balfour letting out a growl from somewhere around Ren's feet, he shook his head, letting his blond hair fall around his face. Like magic, it lost its glossy, crisp sheen from the pomade, falling in unkempt waves.

"I read a lot of romance," Soren said. His voice was light, airy, the smile on his face broad. Nimue choked on the sip she was taking at the nicer version of the man's confession. "And, I know I'm a bit old, but I really like YA, too. When it's fantasy or dystopian. Books like Shawna Higgins's. My favorite bookmark is decorated with the covers from her Ruin and Wreckage trilogy." At least Soren used bookmarks like a civilized reader, unlike Ren. Well, Nimue realized she was just being unnecessarily harsh on Ren. All readers were civilized, regardless of bookmark choices.

Soren peered out at the nearby table with the author best friends, including Shawna Higgins herself. "I think a teen protagonist allows authors to grapple with issues like finding one's identity, even in the midst of unimaginable circumstances."

"*Romance*?" sneered Rona. The conversation coming from Lola and Shawna's table died down, the authors and their companions drawn to Rona's volume. "*Young adult*?"

Nicola jumped in her chair. Nimue wondered how much Nicola knew about Soren's two personalities, but she seemed more concerned about Rona's bulging forehead vein at the moment. "Yes, well, some readers enjoy a variety of genres. Bookshop owners especially like to keep up with all of the trends. I'm sure Mr. Southern also enjoys mystery—"

"Not really." Soren patted Balfour's arched back as she jumped up onto his lap. "They can be rather frightening."

"Oh, but I suppose dystopian futures where children are assigned a life partner or told to murder one another in cold blood, *that* isn't frightening!" Rona was practically frothing at the mouth now, clutching at her throat, at the simple silver chain that was now mostly tucked beneath her sweater. "Or tried and overdone." She narrowed her eyes at Shawna, who gasped.

Lola and Shawna whispered amongst each other. Nimue knew Rona had been describing the books Shawna had written that had become a few hit movies.

"And like happily ever after, same old, same old isn't trite, either," Rona said, narrowing her gaze at Lola this time. Lola's jaw dropped, but Rona wasn't done. "Try writing without magic in your worlds sometime! Might be more interesting to see how a couple falls in love without the help of a witchy godmother or a series of 'cute' misunderstandings caused by the witch next door." She scoffed. "Though worst of all: Making up new kinds of magic entirely. Like all those animal shifter heroes."

"Excuse me?" Lola jumped to her feet.

"Ren—Soren," Nimue said quickly, moving her napkin back to the table as she stood, too. "Perhaps we should see Rona back to her room now that she's finished with her dessert. Especially considering Sherman is about to show up—"

"Sherman is *what*?" Rona smacked her fist on the table as Shawna tried unsuccessfully to get Lola to sit back down. "Did you not assure me that lout would be absent for tonight's dinner?"

Soren blinked. He and Ren shared enough of a conscious mind that they could access each other's memories in a pinch, and no doubt Balfour could fill them in on the necessary details, but they were two separate personalities. From what Nimue knew of the gentler warlock, Soren generally didn't like to think too hard about Ren's frame of mind during his turn at bat.

"As you can tell by the fact that you've been welcome here this evening as well," said Nimue, stepping up for Soren while Balfour or his memories caught him up to speed, "we don't believe in excluding any guest from the special activities we have planned for them." It was so quiet in the room otherwise that Nimue could have sworn she heard a fork drop on the carpet.

But it worked. Lola offered Nimue a satisfied smile and sat back down next to Shawna, pointedly turning her back on the reclusive bestselling author who'd insulted her.

Rona bristled at Nimue's words, even if couched in her best customer service speak, and before she could do more than mumble an incoherent response, Cassie's voice carried down from the hallway.

Nimue had almost forgotten about the assistant who'd "forgotten" to update Nimue about Ren's change of plans.

Cassie's heels clicked into the silence of

the room, a broad smile on her face as she gestured Sherman and Linden inside.

The smile dropped when she found the entire room staring at their arrival.

Rona pounded the table and stood. "Nicola," she snapped. "I'm leaving. One more hack author in here, and my brain is sure to rot from their uncreative stank."

"Oh, jump in the lake!" shouted Shawna. "And take your anti-magic books with you!"

Lola's eyes widened as she stared at her best friend. Then the both of them devolved into giggles.

Soren leaped to his feet, Balfour letting out a little mew as she jumped onto the table.

"She told her warlock all about the stunt Ren pulled, excluding you," came Gowdie's voice in Nimue's head. *"With pride, I might add."*

Balfour hissed at him and Gowdie let out a little puff of smoke.

Rona and Nicola were already halfway to the door, Cassie doing her best to usher Sherman inside and give the approaching grouchy author a wide berth. Linden stayed by the door, his gloved hands clasped in front of him in his most customer service of poses.

"Miss Brynhild," said Soren, trailing after her and stumbling. "I have to apologize for-for anything I may have done or said to offend you—"

The words carried around the enraptured room, the gathered crowd just small enough to pay attention to the goings-on in detail.

"Stealing the plot of an Agathe Christo novel and just swapping the names and removing the magic—*that*'s truly offensive to those of us in the mystery genre." Sherman didn't keep his voice quiet as he took the seat Cassie had shown him to between Penny and Wayne, straightening the lanyard holding up his badge around his chest. Actually, he had two lanyards for some reason. Some people did like to think of the complimentary lanyards as souvenirs of the convention.

Murmurs and gasps broke out around the room.

Rona swirled on her heel to face Sherman, though she didn't take a step toward him. "It's called *an homage,*" she said. "Not that you'd recognize the act of paying tribute to great works of literature if it jumped up and slapped you in that disagreeable face!"

"*Rona!*" said Nicola beside her, as if, between all the insults about other authors' works, the worst one that had been lobbied had to do with a man's appearance.

Besides, it was clearly more hyperbolic than anything. Sherman was older and had a rather sour attitude that reminded Nimue too much of her treacherous co-manager, but he was handsome enough.

"Oh, but I suppose insisting your ARCs be printed in hardcover against industry standard so they look 'nicer on your shelf,' that makes you a bona fide special author somehow?"

"*You're* the one who…. Forget it, you numbskull!"

"You call yourself a writer?" Sherman stood back up, clutching the table in front of him. "Only hacks resort to base insults."

Rona sputtered and launched herself at

the table. Luckily, both Nicola and Soren jumped in, dragging her back. Nimue made her way to block the view between the two authors as Rona let out a string of curses that would have made a sailor blush.

Sherman, for his part, brushed a bit of lint off his shoulder and sat back down.

"You're dead!" shouted Rona.

Cassie let out a little gurgling gasp as Gowdie flew around in the air overhead, taking in the scene.

"You're dead, Sherman Narcissist, Thankless Abbott!" repeated Rona as Soren and Nicola dragged her to the door.

"Not before I manage to kill a character called Morona Brynbuild in my next book." Sherman smiled wickedly and gestured both hands in front of him as if imagining the story on some billboard up in lights. "I'll call it *Death by the Written Word: The Last Gasp of the Plagiarizing Hack.*"

"*Mr. Abbott,*" snapped Nimue, turning on her heel to face the man.

He shrugged and offered a bemused smile, crossing his arms as Rona shrieked and shrieked as she was dragged to the door.

Sherman lowered his voice and spoke to Penny. "My agent would stop me," he said. "No way would my publisher's lawyers put up with such a book."

"What are you looking at?!" shouted Rona.

Nimue turned to find Rona finally free of Soren and Nicola, straightening her oversized cardigan and directing her purple face toward Linden at the door, of all people.

Linden offered a tight, customer service smile. "My favorite author, of course."

After the indignity she'd just suffered, that seemed to be the last thing Rona had expected. She *harrumphed* and made her way out the door, Nicola fast at her heels.

The swinging door leading to the kitchen opened and the waiter walked in with a single plate full of fish and green beans and rice in one hand, his slug familiar in the other.

Nimue's stomach rumbled as Cassie moved toward Soren to touch base.

Gowdie swooped down near the waiter

and inhaled as everyone else around the room broke out into uneasy conversation.

"I know I don't eat, but that smells delicious," Gowdie said in her head. *"Surely, you can let Soren and Cassie take point on this one?"*

Since Ren and Cassie had caused this issue in the first place…

Not that *Soren* had had a hand in it.

Noticing Balfour's little stuck-up nose, her high tail as she jumped up onto the table beside where Soren was standing, Nimue shrugged.

At the very least, she deserved a good meal after the mess made of the evening, whoever was to blame.

CHAPTER EIGHT

By the time Nimue got home and had spent an hour in a bubble bath reading the latest—she found a strange surge of pride in the thought, considering how it had bothered Rona Brynhild—Dora Boberts romance, she had exactly four and a half hours to sleep before she had to get up again.

Gowdie was already getting the most of what time he had, curled up on top of his castle-themed cat tree Willow had insisted Nimue buy for him when they'd moved back to Cauldron Cove.

He did look like a little dragon conqueror, snoring steam from his slitted nostrils, his spiky tail draping down off the carpet-covered "castle" turret.

Nimue had just finished putting on her body cream and pulled back her purple comforter and red satin sheets when the doorbell rang.

Gowdie smacked his jaw together sleepily but didn't rouse from the cat tree beside Nimue's bed.

He would have sensed if it were any-thing she needed to be concerned about, surely.

The doorbell rang again. Pulling on her robe from the hook behind her bedroom door, Nimue made her way downstairs and to the front door of her narrow brick town-house just on the outskirts of downtown Cauldron Cove to peer through the peephole.

On the front step stood Soren Southern, his floppy hair covering his eyes.

Despite herself—and realizing it had to be Soren, not Ren, not only because of his appearance, but because Ren wouldn't have been caught dead on her doorstep—Nimue winced and had to shake out her arms before she took a deep breath and opened the door.

"Soren," she whispered, as if her neighbors could hear her. Their townhouses did touch hers, leaving only a small fenced-in back yard for each, but this being Cauldron Cove, even the smallest patch of yard was forest-like in nature. Nonetheless, everyone else was likely fast asleep. As she and Soren ought to have been, considering Bookshop Con began in the morning.

Before Soren could reply, Nimue felt a furry tail brush her bare leg. Which made her realize with a start that her silken robe was rather short, her usually tights-covered legs fully exposed. She clutched the top of the robe tighter together as she watched Balfour stride in and jump up on the nearest plush armchair.

"Well, make yourself at home, why don't you?" Nimue muttered to Soren's cat.

"Thank you," said Soren, apparently not picking up on her sarcasm—or the fact that she'd been speaking to Balfour—at all. Nimue wondered if she was imagining Balfour's sly smile as Soren stepped in, wringing his hands and having a seat on the two-seater couch beside the armchair. The fireplace, as it had been perma-charmed to do when Nimue had moved in, sparked to life at the sensation that someone was seated near it and felt cold. Soren stroked his arms quickly and then rubbed his hands together in front of the fire.

Nimue, still at the front door, cocked an eyebrow but shut the door. On bare feet, she padded closer to the fire, grateful for the warmth on her exposed skin.

"Soren, it's one in the morning. We have a big day tomorrow—"

"I'm sorry," he said, and for a moment, Nimue figured he was apologizing for the intrusion at the late, late hour. But then he looked up at her from behind his uneven bangs and Nimue melted at the sincerity she found there.

She staggered, seizing the back of the armchair in which Balfour was seated to keep herself standing.

She did not relish the thought of being barely presentable *and* finding Soren Southern a little bit attractive.

"Balfour reminded me of everything Ren did, and well, I… He shouldn't have kept the dinner start time change from you."

"So it *was* done on purpose?" she asked. Balfour looked up and whapped her tail, and Nimue wondered why Gowdie wasn't picking up on the fact that his rival was in the room just below him.

She'd never really doubted she'd been "overlooked" on purpose. It would just be nice to hear the words from the lips of the man at fault—or at least, the right lips, even if the wrong man.

"Cassie wanted to let you know, but Ren assured her you were too busy to be bothered and that you would shut down his idea, anyway."

"Only because apparently, Linden and Ren offered Sherman Abbott a *tour* behind-the-scenes!" said Nimue, her voice rising. "I wouldn't have cared about the dinner time changing, as long as I was made aware of it."

Balfour let out a long, audible sigh, her tail continually whaping against the chair.

"I know," said Soren. "Believe me, I

know. I don't get what Ren was thinking on either point. He doesn't always approve of your ideas—"

"I've noticed."

"But it's not on principle or anything. It's because he genuinely sees the need for improvement in them."

Nimue glowered and crossed her arms, making Soren sink further into the sofa. Still, he continued.

"But he seems to think you would shut his ideas down *just because* they're his ideas."

"That's ridiculous!" She threw her hands in the air as the flap, flap, flap of thinly membraned wings drew her attention to the narrow staircase. Gowdie settled down halfway, peering into the living room. The firelight sparkled off of his blue scales and Nimue shook her head to tell him he needn't interfere. "Who's the one who called my Book Scene Booth idea too *whimsical*?"

"Book Scene Booth?"

Nimue explained her idea to Soren, whose eyes lit up at the mention of interacting with one's favorite characters in a cherished scene straight out of a book's pages.

"That sounds *magical*." He sighed wistfully.

Nimue softened a bit at Soren's unexpected support of her idea. "So do you see what I mean? Dealing with him? He can be so dismissive."

"I know," said Soren, entirely empathetic. It was almost infuriating to Nimue how empathetic and sweet and perfect this man was if he was going to have the gall to show up the minority of the time she had to deal with him. "But he thinks you have it out for him."

"*I* have it out for *him*?"

Balfour let out a little grumbling purr that sounded like she was laughing.

Nimue chose to ignore it. "He's had it out for me from day one! Ever since I moved back to Cauldron Cove and showed up for work!"

"He thinks… He thinks you're too creative." Soren stumbled over his words.

"That is, I mean… *I* don't think that's a bad thing—"

"Balfour just told him you remind Ren too much of Soren," Gowdie said in his witch's mind. He snickered.

Nimue was nothing like Soren. She wasn't as sweet or as patient…

She took a deep breath, trying to focus on Soren's rambling.

"And well, he's rational, maybe too rational, and he always thinks he knows best—"

"Soren." She walked around the armchair and, forgetting her shame at being caught in her silk robe, took both of Soren's hands in hers.

"Congrats," Nimue said.

Soren's mouth fell open, his skin coloring red. "I'm-I'm sorry?"

"On becoming co-manager, you dope." She dropped his hands. "Let's do our best to work together, okay?"

"Right. Yes, yes, of course." Soren's eyes blinked rapidly and he ran a hand through his loose hair. "Congratulations to you, too."

"I appreciate the apology," said Nimue. "But you didn't exclude me from the decision. Ren did."

Soren chewed his lip. "He won't apologize—"

"I don't expect him to." Nimue sighed and, realizing her robe had fallen slightly off her shoulder, exposing the tank top she'd worn to bed beneath, she moved quickly to fix it. "I'd just… appreciate it if you could pop up more often. So Ren isn't fully running the show."

"Ren thinks you'd walk all over me," said Soren, his eyes darting rapidly to Nimue's bare feet.

Balfour let out a little chirrupy, giggling purr again.

Nimue bristled.

"He's not entirely wrong," said Gowdie in her mind.

"I would *not*," said Nimue, more to Gowdie than Soren, but Soren jumped in place on the chair.

Letting out a harried sigh, she walked over to her mantelpiece, focusing on the knickknacks she'd accumulated there since her life in Cauldron Cove had begun anew.

"So let's put that issue aside for now. How did things go with Rona after that disaster at dinner?"

She could hear Soren tapping his heel against the hardwood floor behind her.

"I escorted her as far as her room, but she wasn't interested in discussion."

Nimue wasn't surprised. Soren's love of romance and young adult books—something Nimue hadn't known about him—had started the whole cascade of insults volleying across the banquet hall.

"She did comment on my 'change in demeanor,'" Soren continued. "Nicola tried to explain about Ren and me, but Rona wasn't interested in listening. She was rambling, complaining about no one warning her Sherman Abbott would be at the convention, how she was the only author of her caliber present—"

"How humble of her."

"Yes, well... I mean, she does sell the best out of all of them."

Nimue rolled her eyes. And Rona had

TV adaptations and a movie or two to boot. "Still… Bestseller or indie author, we don't discriminate. Whoever the sponsoring bookstore booth wants to bring along with them. They know better than we do which authors will drive sales to their booths."

"Speaking of," said the warlock, clearing his throat, "right before she went inside her room, she was insistent the Delgados' booth not sell a single one of her books."

"*What*?"

Soren shrugged. "I told her I didn't think she could stop another bookstore from selling her books if they wanted to, and Nicola told her she couldn't punish them because they'd booked Sherman Abbott, but Rona said, and I quote, 'Booking that pompous try-hard for this convention is the *least* of what those bookstore owners did to me. I want every one of my books out of their booth.'"

"That's not her call. At all." She wondered what in the world Rona could be referring to. Then again, Virgil and Penny themselves had hinted at some sort of history with the reclusive author.

Soren lifted one shoulder. "Still. I wonder if they'd even care if they don't stock any of her books. At least at the con. Most con-goers will flock to the booth where she's signing autographs anyway."

"True, but we can't just ask them to remove books they bought wholesale." Nimue let out a sigh. "I'll talk to them tomorrow. See how many—*if* any—of her books they brought along. Maybe they didn't bother and we'll be worrying for nothing."

Soren yawned and nodded, then stood to go, extending his arms out for Balfour to leap up into them. "Well, you're right. It's late. I'm sorry to disturb you when we've got a big day tomorrow—I just wasn't sure when I'd be in control next and I thought it only right that *someone* wearing this face apologize." He grimaced.

Nimue offered a wincing smile back. "I appreciate it. I do." She started walking him to the door, Gowdie taking to the air and flapping behind them. Balfour peered over Soren's shoulder to keep a careful, narrowed eye on him.

"Soren, wait," Nimue said as he stepped outside to the front porch.

Soren turned around, his head tilted. "Hmm?"

She didn't know why she felt it was important to ask him, but after the way he'd continued to speak of her so familiarly, a thought had wormed its way into her mind —and she knew for certain she'd never get a straight answer from Ren.

"How do you know Nicola? I didn't think you or Ren had a lot of connections to the human world."

"Oh." Soren's face fell, his eyes staring downward—specifically at the fingers of his left hand, which were curved around Balfour's hind legs. "She was Lydia's best friend. Lydia met her when she did her study abroad in the human world as a teen."

"Oh," said Nimue softly. She hadn't meant to dredge up bad memories. She did vaguely recall the witch having left for a year before Nimue had even had any interest in doing so herself. "I see. So you… You two kept in touch."

Soren nodded, looking back up to meet Nimue's gaze. "She's real sweet." For the first time since he'd shown up tonight, his features completely relaxed, his smile broad and the corners of his eyes wrinkling.

For some reason, the thought of Soren complimenting this human woman so genuinely, so kindly, like he couldn't wait to sing her praises, filled Nimue's stomach with lead.

CHAPTER NINE

Nimue had just landed her broomstick at the employee entrance ledge, a cup of Sylvie Palmer's rich, aromatic hazelnut coffee in her hand, when her daughter appeared in front of her in a shimmering mirage.

"Mom!" said Willow. "Good luck on the first day of Bookshop Con!"

Nimue offered her a prideful smile. Willow had already admitted to knowing about Bernadette's "surprise" in detail when she'd managed to text her last. "Willow Toothaker, using a Communication Charm to wish her mother good luck at her new position?" She'd made it sound surprising, but only the fact that her daughter was breaking her vow to use magic as little as possible while at human school was re-markable.

"Well, I knew you wouldn't bring your smartphone with you to work." Willow pet Reoch, who barked from behind Willow on the young woman's neatly made bed.

"No," admitted Nimue, stepping inside and taking another sip. Gowdie was showing off for Willow, doing diving ma-neuvers in the air behind Nimue. "You're sweet, Willow. Thank you."

"Well, I blew my Communication Charm for the day, so if for some reason I need to be in touch in an emergency, I guess I'll have to call Daddy." Willow seemed playful but not entirely insincere as she gathered a stack of books and a tablet and shoved them into a shoulder bag. With a flourish, she ro-tated her wand in the air, transforming it into a white ruler. Reoch shoved aside the books and snuggled inside, poking his head out of the top.

"Don't even *joke* about that!" Nimue's heart thundered. As if the stress of today, the lack of sleep, and the prospect of guests having it out for one another weren't enough on her plate, the thought of her daughter needing her and being unable to reach her…

Willow swung the bag over her shoulder and put a hand on her hip, her ruler-disguised wand out in front of her with the other hand. She looked the perfect mix of human and witch that she was, donning a long, black robe over a puffy blouse and a frilly skirt, eschewing the pointed witch's hat for a broomstick barrette and a side bun. "Sorry. But that's what smartphones are *perfect for*, Mom. None of this once-a-day nonsense. Always reliable."

"Well, except, if I remember your father complaining right, when there are no 'bars.'" It had taken Nimue a while to figure out he'd been referring to some kind of indicator on the screen and not the establishments for serving alcohol, which she'd had to admit, had never made sense to her in relation to why cellphones ought to work.

Willow rolled her eyes. "Service is a lot

better these days than it was in the early twenty-first century."

Gowdie chuckled in Nimue's mind as he landed on his witch's shoulder.

"Oh, please. That wasn't that long ago. You make me sound so old."

"Maybe not for a witch, but most humans—"

"Forty is *not old*," Nimue reiterated.

Willow giggled and walked to her dorm room door.

"Where's Veronica?" Nimue asked, standing outside of the employee break room and finishing the last of her coffee.

"Already at classes. And I guess I should get going, too." Willow yawned.

"Are you sleeping well?" Nimue couldn't help herself from being ironic and yawning, too. "You can't focus without a good night's rest."

"Yes, Mom." Willow peered closer to the projected image. "I could ask the same of you."

Nimue ignored the comment and sent her daughter air kisses. "I'll let you go so I can get to work, too. Take care. Have fun—but not too much fun!"

Willow groaned. "You sound like Daddy."

Despite her generally amiable feelings toward her ex, Nimue shuddered at the thought.

"Take care," Nimue reiterated.

"Bye, Mom! Good luck!" Willow waved her ruler-wand.

The Communication Charm dissipated and Nimue tossed her empty cup into the garbage can. The perma-charmed can did a scan of the material and disintegrated it, having found the item to be genuine garbage no one ought to regret tossing out. She found only Merga inside the break room, affixing her black witch's hat on her head in front of her open locker. Nimue was pleased to see so few in the break room. That meant they were out on the Bessa's floor. There was still so much to do.

"Good morning," Nimue said, opening her own locker as Gowdie landed on the nearby break room table, Merga's red miniature llama, Spandemager, doing a kind of bucking dance across the room to extend his nose out to his fellow familiar.

"Good morning, Miss Toothaker."

"Please. 'Nimue.'" She looked in the mirror on the inside of her locker and fixed her red witch's hat into place, admiring the look. Puffing her shoulders back, she gave the reflection her best "serious" face. New Head Witch General Manger. Co-manager.

She fluffed the red, puffy sleeves of her dress.

"Hey, Merga?" she asked as the young witch shut her locker door and went to grab a drink from the array provided by Tituba and her catering team. "You don't think forty is old, do you?"

Merga choked on the sip of sports drink she'd just taken.

Nimue felt her cheeks burning as Gowdie stifled a laugh from behind her. She took out her staff badge, removing her hat briefly to slip the lanyard over her neck, and shut her locker door fast. "Never mind."

"Well, I mean, *no*, most witches live hundreds of years—" Merga was quick to get out.

"But what if I were human?" Nimue held an arm out for Gowdie to land on.

Merga finished her drink and then tossed it in the nearest garbage can, the metal bottle being processed for reuse, sent off to the metal refinery that had contracted with Cauldron Cove's recycling program.

"Did Willow say something?" Merga guessed as Spandemager directed his little bucking dance around her legs.

"Oh, well, just... Just thinking." Nimue whapped her hand in front of her face, trying to cool her skin. "Good luck out there on the first day of Bookshop Con!"

"You, too," Merga said, and the two exited the break room, making their way to the nearest teleportation pad.

"Don't you have to check in with your office?" Gowdie asked Nimue telepathically as Merga stepped through, the glow on the teleportation pad blinking from red to aqua.

Nimue thought about it a moment, wondering if it was Ren or Soren she'd find in the shared office across from her.

Ren. It had to be Ren. He wouldn't have handed responsibility for something like the first day of his first con as co-manager over to Soren.

"Let me send a note to Cassie." Nimue tapped her wrist crystal to bring up the projected witch network screen and thought her message to it. She realized with a start that it was a lot like the smartphone texting communication she disparaged so often to her daughter, though at least she could just *think* or say her message and have it dictated, rather than attempting to type it all out.

"You know, you can dictate into a smartphone, too," Gowdie told her.

But I couldn't think *a message to it, now could I?*

Gowdie shuddered, his talon digging into her shoulder just a bit. *"I'd shudder to think of the text messages humans would accidentally send to one another if they could."*

Nimue finished up her message about checking in with the Delgados' booth, which she'd discussed in advance with *Soren,* she was sure to add, then did a quick double check for the booth in question's location on the show floor. Dismissing her witch network screen, she stepped through the teleportation pad, activating the aqua blue.

Stretching out his wings, Gowdie took to the wide, open space overhead almost as soon as they stepped through.

The showroom floor—any convention's main event—was larger-than-life. Witchy ExS staff had outdone themselves. If only the sun, which appeared to have retreated behind a thick cover of clouds, would come out, the whole place would come to life in natural bright light. As it was, the artificial lights did just fine, especially as every few feet was peppered with glowing orbs filled with perma-charm-lit magic candles.

Every individual booth had its gimmick, but they all came together cohesively, a veritable bookworm's dream. In addition to all the promotion for upcoming new releases, there were goods for sale. Charmed bookcases that a witch could install to slide away to reveal a secret reading cranny or another section of the shop for bookshop owners. Bookmarks, tote bags, T-shirts, tea cups, mugs, tights, socks, stuffed animals—all sorts of goods related to books old and new, classics and the hottest new releases. One tote, a few years out of date and featuring an illustrated tea cup design, celebrated a milestone anniversary of Rona Brynhild's first book in 1987. Beside it was a tote with the cover of Rona's latest Miss Elwes's Cheery Mysteries installment on the front of it. *Poisons and Peppermints and Little, Licorice Lies.* That was a whole lot going on in one book. If Nimue ever read it—and that was a big *if* after meeting the author in person—she'd keep an eye out for any character eating peppermints or licorice. Chances were, they were going to show up dead in the next chapter or two.

As soon as Nimue turned the corner, one of PuffinHouse's flickering illusions of a child super spy who starred in one of their most popular lines of books leaped out in front of her.

"Hi! I'm Kitt the Spy! I go on adventures all around the world, and my parents have no clue! Would you like to learn more about my books?" He put on a pair of illusory glasses, which sparkled in the overhead lights.

"No, thank you." Nimue offered a fleeting smile to the humans behind the booth, just adding the finishing touches on their displays.

They smiled back, one woman turning to the man beside her and whispering behind her hand.

"A witch!"

Nimue caught at least that much as the illusion in front of her dissipated and she made her way forward.

Even in the middle of Cauldron Cove, which was teeming with witches and war-locks, and in a world where independent magic users mingled within human com-munities, humans could still be in awe of them.

Nimue's chest thrust forward, and then she heard someone shout, "A dragon!"

Her familiar was worthy of more than hushed whispers.

Chuffed, Gowdie swept downward and landed on Nimue's shoulder just as they reached the end of the PuffinHouse booth.

Harsh, clipped voices reached her before she even managed to make it to the booth set aside for Delgado Books.

"Do you think we *want* to be right beside you?" Virgil's voice was deep, clearer to Nimue's ears even though she was still a few feet away.

Penny and Virgil stood in front of their booth—decorated like a miniature medieval library, probably a magic request to reflect some of the look of their bookshop back home—and in the walkway in front of them was Nicola.

Behind Nicola, a few feet away, was a large booth decorated like a proper English tea party. Fine porcelain teacups rested on floating vintage tier dessert towers, a doily-like linen tablecloth covering all of the massive booth. Some books were available for perusing on one side of the booth, but the entire second half of it was devoted to Rona Brynhild.

An assortment of tote bags and posters and even shawls were emblazoned with a number of her books' cozy covers. All that was missing were the books themselves. Behind a plush high-back chair, an illusion dotted the air, words emblazoned against a jovial, stationery-esque background:

Meet the Queen of Killer Cozies. Rona Brynhild, Signing Books Only at Nicola's Nook Bookshop Booth!

"What's going on here?" Nimue asked, drawing closer. Neighboring booth attendants were fussing about with the final touches at their booths, their attention clearly drawn to the altercation.

"I was just saying…" Nicola rubbed her forehead and closed her eyes, and Nimue wondered for a moment what this stark, stylish woman and the jolly, charming witch Lydia Southern had ever had in common. According to Soren, though, Nicola was sweet, so she'd have to give her the benefit of the doubt.

It wasn't like she was best friends with the author she'd managed to score for her booth at the convention.

"She was just telling us not only do we have to *sell no Rona Brynhild books*, we have to figure out how to move our booth!"

"*Oh, that's a pickle,*" Gowdie said in

Nimue's mind. *"When PuffinHouse asked to move their booth, Herne couldn't have known the bookshop he was swapping with would pose a problem with our star author."*

Right. The rearrangements of the booths. That Nimue herself had signed off on.

Drat, she thought.

She held out her hand as Nicola and Virgil and Penny launched into another argument. "It's too late to switch booths," she said, stopping them all cold in their tracks. "There's magic involved in the setup and—"

"Rona won't be happy signing in sight of them." Nicola winced as she spoke, as if it pained her to deliver the news.

"She'd be facing the other way!" Virgil pointed out, exasperated. Sure enough, Rona's signing area was set up to face the front of the convention, almost as soon as the crowd entered, and the Delgado Books booth would be nothing more than an annoying gnat in the corner of her eye.

But from what she'd seen of the moody author, even a gnat would be enough for her to cause a scene.

Penny shouted. "And as if we'd *want* to sell any of her books after what she did to us!"

Virgil hushed his wife, whispering softly in her ear, and Nimue's curiosity burned to know more. But she had quite enough to handle already.

"So you don't have any of Rona's books in your booth?" Nicola asked, arching a brow. "Because I'm *pretty sure* someone has them…"

"We most certainly do not," Virgil said. "Not a single one here or at our actual bookstore location. Check through our stock if you must." He stepped back and gestured for Nicola to enter his booth.

She did, after a moment's hesitation, looking from Penny to Virgil to Nimue and even to Gowdie. But no one stopped her from accessing the booth.

When she'd stepped a few feet away, Nimue spoke to the Delgados in a hushed tone. "Is the booth placement really a problem for you?"

The couple exchanged a look.

"Not really," said Virgil, his shoulders

slumping. "If Rona—and Nicola—just leave us alone, we don't mind."

"We're grateful for the increased foot traffic," said Penny, gesturing to the show-room floor badge check station entryway. Nimue tapped her wrist crystal to project her witch network screen and saw the con was just fifteen minutes from opening the front doors for registration. There was a blinking message from Cassie about the day's schedule, but she ignored it.

"So only Rona has an issue with this," she offered, wiping the screen away.

"Oh, *Rona* definitely has an issue." Penny almost spat the author's name. "She's probably gone to find someone to complain to. But she never said anything to our faces."

Nimue wondered what to do. Moving booths this late in the game would be nigh on impossible, even for a team of witches and warlocks with access to magic. If they did find an exhibitor willing to swap—perhaps not impossible, considering the good foot traffic the Delgados were sure to enjoy —that would still involve too much clunky magic when guests were already lined up outside the Bessa's doors. The skywalk would be closed off until the clock struck eight, but she was sure there were people lingering at the other end of it in the Southern Hotel lobby, too, and people lining up by the hotel's teleportation pad.

Besides, the Delgados deserved the extra business this prime spot would bring them. And they had a popular author signing at some point, too.

She wondered where, in their booth, he'd fit, then spotted an empty chair at the edge of it, a red velvet one more at home in front of a medieval castle fireplace, a stack of books piled high beside it and a small, circular end table. Nicola was currently peering through those very books.

If the bookseller complained to Ren about the situation… Would he jump to accommodate? Would he lay the blame at Herne's and Nimue's feet for rearranging the booths, long before Nimue had had any clue Rona would find either Sherman Abbott or the Delgados being in her vicinity so objectionable?

Rona Brynhild seemed to find it objectionable for virtually *anyone* to be in her vicinity.

"Hey," said Nicola, snapping up with a sour twist to her lips. "You have Rona's latest right here!" She lifted a book out from under a stack of dark blue and black spines that had Sherman Abbott's name written all over them.

Virgil and Penny blinked rapidly as Nicola held out the bright pink hardcover, the candy store illustration making it as clear as day this book was not like the stark, dark thriller mysteries all around it.

"That's not ours," Penny said firmly.

"Is it *mine*?" Nicola snapped.

Did she really think the Delgados had stolen a book from her? Why?

"Must have been a mistake in delivery," Virgil started. "We would never sabotage another bookshop! To be part of the Bookshop Owner's League, you have to agree to the Bookseller's Code. Didn't you agree to the same thing to rent a booth here?"

"Yeah, but a code isn't a binding oath or

anything," Nicola pointed out. "It's not a *law*."

"It is if you want to stay in the Bookshop Owner's League," Penny said.

Nicola looked over her shoulder. "Well, since it was the only copy I found, I'm inclined to believe you. But—"

Before she could finish, a great, echoing scream shattered the air, quieting all other sounds.

The shimmering illusion of fairies in flight over the Delgados' booth crackled and twinkled, the only sound in anyone's ears for the moment.

And then came the thundering crash.

Like an entire library's worth of bookshelves had fallen over, the books scattering out across the floor.

"That came from the lobby," Gowdie said.

And so did the second set of screams, these ones louder than even the first.

CHAPTER TEN

"Stay here," Nimue told the Delgados and Nicola, who, like everyone else in the vicinity, had turned toward the entryway to the lobby, as if waiting for an explanation to emerge onto the showroom floor. She didn't wait for their response, jogging the last few steps toward the entryway, just as Morpheus Fowler jogged toward the badge check station from down another aisle on the showroom floor.

In the darkened hallway—there was a skylight overhead, but not much light was filtering through on this cloudy morning—he didn't even seem to notice her approach, his tortie-patterned red squirrel familiar,

Horsnas, as slack-jawed as he was, staring at…

Books. Books everywhere. Opened books, closed books, books awkwardly leaned up at an angle, spread out across the lobby floor.

One of Linden's Guest Services warlocks, a young, skinny man with a pale brown complexion and cropped dark hair, stood at the edge of the mess, looking downward.

At a hand reaching through the array of scattered books, the fingers awkwardly bent, a few feet in front of the concierge desk.

"Communication Charm with Ren, Cassie, or Zelena and message the rest," Nimue barked to Morpheus.

"But what…?" Morpheus started.

"Someone's hurt," Nimue snapped.

She ran forward until she got to the edge of the pile of books, then realized with a start that she recognized them. From storage.

She looked up and Gowdie swallowed.

All of the books she'd used the item

storage crystal to make hover whimsically over the lobby. They weren't hovering anymore.

"Help me," she said to the Guest Services warlock, bending down to remove the books covering the human hand.

The warlock jumped into action, whipping his wand out of his holster at his belt with a shaky arm.

"Wait," Nimue said, putting a hand to his ankle. "If you're thinking of a Movement Charm of some kind, you might get the person caught up in it, too."

"Right." He swallowed and put his wand away, then bent down to help Nimue sort through the books.

It felt like forever, revealing the person's limp form bit by bit, but it had to be no more than ten seconds. Gowdie jumped down off Nimue's shoulders and dragged a book away with his teeth, and the warlock's familiar, an owl with teal-colored feathers, did the same with her talons.

"What happened?" Nimue asked. She tossed a book aside and it echoed out into the lobby with a clatter.

The warlock winced. "She was... She was just standing there, upset about something. I tried to get her to slow down and explain and then... And then..."

Her. Nimue recognized the overly large cardigan she revealed, the chain at the woman's neck. There wasn't a pendant of any kind on it.

But most of all, there was the wild, red-orange hair.

Rona Brynhild's stone-cold face.

With shaky fingers of her own, Nimue removed her wand. "Healing Charm!"

Magic soared out from her wand and clashed against the limp body beneath her.

"Try it, kid," she said to the warlock. Her throat was dry. Rona wasn't responding.

"Heal-Healing Charm," he said, his wand only halfway out before he began the charm.

The magic bounced out and ricocheted against Rona and then a book beside her bent fingers.

Maybe he hadn't cast it perfectly. "Communication Charm," she said, waving her wand in the air. "Medics."

The short, pixie-cut silver hair under the rainbow-colored witch's hat of Florence Thornton popped into view. "I'm here. Status?"

"Medical emergency, building lobby," Nimue barked.

Florence nodded and dismissed the charm.

The warlock beside her started hyperventilating, his owl flying up to his shoulder and letting out timid hoots in time with his fast breaths.

Nimue grabbed him by both shoulders, her wand flat against the man's shoulder. He was wearing the same outfit as Linden, though he hadn't opted to wear gloves.

"What's your name?" she asked.

"Humphrey." He gasped. "Humphrey Bruce, Miss Toothaker."

"Humphrey," she said, remembering him in the employee roster now. A little older than Willow. Been working convention hospitality for seven years.

"Take a deep breath," she said.

He tried, swallowing hard.

Frowning, Nimue let him go to wave her wand over him. "Calming Charm."

Humphrey's tense shoulders loosened almost immediately, his expression growing lax.

She was about to get the full story out of him when the teleportation pad blinked red, then purple, then aqua blue, a new figure or several figures approaching from the spot after every color change.

"What's going on?" snapped Ren. Balfour trotted behind him, her tail straight up in the air. When she spotted Rona, she hissed.

Ren's gaze snapped toward the victim's face, his eyes bulging as his mouth parted. "Medic!" he called.

But Florence was already behind him. "Right here." She was joined by two other medical witches, who gestured for Humphrey and Nimue to step aside and surrounded Rona's prone form.

Florence's lips were set in a grim line as she poked and prodded the fallen author, but they all removed their wands and went to work.

"What in the flying broomsticks happened here?" Zelena hovered behind Ren, followed by a wan-looking Cassie.

Nimue winced despite the fact that it hadn't been her fault.

Actually, now that she thought about it, perhaps it *had* been. Ren had warned her about the danger of the hovering books display.

Gowdie flapped his wings and landed, digging his talons into her shoulder. *"This wasn't you,"* he assured her. But she wasn't too sure.

"I was just… This guest…" Humphrey was calmer, but he still looked a bit peaky every time he checked over his shoulder at the medical witches at work.

"This *guest* is our guest of honor!" Ren snapped.

The poor young warlock practically melted into the ground under his glare. "I… I know…"

"Stop." Nimue held a hand out toward Ren before he could respond again. "Let him finish."

Ren opened his jaw, a vein bulging at the

corner of his exposed temple, but Zelena nodded stiffly at him and he went quiet, pinching his lips together.

"She was... She was shouting at me, almost as soon as she walked up to me," Humphrey said. His owl familiar rubbed its feathery head against his cheek, seeming to give him the courage he needed to go on. He stood straighter. "I couldn't understand what had upset her so much. She kept pacing and ranting and demanding I fix things and before I could get her to slow down..." He looked up. "They fell." He pointed upward, at the now-empty skylight above them all.

They all turned up and looked. As if the wide-open glass ceiling would have answers.

Nothing.

"Bad news." Florence stood, drawing everyone's attention. Her brow was drawn into a dour line. "She's dead. There's no saving her." The other medical witches stood beside her, looking chastened, clutching wands that had proven useless in this, Witchy Expo Services's, first major crisis in decades.

Cassie let out a little yelp and stumbled. Zelena leaned out to catch her.

The first major crisis in decades.

And it had happened on Nimue's watch. On her very first convention as co-manager. In relation to something *she* had pushed for…

Belatedly, the realization hit her that Rona was truly dead. More than a crisis for the con staff, a human being was no longer. Lying there. In her convention center lobby. A world-renowned author whose fans were legion—likely because her reclusiveness made it so no one knew her beyond her books—and she'd died at Bookshop Con.

Ren snapped into action before anyone else. "Medical curtain." He grunted to Florence and the other witches, kicking books across the floor to make more space around Rona's prone body.

The assistant medical witches looked puzzled, but Florence nodded, charming a sort of privacy curtain around Rona—necessary for fallen humans who'd fainted and felt a bit overcrowded, Nimue knew—so that the prone body was no longer visible.

Ren's gaze went beyond Florence to the milling crowd on the other side of the doors.

Nimue checked the time on her projected witch network screen. One minute until opening.

"You can't seriously expect to still open on time?" Nimue asked.

The room went quiet. For one long, harrowing moment, everyone just stared.

"Back to position," Ren barked at Humphrey. "Get ready to register guests and pass out badges. Where's Linden?" He looked around the empty lobby.

"Here!" Linden's voice carried across the atrium as he slipped through the crowd of staff members gathered in the direction of the teleportation pad. "Got the message."

Nimue cocked her head, but then her own witch network screen lit up in red. She looked past it to find Cassie having recovered herself, staring with intense focus at her own screen as the screen picked up her thoughts and dictated an emergency message.

Code Red. Medical emergency in lobby. Thirty seconds until Bookshop Con begins.

Nimue blinked. Then blinked again.

Of course Bookshop Con was going to go on as usual.

Cauldron Cove's magic could collapse without it, now that all the prep work had been done, the convention signed, sealed, and about to be as delivered as possible.

Witchy Expo Services existed to entertain the masses, to offer them a one-of-a-kind venue in which to celebrate their interests or exchange ideas.

But it existed first and foremost to sustain the massive cauldron that slept beneath the soil, feeding on the magic of passionate gatherings.

She swiped her witch network screen away and jumped to work, the rest of the staff scattering.

Ren was conferring with Florence, even as he waved his wand and all of the scattered books gathered into piles that he shifted on top of nearby tables. Nimue caught just one sentence: "Get her out of here."

"Wait!" said Nimue, jogging up to them. Balfour darted out and practically tripped her at one point, but Nimue pressed on. "We have to investigate what happened—"

Ren's eyes grew narrower even as his hands still waved and his wand went to work.

"An item storage malfunction, obviously."

Almost as if on cue, Zelena jogged over, the cracked item storage crystal in her hand. It looked as if a hard object had slammed against it, resulting in spiderweb cracks down the crystal.

That wasn't a *malfunction*. It was broken. Someone had broken it.

Which meant… Someone had killed Rona Brynhild.

Accidentally… or on purpose.

"Prepare to greet guests, people!" Linden shouted, both to Humphrey in his department and the rest of the staff milling about. He approached the front door, reaching for his wand in his holster. Only it was Dyer, his chinchilla familiar, who had it. She darted around the books remaining on the floor, his wand in her mouth, and climbed up his leg, handing it to him so he could unlock the front door. He must have dropped it in the chaos.

Whoever had gotten into the lobby to destroy the item storage crystal hadn't gotten in—or out—through that front door. Not without taking the time to lock it after them—and no one had mentioned a suspect running to the front door.

Not to mention all of those witnesses gathered out front.

But who could have done this? A witch? A wizard? Who had had it out for Rona from the first moment she'd set foot in Cauldron Cove?

Humans. Multiple humans.

Though it may have been more accurate to say Rona had had it out for *them*.

"Nimue, focus," said Gowdie in her mind. *"Bookshop Con is about to begin."*

The show must go on, she thought, *no matter the tragedy that occurred.*

And in mere minutes, a stampede of eager readers, librarians, and publishing industry professionals would step through those front doors to see what all of the book-shops had on display.

And somehow, they would have to move the dead author they'd all come to see out from behind that curtain without anyone noticing.

CHAPTER ELEVEN

Bookshop Con was off to a great, great start.

Nimue thought that both sarcastically and literally. Even though it was still a weekday, when only the industry insiders and the most devoted con-goers managed to show up, Herne and the rest of the floor crew counted attendance at over four thousand.

Over four thousand people… who could have been walking through the lobby in which a curtain blocked off the dead body of a famous author.

Not for too long. Ren and the medical team worked quickly to transport the body.

During brief moments while directing the flow of the crowd around the tent, Nimue tried to take note of anything that seemed off about the scene before Rona was removed entirely, but Zelena told her, "We know what went wrong. *Someone* messing with the item storage crystal overloaded it."

That someone being Nimue, of course.

The medic team created an emergency teleportation portal behind the curtain and took Rona's body to Florence's clinic downtown, closed whenever she had con duties to attend to.

Merga, who'd never seen the author lying prone on the floor, was finished with her con setup duties and had been called to get the lobby back into presentable shape.

"Nimue, is that—?" Merga pointed at a small dab of red over which her wand hovered, in the midst of the Cleaning Charm. Spandemager, her llama, sniffed at the spot and wrinkled his nose.

"Clean it up," Nimue said behind her. Voices carried from the other side of the curtain. "Then charm away the medical curtains."

"Usually, the medic team—"

"They're busy," said Nimue quickly. "When you're finished, gather all of the books Ren piled around the lobby and send them to my office. Our office. Ren's and mine."

Gowdie flew over to Spandemager and landed on the fluff of his back, the two familiars exchanging a silent conversation that would no doubt have news of Rona's demise spreading quickly throughout the staff.

If it hadn't already.

Though everyone who'd been gathered was currently busy dealing with the con being off the ground or the aftereffects of the… incident.

Nimue's witchy network connection flashed red and she brought up her projected screen. Cassie told her Ren wanted her back in the office ASAP. Tituba sent a message asking what had happened.

Zelena stormed past the ConSuite in a huff, Tituba wrote. *Her face was so red, I asked her if she needed a drink, but she just said, 'Con Emergency.' What happened? Who was hurt?*

Sighing, Nimue touched her wrist crystal and thought her message back to her: *Talk later. Don't let guests know anything is wrong.*

Gowdie's wings flapped as he perched back on Nimue's shoulder. *"Well, if that isn't an ominous message to send to your best friend without explanation."*

Nimue was already making her way to the teleportation pad, though she had to get in line behind a family of human guests that was warily approaching it.

"It says here Shawna Higgins is going to be on a panel in Room 3C," said the mother, a tall and broad-shouldered woman who was staring at the free con program guide, each with a miniature perma-charm crystal embedded in the spine. A little cartoon witch hovered over the booklet and pointed to the room in question, having sensed the guest's desire to locate a panel.

A pre-teen and teen girl who looked a lot like their presumed mother leaned over either of the woman's shoulders, their jaws dropped.

"She's cool, but it says it's about Writing

the Teen Experience," said the older one. "Sounds boring. Can't we go check out the shop booths first?"

The younger one waved her hand over the cartoon witch. Her fingers reached right through. "Whoa. Magic."

Her mother *tsked*. "Now, remember, girls, this is for class credit. I am your teacher as well as your mother."

"Yes, Mom," both girls said, clearly not for the first time.

The older girl leaned back and let out a huff of air that sent her bangs fluttering.

"I think learning about writing is the perfect way to start the day." The mom frowned, staring at the white light of the teleportation pad. "I just… don't know…"

"Oh," said Nimue, piping up, glad to be of service beyond dealing with one of the worst catastrophes Witchy ExS had ever seen. "You just step inside and think of your destination. The magic will take you to the nearest portal."

The mother jumped and took a step back, nearly dropping the con guide. The younger daughter squealed and held on to her mom's shirt as she took in the witch before her, and the older girl crossed her arms and continued to look bored.

"It's perfectly safe," Nimue assured them. She gazed over their heads to where one of the warlocks was taking items in for item storage and… just stacking everything on the floor.

There was plenty of space for that. As Ren had—rightfully—pointed out, the reason why the item storage was located in that corner was because the items floated over an alcove beneath which no one was in danger of walking.

Unlike Nimue's books in the lobby.

She sighed. And wondered if it was safe for the booths to have floating displays, too, now that she thought of it.

But those relied on individual witches or warlocks casting Hovering Charms. The item storage alcove would have required too many charm castings, thus the reliance on the perma-charm crystal.

Which had backfired on Nimue spectacularly when she'd used that same crystal to hover the display books.

"Or not?" the mother guest in front of Nimue asked.

Nimue shook her head, snapping herself out of her thoughts. "Sorry?"

"I asked if your pet dragon is safe to pet?"

The two girls—even the older, jaded one—looked eagerly at Nimue's shoulder.

Gowdie puffed out his chest, spreading his wings and smacking Nimue in the cheek with one.

"He's my familiar." She held out her palms cupped together for him to jump into and then thrust him toward the girls for careful, cautious pets. As the older one held out a single, bent finger, he stuck his nose in the air, inviting her to scratch his chin.

Both girls beamed when he took to the pets, scratching his cheeks and head and even his scaly body. He arched into the strokes like a cat.

The mom looked behind her at the showroom floor, beyond the badge check station. The teleportation pads would also check to make sure everyone who stepped through was wearing a badge that would allow them to reach their destinations. A staff badge granted access for employees-only areas, for example. "It's quite a magical place you have here."

"Thank you," said Nimue. Her wristlet flashed with another incoming message. She sighed as she moved toward the teleportation pad. "Just think where you want to go, and it'll get you to the closest spot," she repeated. Then she stepped through, and the portal grew red, depositing her on the second floor, near the employee break room. Even if a guest wished to go there, though, this location only responded to a staff badge.

Nimue's footfalls echoed out against the long hallway amidst the murmurs of the crowd below. Below her and partially visible beyond the glass railing, the activity of the showroom floor brought the Bookshop Con to life. Normally, she experienced excitement at the start of the con. Now she was mostly weighed down by dread.

She stepped into the Head General Manager office reception area, finding Cassie's post empty, and walked farther inside.

A familiar sight awaited, with various heads of departments gathered around Ren's forward-facing desk, Nimue's own perpendicular one lost behind the crowd.

"Got here as soon as I could," said Morpheus from behind Nimue. Startled, she stepped aside and let him in, just as Tituba crossed the room and whispered to Nimue, her mouth in a grim line. "Ren got us up to speed."

Nimue offered a flittering smile, taking in everyone's expressions. Herne and Morpheus exchanged a few words. They worked together to make sure everything on the showroom floor went smoothly. Zelena and Linden stood side by side, Zelena grim and Linden offering one of his almost-always-present customer service smiles—the kind that may have been hiding anger or annoyance beneath the amiability. Cassie stood in front of Ren's desk, her back straight and her ferret curled in her arms. Ren stood behind his desk, conferring with Florence. Both looked bleak.

"Nimue. Update," Ren said, gesturing for her to speak.

Ren had assisted Florence and Zelena in removing the body to Florence's clinic while Nimue and Linden had spread out to make sure the Bookshop Con got off without a hitch. Without *another* hitch, that was.

"No other *incidents*," she said quickly. "But Nicola tried to get my attention shortly after you all left and I… dodged her." Nimue winced and looked to Linden. "I could have used some tips on how to let her know about what happened to her guest."

The corner of Linden's lips cocked up into a wary smile. "Even I haven't had experience in passing on that kind of news."

Zelena shifted her weight from one foot to the other beside him. Dyer the chinchilla skittered up to her warlock's shoulder to twitch her nose at Messenger, Zelena's slow-moving sloth still draped around her neck.

"I'll take care of Nicola." Ren crossed around the desk and sat on the front of it, which Nimue felt was entirely out of character.

Dark bags hung under his eyes and a lock of his slicked-back hair was hanging out of place. The stress of the morning was wearing on him more than he let on.

"I won't keep you long," Ren said, gesturing to Florence. The familiars in the room all seemed rapt with attention, quiet and stiff, as the head medical witch stepped forward to give her report. "The… body is at my clinic. I've never had to deal with an accidental death at a convention before—"

Cassie raised a timid hand. "Are we sure it was accidental?"

Ren sent her a withering look and she shirked back, clutching her ferret for support. "We're proceeding on those grounds. The problem is, we have to alert human authorities—Huntsville has the closest jurisdiction—and we don't want that kind of news leaking out. Not yet."

The room went quiet again.

Tituba frowned. "You don't want the con cancelled."

"It can't be," said Zelena flatly. "Cauldron Cove would implode without the convention the cauldron was promised to feed on—and we might not even be able to evacuate in time. With tens of thousands due for

Bookshop Con, not to mention all of us who've made homes here, that's a far greater disaster waiting to happen."

Nimue nodded. They couldn't cancel Bookshop Con. And they couldn't scare away all of those con-goers, either, effectively leading to the premature end of the convention even without a formal closure.

But if it was just an accident, couldn't they make the public aware?

No. An accident might lead to the con closing for safety issues.

Though maybe, if the whole town didn't depend on it, it should be.

"Beef up security," Nimue said to Zelena. "Ensure the rest of our guests' safety first and foremost. Cassie, is there anything else operational that wasn't approved by Bernadette?" Nimue stepped closer to her assistant, who quickly scanned through her projected witch network screen.

Nimue's own whim had led to this incident, at least in part. Ren had been right. She shouldn't have tried to get creative, least of all with the con just days away.

"No, nothing but the booth change,"

Cassie said. "PuffinHouse swapped with Delgado Books."

"That'll be fine." Ren rubbed his forehead and exchanged a look with Nimue that seemed almost… surprised. That Nimue had stepped up to admit she'd been wrong to want the hovering books?

"So here's the plan," Ren said. "Medical witches will keep the body in stasis until convention end. I'll tell everyone Rona is ill in her hotel room, and then…" He left the rest unsaid as Balfour jumped up on his desk and rubbed her cheek across his chest.

"Then we tell the world she actually died during an accident at Bookshop Con?" Tituba said. "And… maybe make future clients hesitant to book with us?"

A heavy sensation settled over the room. Ren cleared his throat. "We can't lie. It'll be bad enough we're keeping the truth from the public through Bookshop Con's end."

Herne chewed his lip. "We've got some smaller industry events coming up next," he pointed out. "Just enough to keep the cauldron fed, but not satiated. What's the next big event?"

Cassie didn't even have to consult her projected screen to answer him. "Comic Hero Con. In a month. Expected turnout forty to fifty thousand."

"And more than half of those badges reserved in advance." Ren chewed his lip.

If clients started pulling out of Witchy ExS, all because of Nimue's foolish, whimsical idea…

"Who was manning the item storage station right before the books fell?" Nimue asked.

Most eyes turned on Morpheus. He usually oversaw the badge check station and item storage. He shirked under the glaring eyes. "Most of the showroom floor staff was scrambling to get things done. No one needed to be posted there yet."

"So no one was there?" she asked.

He shook his head. "Merga was supposed to be first on duty, but I asked her to do a final showroom floor check. Then you called her over to help with the…" He indicated Nimue.

With the cleanup. "And you?" Nimue asked. "Shouldn't you have been posted at the badge check area?" Only she knew he hadn't been. He'd been drawn to the screaming at the same time she had.

Morpheus shrugged again, his squirrel familiar scurrying under his longish hair. "I was wandering the showroom floor, too. Quite standard right before a con starts. Guest Services usually handles the lobby until then." He turned to Linden, as if passing on a baton.

Linden didn't flinch at everyone's stares. "I didn't see anything unusual. I had to quickly run back to the lockers before the con was to start." He held up a gloved hand. "Forgot my gloves this morning." Nimue wasn't sure she'd ever seen the man without them. She imagined even a fastidious worker like him would have found them worth retrieving with minutes to spare before the con began. They were practically his second skin. "Either way, none of my staff would have seen anything around the corner from the front desk. Item storage is off in its own little alcove."

Nimue knew as much. Still, she'd been

hopeful. "And it was just you and Humphrey this morning?"

"Glinda took her vacation days this week." He frowned, his eyes darting to Ren. "Though she's staying local. Just enjoying her time off."

Nimue wondered if Linden's look meant anything, but Ren completely ignored him.

"Where's the item storage crystal?" Nimue asked. She didn't know how that would help, but she just… didn't understand. How she could have failed as co-manager so awfully.

She needed concrete answers.

Gowdie flew off her shoulder and soared over Ren's head, landing on his desk. "Here."

Nimue strode ahead, weaving around Cassie and Florence to take hold of the crystal. It was vaguely still spherical in shape, though the shattered pieces threatened to chip off in her fingers.

"Careful with that," said Linden, scurrying forward, his gloved hands extended. "The charm could backfire. Injure even more. And you can't toss a magic item away in the trash. I'll contact the sanitation department and we'll arrange—"

"No," said Nimue, carefully putting it back. Linden stepped back, giving her a deferring bow as he clutched his hands together in front of his waist. "I'll take it to my grandmother. Have her dispose of it—far from the Bessa." She looked to Ren, as if asking for permission, and then realized she didn't need to ask it. "I think we owe it to ourselves to investigate this thoroughly. Just so we know… what to tell the press when we reveal the truth." She blinked, realizing that tears had been starting to form in her eyes. "Maybe… Maybe we can explain how this broke and why it should never happen again." She turned to Cassie. "And maybe we need to get rid of any floating displays over the booths, just for appearance's sake."

"But that's a different kind of magic," Herne protested. His crew had worked hard to get it all ready. And Nimue was asking them to undo all of their work—in just a day. There wouldn't be enough witches and warlocks to use charms to undo it all within the same day.

"Agreed," Ren said. "Those items are hovering in a safer way. Guests will notice something is strange if we start messing with the booth displays while they're all still wandering the floors." He stood, accepting Balfour into his arms. "But I think you're right. That's what having a co-manager is for, isn't it? Let me hold down the fort. Bring the crystal to Bernadette and report back."

Nimue nodded.

It felt good to be trusted with something after the way she'd messed things up.

"Okay, everyone, back to work. We'll keep you updated." Ren gestured for the rest of the gathered staff to make their way to the doors. They shuffled out reluctantly, Tituba sending an empathetic look Nimue's way. Zelena and Linden stopped in the waiting room, the two speaking in hushed whispers. After just seconds, Zelena, red-faced, tossed her hands in the air, her sloth familiar slowly tossing one hand just the same, and walked away.

"This doesn't seem safe to carry all the way to Bernadette and Prue's," Gowdie told her,

darting around the crystal on the desk and examining it from every angle.

Without even hearing what Gowdie said, Ren pulled out a black handkerchief from the pouch at his waist and then his black wand from its holster, pointing it at the crystal. "Securing Charm."

The handkerchief wrapped the crystal, tying itself into a handle of sorts at the top.

"That should keep the magic inside from leaking for a day, if necessary," Ren explained. He turned to Cassie. "Cassie, forward me anything Nimue was due to check this afternoon, and we'll squeeze it between my tasks."

Carefully, Nimue took the crystal by the handle, Gowdie jumping on her shoulder as Balfour took the dragon's former place on Ren's desk.

"It shouldn't take all day," Nimue promised.

"We've got things handled," said Ren, not meeting her eye.

Nimue waited for him to scold her, to blame her again for the incident.

Maybe he was waiting for Bernadette's official report.

"Don't forget… Rona's first signing was supposed to be at four today," Nimue pointed out.

Sighing, Ren sunk back into his seat. He swirled around, facing the sparkling waters of Lake Salem. "As I said, I'll speak to Nicola," he said. "Her alone, I'll tell the truth."

Nimue swallowed, fighting down the surging nausea. At the loss of Rona Brynhild. At Witchy ExS's impending doom. At the mistake *she'd* made that had contributed to the woman's demise, and all of the horrible things that were due to come with it.

And even, she hated to admit, at the thought that Ren thought highly enough of Nicola to know without reservation that she could be trusted to keep the convention's most dangerous secret.

CHAPTER TWELVE

Though it was true that a week ago, she'd never have imagined being Head Witch General Manager—co-manager —of Witchy ExS so soon, she also, if pressed to imagine such a day, would definitely not have imagined fleeing to her retired grand-mother's on her first con's opening day, cradling evidence in some kind of freak ac-cident… or worse.

The town of Cauldron Cove was busier than she'd imagined on a con's opening day. Flying carriages, tourists and locals walking down below or, in the latter case, flying by on broomsticks. She'd never had the chance to observe Cauldron Cove while a con was happening, as she'd usually been so busy on opening day.

"You know this isn't your fault, right?" Gowdie soared overhead, his two wings outstretched, diving toward her.

She leaned on her broomstick and made a sharp turn, taking her hand off briefly to offer a flittering smile and a polite wave to Klaus with a new batch of tourists in his flying carriage.

"I probably overloaded it," she shouted into the wind. The crystal in question dangled from under her broomstick, affixed by the part of the handkerchief fastened into a loop.

They'd established that the item looked smashed on one end, but magic worked in ways that defied gravity and other human laws of physics.

Overloading it may have forced it to collapse from the inside.

"Ridiculous," Gowdie said as they hit the outskirts of downtown and the forest grew more dominant on the landscape. *"You've seen how much stuff that crystal handles on a packed con day."*

"Well, it's all going to be stacked on the ground in item storage now." Nimue sighed and gave her broomstick a boost, aiming straight for her grandma and Prue's cottage. She hoped they were home. She hadn't even thought to ask someone to Communication Charm ahead for her. But considering everything going on, she hadn't been sure she'd wanted to waste someone else's charm for the day.

She pulled to an abrupt halt, leaning her broomstick against the hitching rail her grandmother provided for her and Prue's broomsticks and for visitors'. Gowdie flapped down and settled on her shoulder as Nimue untied the handkerchief from her broomstick's shaft.

She was heartened to hear the chirping of lovebirds, the crackling of fire.

"Nim!"

The cottage door opened and out stepped Prue. She crossed her arms, tucking her oversized shawl under her arms, reminding Nimue with a sharp twinge of the fallen author' and her over-sized cardigans.

"What in the cauldron are you doing here? On the first day of Bookshop Con?"

Nimue couldn't tell whether her step-grandmother's look was one of reproach or pity—or both.

"Is Bernadette in?" Nimue asked, all business. She held the handkerchief out in front of her, almost with reverence.

Prue frowned but stepped aside, gesturing for her to follow.

Bernadette's humming mixed with the sweet birdsong. Nimue found her at her fireplace, stirring a concoction she was making in a cauldron. Potion brewing took years of experience. Witches and warlocks usually specialized in crafting perma-charms resulting from potions woven into the charm like the one Bernadette had used to create the item storage crystal.

It wasn't like she could just wave her wand and charm a new such crystal into existence.

But item storage issues at Bookshop Con were the least of Nimue's problems just then.

"Prue," said Bernadette, not bothering to

look behind her. "Can you pass me the dried lavender, please?"

Without responding, Nimue followed her grandmother's extended hand in the direction of the ingredient storage, a collection of pots and jars and dried plant life lined in rows on a shelf. By the time she found the lavender and returned to her grandmother, Bernadette realized who was standing beside her.

Her expression soured as she took the lavender. "Don't you have a convention to oversee? I know it's a weekday opening day—"

"We have a problem." Nimue held the cloth-covered crystal out in front of her.

Bernadette frowned and tossed the lavender into her cauldron. Whatever she was brewing let out a puff of smoke, pink and almost shimmering. "Well, I can't stop this," she said, continuing her stirring. "Part of the reason why I finally retired. I like doing this. But brewing perma-charms takes focus—and time. Time a Head Witch General Manager just doesn't have."

Prue took that as her cue to brush past them to the kitchen. "Tea, Nimue?"

"I won't be staying long," Nimue said, meeting her grandmother's eye. She didn't want her to think she wasn't up the task of co-manager. Though today, she felt she truly wasn't. "It's one of the perma-charms that was the problem."

She untied the knot and gently unfolded the handkerchief, revealing the crystal with its flattened edge, the spiderweb cracks traveling throughout the sphere.

Bernadette peered over to get a closer look, and though Prue had still turned on the kettle for tea, she stepped forward, too, the two lovebird familiars flying off their perches to join their witches on their shoulders.

"The item storage crystal," Prue breathed. She spoke with reverence, as if unable to believe the convention stable was here.

As if unable to believe it was shattered.

"What happened?" Bernadette asked bluntly, Naismith's birdsong harsh and clipped from her shoulder.

"A guest died."

Prue gasped, and only the whistle of the kettle a moment later spurred her into action, flittering around the kitchen as if looking for something to do.

Nimue explained everything she knew to her grandmothers, and by the time she'd finished, Prue had poured herself a cup and then sat at the table behind Bernadette, stirring honey into her tea almost in perfect reflection of her wife stirring the cauldron behind her.

"Hold it closer," said Bernadette, her mouth in a thin line.

Nimue did as bidden. Gowdie and then Naismith flapped backward to land on the table at which Prue sat with her bird, Dunlop, to allow the both of them some room.

"The magic on that should have held," said Bernadette, turning her focus back to the cauldron in front of her. The concoction boiled and bubbled, a murky purple color. "Forever. There was no danger of ever overloading the thing."

"Not even with my flying books?"

A twitch of a smile raised the corner of

Bernadette's mouth. "No. And I, for one, think that was a brilliant idea."

"Obviously not now." Nimue sighed and carried the crystal with both hands to the table. Gowdie and the lovebirds jumped back to allow it space.

Prue offered her a sympathetic smile before taking a sip of her tea.

"It wasn't anything *you* did that led to that tragedy." Bernadette's spoon continued to move round and round in the bubbling brew. "And I'm proud of you all for continuing forward as you have."

"We just… We need to know what happened to her. Before we tell the authorities."

Prue put her tea down on its saucer, still clutching the cup with both hands. "You need to know who *did* this to her. In case they intend to hurt anyone again."

Nimue's eyes blinked rapidly. "You don't think…?"

"That was no accident," said Bernadette, sniffling. "And that damage had nothing to do with magic. If I'd have thought human hands might have gotten a hold of it, I might have threaded even more strength and protection spells into the perma-charm brew all those years ago."

"Human hands?" Nimue whipped around.

"Told you it wasn't your fault," said Gowdie in her mind's ear.

"Well," said Bernadette, sparing a look over her shoulder. "A witch or warlock could have done the woman in in all sorts of manners. They could have just tapped their wand to the crystal and had the books fall whenever they'd have liked them to."

"But a human," said Prue, reaching across the table and tugging the crystal closer by the edge of the handkerchief, "would have had only one option: break the crystal."

Nimue stiffened. "Timed at just the right moment!"

So someone had been there, around the corner, by the item storage alcove, just biding their time?

How had they seen when books were flying perfectly in position over Rona's head? The alcove was in the lobby, but around the corner from the reception desk.

Maybe they'd figured there were enough books, it'd be hard to miss her.

Maybe they'd heard her carrying on and assumed she'd been in position.

Maybe they'd assumed she *hadn't been* in danger of being hit on the head just right and had only intended to scare her.

Either way, now that Bernadette Toothaker had assured Nimue it hadn't been a matter of overloading the crystal's magic, Nimue and the rest of Witchy ExS had another problem on their hands.

A human con-goer had murdered Rona Brynhild.

And there were plenty of suspects Nimue could think of who would at least liked to have seen Rona frightened—if not dead.

CHAPTER THIRTEEN

Nimue finished her chat with Cassie via Cassie's Communication Charm. She'd called to check in.

Cassie nodded, her face grim. She was on the second floor of the Bessa overlooking the main showroom floor. Nimue recognized some of the flying displays, as seen from above.

"Herne will be glad to hear we definitely don't have to take the floating displays down from the booths."

"We might be told they were in poor taste if and when we reveal what happened to Bookshop Con's star attraction." Nimue stood outside of her grandmothers' cottage, unwilling to chat and fly—too many broomstick accidents happened that way—despite how dire everything was.

Cassie winced. "Soren won't want *anything* leaking to the public until we know exactly what happened. And now—who was responsible."

"I wish we could end the convention…" Nimue thought she just imagined the trembling at her feet, but Gowdie bristled from atop the hitching rail beside her, too. "For the guests' safety, that's all," she said, to the cauldron below if that was what needed to hear it. She straightened, clutching her hands into fists at her side. "We'll just have to protect them. Find the person responsible—and fast."

Cassie tapped at her wrist crystal, bringing up her witch network projection screen. "Soren will probably want you on top of that," she said. "He's juggling enough as is—*and* once he hears that us fiddling with the item storage crystal wasn't responsible for the incident—"

"We weren't *fiddling* with… Hold on.

You keep saying 'Soren'?" What had happened to "Mr. Southern?"

Cassie grimaced, but she quickly tried to school her features. "Yes, he came out not too long after you left. And… it's all been a bit overwhelming for him."

What in the broomsticks was Ren doing going into hibernation *now*? He knew Soren wasn't that reliable in a pinch, let alone a multi-pronged crisis unlike anything Witchy ExS had seen before in their lifetimes.

"Where's the item storage crystal, then?" Cassie asked.

"I'm leaving it with Bernadette. She's busy, but Prue is going to cast the proper charms to safely dispose of it. Bernadette will make us a new item storage crystal, but it might not be ready today. She's working on something else."

"Merga is currently on item storage, and she's making do," said Cassie dismissively. "Some regulars have expressed disappointment in not watching their bags and coats fly up into the air like usual, but we've let them know the storage magic is undergoing maintenance. Morpheus went out to the tailor's and asked for some extra clothes racks. It's working out fine."

"It's just not special," Nimue said, her stomach sinking. "Not how Witchy ExS does it."

"No," said Cassie. "That's part of why Soren…" She bit her lip.

"Why Soren what?"

"Wants something grand to take their mind off of it. So they remember that and not the broken-down parts or"—she winced, Laveau the ferret's fur bristling at her shoulder—"or anything *unpleasant* that might come out of the experience by the time we spread the news."

What was she talking about? Ren would never step out of his comfort zone to come up with "something special," not when the tried-and-true method had been proven successful. Especially not with so many unknowns on the table. Even if the cauldron could probably sense the guests' disappointment in the lack of floating item storage, it was just one small piece of the experience gone, nothing for which anyone came to a convention in the first place.

They came for... Magic. Wonder. Whimsy. And *whimsical* was, in a rather insulting manner, how Ren had described her experience-a-book-scene idea. "He can't be trying the Book Scene Booth!" Nimue sputtered, waiting for Cassie to correct her.

Cassie cleared her throat. "Maybe...? If he can get it to work?"

Nimue's jaw dropped. "But the time it would take to imbue a perma-charm crystal, something that could handle hundreds, thousands of guests, stepping through—"

"He put in an order with Bernadette almost as soon as he took over," Cassie explained.

Nimue looked over her shoulder at the cottage door. So that was what had her grandmother's attention. Soren had Communication Charmed with her grandmother to place the order but had still left it up to her to explain the *disaster* that had prompted it?

He hadn't even told them to expect her to show up.

She shook her head. That was so typically Soren, though. His head was in the clouds, even when he had control of it.

"Even with my grandmother working on it, it won't be ready—"

"Until later tonight," Cassie said, her shoulders drooping, as if a few hours' wait was too much to ask from an untested, multi-pronged Illusion Charm of that caliber.

"Where's he going to set it up?" Nimue practically shrieked.

"There's room in Section 3F of the showroom floor," said Cassie, swiping in the air at her witch network screen. Some conventions needed more space than others, and it was true that Bookshop Con was only taking up about three-quarters of the showroom floor. The rest was roped off with temporary curtains, hiding nothing but various equipment and extra chairs and the like behind it.

For a second, Nimue pictured it. That empty space filled with interlocking cushioned mats, the curtains pulled back. And then Nimue herself tapping her wand to a perma-charm of an Illusion Charm of an unimpeachable caliber, asking the con-goer for the book scene of their choice, which would come to life around them, drawing from the con-goer's own memory of the scene to make them a part of it.

She imagined the joy on a child's face as they faced down Long John Silver for a bounty of treasure. The blush on a romance reader's cheeks when they found themselves swept up into one of Lola Jackson's heroes' arms.

Lola. A human who hadn't exactly gotten along with Rona. Like so many others.

"Never mind that," said Nimue, dismissing her own flight of fancy. "I'm sure Ren will put an end to that when he shows back up."

Cassie shrugged a single shoulder helplessly. "Have you ever known Ren to leave Soren to handle a crisis?"

No, Nimue did not. Ren had settled into Soren's body in the potions-brewing accident that had killed Lydia, and he'd made his way to the surface more and more often, certainly every time Soren was in danger of letting his grief or stress take hold of him.

Ren bailing on him now felt weird. Almost as weird as Soren being gung-ho and moving forward with her idea that Ren himself had dismissed out of hand.

Unless that was Soren's way of apologizing for Ren's behavior.

Which was sweet, but... Now was hardly the time.

"When, exactly, did Soren take over?" Nimue asked, getting ready to mount her broom.

"After he came back from speaking with Nicola Nash."

So after he'd told Nicola the news. Perhaps her reaction had sparked some sort of change, brought out the version of the man who'd known her best friend. Perhaps the stark reminder of death had brought up memories that would have caused the both of them hurt.

Gowdie took to the air, looking back over his shoulder to wait for his witch to join him in the skies.

"Cassie, I'm heading back." Nimue

started hovering on her broomstick. "I trust you'll let Ren—Soren—know?"

"Of course." Cassie nodded, waving her wand to dismiss the Communication Charm.

Nimue took to the air, Gowdie doing loops around her. There was no point in asking her grandmother not to bother with the new crystal Soren had ordered. Whether or not it wound up being used at the convention, Nimue knew her grandmother would see the crystal's creation through. A witch didn't leave a brew half-finished.

"What's our plan, then?" Gowdie asked in Nimue's mind a few minutes later as they reached the edge of downtown Cauldron Cove. *"Is it really going to be your job to find the killer?"*

Nimue winced at that term. But intentional or not, someone *had* killed Rona.

And finding that person—despite everything she'd have preferred to have been focusing on during the first day of Bookshop Con—was the highest priority.

"I'll have to speak with Zelena," she said, a shiver running up her spine even as she spoke. But surely, the Convention Security Manager would put aside her obvious disdain for Nimue in the face of ongoing danger to the con-goers. A second such incident would be unforgiveable—and the convention couldn't be stopped.

"What about Soren?" Gowdie asked, the flap of his wings louder as he swooped down.

"One of us has to attend to con matters," she said. She found herself, strangely, wishing it were Ren and not Soren handling everything alone.

But then again, she didn't want Ren to see just how well he could handle things without her. Because future cons wouldn't have crises of this proportion that would take up all of her attention.

She came to a stop at a light, only for it to turn green again a moment later. About to head forward, she saw something out of the corner of her eye. She took a sharp turn, Gowdie having to double back to catch up to her.

"Why are you going this way?" he asked.

She pointed ahead. There, in Iron Cast

Park, was a recognizable figure, a man with silver hair sipping a familiar cup, a folio bag on his lap. The cup held a hot drink from Sylvie's Sweets Bakery, which was just around the corner from the park.

"Is that Sherman Abbott?" Gowdie asked in her mind.

"Yes," answered Nimue, slowing her speed and descending down to the sidewalk at the entryway to the park. Her booted toes scuffed the ground before she'd fully descended, leaping off in her eagerness.

Here was the human at the con who'd had the biggest, most public beef with Rona Brynhild.

If he needed to be taken in, best to do it away from the convention.

Sherman sensed her approach, looking up from the phone in his right hand and taking a sip of his coffee from his left as she approached. Nimue narrowed her eyes to get a better look at the angled screen. A call was coming in from someone named Print More.

A printing business or something, Nimue supposed.

"Ah, Miss… Toothaker, was it?" He glanced at his phone screen again and dismissed the call before sliding the phone into his bag and fastening it shut. "Am I running late for the signing?"

"No," said Nimue. At least she didn't think he was. That wasn't why she'd approached him anyway. "Or… I guess you'll have to ask the Delgados."

"Okay…" Sherman cocked a silver eyebrow. "So may I ask what you're doing out here, blocks away from the convention? It's started, hasn't it?"

"Yes, well…" Nimue clutched her broomstick tighter against her. Gowdie, having circled overhead like a vulture after carrion, landed on a nearby bronze statue of Bessa Toothaker herself. The witch who'd founded the town looked forever young, flawless, in metal, looking off to the horizon, as if to say that there was still so much to be done.

But her job was done. The town had been founded. It had flourished. Until darkened with this tragedy, teetering on the edge of full-scale danger.

"What are *you* doing out here?" Nimue asked.

Sherman bristled at the accusation in her voice but seemed to dismiss it with a shrug. He took another long gulp of his coffee. "Enjoying the fresh air. Seeing the town. I do like a little solitude in the mornings." He stood and tossed the cup into the garbage can beside his bench. The perma-charm inside it whirred to life, processing the trash for proper disposal.

Sherman stretched, one hand clutching his folio bag handle, then looked back at Nimue, as if surprised to still find her standing there.

"Do you need something from me?"

"Enjoying the fresh air, huh…" Nimue frowned and took up the slow, steady gait of the man she was determined to follow as he made his way through the park in the general direction of the Bessa. "You don't stick around at cons for opening?"

"Should I have to?" Sherman watched as Gowdie took to the air and flew above her, but he didn't say anything. "I'm a convention *guest*, not a prisoner, am I correct?"

Nimue winced at the label "prisoner." If he'd killed Rona…

"It just seems odd, is all. Most guests who travel to Cauldron Cove for a convention tend to stick around the Bessa when the con is on, at least until showroom hours are over."

"In a town as wonderous as all this?" Sherman gestured around him at the park, stuffing his free hand into his pocket. It was quiet, and they encountered few others on the paths in different directions. Witch and warlock children were at school, and human guests were likely for the most part at the convention, especially now that it had been open for a few hours.

"There's usually enough to keep them entertained…" Nimue let her thoughts carry that sentence off as Gowdie flew into the boughs of trees overhead. She remembered Huntsville parks well—Willow had loved playing in them—with their broad, open spaces and impeccably mowed grass, but this was more like a carefully cultivated patch of proper forest, right in the middle of the town.

"Yes, well, you live as long as I have, and you have enough of *entertainment*." Sherman spat the last word. "Of frivolities. Makes you want to run off and get lost in the middle of the woods somewhere." He chuckled and brought his left hand out of his pocket to gesture in the speckle of leaf-filtered light. A plain golden wedding band caught a snatch of overhead sunlight through the lattice of trees before he tucked his hand back into his pocket. "Can't say I blame Rona for being so reclusive some-times…" He winked at Nimue, and she was taken aback by how casually he spoke of his now-dead author rival. "Granted, I do enjoy meeting readers and partaking in the adulation of fans. I imagine even Rona can't resist on occasion. Probably why she dragged herself out of her hidey-hole for this."

Was it possible he didn't know about Rona's untimely demise? She wondered if she might get him to slip up somehow, if this was all an act.

"Is the argument about the award she received really all there is to the bad history between you two?" Nimue asked. "It seemed like it runs… much deeper."

Sherman slowed his gait even more, stopping to turn and look at the witch beside him. "Miss Toothaker—"

"Nimue," she corrected.

"Nimue." He winked at her, and she found herself taken aback. "Are you a fan of my books?"

Nimue wasn't sure where the question had come from, other than narcissism on the man's part, but she supposed from what little she knew of him, that didn't seem entirely out of character.

"I've read a couple," she admitted. She didn't want to tell him what she thought about his witch and warlock characters always being at fault for whatever heinous crime had been committed.

"I was just going to say you seem a lot like my most frequently-appearing detective, Mallie Fitzroy." He tapped his chin with one finger. "Asking some strange questions."

Except that Mallie Fitzroy was a human, and her suspects almost always of the magical variety. Here, the situation was reversed. "And you're like a suspect, evading an innocent question."

"Except a question is hardly ever *innocent*, is it?" He held a finger up.

Did he know about Rona's death, then? Why else be so coy about the answer?

Sherman sighed and picked up his feet again. Overhead, Gowdie jumped to another bough to keep slightly ahead of them on the paved path through the trees.

"I take it Rona's been talking, has she?"

Actually, quite the opposite, Nimue held herself back from saying.

Gowdie chuckled darkly in her mind from where he'd hidden amongst the trees.

"We met once before," Sherman said, tugging on an earlobe. "Any writer who's been friends with either of us knows that much. And that was years ago—back when we were both just starting." His lips made a puttering sound. "Had to be thirty-five years ago, give or take."

"So the comment about her book not deserving the award it got—that wasn't just about you thinking the book itself didn't deserve it?"

"Oh, the book didn't deserve it—don't get me wrong there." He dipped his head to avoid the bough that hung down just a little too much ahead of them. "I've made a point of reading every single one of Rona Brynhild's releases, and while I can forgive the masses for being attracted to tripe, I couldn't forgive our peers for finding it worthy of particular attention."

Nimue ignored his *professional* criticism. She hadn't been a fan of Rona, either, mostly because of her comments about how her worlds without magic were some kind of superior fantasy to the real world. But her books—the few she'd read—had always been solid. Innovative, even.

"You found her books *trite*," Nimue pointed out, "and yet you've read every one?" He *had* had an awfully thorough knowledge of her books to whip out when it came to handing out insults. But hadn't he insinuated he hadn't read the books?

Sherman kicked a pebble down the lane. "I can read fluff like that in half a day."

"I wasn't asking how you managed to *find time* for them."

They'd reached the other end of the miniature forest in the park now, coming out to a few more benches in an open space, a bronze statue of the giant cauldron beneath the town in miniature and a clear view of the Bessa ahead.

"I was… looking for something."

"For what?" Nimue stopped, and Sherman stopped with her.

"Genius," he said, smiling coyly.

Nimue cocked her head. "But you said—"

"She couldn't write." He shrugged one shoulder. "She could once. Or so I thought. We met in a writer's workshop. She and I swapped stories for critique. I thought her short, thrilling murder mystery was marvelous."

"You did?" Nimue would never have guessed he'd ever say something complimentary about her.

Bringing his hand out of his pocket, he fiddled with his wedding band. "And she told me my story, and I quote, 'Needed more than a little improvement. It needs a match and a blowtorch for good measure.'"

Nimue blinked rapidly, Gowdie taking his favorite place on her shoulder, his tail whapping across the top of her broomstick's shaft.

"*Never one to mince words,*" he said in Nimue's mind.

"You must not have taken that well," said Nimue aloud.

He shrugged, tucking his hand back into his pocket. "She wasn't *wrong*. I didn't see it then, but… I did a few years later." His nose jutted up in the air as they made their way to the edge of the park. "And the tables have turned, in all the best people's opinions. Her stuff is for the masses. Mine has mass appeal, but it's truly for the intellect." He tapped the side of his head.

"*Modest,*" said Gowdie.

Nimue stopped herself from snickering.

"Mr. Abbott—"

"Sherman." A twinkle danced in his eye as he threw the first-name insistence back at her.

"Sherman," she said. "What time did you leave the hotel this morning?"

All mischievousness dropped from Sherman's face as he flinched back. "Why do you ask? Did Rona say something?"

"No..." Nimue pursed her lips. What was she missing? Wasn't it a simple enough question?

Sherman scoffed, and she noticed the way his left hand balled into a fist inside his suitcoat pocket. "I didn't check the time, but it was before six." He pulled out his phone. "By the time I walked down to the bakery, got my order, and went to the park to check my emails, it was 6:15, so I had to have left much earlier."

"6:15?" She cocked her head. It was approaching eleven now. "That's a long sit in the park."

His body rigid, he licked his lips before speaking again. "As I said, I enjoy my solitude. Now you'll have to excuse me. I have a signing to get to."

Nimue watched him exit the park and cross the road, making his way to the convention center with purpose.

"Talk about cold coffee," Gowdie said.

Nimue chuckled despite everything. There was that, too. He'd been sipping on the same cup since nearly five hours beforehand? Doubtful. So what had he been doing? Brainstorming a new book? Talking on the phone? Waiting for someone who'd never shown?

Nimue was glad she hadn't let slip the fact that Rona had been killed just yet. She could see at once how defensive the man got at even a simple question.

She'd have to keep an eye on him and figure out another way to learn more.

Nimue brought up the witch network projection screen from her wrist perma-charm crystal almost as soon as she stepped inside the employee entryway. Projecting a mental command to send a message to Zelena—it wouldn't be as pressing as a Communication Charm, but she'd used that up for the day—she asked the Convention Security Manager to meet her as soon as possible in the General Manager's office. Then, thinking for a moment about what to say, she sent another message to Soren, asking if he might have a moment to spare to meet her there as well. Whether he arrived before or after Zelena, she'd get him caught up with matters. After dropping off her broomstick in the empty break room, she checked her witch network projection again for a reply from either of them and found a message instead from Tituba.

Crisis in the ConSuite. Are you back yet?

Gowdie peered at the message. *"Well, that doesn't sound good."*

On my way, Nimue thought to the witch network.

"How big of a crisis can it be if she contacted you instead of Zelena?" Gowdie pointed out as they made their way to the teleportation pad down the hall.

Nimue's heart had been pounding loudly in her ears and Gowdie's observation mellowed her slightly. Her steps slowed. "True…"

Maybe this was a normal crisis. Of the catering variety. Which would otherwise have been a major crisis when a convention was up and operational, but…

In any case, Nimue walked through the teleportation pad, the white light glowing purple.

She stepped out in the corner of the Con-

Suite, an array of guests with badges dangling from their necks selecting snacks and drinks from the food tables. One young woman looked wide-eyed at Graves the frog familiar as he did a little dance between the cups and bottles of drinks, laughing as he kicked his long legs, her joy spurring him to do more tricks. But most of the guests kept stealing glances over their shoulders at the far corner of the room.

At a table with only a napkin dispenser and a single bottle of water in front of them were Lola Jackson, Shawna Higgins, and Tituba. As Nimue approached, she noted that Tituba and Lola each had a hand on Shawna's shoulder as she sobbed into a limp and torn napkin.

"Can I be of any assistance?" Nimue asked, looking over her shoulder at the other con-goers. A number were at their own tables, eating, popping snacks into their mouth like the YA author was putting on a show. "Concealment Charm," said Nimue, almost the instant she'd pulled her wand out of its holster. A curtain like the one the medical team had placed around

Rona's prone body appeared around the table in time with Nimue's wand movements. She suppressed a shudder at the mental comparison as she took a seat.

The flap of Gowdie's wings filled the air as he flew overhead, landing on the table with Graves the frog on his back. The little frog skipped over to Tituba, who stopped patting Shawna in order to run a finger under his chin.

Shawna's sobs echoed hollowly in the confined space, but the charm should damper some of the sound to passersby's ears as well.

"It's, uh... It's..." Shawna pointed a shaky finger in front of her.

Frowning, Nimue pushed aside the napkin dispenser that wove napkins out of thin air at the push of a button, using dust particles in the air and pre-fed recycled fibers in an eco-friendly witchy manner to produce the napkins humanity was accustomed to. In front of Shawna was a piece of paper, unfolded but bearing the creases of having been folded in three spots lengthwise.

"I asked her if she wanted me to perform a Calming Charm or call the medical team" —Tituba shot Nimue a look at that, as if asking if the team would be up to the task after Rona's demise—"but she said she'd prefer not to."

"I don't…" Shawna hiccupped, rubbing her hand on the front of her forest-green sweater. "I don't *want to be* calmer. Not if I have to watch out around every corner." The last few words tumbled together and she leaned against Lola's arm, sobbing harder.

"There, there," Lola said, tapping her back.

Nimue took the letter.

In flowing, cursive font, it read:

One book down, and still more to go. Jump in the lake or I'll push you in myself.

A sudden sensation of coldness hung heavily in Nimue's body as her fingers shook on the letter.

A death threat?

She turned it over. It was blank on the other side.

"One book down?" Gowdie said in her head. *"And still more to go?"*

Rona, Nimue thought back to him. She'd died when a book had literally fallen. Or many books, Nimue supposed. But if "book" in this context represented an author…

"Is there a serial killer at Bookshop Con?" Gowdie asked.

Graves croaked wildly, his gullet expanding and contracting. Tituba hushed him and pet him soothingly as Shawna's sobs quieted and she sat back up, wiping her eyes while looking at the frog.

"May I have this?" Nimue asked, folding it up and already tucking it into a pouch at her belt.

"Ye-Yeah…" said Shawna, her throat cracking. "But…"

"Readers can… cross lines sometimes," Lola said, folding her hands over the table. "We've both gotten some wild mail—usually angry at us for doing this or that with beloved characters—but usually, our PAs, or in Shawna's case, her agent, handle that."

Nimue frowned. "You've gotten death threats before?"

"Well…" Shawna frowned. "I didn't like to know the details—it was too upsetting for me—but my agent and my assistant did find some threatening things online when the last movie in my Ruin and Wreckage series never got made. As if *I* had any say in that! I wanted it made, too!" She started sobbing again.

Tituba pushed the button on the dispenser and another napkin wove itself into the air. Shawna thanked her timidly and traded the flimsy remnants of her sodden napkin for the new one.

"Police wound up looking into it and it was just some thirteen-year-old girl," Lola explained. "They stressed to her and her parents the seriousness of saying these things, even hidden behind an online handle, and we thought that was the end of it. The girl was sorry—and upset."

"Upset she got caught maybe." Shawna laughed darkly.

"How long ago was that?" Tituba asked.

"Good thinking," added Gowdie. *"Maybe*

Miss Disgruntled Fan grew up to follow through with her threats against authors who displeased her."

"Just last year," said Lola. So there went Gowdie's suspect, though Nimue wouldn't entirely rule out a fourteen-year-old if the clues eventually led that way. More likely than not, some kind of restraining order would have kept the girl away from an event where Shawna Higgins had been publicized to be, though.

Unless she was just *that* passionate enough to kill her. And take Rona—and possibly others—out at the same time.

That would have to be one angry and genre-hopping prolific reader.

"How did you get this letter?" Nimue asked, tapping her pouch to indicate where she'd tucked it away. She'd show Zelena and maybe they could cast an investigative Origin Charm on it. Zelena was more practiced with those.

"In our room," Shawna said, blowing her nose. "It was slipped under the door. I don't know when. It was already there when we got back this morning."

"Back?" Nimue asked.

Lola and Shawna exchanged a look. "We went out for breakfast."

"At the hotel restaurant?" Nimue suggested.

"Um—" started Shawna.

"Somewhere downtown." Lola waved her hand in the air.

"And when was that?" Nimue asked.

Gowdie's talons dug into her shoulder. *"Are they suspects?"*

Sherman wasn't the only one who'd had a public argument with Rona.

Just covering all our bases, Nimue thought to her dragon familiar.

"Like seven?" Lola said. "What does that matter?"

Nimue bit her lip. She wasn't sure how best to approach this without giving away what had happened—and that she was checking the other authors' alibis.

"There was… well, a little incident with some magic shortly before the con opened. I just wondered if whoever sent you that letter used the chaos and distraction to slip it under your door." That seemed as good an explanation as any.

Shawna let out a little gasp.

Lola leaned back in her chair, arching a brow. "What kind of *incident*?"

Nimue ignored the question. "It happened around a quarter to eight. In the convention center lobby."

Shawna had taken her latest napkin and was tearing the soggy pieces up in her hands. "We didn't get back to our room until 8:30. I remember because I was scrambling. I was going to be late to my panel at nine. I like to get there a little early and I still had to run to the bathroom."

That checked out. Nimue remembered the guests she'd run into who'd been about to attend that.

"And I reminded her with the teleportation pad, getting there in time would be a piece of cake." Lola waved a hand. "We noticed the note right away, but I picked it up and told Shawna to hurry and get ready. When she was in the bathroom..." She stopped, looking to her friend, almost as if confirming whether or not she should continue.

Shawna sat up straighter. "Lola read the letter but kept its contents from me until after the panel. I was so panicked about being late, I almost forgot about it entirely."

"Yeah," said Lola softly. "It worried me during the panel, and I wanted to go find security, but I didn't want to alert Shawna as to *why* or leave her alone for even one second, so… I just kept an eye out at the panel with her."

"She was acting kind of strange," Shawna said. "But I had to focus on the panel. I hate public speaking." She shuddered.

"The panel was just down the hall," Tituba said, gesturing in the northern direction. "And I heard a scream as I was refilling some of the ConSuite snacks and headed out into the hallway to find them."

"Just a little scream," Shawna said, her cheeks flushing. "I just… When Tituba told me, I got flashbacks to last year—the fear, like I had to look over my shoulder, like anyone I met in public could be the person who wanted me dead—and I panicked a little."

She let Lola give her another hug.

Nimue thought over what they'd said. Another vague answer as to where the two authors had been during Rona's murder, but if Shawna herself was also a target…

She thought back to the threatening letter. There'd been nothing on the back of it.

"How did you know the letter was intended for Miss Higgins?" Nimue asked.

Shawna and Lola broke apart, seeming to have a silent conversation in their heads.

"I can see now why you find that kind of vexing," Gowdie said. *"Watching familiars have conversations with one another and waiting for me to translate for you."*

"If you tell me at all," Nimue pointed out quietly.

"What was that?" Lola asked.

"Just talking to Gowdie," Nimue said, rubbing her dragon under his chin. *Maybe I should have said that telepathically.*

Gowdie's little cat-like movement seemed to cheer Shawna up slightly as her gaze focused on the dragon.

"Time for me to shine." Gowdie hopped onto the table and took careful steps toward Shawna.

Her face lit up and she held out a tentative hand. Gowdie leaned into it, rubbing her hand and turning his head. He winked back at Nimue, but she could tell he was enjoying the pets nonetheless.

"Well, Shawna had that incident before." Lola smoothed the front of her skirt. She wore a cherry red dress today, her makeup bright and bold to match.

"And the… the…"

"'Jump in the lake,'" Nimue quoted, suddenly making the connection herself.

Shawna and Lola went quiet, Shawna's petting getting slower.

"What am I missing?" Tituba asked.

"Last night, at the author guest dinner," Nimue started, "things got *testy*. Some things were said—"

Shawna gasped. "You don't think it was *Rona*, do you?"

Tituba visibly winced and Gowdie slammed his head against Shawna's extended hand harder, as if demanding to be pet. It worked for a bit, as Shawna went back to focusing on running her hand under his chin and over his scaly head.

"Rona couldn't have done it." Nimue stood up from the table, unwilling to explain more.

"I don't know." Lola shook her head. "Seems like something she'd do."

"We don't even *know* her," Shawna pointed out.

Lola scoffed. "I know more than enough."

"I need to alert our Convention Security Manager," Nimue said, extending her arm to signal Gowdie to join her. He soared over and landed on her forearm like a hunting hawk. "And I have a meeting with her right now. Tituba, could you escort our guests back to their hotel room?"

"Oh," said Shawna, her face falling. "But we both have signings this afternoon."

"Security will escort you from your room to the signings," Nimue said, bringing up her witch network projected screen as Gowdie climbed up her arm and settled on her shoulder. She sent a mental message out to Cassie and Zelena that all authors would need beefed-up security.

"Is… Is that necessary?" Shawna asked. She looked to Lola, her eyes widening, as if hoping her friend would tell her Nimue was overreacting.

"Last time, it was just a foolish little girl," Lola pointed out.

"Better safe than sorry," Nimue said. She tapped a finger against her pouch. "Like I said, I'll look into it. Outside of your scheduled events, please remain in your room until I can have more security sent."

Tituba bit her lip but nodded, Nimue's message clear.

Nimue knew Tituba had plenty to do, but this convention wasn't going to be marred by another death. Her guests were going to be safe—her remaining ones, anyway.

"I'll be in touch," she said, looking at Shawna and Lola—but Tituba, too.

"Graves said Tituba thinks they're acting suspicious," Gowdie said as Nimue pulled back the curtain and made her way to the teleportation pad.

Nimue had certainly seen more suspicious behavior. Less than an hour earlier in the park, even.

But still…

That makes two of us, Nimue thought back to her familiar.

"Four," Gowdie said. *"Familiars can have opinions of their own, too."* While that was true to an extent, Nimue had never known one's opinion to vary so wildly from their witch or warlock. She'd taken it for granted that Graves and Gowdie would share their witches' opinions. Gowdie tapped his talons into her shoulder as they stepped into the white teleportation pad and it turned red. *"I do think anyone who could give such good scritches can't be all bad, though."*

At least Shawna Higgins had that much to say for her character. Nimue wondered if the super spies in movies who went up against all of those villains with cats on their laps would disagree, though.

CHAPTER FIFTEEN

The threatening letter metaphorically burning a hole in her pouch, Nimue made her way out of the teleportation pad to her and Ren's office. Cassie wasn't at her desk, which was piled high with books stacked sloppily. Books were also stacked on either side of the desk on the floor. Merga must have dropped them back off without shelving them in the Head Witch General Manager's office, not that Nimue would have expected her to. Nimue could deal with it herself once she had a minute—whenever that would be—though poor Cassie might feel like she had to, considering her workspace was now cluttered.

Cassie's absence didn't necessarily mean Ren—Soren—was still out on the showroom floor with her. If Soren was still in charge, she might have welcomed his presence when she opened the door, despite her thoughts that Ren could better handle the series of problems unfolding for them.

However, it was only Zelena Varlett she found waiting in the office.

Her sloth familiar, Messenger, slowly pointed an accusing finger from where she dangled around Zelena's neck.

"You'd think I didn't have enough to do without you *summoning me* here despite not being here yourself." Zelena tapped her boot on the carpeted floor impatiently.

Gowdie hissed at Messenger but didn't translate whatever the sloth familiar may have said to him.

Nimue shirked back for a moment, letting the taller, broader witch intimidate her. "Sorry," she mumbled, but then she straightened up and fished the letter out of her pouch. "I was on my way when another situation came up."

Narrowing her eyes, Zelena took the

letter from her smaller superior and read it over. "What's this?"

Nimue explained the situation with Shawna and Lola, then added on Bernadette's verdict about the item storage crystal having been damaged through human means. For some reason—perhaps because she didn't know what he was hiding yet, perhaps because she feared Zelena saying it was *her* job to investigate—she didn't tell her about her encounter with Sherman Abbott.

A deeply-lined scowl on her face, Zelena set the letter down on a clear spot on Ren's desk. "Have you performed an Origin Charm on it?"

"I was going to ask you. I figured you were more experienced with that kind of thing." Origin Charms could be murky, if a witch didn't know what she was looking for. They weren't as clear as History Charms, and a witch could only perform those on a place, not a thing.

Come to think of it, Zelena or someone else on security could probably perform a History Charm outside of Shawna and

Lola's hotel room door to see who'd left it. Nimue was about to suggest that if the Original Charm didn't provide answers, but Zelena grunted in response, pulling her wand out. "Origin Charm."

Gowdie flapped over and sat on a perch in the corner of the room Bernadette had left behind for her lovebird familiar.

The paper fluttered in a miniature cyclone of power, the results of whatever the magic could tell Zelena going straight into her mind in a series of images.

Gowdie? Nimue thought to her familiar.

He cocked his head at her.

Keep an eye on Messenger's thoughts. See if she picks up anything Zelena sees.

"She's too slow," Gowdie told her, and she could feel the curiosity behind his words. He'd been trying to read the sloth and failing, apparently. Messenger's arm moved out again, slowly, a single finger pointing at the dragon in the room, but Zelena didn't seem to notice.

"Well?" said Nimue as the letter fluttered back down to the desk.

"Nothing useful." Zelena snatched the

letter and tucked it in her own pouch at her waist. "But sometimes another angle can bring things to light. I'll have my team look at it."

"What about a History Charm? Outside of the hotel room door?"

"Yes, of course." Zelena swirled on Nimue, the letter already put away. "Though I'd bet my last brisket whoever left this note covered their face in the hallway, just in case they were spotted delivering it. In the meantime, I assume we need to beef up security on Shawna Higgins and Lola Jackson?"

Nimue twisted her wrist in one hand. "Yes. I was just going to tell you that. They're back in their hotel room waiting for security."

Zelena spun on her heel and headed toward the door.

Nimue wouldn't let the intimidating witch intimidate her. "And I want security for *every* author."

That stopped Zelena, allowing Gowdie the chance to take to the air and hover over his witch's shoulder.

"How much witchpower do you think I have to spare?"

Nimue ground her foot in the carpet. "You saw the letter. We could have a serial killer on our hands. What if authors are their intended victims?"

Zelena chewed her lip, thinking for a minute.

"And don't forget, all of our suspects are authors, too. Other than, perhaps, that four-teen-year-old fan of Shawna's." Gowdie flapped and flapped, his wings a steady rhythm.

Messenger cocked her head and looked up, perhaps in discussion with Zelena.

"You suspect an author?" Zelena said, her tone not accusatory. More curious.

Nimue sent Gowdie a chiding look. "Well, the security detail would be two-fold. Keep an eye out for threats on any more of our guests and keep track of what they're up to."

Sighing, Zelena brought up her witch network projection, tapping at the crystal on her wrist. It lit up with all sorts of colors as she sent mental messages to her team. "I'll see what we can do." Zelena dismissed the screen and exited.

Nimue was left to her thoughts, the wheels still spinning.

"Wait! Zelena!"

She headed out to meet the other witch in the hallway, startled a bit to feel Gowdie flinch mentally, as if she'd taken her own familiar by surprise. She checked on him, but he seemed okay, flapping his wings a bit too quickly until he got back into the rhythm of it, scrambling to land on her shoulder.

"What now?" Zelena put more effort into expelling the air in her lungs than was wholly necessary. Around her neck, Messenger's eyes were slowly, slowly widening. "I've got a lot to do—and I have to figure out how to get it all done understaffed."

Nimue tossed her head back, clenching her fist at her side. *She* was supposed to be the boss here. "Were there any recordings?"

"Recordings?"

"Of the lobby."

Messenger shook her little head slowly, the slightest edge of a smile widening her face.

"She thinks you've been reading too many Rona Brynhild books," Gowdie translated.

That was, Nimue realized, where she might have gotten the idea.

In Rona's worlds without magic, sometimes human video technology saved the day, picking up suspicious movements or even the act of murder. Cameras hung from ceilings in public places. A business the caliber of Witchy ExS really ought to have such things. She thought suddenly of Ren's idea of hiring a human medic and wondered if they would have known anything to save Rona that Florence and her team of magic medics couldn't have.

In any case, she felt the surly warlock wasn't too off-base when it came to the idea of bringing some of the human world into their convention center.

That, or she could talk to her grandmother about crafting perma-charm crystals for History Charms. She liked that idea, the more she thought of it. It'd require a lot less witchpower if she had a record of events she could always access in a pinch.

"Witches don't have need for *recordings*

when a History Charm will do." Zelena waved her hand in the air. Nimue was struck again by the pale scarring across it. "And if it's only occurring to you *now* to try it, you're two steps behind. My team combed the lobby, looking at past visions. The lobby played out about how you'd expect and it was too dark in the item storage alcove to see anything."

Before Nimue could say more, Zelena stepped through the teleportation pad, the color switching to aqua blue.

"You know that besides our own conversations between familiars, I can only hear one-sided conversations, whatever the familiars say to their witches or warlocks," said Gowdie. *"And that one… Well, she didn't have to be a sloth, and yet that's what she chose. Her thoughts come and go, slow as you might think at times, fast and to the point at others. Mixed up, even."*

"It must be hard to talk to her."

"Tell me about it. It's hard to be around her! Like sometimes, her thoughts or feelings just hit out of nowhere, like bam!" Gowdie swooned, pretending to faint. *"And you have to wonder*

if she just reacts weirdly at the wrong moments or her reaction has been slowed down. Like when you called for Zelena to wait as she was about to leave—boom! Messenger was as surprised as if you'd punched her."

Nimue laughed. She couldn't imagine punching anyone's familiar, least of all that slowly stirring sloth, even if she did seem to share her witch's general distaste for Nimue.

"She always listens, though. Sharp as a tack, that way. Picked up anything I said to you."

"I know," said Nimue, taking a deep breath to avoid snapping at her familiar. Her stomach rumbled, and she wished she'd picked up something to eat while she'd been in the ConSuite. "I just thought… Well… Zelena doesn't like me."

"She doesn't like a lot of people."

"Makes me wonder how she wound up with a sweet warlock like Linden," Nimue spat. But she felt bad almost as soon as she'd said it. Their relationship was none of her business, even if she still couldn't help but feel a pang of sympathy for the Director of Guest Services.

"She doesn't want you to succeed." Gowdie didn't even try to debate that point. *"But her husband seems to."*

Linden Varlett would have wanted anyone to succeed. It wasn't particularly personal. He was just friendly that way. Got along with everyone. He had a special charm with human guests in particular that made him perfect for the job.

"What are you suggesting?" Nimue asked.

Gowdie kneaded her shoulder. *"Well, we have one History Charm we could use today ourselves."*

That was true. But Nimue wasn't particularly familiar with the charm; she hadn't had much use for it as Bernadette's assistant. She wasn't trained in all matters of security.

"Zelena says the team combed the lobby for clues…"

"So maybe we hold on to ours and use it instead to check some alibis?"

Sherman. And even Shawna and Lola had seemed dismissive when asked about their whereabouts during what they hadn't known to be Rona's time of murder. There was whoever had delivered that threatening letter, too. But, as Zelena had suggested, she had a feeling whoever had done that—especially if they were the same person who'd targeted Rona—may have been careful to wear a disguise. Humans knew about security cameras in hotel hallways, after all. They probably would have assumed witches had the same.

Well, they would if she ever got around to asking Bernadette to make the perma-charm History Charm crystals.

"I didn't tell Zelena about Sherman's wonky alibi."

"She would probably just dismiss you. Or claim she has no time to help keep an eye on him. I say, check into that yourself. But I figure you still want to see what happened in the lobby."

That was true. And it was Linden's domain.

She gave Gowdie a little scratch under the chin before checking her witch network projection screen. No messages from Ren, so she mentally projected another one to him, telling him to touch base with Zelena and she'd catch him up.

Then she sent a message to Linden, asking if he had time to meet her in the lobby.

Linden greeted Nimue in the lobby almost as soon as she stepped through the teleportation pad. The Director of Guest Services had his arms behind his back, his chinchilla familiar, Dyer, flittering down his legs to reach the ground.

"You wanted to talk?" Linden asked, his customer-service smile perfectly in place, even for her.

Around them, the crowd had died out, the noise from the main showroom floor filtering out into the lobby like the echoing hum of insects.

"Yes, I was wondering if you might help me." She looked around her, but no one seemed to be paying attention. Over her shoulder, she saw a smiling Sherman Abbott with a long line of people clutching his books at the Delgados' booth. Across from that, a sign flashed "Signing Cancelled" for Rona Brynhild at Nicola's booth, her shop entirely empty of customers.

"Ah," said Linden. "I take it you weren't present for Zelena and her crew's History Charms?"

Nimue snapped back, surprised at Linden's intuitiveness. "Yes. Do you think you could use yours for me?"

Linden arched a brow, his customer service expression slipping just a bit. "You've already used your History Charm for the day?"

"Er, well, I thought I might need to save it. But if you've already used yours—"

"No, that's fine. I don't mind. I don't often have much use for the charm. Dyer?"

Nimue turned to see Dyer sniffing over at the item storage alcove, where Merga looked bored, leaning against the wall and flicking through what Nimue recognized to be a human smartphone. Her llama familiar was curled up, sleeping, on the table separating her from any approaching guests.

Dyer scattered back over to her warlock,

who was already attempting to lead Nimue to the front concierge desk that had been the scene of the accident—or more likely, crime.

"No, let's start over here," Nimue suggested, now that she saw how empty the alcove was. This was where the item storage crystal had been, after all.

"That's fine," said Linden, "but my wife assured me it was too dark at the time to see anything over here. I only have the one History Charm to use, so I thought it best to see where the incident actually happened."

"History Charm?" Merga leaned away from the wall, sliding her phone into her dress pocket. Nimue wondered if she kept in touch with Willow that way or if she, too—as Nimue had been at that age—was fascinated by the human world outside of Cauldron Cove's borders. "Sorry, boss," she said when she saw Nimue staring at her pocket where she'd tucked her phone away. "No one was around and—"

"It's fine." Nimue waved her off dismissively. They had other things to worry about, and someone needed to be managing the item storage alcove, even if the lines had died down. She looked around. They had done a good job in a pinch. Bags were stacked toward the back in neat rows, and coats were hung off of the racks they'd borrowed from the tailor's in town. It looked neat and orderly, and there were even little tags sticking off of each item. In the absence of the perma-charm crystal's ability to match owner with item, it made sense they'd have to keep track of things a more human way.

Cassie was right that it was, despite all of this, just lacking that something special.

"On the contrary, Miss Arriens," Linden said, "I know you're not in my department, but you're close enough in this capacity. I would prefer you present yourself as paying attention and ready to help a guest the entire time you're at your station. *Honestly.* Witches ought to display more decorum. Yet I so rarely meet one who does."

Merga flushed, her pale skin growing red, and Spandemager woke up with a start, jumping down to the ground beside her.

Nimue didn't bother to point out that she bet most human guests would find a sleeping miniature llama on the desk plenty adorable. That made it *professional* in a way. But Linden was clearly not in the mood to hear it, his smile causing his face more strain by the second. A vein was even pulsating slightly at his forehead.

"Dyer's scared," Gowdie told her in her mind.

Remembering that familiars could report on the half of the conversation they heard between other witches and warlocks and their familiars, Nimue just took note of the chinchilla as Linden let out a deep breath and pet the rodent in his arms.

Nimue had never worked under Linden. She wondered if his perfect customer service demeanor made him a strict boss.

"I was wondering if we could cast a History Charm here," Nimue told Merga. She looked to Linden. "Though he's right. I need one cast over by the front desk, too…"

"I can cast one for you." Merga took out her wand. "I don't use that charm much."

Dyer let out a little trembling titter, and Linden stepped back, bending down to whisper into her ears.

Nimue stepped back. *What's she saying?* she asked Gowdie in her mind.

Gowdie cocked his head. *"Nothing right now."*

She seemed to be relaxing more into Linden's touch, though, and the older warlock's smile was becoming more natural and at ease.

It had been a long opening day for Bookshop Con and it wasn't quite even noon yet.

"What time did it happen?" Merga asked, brandishing her red wand.

"Try seven-fifty this morning," Nimue said.

"History Charm." Merga's eyes glowed as she waved her arm and the area was cloaked in darkness, the passing cloud cover that Nimue had noticed around that time making it hard to see, as Zelena had reported.

Since this was a History Charm illusion of the area at the moment and not the alcove's current appearance, no one could cast a Light Charm or anything of that nature to get a better look.

The item storage crystal glowed on the dark table, a muted burnished yellow.

Nothing else seemed to happen.

"Try speeding it up a little," Nimue instructed Merga. She couldn't see her just then since Merga hadn't been where she was at the time displayed in the History Charm. She couldn't see Linden or even Gowdie or herself. The entire area was blanketed with the illusion.

Zelena would have had to put up a Concealment Charm and put the item storage on hold if they'd attempted this when a crowd had been gathered.

A small whoosh of air indicated the movement of Merga's wand and the illusion sped up. The only way to tell that, though, was the shimmering, dull glow of the item storage crystal as it had sat there on the table, not in use.

And then the illusion of the crystal shattered, silently, since it was a History Charm, which only displayed images and didn't recreate sounds.

The top of the crystal caved in at an

angle and then it smashed again, the cracks spreading outward.

Nimue moved closer to the crystal, but there wasn't much to see in the darkness.

"That's what Zelena's team found." Linden's voice carried through the darkness. "It's smashed, but you can't see how or who."

"Wait." Nimue held up a hand, though she couldn't see it.

Merga's whispers paused the charm, the light flickering from the dying crystal pausing in front of them.

Nimue went down on her knees and looked up at the table, attempting to see whatever had struck the crystal from above.

She couldn't see a figure, no sense of the height of whoever had to be standing somewhere around the crystal. But she did see, in the glint of the last bit of the crystals' inert, yellowish light, the tool used to smash it.

It resembled a common human-made hammer.

CHAPTER SIXTEEN

"There!" said Nimue, pointing. But no one could see what she was pointing to.

"What?" Merga's voice carried over the illusion.

"Oh. I'm down on my knees, looking up. I can just make out a hammer."

"A hammer…?" Linden's voice carried through the air. "So it was a human."

Nimue knew as much already. "It'd have to be a strong human. Crystal doesn't break after a light swing of a hammer. Not a perma-charm crystal, anyway."

"Maybe it was two humans together?" Merga's voice carried from closer. She must have been down on her knees nearby.

"Maybe..." Nimue kept cricking her neck, but she couldn't get a look at any figure, one or two. All she saw was darkness, darkness edged in the distance with a stark red glow. "If the handle was long enough to grip together. Merga, can you keep the illusion going?"

The witch did as bidden and Nimue watched as the crystal shattered even more, then went dark, taking with it the very last of the light.

Moments later, a lit wand came into the alcove and Nimue watched as Zelena, her face clear in the wand's glow, grabbed the shattered crystal. Her lips curled as she examined the broken crystal, her grip on it so tight, if the thing had been made of lesser stuff, she'd be about to break it even more. Messenger, her sloth familiar, just stared at the crystal, her wide eyes glossy.

And then Zelena left the illusion and the alcove was empty, the cloud overhead passing back to reveal nothing at all of note. No crystal, no figure, no hammer, no evidence. Just a table and a once-floating pair of keys on the floor behind it.

With a whoosh of air, the History Charm dissipated and the alcove went back into the sunnier, current view. Merga was on her knees behind the table. She stood, slapping her tights clean of any smudges.

Linden stepped forward from where Nimue had seen him last. "So we're looking for a hammer."

"Apparently." Nimue used the table to help her stand. Gowdie flew up from where he'd settled on Spandemager's fluffy back at some point during the illusion and landed on her shoulder. She brought up her witch network projection screen and thought the update to Zelena and then Ren and Cassie. She was just about to put it away, when Zelena sent a message back.

How can you be so sure?

We did a History Charm at the item storage alcove, Nimue messaged back, her pulse quickening. *And at the right angle, there seemed to be a hammer smashing the crystal.*

Zelena's icon flashed, a sign she was writing back.

"Did you still want to look at the moment at the front desk?" Linden asked.

"Yeah," Nimue said, not taking her eyes off of her witch network screen. "I'll meet you there in a second. If anyone has a Concealment Charm left, block off the area in case we get stragglers." Her stomach growled. "It's almost lunch. People might leave the Bessa to check out the town's offerings."

Linden nodded and turned around the corner.

Merga waited until he had left the alcove entirely and then pulled out her phone from her pocket, watching Nimue carefully as if to see if she'd object.

Nimue was too focused on Zelena's reply.

My team did History Charms all over the lobby, she'd written back.

"I think you've made her dislike you more," Gowdie pointed out.

Well, you missed it. I was on my knees, looking up, and I saw a flash of a hammer.

If you say so, Zelena wrote back. *But investigations of this nature are best left to the pro-*

fessionals. They're not for amateurs.

Nimue gritted her teeth.

Who's with you? Zelena messaged her. Why did she care to know?

Merga, Nimue messaged back. Then, with a little twinge of pleasure she shouldn't have felt just then, she added, *and Linden.*

She swept her witch network projection screen away and headed after Linden.

He'd brought over Humphrey from behind the desk to cast the Concealment Charm. Perhaps Linden had already used his for the day or he wanted to keep it safely tucked away. After a day like today, it was true that Nimue wasn't even sure what kind of Guest Services crises may yet require the head of the department to quickly conjure up some privacy.

"Ah, here she is." Linden stood with his arms behind his back. Humphrey, a visible jumpy moment later, echoed his posture. Linden gestured to the curtain, and Nimue slipped inside. "Let's do this quickly," he said. "We have people coming to pick up their badges all day, and lunch hour is bound to increase foot traffic. History Charm."

Humphrey stepped inside the curtain and then he disappeared from view as the area was blanketed in an illusion of the same place several hours before.

Though the cloud cover darkened the lobby somewhat, it was still easy to see what was going on in the lobby at the time, thanks to better lighting and all of the windows surrounding the area.

Now Humphrey—past Humphrey—stood behind the counter. And Rona was in front of him, spittle flying from her mouth as she paced on the other side of the counter.

Nimue heard what could best be described as a "whimper" before Gowdie spoke in her mind. *"Abigail is comforting Humphrey,"* he explained. He must have been referring to Humphrey's familiar owl.

She wasn't sure whether familiar or warlock had been whimpering, but she imagined this wasn't a pleasant scene for Humphrey to revisit.

Humphrey in the illusion brought up his

witch network projection screen and thought a message to it, the screen flashing, then quickly brushed it away. However, his lack of attention for even ten seconds clearly made Rona more irate, as she pounded the counter now to get his attention. Rona continued in her silent ranting, Humphrey doing his best, clearly, to get a word in edgewise, his brow glistening with sweat. Rona pointed toward the showroom floor, her eyes still focused straight at Humphrey, who shirked under her glare. He looked upward. His jaw opened, and he looked like he was screaming.

Rona looked up, her mouth falling into an "o."

And then the books flittering overhead all fell at once, burying her beneath them.

Nimue's heart sunk as she saw the moment unfold.

Zelena's words about investigations like this not being for amateurs hit her like a brick. She dug her nails into her fists. She was strong enough for this.

Linden's voice cut into the illusion as he ended the charm, as the pile of books became more and more surrounded by staff in the illusion, Nimue among the first Witchy ExS staff to respond. The lobby brought back to its current state, Nimue found Humphrey leaning against the counter, his legs trembling.

She stepped forward and offered him an arm with which to steady himself.

"I know it's only been a few hours, but I was wondering if—now that things have calmed a little—you might remember more about what you talked about with her in that moment?"

"First things first," snapped Linden, all business. He gestured at the curtain still up and Humphrey stood straighter, letting go of Nimue's arm, to pull out his wand and undo his Concealment Charm.

Linden offered him a firm customer-service smile in exchange, his eyes wrinkling. "Why don't you take lunch?" he suggested. "I'll man the desk here. Answer Nimue's questions, have some food, you'll feel better. Report back in an hour." Linden brought up his witch network projection and it lit up as he made mental notes. Probably clocking Humphrey out for the moment.

Humphrey nodded, not saying much, and shuffled toward the teleportation pad. Linden dropped his screen projection and slipped behind the counter, all smiles as the front door opened and a group of convention guests shuffled inside. "Welcome to Bookshop Con!" he said. "If you need to register or pick up badges, please make your way here."

Humphrey couldn't have been more Linden's opposite as his slow gait took him across the room, his owl joining Gowdie to fly overhead.

"Come on," said Nimue, taking him by the arm. "You'll feel better with some lunch." She brought up her own witch network screen and sent a message for Tituba to bring Humphrey and her some lunch in the employee break room when she got a chance.

Humphrey just nodded.

"Break room," Nimue told him as they reached the pad.

He stepped through without acknowledging her, the white color turning red.

At least that meant he'd gotten the right destination.

Nimue followed after him then was back at his side to guide the slowly-walking Humphrey the rest of the way to the brightly lit break room. She directed the warlock to a seat and then grabbed him a bottle of water, taking one for herself while she was at it. Familiars didn't need to eat or she'd make sure the two of them had what they needed, too. Especially the owl, whose feathers looked a bit ruffled as she took a seat atop the back of an empty chair. Gowdie sat down on the table in front of her.

"I asked Tituba to bring us some lunch." Nimue offered him a flittering smile and sat kitty-corner from him at the table.

Humphrey just nodded, his expression blank.

"Should I call the medic team?" Nimue offered. "Send you home the rest of the day—"

"No." Humphrey shook his head, a bit

of life coming to his dull eyes. "I already took off last week."

"Have you been unwell?"

"No. No, nothing like that." Humphrey seemed to notice the water in front of him for the first time and opened it up, taking a long drink. He wiped his mouth with the back of his arm afterward. "I just needed a break." He winced. "But since I didn't schedule it in advance, I called in sick. I *had* sick days to use," he scrambled to add. "And I figured it was a good time, a lull between bigger conventions—"

"It's fine." Nimue waved a hand and took a sip of her own drink. "You're not in trouble with me."

Humphrey sent her a wry grin, though it was short-lived. "But aren't you my boss's boss now?"

"Yeah." Nimue smiled back. "But I also understand the need for a mental health day once in a while. It's okay."

Humphrey chewed his lip and squeezed his half-empty bottle in both hands. "Still. I'd appreciate if you didn't tell Mr. Varlett. He already suspects, I think."

Nimue nodded. "No problem." It was true witches and warlocks rarely got sick with something a charm couldn't fix. Linden was a stickler for perfection in his department, it seemed. Nimue wondered, and not for the first time today, if he was a harsher boss than she'd imagined.

She took a deep breath. "Are you ready to talk about it?"

"I already told Zelena and her team everything."

Nimue recoiled at the mention of Zelena. "We're working the investigation from multiple angles," she said, feeling once more like a character in one of those mystery books that may have been at the heart of today's incident. "Please. Just one more time."

"Well..." Humphrey put his bottle back on the table. "She really did talk too fast for me to understand most of her complaints. You saw in the History Charm. She walked right up to me, already shouting."

"Had you ever met her before?"

"No." Humphrey shook his head, then smiled weakly again. "That doesn't matter in Guest Services. You represent whatever thing or person a customer has a complaint against, and they lay it all at you, as if you personally were responsible for the offense. She wasn't the first such customer I've dealt with. Just the first who…"

"Ended up like that," Nimue finished for him.

"Right." His tongue poked at the inside of his cheek.

He was too quick to shut down. Perhaps he was too used to letting others do all the talking.

"So what do you normally do, when facing a customer like that?" Nimue asked, hoping the slight detour would pry open his reluctant lips.

"Call Mr. Varlett," he said without hesitation. "Customers usually want to see 'the manager' anyway, and as head of the department, he's the person best equipped to handle them."

"What does he usually do?" she asked, thinking of how he'd soothed an irate Rona even after being smacked by her and successfully parted her and Sherman until the two of them had calmed down. Mostly.

"He handles them. Usually gets them to calm down and enunciate what's bothering them, assuring them it'll be fixed posthaste. Then he does what he can to follow through on that."

"Even if they're out of their minds?" Nimue asked.

Humphrey chuckled. "Especially if. And especially if they're a VIP like I recognized Rona Brynhild to be. I've read a few of her books." He shuddered. "Never again."

Gowdie jumped up beside Abigail and chirped at her, the owl hooting back.

"Abby says they did call Linden right away," Gowdie translated. *"On the witch network. But he didn't arrive fast enough."*

Nimue nodded. Linden hadn't been one of the first on the scene. He'd been off to get his gloves from the break room, he'd told them.

"Did she ask to see Linden specifically?" Nimue asked.

"No, not by name." Humphrey stared down at the bottle in front of him before taking another sip. "She did demand to speak to my manger, but when I told her I'd already called him, she got angry that he wasn't there yet. She even said, 'You witches think you're so much better than humans.' I told her I didn't think my manager thought that at all."

"That's true," Nimue said. "Linden is the perfect Director of Guest Services. He treats our human guests with nothing but kindness."

Humphrey grumbled. "I think he likes humans *more* than witches and warlocks, actually."

Abigail ruffled her wings.

"'*He's made some strange comments to his staff,*'" Gowdie translated.

Nimue chewed her lip. Merga didn't even work directly under Linden, and she, too, had snapped to attention the moment he'd spoken to her. She couldn't fault Linden some strictness, especially in Guest Services… Still, she needed to know if there were any issues with her staff, but that wasn't what she needed to focus on right now. *Remind me to speak to Guest Services staff without Linden around after this,* she thought to Gowdie. *Maybe he's not the great member of the team I thought he was from their point of view.*

"And how'd she take that?" Nimue asked.

"She didn't hear me." Humphrey shook his head. "It was just one of many things she ranted about."

"What, specifically, could have gotten her *that* upset?" Nimue asked. "Are you sure there's *nothing* in particular she was complaining about when she first approached you that you can remember? What about the Delgados, maybe?"

Humphrey frowned, tapping his finger on the table.

Abigail cooed.

Gowdie flapped a wing, translating. *"Bribes?"*

Humphrey's eyes widened, clearly having heard Abigail's hint. "That's right. She was going on about how she wouldn't have expected a convention center of our caliber to accept *bribes.*"

"Bribes?" Nimue cocked her head. In what universe would Witchy ExS have needed to accept bribes? They were finan-

cially solvent and then some. The only thing that ever really worried her was the cauldron beneath the town receiving enough energy from satisfied, happy con-goers.

Humphrey shrugged. "I had no idea what she was talking about, but Customer Service 101 says you can't tell a customer that, least of all an irate one. I can't say for sure what I told her. I'm sure I fell on the staples we're taught in training. 'I'm so sorry to hear. I'm sure it's a misunderstanding.' I remember saying that because…" He went silent, thinking.

Abigail hooted again.

"Yes! She said there was a bookshop booth that had no business being in the front like her booth was. And it was no *misunderstanding* on her part." He rolled his eyes. "Classic demeaning irate customer."

Abigail let out a little trill.

"*She doesn't like Humphrey working in Guest Services,*" Gowdie translated. "*He's too nice.*"

Abigail cooed again, as if to underscore the point, ruffling her wings.

Nimue would have thought that being

nice was exactly the type of characteristic one needed to work in Guest Services. But she could see that the day's events were really taking their toll on Humphrey. And he wanted to go back for the rest of the day after lunch?

No sooner had Nimue thought about lunch than the door to the hallway opened, Tituba walking in with a broad smile on her lips and three stacked, covered plates in her hands.

"Someone order lunch?"

The door stuck open behind her.

"Yes, thank you. You're a lifesaver." Nimue winced at her poor choice of words, but no one else seemed to notice.

Tituba and Humphrey exchanged *hello*s as Tituba put down a covered plate in front of each of them, though Nimue wasn't sure Tituba knew the young man by name, either. "Mind if I join you?" she asked.

Nimue shook her head. "Of course not."

Humphrey mumbled, "No" as he pulled back the foil cover on his plate.

Tituba took the last remaining seat, Graves jumping up from around her feet to the table, in front of the chair the other two familiars had perched upon. "I hope you like veggie loaf," she said. "Slices are selling like hotcakes down in the food court." In addition to the free snacks provided at the ConSuite, guests had an array of options to choose from down in the food court area. Tituba spent most of the conventions going back and forth between the two locations to make sure her team had everything it needed.

"Hotcakes?" Gowdie perked up his head.

Graves gave a croaking sound that was something like a giggle.

Nimue could feel Gowdie's disappointment as he landed next to her own plate and found veggie loaf instead. The food was great, though, and she told Tituba as much.

"You don't even eat," Nimue pointed out to Gowdie.

Tituba laughed as she looked at Graves. He was probably translating for her.

"I know, I know," said Gowdie. He stuck a little taloned back foot at a piece of Nimue's veggie loaf. *"But pancakes are so springy. I like jumping on them."*

Nimue pulled her plate closer to her. "Then I'm glad I've got veggie loaf and not hotcakes."

"I wasn't totally paying attention when she walked in with the food," he admitted, cocking his head. *"Abby was telling me about something else Humphrey noticed earlier. Before Rona came ranting and raving into the lobby."*

Earlier? Nimue questioned.

She turned to Humphrey, whose face was already glowing more as he just about wiped out his veggie loaf.

"Humphrey, Gowdie says Abigail mentioned something happening in the lobby earlier? Before Rona?"

Tituba's fork paused halfway to her mouth. She may not have realized what it was Nimue and Humphrey were here to discuss. She hadn't seen the crime scene… Hadn't been there to see the body. Maybe the staff hadn't talked about Humphrey's involvement in Rona's final few moments.

"She did…?" Humphrey leaned back, his plate empty, and patted his stomach as he stared at his owl familiar. The two were having a conversation, but Gowdie didn't translate, though she could tell he and Graves were following the half they could hear, Abigail's half of it.

"Well… I don't know. Con guests can get pretty weird."

"What does that mean?" Nimue asked, but Tituba snorted and nodded, helping herself to another bite.

"I didn't think it worth mentioning." He directed an arched eyebrow at his familiar. "But if Abby does… There was a woman. With an exhibitor badge. And another couple of women with VIP badges? That's what I noticed anyway. I had to check to make sure they were allowed on the showroom floor early. Otherwise, I would have asked them to make their way back outside to line up. Happens sometimes, you know. The hotel teleportation pad leads to the lobby even before the convention starts, so exhibitors and special guests can access the showroom floor early. But sometimes just normal con-goers staying at the hotel walk in behind them and think they, too, can get in early."

Nimue knew that much. On occasion, a

con-goer could get pretty irate about it, but the vast majority were understanding. "And did they all come from the hotel?"

"The two VIPs did," Humphrey said. "The exhibitor came from the showroom floor. She headed straight for the teleportation pad. The three bumped into one another."

Nimue couldn't say who the exhibitor might have been with nothing else to go on, but she already imagined Shawna and Lola as the VIPs. They seemed attached at the hip this con and there were no other women VIPs, outside of Rona. And Humphrey would have told Nimue if Rona had been one of them. He wasn't likely to forget *her* anytime soon.

"Do you read YA or romance?" Nimue asked.

"Pardon?" Humphrey asked.

"Never mind," Nimue said. "So they bumped into one another?"

"Yeah," Humphrey said. "The exhibitor lady was, like… a bit agitated? She was pacing in front of the teleportation pad, and when it lit up with the black color indicating the hotel lobby, she jumped up, her face twisted, like she was about to *yell* at whoever walked through there, and then she knocked the shorter VIP clear to the ground."

Nimue chewed her veggie loaf and wondered at that.

"I ran around the desk to help her up," said Humphrey, "but she was just fine. Said she didn't need any help. The exhibitor lady was so apologetic, said she'd been expecting someone else. Then she ducked away back to the showroom floor."

"And the VIPs?" Nimue asked.

Humphrey shrugged. "They huddled together, whispering. The taller one brushed the shorter one's sweater off as I made my way back to the front desk. Then they, too, headed to the showroom floor. They were carrying extra badges, and I realized the exhibitor lady must have dropped hers. They were off to return it."

Nimue cocked her head. "Morpheus or someone at the entryway didn't stop her from entering without the badge?"

Humphrey shrugged. "I'd say maybe he

recognized her—showroom staff is good at that, memorizing the exhibitor faces since they work with them even before the con starts—but no one was at that post yet. I noticed that when I went over there to try to help the VIP up off the ground."

That matched up with what Nimue had seen.

"Do you know who these women were?" Tituba asked. She pursed her lips. She'd probably thought of the VIPs being Lola and Shawna, too. Shawna was shorter and was even wearing a sweater today.

"No." Humphrey shook his head. "I mean, if I saw them again…"

Nimue touched her perma-charm crystal and brought up her witch network projection screen, scrolling to the human Internet Bookshop Con site with the VIPs. "Lola and Shawna?" she suggested, pointing them out.

Humphrey leaned forward a bit to get a better look. "Yeah, that was them."

"So they went 'somewhere in town' for breakfast, huh?" Gowdie reminded Nimue of the two authors' flimsy alibis. *"Think they would have mentioned swinging by the Bessa*

before rushing back to their rooms, picking up a threatening letter, and then rushing right back to make the panel?"

He raised a lot of questions. But Nimue still wondered who else had been involved in the incident. There were no photos of exhibitors to show Humphrey, though.

"Can you describe the exhibitor?" she asked.

"Uh, I have a better idea." Tituba pointed her fork behind Humphrey to the open breakroom door. "Why don't we ask the authors themselves?"

Hushed, muffled whispers carried down the hallway. Nimue turned around and caught sight of a red dress as Lola Jackson walked past them, somehow present in the employee-only section of the convention center.

CHAPTER SEVENTEEN

"Excuse me?" Nimue's voice echoed out into the hallway as she approached Lola Jackson and Shawna Higgins from behind. "What are you two doing here?"

Behind her, Tituba peeked around the corner of the employee lounge as Graves hopped out and Gowdie flew. Humphrey stayed behind, his nerves likely already rattled enough for the day.

Shawna jumped and swirled around, Lola just a touch less startled as she, too, spun in place.

"Ni-Nimue," said Shawna. She looked up to Lola, as if to ask *her* to explain.

"This is an employees-only area."

Nimue stepped forward, her boots echoing out across the floor. She took a look at the badges hanging over the authors' necks, but they were the correct ones. VIP access, which was pretty flexible, but it shouldn't have allowed them back here.

Beyond the balcony, the soft murmurs of conversation from the showroom floor echoed up.

"Well, we're looking for employees," Lola said. As if that explained anything.

"Where is your security detail?" Nimue asked. A security guard escorting them here would explain how they'd gotten the teleportation pad to allow them entry.

Lola stiffened. "They went back." She pointed to the con below. "We wanted to see if there'd been any progress on finding out whoever sent that letter, so they brought us here but were called back to the con." She pointed over the balcony.

That would explain how they'd gotten here. But Nimue couldn't understand why a security witch or warlock would leave the authors here, even if Zelena had said they were spread thin at the moment. She tapped her wrist crystal and brought up her witch network projection and didn't see any blinking lights from Zelena. Not even after she'd sort of cut her short the last time they'd messaged.

There was a message from Cassie, which Nimue dismissed to deal with the problem in front of her.

"The security team has the letter," Nimue said, Gowdie coming to land atop the balcony railing beside her. "And they didn't find anything."

"What does that mean?" Lola frowned.

"It just means… Whoever wrote this letter isn't within the vicinity still."

"Or they hired a witch or wizard to perform a Concealment Charm on it," Gowdie added in Nimue's head.

There was that possibility, too. But usually, there were traces of such a charm left on an object, and Zelena hadn't mentioned it.

"Still, I feel it's in your best interest to stay with your security guard," Nimue said, bringing up a message to Zelena. "Let me contact them—"

"Wait," said Shawna, wringing a large chunk of her purple sweater between her hands. "We said we'd meet them at our signings at one."

"That's not how a security escort usually works," Tituba said. Graves croaked from the floor beside her.

Lola shrugged. "We figured we were safe in the employee section. Is that not true?"

Nimue bristled at the accusation that the Witchy ExS staff would pose them any danger.

"Never mind, then," she said, dismissing the message she was going to send to Zelena. "We'll take you to your signings ourselves."

Shawna looked up at Lola, who didn't return the glance.

Nimue stepped back and gestured toward the teleportation pad at the end of the hall.

Lola gritted her teeth but didn't say anything, heading back the way they'd come. Shawna scrambled behind her.

Tituba arched a brow at her best friend

before they pursued. She brought up her witch network screen and sent a message that wouldn't be heard aloud.

You believe their story?

Nimue chewed her lip as she watched them head down the hall. She shook her head slowly but picked up her feet before the two sneaking authors left and got lost in the crowd below.

"Wait! Before you go through, I was wondering if you might answer some more questions."

Shawna stopped. Lola grabbed her wrist and tried to drag her to the teleportation pad, but Shawna's eyes widened and she shook her head *no*.

"About what?" Lola asked through a harsh breath.

Nimue frowned. What reason did she have to be so defensive? *She'd* been caught in an area that was off-limits.

"This morning, you said you were in town having breakfast shortly before eight."

Shawna practically ripped a hole in her sweater as she rung it between her hands but didn't say anything.

"And?" Lola put a hand on her hip.

"And we have reason to believe you swung by the convention center lobby around 7:30 and ran into an exhibitor."

Shawna gasped, but Lola elbowed her and quickly put an end to the outburst.

Tituba appeared behind Nimue, picking up Graves from the ground as Gowdie settled on Nimue's shoulder.

"You have security cameras?" Lola asked.

That was a strange segue.

"We do not," said Nimue. It wasn't a lie. "But we have something similar. A History Charm."

Shawna let out a little squeak and Lola shook her head at her. Just slightly. Nimue thought she might have imagined it.

She wondered if it would be a good idea to do a History Charm in the lobby again, perhaps ask Tituba to use up hers or use her own for the day.

What had happened at 7:30 in the lobby that these two seemed so eager to hide?

"The staff," said Shawna, under her breath.

Lola's hardened expression grew slack. "Right. That kid who helped you up."

"Yes, well, I was wondering whom you might have bumped into? He said you were carrying her badge when you went back inside the convention center."

Shawna let out what seemed like a deliberately quiet exhale. "Yes, one of the bookshop owners. We just returned her badge and—"

Lola elbowed her. "She was right at the front, behind a booth. We returned the badges and made our way right back to the hotel to freshen up before the con started. That's when we found the note under our door."

Nimue frowned. That wasn't adding up. Earlier, they'd said they'd been running late to make Shawna's panel at nine by the time they'd gotten back to their room.

"Which booth?" Tituba asked, making Nimue file her own question away for later. These two clearly would just get defensive. Or at least Lola would. Nimue wondered if she might be able to corner Shawna by herself at some point.

Lola waved a hand. "The one with the Rona Brynhild signing."

Nicola? It was Nicola whom Humphrey had seen waiting by the teleportation pad.

"Did you hand over her badge in person?" Nimue asked. Perhaps Nicola could back this story up.

"No," Lola said. "Does that matter? We left her badges on her table."

Did it matter? Leaving a badge unattended meant anyone could have picked it up…

Shawna threaded her hands together and repeatedly tapped her palms against one another. "We saw Rona Brynhild's first signing was cancelled. Did she—"

Lola waved a hand, then dug into the small red purse strapped over her shoulder and pulled out a human smartphone. "We're going to be late for our signings. And Shawna is with *PuffinHouse*," she said, as if the publisher's name would add extra urgency.

Nimue gestured to the pad, and Lola didn't hesitate, taking Shawna by the wrist and stepping through, the light flashing aqua blue.

"Want me to make sure they get where they're going?" Tituba asked.

"Sure. Thanks." Nimue smiled at her friend, a small bit of sunshine in an otherwise cloudy day. She looked up. The clouds had retreated, and the sun was thick through the overhead skylight. Little of it reached the floor where the employee area was, though. "And thanks for lunch."

"Anytime!" Tituba stepped through the pad's light, turning it aqua blue.

Nimue stood there a moment, looking down over the Bessa's crowded showroom floor.

In one area behind the wall of curtains, two figures moved, one directing his wand to spread the cushioned mats Witchy ExS put on high-traffic areas of the showroom floor in a large, otherwise empty area.

Nimue recognized Cassie's green witch's hat and Soren's floppy golden hair.

She tapped her wrist crystal to bring up that message she'd dismissed from Cassie.

We need Ren back, she'd written. *Any suggestions?*

Her assistant was asking her to bring out the side of Soren Southern who didn't get along with Nimue at all.

But if Soren was still prepping the closed-off area for the Book Scene Booth, in the middle of the convention's busy opening day—a day in which the guest of honor may very well have been murdered—Nimue thought perhaps she had no choice but to facilitate the change.

CHAPTER EIGHTEEN

"*Are we headed to Soren or Nicola?*" Gowdie asked as they stepped through the teleportation pad and appeared on the showroom floor.

She *did* want to ask Nicola about her run-in with Lola and Shawna, but she was sure to be at her booth for the rest of the day. She'd know where to find her.

Cassie had sent that message a while ago, and they really needed all hands on deck.

Especially Ren's hands.

She wove past a couple of teenage girls carrying stuffed-to-the-brim black tote bags with "Book Squee" written across them in neon pink, looping letters, then shimmied around a man in a dress shirt and tie who was droning on about his "manuscript that totaled 700,567 words and counting" to a salesperson at the PuffinHouse booth. She smiled awkwardly and told him, "I'm not authorized to buy books. You have to secure an agent and they'll send it to the right people at the company."

"I've tried getting an agent." The man bristled. "They told me it was too long, for starters, and I haven't even finished it—"

Nimue tuned him out as she made her way through the crowd, not surprised to see a small group of women all in flowery bonnets that were clearly an homage to Miss Elwes of Rona Brynhild's Cheery Mysteries sorting through the book goodies with Rona's latest book cover printed all over them.

A pit grew heavy in her stomach and Gowdie rubbed the top of his head against hers.

"We'll get to the bottom of this," he told her.

But too late, she thought back.

Rona had been rude. A diva. Completely unlikable. But her characters had made an impact on countless people's lives. And now she was gone. Snuffed out at Bookshop Con. Under her watch.

Her first time as Co-Head Witch General Manager would likely be her last.

She felt her skin prick as she approached the curtains she knew were hiding Soren and Cassie.

No. Witchy ExS would survive this. It *had* to.

She pulled back the curtain.

Cassie was busy at her witch network projection screen, brushing aside this message and that.

Soren was still putting down interlocking padded flooring panels. The closer Nimue got to him, the clearer his humming became.

"Soren?" she said.

Cassie looked up and let out a visible sigh of relief.

Soren swiveled aside, his hand still moving his wand. Balfour was watching as the last of the padded panels lowered in place to the ground, shaking her butt and leaping up to pounce on it before it settled in place.

"Nimue! Isn't it wonderful?" He gestured around him and slipped his wand into its holster. Balfour jumped one more time on the lowered panel and walked away, her head and tail held high, clearly satisfied she'd successfully "attacked" it.

Nimue looked around at the wide, empty space with interlocking floor pads in place and one small table near the curtain and saw… nothing but potential.

"It's… It's a big, empty space."

Soren's soft features brightened and he brushed his long bangs out of his eyes. "Which will be filled with readers' favorite book scenes!" He nudged Nimue with his elbow and she found herself stumbling at the unexpected touch. "It was *your* idea."

"And Ren rejected it out of hand."

"It's *brilliant!*" Soren put both hands on his hips and Balfour came to rub his legs, staring beady-eyed up at Gowdie as she wove around and between her warlock's calves.

"Balfour thinks he cracked," Gowdie translated.

How did *Soren take over?* Nimue wondered.

"Nimue, if it's all right with you, I'll take my lunch hour…?" Cassie's stomach growled on cue, and Nimue felt bad that she'd felt the need to "babysit" Soren during all of this.

Cassie took Nimue's pitying look wrong and blinked rapidly. "I'll keep working as I eat," she said. "I know we have a lot to do." Her ferret familiar popped out from under Cassie's wide-brimmed witch's hat.

"No, don't worry about it." Nimue waved a hand dismissively. "Meet us back in the office afterward." She leaned forward to catch Cassie's attention once more before she left. "I take it Zelena updated you and Ren on everything?"

"*Soren* and me, anyway." She looked over Nimue's shoulder to the other Head General Manager behind her. "He said it sounded like she had everything in hand, so he'd leave it up to her to 'crack the case.'"

Then Nimue and Soren had very different definitions of having "everything in hand." *She* was the one who'd spotted the hammer in the History Charm.

She nodded and Cassie pulled back the curtains, a quick reveal of the women with the Miss Elwes hats passing by reminding Nimue that she couldn't rest, couldn't return to her con duties, until she knew what had happened to Rona.

And she needed Ren to be alert and aware to step up and fill in whenever the con had need of a leader until then.

She sat on the table in the big, empty space, trying to see what Soren did on the plain mats.

Wonder. Whimsy. She'd imagined a space like this brought to life with books.

It would be the talk of the con—maybe the world once it hit the news shortly thereafter. She really did believe in her idea, and she knew her grandmother was just the witch to craft the perma-charm to make it happen.

But Ren was right. Now was not the time to rush through ideas—maybe *dangerous* ideas. The con had already started and they should test such a charm first. There was no time for that.

"Soren, do you remember anything from this morning?"

He grimaced. "I do…"

Balfour jumped up into his arms as he stepped closer.

He petted her absentmindedly. "She reminded me of everything I missed, and Ren left so abruptly, our memories, they got kind of co-mingled…"

"Why did Ren leave?" Nimue asked. Gowdie hopped off her shoulder and sat on her lap, looking particularly cat-like as he lifted his chin up for scritches.

Soren blinked heavily, his long bangs getting caught in his eyelashes. "I would have thought you'd be happy to see me instead."

"I *am*," Nimue said, and her mouth, meant to smile, twisted a bit grimly. "I always prefer spending time with you."

He gestured one hand around him. "When I took over and all of that… that… *horror* came crashing into me, your idea was like a beacon in the darkness. I thought, well, as long as I was in the driver's seat, I'd make the most of my time and show you what your creativity means to me."

"I appreciate that," she said. "Though I'm surprised Bernadette agreed to try it."

"She thinks she'll be done sometime this evening."

Nimue's breath hitched. All the more reason not to open the booth without testing it. How could Bernadette finish so quickly?

Chewing the inside of her cheek, she pointed around the perimeter of the mats. "We should put up cushioned walls," she said. "There'd be no way to contain a guest to a safe area without them. Some people might illusion themselves in the midst of broad moors and endless horizons."

"*Jane Eyre*?" Soren ventured, his eyes twinkling.

She swallowed. She'd thought her days of romance were long behind her.

So why was she picturing Soren as Mr. Rochester?

Not to mention, Ren, with his surly grumpiness and cagey secrets, would have made a better match for the character.

"Soren, did you—did Ren—tell Nicola what really happened to Rona?"

A dull sheen grew over Soren's eyes. "Yes. She… She didn't take it well."

"I imagine." Nimue swung her legs, feeling for all the world like a teenager again. Complete with the strange awkwardness of being left alone with a boy.

Which was ridiculous. She'd *known him* since they'd been kids.

And she was forty years old. With a grown-up daughter.

She needed to focus.

"She's telling everyone Rona is too ill to sign today?" she asked.

"Yeah…" Soren cocked his head and looked at Balfour, then turned back to Nimue. "I only came back at the end of their conversation, but she and Ren hashed out all of the details." His face flushed.

Gowdie sat up straighter, digging a talon into Nimue's thigh.

Balfour was looking straight into his eyes.

"She said Soren took over to find Nicola in his arms, sobbing against his chest."

Nimue's legs stopped swinging. "Are Ren and Nicola close, too?"

Ren and Soren *were* one warlock in some ways, but…

Soren cleared his throat and took to petting Balfour with extra intensity. "I wouldn't say that. She and I are more… But not like…"

He didn't finish his sentence.

Balfour looked up at him and then to Gowdie.

"She says Ren sputtered worse than this when Nicola embraced him. That's probably why he went into hiding."

Well, that explained that much, Nimue supposed. She was surprised she'd ever thought for a second that Ren could have had a secret love affair with a beautiful human. Soren, maybe, but… That was just because she knew him to possess a heart.

But maybe a cold, emotion-less mind was what they needed right now.

"Soren, I'm trying to figure out who's responsible." She was afraid to say the exact words, to accuse an unknown human guest of murder. "Everyone's being cagey…"

"Isn't Zelena looking into it?"

"Zelena and her whole *team* missed something that was key. They're stretched thin," she added quickly, keen to let Soren know she wasn't trying to start something with the Security Manager who disliked her.

"The hammer?" Soren asked.

So Zelena had told them. Or maybe just Cassie, who'd passed the message along. She'd probably tried to keep Soren focused, maybe bring out Ren, get the con back on track, remind him of the potential for *danger* that was out there.

"There's a lot to be done," Nimue said. "And I can't leave this to Zelena and her team alone to solve. I'm tackling this from another angle, bringing my own observations to the fray. There was… a lot of suspicious activity this morning."

Soren stopped petting Balfour to cock his head. "Such as?"

"Well, Nicola was acting weird in the lobby not too long before the… Before the incident."

Soren clenched his jaw, a flash of something dark crossing his eyes. "She would never hurt anyone."

Nimue recoiled, startled by *Soren's* harshness. Because of Nicola, Lydia's best friend. Nimue hadn't even specifically accused her of hurting anyone. "Do you… Do you know what she was doing? Witnesses all agreed she seemed to be waiting for someone."

Soren shrugged. "I have no idea."

So it wasn't… him?

"Ren was busy with Cassie at the time," Gowdie pointed out in her head.

Sure, she thought back. *But maybe Soren had promised to meet her, and then… Ren wouldn't let him out.*

"Why would Soren do that? He knows Ren doesn't like to give up control at all when they're busy with work. Least of all on the opening day of their first con as co-manager."

And yet… Nimue gestured one hand at Soren in front of her.

"When was the last time *you* saw Nicola before, um, you woke up in your body, being held by her?"

Soren's jaw dropped and he looked down at his familiar cat. "Balfour!"

She lifted a single shoulder as if to shrug and licked her paw as Soren clutched her against his chest.

It took a moment for Soren's cheeks to approach something of their usual color. "Last night. I went with her to escort Rona back to her room. And then we chatted in the hall and… parted ways."

"Chatted about what?"

Soren's lips grew a bit thin. "Are you accusing Nicola of something?"

"No."

"Are you accusing *me*?"

"No!" Nimue fidgeted in place, the table suddenly noticeably hard and uncomfortable. "I don't *think* either of you would hurt anyone—"

"Good," said Soren succinctly. "Because you know me better than that. And I know Nicola. Trust me. It would *kill* her to know she'd hurt a fly."

"All right." Nimue held both hands up in surrender. "I'm just wondering, then… What did you talk about? Anything that might explain why she was waiting for someone in the convention center lobby this morning?"

"She was probably waiting for Rona!" said Soren, his voice growing louder in turn. "What else do you think? Why are you even focusing on this and not finding out whoever wielded that hammer?"

He was starting to pace now, and if Nimue hadn't known better, she would have thought that Balfour smiled as she looked up at her warlock.

"Right," Nimue said quickly. That *did* make sense, actually. "Just… covering my bases."

"We just talked about Rona. Mostly." He added that last part to Balfour, turning down to look at her.

"*And Lydia, too,*" Gowdie added, translating, no doubt, what Balfour had told her master.

No wonder he was in such a tizzy.

"I apologized for putting her in that position, asking her to deal with a woman so unreasonable like that, but Nicola thanked me." He looked at Nimue, his eyes growing wider. "She was dealing with that monster of a woman, and she actually *thanked* me for pushing her to contact Rona's agent and secure her for the signing. Her business is doing poorly, and she figured selling all those Rona Brynhild books here, at the con, it just might make her stay afloat."

Some people would put up with almost anything to save their businesses. But now, without the famous reclusive author, Nicola's business might be ruined.

She'd have had to have been pushed *very* far to hurt Rona and give up on all of that.

"Remember, she wouldn't hurt a fly," Gowdie said in Nimue's head. His tone was dripping just the slightest bit with sarcasm.

Balfour meowed a little chirp and looked up to Soren, probably, Nimue realized, translating what Gowdie had said.

"You don't understand—" Soren started, shaking a finger at her, his face purpling.

And then, in front of Nimue's eyes, his hair slicked itself back, growing wet and stiff, the red in his skin evening out and dissipating.

Ren grew stiffer, patting Balfour on the head.

His gaze flitted just slightly to the wide, open space beside him. "I see I haven't missed much." His glare rested heavily on Nimue, seated on the table in front of him.

Nimue jumped down. Not that she'd planned it, exactly, but she'd had a feeling getting Soren angry would bring Ren to the surface, just as embarrassing Ren had brought Soren back. They tended to hand over the emotions they disliked the most to the other. "Have Balfour and Cassie, when she's back from lunch, get you up to speed. Make sure all of the con business is taken care of. Zelena can keep you updated on security business." She grabbed hold of the curtain, about to shift it aside.

"And what, pray tell, will you be doing?"

"Catching a killer," she said softly. "Before they potentially strike again."

CHAPTER NINETEEN

Nimue checked the time on her witch network crystal. As long as Lola and Shawna were signing books for another forty minutes, there were two other people she needed to check in with.

Sherman's alibi was shaky. His dislike for Rona was clearer than anyone's, though his past with the other author was a little murky yet.

But she still wondered if Soren was right and Nicola had just been waiting for Rona that morning. It couldn't hurt to ask her what she knew about the author, either, having spent the most time with her of anyone at the con.

She flicked through the con guide, searching for Sherman's name and finding him about to join Wayne Gomez on a panel about incorporating real history into mystery. She headed to Nicola's booth instead.

Only once she wove her way through the crowd to the front of the Bessa, she was surprised to find the crowd growing thinner and thinner, the booths with prime real estate just past the front entryway rather empty. A few con guests wove in through the Delgados' high-stacked shelves.

No one was attending Nicola's Nook Bookshop booth at all, the "Signing Cancelled" flashing in red text over the floating banners like an alarm keeping everyone away.

"Hello?" Nimue leaned over the table beside a powered-down cash register but didn't find Nicola or anyone else manning the booth.

She wove through the bookshelves, seeing book after book on display, but no one to stop a would-be thief from snatching one and taking it elsewhere.

Strangely, though, there was one large

mostly-empty shelf right beside where Rona would have sat had she done her signing. A few copies of Rona's books were shelved at the bottom, two empty boxes beside the shelf. Almost as if someone had cleaned out the shelf since it'd been left unattended or been called away in the middle of stacking the shelf. Only then the boxes would have been full with books yet to have been put out on display, wouldn't they?

"Hello?" Nimue called again. Gowdie flapped off her shoulder and sat on the top of the empty bookshelf, peering around.

"Do you think she stepped away?" he suggested. *"Lunch?"*

Nimue's heart went cold as she approached the cash register and hit the *cash* button to see if it would wake up and open. No dice. At least she'd remembered to lock up after herself.

"Looking for Nicola?"

Virgil's voice carried across the empty aisle between them. He was walking between shelves in his booth, eating veggie loaf he carried on a plate. Several shelves away, his wife was checking out a customer at the edge of the booth.

"Yes," Nimue said, raising her voice to be heard over the din of the crowd echoing out over the wide space. "Did she step away?"

Virgil frowned, then finished up his loaf with a couple of quick stabs of his fork. He raised a finger to indicate Nimue should wait a second and then, moments later, stepped out from his booth and crossed the aisle, standing across from her at Nicola's booth as if a customer, and she the cashier.

He crossed his arms gruffly. "Nicola hasn't opened her booth at all." He *tsked*. "I keep having to shoo potential customers away. But I usually have what they're looking for. Unless they're looking for Rona Brynhild's books." His expression soured at that.

Frowning, Nimue pulled out her wand and pointed at the empty space beside the cash register. "Create Charm," she said, envisioning a sign reading "Closed." It appeared on the table, fashioned out of recycled fibers that went through the waste management system, no doubt.

"Should have thought of that," Virgil said. "Well, I could have just made a sign with a piece of paper, but… Then again, if I didn't have to tell them she's closed, I wouldn't have the opportunity to direct them to my booth instead." He winked.

Penny thanked the customer she'd been helping and told him to enjoy his books. She waved at Nimue and Virgil, then disappeared somewhere behind the bookshelves.

"Helps to have a partner help you run the booth in case you need to step away," he said.

Nimue nodded. "Do you have a minute?" She gestured behind her, inviting Virgil to step inside Nicola's unoccupied booth.

He scratched his chin, his beard rustling. "Sure."

As Virgil followed Nimue farther into the booth, his eyes caught on Gowdie flapping his wings atop the nearly-empty bookshelf. He whistled. "I have to tell you. Your familiar has to be the best one I've seen."

Gowdie flapped his wings harder. *"I like this guy."*

Nimue ruffled his scaly head. "Don't give him a bigger ego than he already has."

Gowdie looked at Nimue. *"I do not have a big ego!"* He began cleaning himself, pecking at a bit of scale under the crook of one wing. *"Can I help it if your soul shaped me into this shiny, beautiful creature?"*

Well, at least Nimue knew that there were plenty of other people with bigger egos than her beautiful little dragon. She'd met a few of them during this con alone.

"Nicola hasn't been at her booth at all?" she asked.

Virgil looked around, taking in the empty chair Rona would have sat in to sign, the flying tea cups flashing with "Signing Cancelled" in front of them.

"Well, you were here when she was having a fit about searching our booth."

Nimue nodded. Right before… All the books stopped hovering. "She thought you were selling Rona Brynhild books."

"Which we most certainly were not."

Nimue cleared her throat, wondering

how she could ask about Rona without letting the cat out of the bag.

"Oh, can you put cats into bags? I'll have to remind Balfour of that next time she gets sassy."

Nimue rolled her eyes at her familiar but tried not to let Virgil see. "Did Rona herself accuse you of that?"

"No." Virgil cocked his head. "Probably didn't have the guts to confront us herself. If she really remembered us... She's sick, then?" He *tsked*. "Be nice if she'd got food poisoning."

Nimue's eyes widened.

Virgil had the sense to look a little abashed. "Well, I mean..." He scratched his jaw and lowered his voice. "I suppose you're wondering why Penny and I hate her."

Hate was a strong word choice. One especially strange to admit to when the object in question had been murdered. But if he were innocent, he wouldn't know that fact.

"She's easy to dislike," Nimue said, trying to keep the conversation casual. Gowdie did his part by hopping down the shelf toward Virgil and rubbing him with his scaly head, begging for pets.

Virgil chuckled and scratched the dragon under his chin.

"Well, this was about five years ago now," he said.

Gowdie interrupted the flow of the conversation to report to Nimue that Virgil gave good scritches so he was clear of all suspicions. Nimue tried to refrain from rolling her eyes and nodded along with Virgil's recollection.

"Penny and I were just starting out with the bookstore. I used to work for a literary agency. Penny was a homemaker, took care of our kids. They were both out of college by then and our bank account had survived—just barely. We thought, rather than me retiring, why not try to make one more dream come true? We decided I'd quit my job and we'd open a bookshop together."

"I always admire a person willing to take a risk," Nimue said.

Virgil chuckled darkly. "Well, I wish I weren't one of them. We struggled so much back then—even these days, we're just barely keeping our heads above water." Virgil gazed down at Gowdie, then reached beyond him to pick up one of the sole copies of Rona's books that was actually on the shelf. "Hardly have time to read these days, what with worrying about keeping the shop going. Penny does." He put the book back, this time on the top shelf beside Gowdie. "I don't mind her taking some of her day to keep reading. We need *someone* to know which of the latest books to recommend to customers."

"Bet that was a change," Nimue said. "You were an agent before that? You must have read all the time."

"Well, I worked *for* an agent," he said. "But that included getting first crack a lot of the time at the slush pile. You don't have time to read a lot of the most popular books already published, but it's all worth it when you can say you were among the very first to read what eventually becomes a world-wide bestseller." His forehead was positively rosy.

"Did that happen a lot? You discovering future bestsellers?"

"I discovered *two*—well, I kicked them up the slush pile and got my boss to hurry up and read them to sign them." He tapped Rona's book. "Rona was one of them. Had to be, wow, time flies… Thirty-five years ago now?"

There was something about that timeframe that jolted Nimue's memory.

"Back when Sherman and Rona had that writing class together," Gowdie reminded her.

"*You* discovered Rona Brynhild?"

Virgil chuckled. "Well, I had a role in it. As far as she knew for decades, it was all my boss. I was just an assistant working the slush pile."

"'As far as she knew for decades,'" Nimue repeated.

Virgil scratched his beard again. "Yeah, well, Clint Moore, my boss and Rona's former agent, he applauded me starting up a bookstore. Kind of the booklover's dream, you know? Outside of writing a book themselves. Kind of a *wistful* dream, one that most people don't have the money or drive to see through to the end…"

Clint Moore, thought Nimue. Her mind scrambled for where she'd heard that name, but Gowdie had nothing to offer her.

"He pulled some strings and got Rona to crawl out of her hidey hole for our store's grand opening. Sort of a retirement gift, you could say." Virgil let out a sigh, his eyes drawn to Rona's book. "Clint and I were more than just co-workers. I considered him a good friend."

Nimue wondered, based on how Virgil spoke about the man, if he'd passed away, if that was why Virgil had called him Rona's "former" agent.

"She agreed—I can't tell you why." He scoffed. "She had a brand new series starting up, a spin-off of Miss Elwes that everyone and their mother was excited to own, and *our* little shop was to be the only place *in the world* where you could get an autographed copy. Not only were we booking tickets for the in-person event, but we were promised another thousand copies we could sell online or for locals who couldn't get a ticket to be there to hear her read her first few chapters."

Virgil spread his arms wide. "We thought we had it made. We were due to be out of the red within a month of opening. It felt like all my decades working behind-the-scenes in the industry were really paying off."

"But something went wrong," Nimue prompted him. From what she'd seen of Rona, she could definitely imagine.

"At first, Rona got cold feet. Didn't want to be out in the spotlight. Changed her mind." Virgil's face grew redder. "We'd taken money for most of the pre-orders, promised payment to creditors on the hope of the rest of that money coming in. Now she wanted to *cancel*?

"Clint knew what a bind we'd be in after all we'd sunk into marketing the event, so he appealed to her *better nature*. Ha. It was more *appealing to her ego* that worked in the end."

Nimue was taken aback. "She did wind up attending the signing?"

"Only now I wish she *hadn't*!" Virgil pet Gowdie's head a bit too roughly, like he were some kind of stress ball.

"I take back… What I said…" Gowdie sent to Nimue, his eyelids peeled back under Virgil's rough pets.

"Maybe we would have had to close the shop to issue all those refunds, go bankrupt to avoid the lenders. But we wouldn't have had to put up with *her* for the day." He gestured to the empty seat. "And I wouldn't have severed a decades-long friendship."

Gowdie managed to wriggle free and out of range of Virgil's hands, seeking refuge on Nimue's shoulder.

"Your friendship?" Nimue prodded.

"With Clint Moore." Virgil rubbed the back of his head. "She dropped him like a hot potato after the signing event. She had her pick of replacements. *Decades* with Clint and she turned on him. Clint blamed me. His agency wasn't even in that much danger—least of all because he'd always get a cut of the books she'd sold through him—but losing Rona still dealt a blow to his reputation."

"But why blame you?" Nimue couldn't imagine what had gone so wrong during a one-day event. Had Virgil and Penny failed to remove all the green M&Ms from a snack bowl in the lounge or something?

"Rona was crabby from the moment she stepped inside. Made it clear she wasn't there because she wanted to be." Virgil's lip trembled at the memory. "Saw a line a block-long out front, a stack of hardcovers in the back for her to sign for other customers, and claimed she had a hand cramp and only wanted to do the reading.

"I tried to reason with her, said she could come back and sign the books for the people who didn't get event tickets later in the week, the month—whenever, as long as it was soon—and she told me to 'take it up with Clint.' As if *my friend* of several decades would just tell me I was out of luck, despite the efforts he'd gone to to arrange the thing."

Virgil tossed an angry look at Rona's book. "And the worst was how she treated Penny. Penny *loved* her books. Read every single one. Clint usually got her ARCs, too. But she was good at keeping the twists and turns secret. Not even her dearest friends in Book Club could pry a word out of her."

Virgil was pacing now, the red lettering indicating the "Signing Cancelled" casting a warm glow over his face.

"She bent over backward to accommodate that… that *writer*… and Rona treated her like 'the help.' At one point, when I was opening the doors and finally letting the crowd inside for the start of the event, I heard a *shriek* from the back of the store."

Nimue thought horribly of the sound she'd heard in the lobby earlier that morning.

"Not unlike that child's squeal the security staff told us was responsible for the screaming in the lobby this morning." Virgil gestured toward the lobby and Nimue realized that was the cover story Zelena had gone with. If only he knew how attuned his ear was for Rona's specific wailing, apparently. "As loud as *that*," he continued. "So I ran back there and I see Rona… Well, Rona *hitting* Penny. Slapping her! Clear across the face, over and over!"

Nimue's jaw dropped. "What? Did you call the police?" She was more than positive human law enforcement would interfere in matters where someone was hitting someone else. She thought uncomfortably of how Rona had smacked Linden of all people, stoic, ever-cheerful Linden, and none of them had done much about it.

Because she'd been the VIP.

Because the convention had sold tickets for her fans to come see her.

"I-I wanted to." Virgil's eyes glistened with tears. "Penny, she tried to talk me out of it. The customers were filing in by then, some even coming over to see their beloved author with her face all red and purple. I don't know what it was all about. Something Penny said about... right." He stopped himself.

"You *do* remember?" Nimue prodded.

"Well..." Virgil let out a sigh, his gaze focused over the witch's head across the way to his own booth. "The other big-time author I picked out of the slush pile for Clint?"

"Sherman Abbott!" cried Nimue, remembering the name she'd seen on Sherman's screen. *Print More.* Clint Moore. Maybe the older writer's strange joke to himself or a wish for his agent to help him sell enough copies for second printings.

"Right." Virgil nodded. "And I remember telling Penny, how despite the difference in their subject matters—I mean, they both write mysteries, sure, but one's much grittier, the other all fancy—I thought they had a similar… *style* to them. Both amazing, don't get me wrong, but for some reason, I'd even thought Rona had been being cute, submitting another manuscript to her own agent under the slush pile, seeing if he could pick her out among the masses…"

"Authors do that?" Nimue asked.

"Well, we'd done cold editor submissions for other authors before. New pen name, new genre, see if an editor picks it up on merit alone, without the bestseller name attached. It's rare, but it happens.

"Anyway, yeah, that wasn't the case *at all*, as we now know, but Penny, looking for some topic of discussion with which to fill the awkwardness with this grumpy, uncooperative diva, and with Sherman Abbott about to publish another book around then, too, said something about how she and her husband found the books to be similar. She didn't even get to explain herself before Rona threw a fit.

"A fan helped me pry the author off my wife, and we agreed not to call the cops, but Rona called Clint and stormed off. Didn't read a word of her book to my customers. Didn't sign a single copy. Never did. We had to issue all of those refunds, since most people were upset about not getting their copy signed and not seeing the reclusive author. Clint called back and said he'd been sacked, it had been a disaster, and he'd never have arranged it if he'd thought…" He sighed. "Well, he gave me one more parting gift. Arranged for Sherman Abbott to do a signing the next month and despite the bad press our previous incident had garnered us, enough fans showed up. Just barely kept our heads above water. Things were touch and go for years."

"Awful," said Nimue, staring at Rona's bright and cheery cover and having trouble reconciling it with the author she knew in her head. "I get why you didn't want anything to do with her now."

"Well, she didn't seem to recognize us. Not at first." He shrugged. "I didn't want to even look at her face, but this convention is important to our business. And we could rely on good ol' Sherman." He smiled faintly. "We wouldn't let her scare us away, even if she *had* remembered us. But, of course, she remembered *Sherman*, no problem…"

Rona had clearly been the most volatile around Sherman.

And Sherman's alibi was so weak.

Virgil and Penny—and Nicola, for that matter—had been right here with Nimue when the murder had occurred. Now she felt like she understood more about the Delgados and their contentious relationship with Rona Brynhild, and she was sure they were in the clear.

And Nicola's strange absence could be easily explained since she knew the truth of the matter of the "sick" reclusive author.

Still, not everything was clear…

"What prompted Nicola to check your booth for Rona's books this morning?"

Virgil rolled his eyes. "Bless that girl. I think she's in over her head—in more ways than one."

"What do you mean?"

"Well, owning a bookshop is no simple business. I don't know if hers will make it." He gestured around him. "She seems to have been betting everything on selling Rona's books."

Nimue stared at the mostly empty shelf with a few of Rona's books.

"So where *are* all of Rona's books?"

"She thought we might have taken them, to be honest." Virgil scratched his jaw. "That's what it seemed like she was saying to me. But that's outright theft. We'd never! And we certainly have no interest in stocking Rona Brynhild's books." He spat on the carpet. Then he had the wherewithal to at least look sheepish about it.

"So why was there a copy of Rona's latest book at your booth?" Nimue asked, remembering what Nicola had found right before the scream.

Virgil shrugged. "Beats me. Sherman brought a stack of his own books to the signing. Good guy that he is—he knows he often gets more people to come than a book-seller plans on, or he'll let you keep the signed extras for future sales. He pulled his stack of books out of his folio bag and put them there beside his signing chair, atop the pile of the other books we ordered, early this morning. Then he spent a bit of time looking around the booths in our aisle, and he left."

"That was Sherman's copy of Rona's book?" Gowdie asked.

"What time was that?" Nimue asked.

"Oh… I don't know. Around seven?"

When Sherman was supposedly out in the park, beginning to drink his coffee over the next several long hours.

Seemed like Nimue couldn't put off grilling the man any longer.

Nimue wandered the convention floor, trying to feel the enthusiasm so many of the con-goers were exuding, feeding the giant cauldron below the ground with riotous energy. Her heart wasn't entirely in it, though, despite the laughter and the mirthful faces. She didn't think she imagined a pocket of negative energy in the food court, where the group of Miss Elwes enthusiasts had gathered for a late lunch. She supposed if they'd come to the con specifically to meet Rona Brynhild, a cancelled signing *and* a cancelled panel had to weigh on them. The only bit of hope keeping them good providers for the cauldron was likely that

Rona was scheduled to sign at the convention again.

Only she would never "feel better" and show up. Once her fans knew that…

"Hey." Gowdie flew down from overhead, landing on her shoulder in front of the teleportation pad. *"You know, your funk isn't exactly helping the convention's energy, either."*

She sighed, but she knew he was right. Only, she was so tired, and she was still no closer to uncovering who could very well still pose a danger to her guests at this convention.

"Hey," Gowdie said again, softer this time. He nuzzled his scaly maw against her cheek. *"We'll figure this out."*

Nimue didn't know how, but he was right. She had to. And Zelena and her team were working the case from other angles. She wasn't entirely on her own. Somehow, they'd bring it all together.

She tapped her witch network crystal to bring up the con guide and find the room Sherman's panel was in. Best to catch him as he was leaving rather than offer him the chance to give her the slip.

The teleportation pad glowed brown and she found herself in the basement of the Bessa, in the convention's second-largest panel room. No one had bothered to move the panel to the largest, considering Rona would no longer be using it.

But, she found as she approached the open doorway of the panel, they wouldn't have needed it. The chairs were only half taken, the room perhaps less crowded even than the Sherman Abbott signing line she'd seen at the Delgado Books booth earlier.

She nodded at one of Zelena's security team as she approached the open door. He stood there, broad shouldered, one hand over his wrist, and thin lips stuck in a straight line. A mint-green, sleek-bodied hare stood at his feet, rigid, her nose twitching.

Nimue recognized him and ran through her mental database to come up with his name.

"Cary," provided Gowdie.

Did you remember that or ask his hare?

"If you must know, I remembered her name, but not her warlock's. Miller is something of a

legend among familiars when it comes to the occasional foot race."

Nimue thought she saw Miller's chin tilt up in a sense of pride.

You race other familiars on foot? I'd like to see that.

Gowdie lifted a taloned claw, unsuited to running any length of distance. *"Only when you're not looking. I do better in the winged races."*

I'd definitely notice those.

"You'd be surprised what a familiar can get away with." Gowdie winked at his witch.

As long as the familiar's witch or warlock was still nearby, she supposed.

The crowd in the panel room laughed at something Wayne Gomez had said, projected to the loudspeakers through a perma-charm microphone. Nimue shuffled past Cary to head inside the room, standing at the back wall.

"Now, I don't know about *that*," said Sherman, turning to face the man with whom he shared a panel. "I wouldn't write about witch and warlock spies if there was a chance I'd get any real-life details *too* accurate. They *know where I live.*" He added the last bit with a dramatic flair, wiggling his fingers in the air like rain.

That got a reaction from the audience, too.

"Distinguished guests, and on that note before any spies in the audience get ideas, Sherman Abbott and Wayne Gomez!" A witch Nimue knew to be the Panel Programming Coordinator stood up from her seat beside the table at which the authors were seated and gestured to the older men, leading the crowd of about fifty or so into a round of applause. She was tall, willowy, with long, silky, black hair that was totally shaved on one side, giving her a bit of a punk-rock look below her orange witch's hat. Her familiar, a tiger with black fur and golden stripes forever the size of a cub, prowled at her feet.

"Mercy and Ward," Gowdie said in her mind.

"Yes, I know that," she said aloud. She was determined to keep track of everyone at Witchy ExS now that she was supposed to be in charge of it.

She still didn't really feel in charge of it. Even half in charge of it.

Mercy directed the crowd to exit, then turned to the authors and shook both of their hands.

Sherman's grip on her hands lasted a moment too long in Nimue's opinion, and she couldn't help but notice that despite Mercy's broad customer-service smile—Linden would have been proud—she was clearly trying to get out of his grip before he would let her go.

"Marvelous job keeping the rabble in check," Sherman told her.

Mercy laughed politely, but Ward growled at her feet, and Sherman finally broke away.

If she hadn't been so focused on the grip the author had had on her employee for two beats too long, Nimue might not have noticed the fact that Sherman Abbott's wedding ring was missing.

"Mr. Abbott," she said, "I was wondering if you had some time?"

Sherman's face fell when he saw her, but he quickly plastered on a friendly smirk.

"I thought we were past such formalities, Nimue."

"Ward doesn't like how chummy he's been with her witch," Gowdie reported.

I can tell that, Nimue thought back to him. She wondered if Sherman hadn't lost the wedding ring at all. It could easily have been in his pocket.

Gowdie flapped his wings and jumped down to the table between Nimue and the authors, startling the thriller writer.

"Oh—my, uh, pardon?"

Gowdie sniffed Sherman's suitcoat and nudged at the pocket in which he'd so often stuck his left hand during their walk through the park that morning.

"Gowdie," said Nimue, pretending he were no more than a base animal sniffing around.

"Yup, gold," said Gowdie. *"I smell gold in his pocket."*

Do you smell a hammer, too? Nimue asked, only half-joking.

But Gowdie took it seriously, sniffing all over the man.

Gowdie, it's fine. Nimue pasted on a tight

smile as she looked at Sherman. *He wouldn't be able to hide a hammer in his pocket.*

Sherman took an awkward step back, chuckling, and gestured to Wayne. "I'm not sure if you've become acquainted yet? Wayne, this is Nimue Toothaker, one of the heads of Witchy Expo Services."

"Ah, yes, I remember her from the dinner." Wayne extended his hand for a shake, a brief but firm one. "Shame Bernadette didn't show this year."

"Have you met my grandmother before?" Nimue asked.

"If you'll excuse me," Mercy said, interrupting. She smiled at Nimue. "I've got another panel to get to."

Sherman watched Mercy and Ward leave, his eyes on the willowy witch almost the entire way. Nimue found it hard to focus on Wayne, who was packing up some note cards in front of him into a leather folio case.

"Well, I've been to previous Bookshop Cons," Wayne said. "Sherman here, too." He nudged the other author, bringing him back to the moment. Sherman smiled and stepped around the table, his own folio bag already in hand.

"She always made me feel so welcome. So personable."

Nimue turned over her shoulder to keep an eye on Sherman, who stopped by the panel room door to speak with Cary. He must have been his assigned security detail.

"We've… We've, uh, had some kinks to deal with," Nimue explained. "I'm so sorry if you feel anything has been lacking in your experience this year."

Gowdie took off to the back of the room, landing on the top of one of the chairs near the room's exit.

"Oh, no." Wayne waved a hand at her. "It's been fine. Mostly."

That got Nimue's full attention. "Mostly?"

Wayne chuckled, coming around the table. "Oh, nothing to worry about. And more of a hotel issue than a convention issue, I must say."

Nimue waited for him to come around, then matched his pace as they headed toward the exit. "What kind of hotel issue?

What's your room number? I can look into it for you. Witchy Expo Services and Southern Hotel work closely together."

"Room 425, but it's nothing so terrible as all of that." Wayne stopped by the exit and clutched his bag to his leg.

Sherman and Cary stepped out into the hallway, Sherman talking the warlock's ear off and the warlock not responding.

"I'll head out into the hall after them," Gowdie told her.

She sent a grateful *thank you* and knew she'd have to go out there soon or Gowdie's ability to follow them would soon hit an invisible wall.

"Besides," Wayne said, "it seemed to have resolved itself, with her being sick and all. Not a peep from her room."

Nimue snapped back to face the non-fiction author in front of her.

"Her room? Rona Brynhild's?"

"Yes." Wayne grimaced. "I don't mean to complain about a guest, but first the scene at the dinner and then the *shouting* coming from her room last night... Around a quarter after eleven, I think?"

"She was shouting? At whom?"

"I couldn't say." He chuckled darkly. "She could have been screaming at herself for all I knew, but there were several times a door slammed and I don't think even *Rona* would go around slamming doors for attention in the middle of her rants."

That "even Rona" made Nimue wonder... "Have you met Rona before?" The author had been so reclusive, she wondered how.

"Oh, yes," Wayne said. "And I can't say I'm new to her moods. She used to at least balance them out with bursts of spontaneity and creativity, but... Every time I've seen her in the past couple of decades..." He blew a strong breath between his lips, emitting a puttering sound.

So it hadn't been a close friendship.

"You seem friendly with Sherman," she said. She added mentally to her familiar, *Where's Sherman off to?*

"The gent's," Gowdie said, which she knew to mean the bathroom.

"Oh, friendly enough. The three of us met each other way back."

"During that writing class Sherman mentioned?"

Wayne leaned forward. "He told you about that, did he? Yes. Thirty-five years ago, I think."

That number was starting to be a refrain.

"Of course, it was hardly friendship from the start between the two of them. I remember in class, Sherman was all smiles and praises for Rona's writing and she..." He shrugged.

"He told me she ripped apart his work—and that she wasn't wrong."

"Well, he didn't believe that back then." Wayne shook his head. "To tell you the truth, I'm glad I got out of fiction writing. I wasn't particularly suited for it, either."

"'Either'?" Nimue quoted. "But surely, Sherman's improved."

"Oh, yes, yes..." Wayne's gaze wandered around the room.

Nimue's eyes followed suit and she found herself staring at the perma-charm crystal projecting the covers of Sherman's and Wayne's latest books behind where they'd been seated for the panel. Wayne's was an account of witch and warlock activity during the 1980s.

Nimue bristled. As if Sherman's flights of fancy about witch and warlock spies—for whom? Other countries' governments? Some shadowy evil witch society that Nimue herself didn't know existed?—in his novels had any basis in the truth.

It was that bristling feeling that made her ask, "Where were you this morning? At around a quarter to eight?"

"Right before the con opened?" Wayne cocked his head. "Well, I didn't have to be here for a couple of hours, so I stayed in."

"In your hotel room?"

"Yes…" Wayne's voice carried with it some curiosity.

"Just wondering if… you heard any loud noises from Rona's room," she mumbled, making up an excuse.

"Well, no, but I was on a video chat with my daughter and grandkids from about seven till eight, before they headed off for school. It's possible I was distracted. Then I took a shower and I left my room around nine."

So he had an alibi of sorts Nimue could check out. If she needed to.

She was seeing suspects everywhere now. But everyone seemed to have some sort of connection to Rona.

Most of them had been on the wrong side of one of her outbursts.

Then again, Wayne hadn't spat her name like so many others she'd talked to.

"You said you haven't been that close with Rona the past few decades?"

Wayne frowned. "Well, I suppose not. We've mostly chatted by email the past few decades, me and Sherman and sometimes Rona."

Nimue stiffened. Did he mean Sherman and Rona had chatted by email, too?

What else was the man lying about?

Gowdie? She sent out a message mentally.

"Still in the gent's room. I've told Miller we want to talk to him. But she claims her warlock is waiting out here for Wayne, too."

Let me guess, Nimue projected. *Zelena's too short-staffed to send one security guard for each of them?*

"Right," Gowdie sent back.

"Did you talk about writing?" Nimue asked.

"Yes. Sherman always loves consulting me for help with facts with which to embellish his fiction." He winked. "You'll find me credited in most of his acknowledgements."

Nimue nodded. Short of the man pulling a hammer out of that folio case, she was mostly just interested in what he knew about Sherman and Rona. "And did Rona and Sherman email each other?"

"You'll have to ask them. We didn't have a single group message, as far as I can recall. No, Rona and I just usually email to congratulate each other on our latest releases. Or life events. My marriage, my daughter being born, my grandchildren, my tenure."

He didn't list a single life event for Rona. "Did Rona never marry?" She supposed the information was out there, somewhere on the human Internet, but she'd have to ask Willow or another savvy young witch to do the digging.

"No." He grimaced. "But she keeps her

life pretty close to the vest. For all I know, she could have secretly eloped and kept her lover at her cabin outside of Portland all these years. She has a reputation for being a recluse for a reason."

Nimue thought suddenly of Sherman's hidden wedding ring, which she'd *seen* on his finger that morning. Why had he taken it off? To hide his marriage status when there was a pretty face to flirt with?

"Is Sherman married?"

Wayne cleared his throat. "Well, yes, I think so. He doesn't like to talk about his private life, either. I can tell from the few comments he's made that it's… rocky. But I don't ask."

"So no kids, either?"

"No."

"I'm surprised either kept such a close eye on your life events, then," Nimue said. "If both are pretty private themselves."

"Well, that's no big mystery. We share— er, shared—the same agent for years. He kept all his clients on an email loop about news like that for each of our milestones.

Before the Internet, he even sent out newsletters in the mail."

"Clint Moore," Nimue said.

Wayne nodded. "You *are* informed, aren't you?" He checked his watch.

Nimue felt like she was on the cusp of learning something important, though she couldn't say why. But she was about to lose him.

"Rona doesn't seem like the type to care about 'staying in the loop' with her fellow authors, does she?" she blurted out. It was true, though. From what little she knew about the woman.

"True." Wayne dropped his wrist and stared again toward the exit. "There was one time…" He shook his head.

"One time what?" Nimue prodded.

"Well, I got an email from her asking a question about history." He pursed his lips, as if in thought. "I asked if she was writing a new genre—her fantastical worlds don't often require that level of scrutiny—but she just never replied. For some reason, that email stuck with me."

"Why?" Nimue asked. Was it so strange

Rona might have incorporated some factual detail into her writing or thought about writing something new?

"She never wrote back since. My youngest grandson was born, but she didn't send a congratulatory note."

"When was that?" Nimue asked.

"Four years ago."

"But Rona left Clint Moore nearly five years ago," Nimue pointed out. So it would make sense she hadn't been kept abreast of Wayne's news, if she'd been getting it from their agent all along.

"True… Only…"

"Only what?"

"Last night, at the dinner, before you showed up… We chatted a little. She asked after him. Knew his name and everything, in addition to the two older grandkids'."

"That's quite a memory," Nimue said.

"Yes." Wayne cocked his head. "I was going to ask her about that historical fact she'd asked about, if she ever wrote a book with it, but well, she didn't seem in the mood. She may have shelved the manuscript. Even the most prolific of writers can do that, especially when trying a new genre."

He headed toward the exit and Nimue matched his pace. "What kind of fact was it?" she asked, for want of something better to ask.

"Oh, something about the American Witch Brigade in World War II. I can't remember, precisely…"

In the hallway, Cary opened the door to the bathroom and called out inside. "Mr. Abbott?" His voice carried down the largely empty hallway.

Gowdie flapped his wings from where he'd been resting atop a potted plant and flew over to peer inside.

"So, apparently, security is guarding the guests this year?" Wayne asked, nodding toward the security warlock in front of them.

"Yeah…" Nimue said. "Just taking a few extra precautions."

Cary let the door swing closed and swiped at his witch network crystal.

"What is it?" Nimue asked as Gowdie settled on her shoulder.

"I lost track of Sherman Abbott," Cary said, wholly focused on his projection screen. It lit up with a blinking light, signifying a message.

Nimue turned to look at Gowdie, who looked equally as puzzled. "What? How?"

Gowdie took to the air and opened his jaw, blowing a puff of steam against the bathroom door. The door swung open and Nimue remembered the bathrooms on this floor had two entrances. At the other end of the long array of stalls and sinks and urinals was another door leading to the hallway around the corner.

Miller the hare zipped around inside and out, coming back and shaking her head.

Gowdie stopped his smoke breath and settled back on the potted plant beside the door. *"Why would he run from his escort?"* Gowdie asked, either for himself or translating for Miller. *"They're here to protect him."*

"Maybe he's the one people need protecting *from*," Nimue said, ignoring Wayne's "Pardon?" and turning on her heel, heading down the hallway with clopping footfalls.

CHAPTER TWENTY-ONE

"What, exactly, do we know about Sherman?" Gowdie asked.

"He lied about his alibi. He lied about only meeting Rona the one time before yesterday—"

"Unless they didn't meet and just kept in touch online."

"I suppose," Nimue said. "But he made it seem as if they'd never spoken since that first meeting."

"We don't know that they did. Just because they both emailed Wayne doesn't mean they emailed each other."

"Someone told Rona about Wayne's latest grandkid."

"And you think it was Sherman? In between insulting her ability to write and demeaning her choice of genre? 'Oh, Wayne's newest grandchild is so cute! Also, your books are a waste of the pages they're printed on!'"

"I don't think you're going to win any prizes for impressions," Nimue muttered wryly. She'd reached the nearest teleportation pad, only she wasn't sure where to go.

"Hmm. If only you kept your smartphone with you, you could look up more about Sherman and Rona. Human Internet is surprisingly informative."

"If you tell Reoch about this and he blabs to Willow…"

"Of course he would! Familiars don't keep secrets from their witches." He nudged Nimue with the tip of his wing, and she was about to point out she hadn't known about familiars racing until he'd just mentioned it. But he seemed to anticipate what she'd say. *"Not important ones. So no, I won't tell him next time I see him about how you solving this mystery hinged on a smartphone his witch insisted you carry with you and yet you still can't figure out how to even turn it on without having a fit."*

"Ha ha," said Nimue. The thought of recounting this entire experience to Willow… No, she needed to know what had happened before she made anyone else worry about it. "I'm going to assume Cary and Zelena are on top of locating Sherman."

"But do they know that it's pressing?"

"I'm not *positive* he's our guy," she said. "I just need to know more."

"The Delgados seem to know plenty about him," Gowdie offered.

"But they're fond of him, too. We need someone neutral. Someone who can navigate the human Internet."

"Cassie?" Gowdie suggested.

"Merga!" Nimue said, remembering the young witch bringing out her smartphone.

She stepped through the teleportation pad, which turned brown and brought her to the convention center lobby.

Humphrey was back behind the counter, Linden over by the skywalk entrance, pointing out something on a map projected from the perma-charmed con guide that a group of four con-goers held between them.

Nimue slipped past them into the item storage alcove.

Merga was helping a con guest claim a jacket, and no sooner had the man stepped away than her customer-service smile slipped and she picked up her phone.

"Merga," Nimue said, jogging up to her.

She jolted and looked up from her phone, setting it carefully back on the table in front of her. "I only use it when it's not busy. It can get dull here between con opening and closing."

If con opening was when the perma-charm crystal had been smashed, then yes, Nimue imagined the rest of the day to be rather dull in comparison.

"It's fine," she said. Gowdie leaped off her shoulder to land on Spandemager's fluffy llama fur. "In fact, I could use your help with that."

Merga arched a brow and picked up her phone. "With my smartphone?"

"Yes. Can you look up Sherman Abbott? Willow does that sometimes, sees something in a movie, then lists back a bunch of facts—"

"Wikipedia," Merga explained, as if that explained anything to Nimue. She tapped at the screen, then swiped up, her eyes darting across it. "What, exactly, do you want to know?"

"*Good question,*" Gowdie said.

"Is he married?" Nimue asked.

Merga's eyes just about popped out of their sockets.

Nimue felt her face flush. "Not-Not asking for me."

"I thought Tituba wasn't into dating—"

"Not asking for her, either. Just… does it say?"

Frowning, Merga turned back to her screen. "No. Though not everyone's wiki entry lists personal relationship information like that. Depends on how famous they are, how public their lives are."

So Sherman did indeed keep his life close to the vest, if even the great human Internet and all of its information potential didn't have much on him.

"Says his first book was published in 1990," Merga read off her screen. "*The Cold Witch War.*" That one. The instant bestseller where it turned out the sexy heroine witch was actually spying on America for another country.

"1990. That's three years after Rona's debut," Gowdie pointed out.

That tracked with what Virgil had said about finding both of their manuscripts in slush piles, and how there'd been something about Sherman's writing that, despite being so different in subject, had actually reminded him of Rona's writing.

"'Other bestsellers and those adapted for TV and film include *Redcoat Warlock, The Magical Assassination, The Axis and the Witch Brigade, No Time to Fly...'*"

"Yeah, I get it. Book after book of bad, nasty witches and warlocks," Nimue mumbled.

"You guys need better PR," Gowdie added.

Merga twirled a curl of her red hair around one long finger. "It's just fiction. I mean, he incorporates some aspects of history, but—"

"Wait. What did you say about the Witch Brigade?"

Merga tilted her head but did some more tapping on her screen. "Oh. It's going to be a streaming TV series soon, starring Rachel Lawrence as Zethica Gala. '*The Axis and the Witch Brigade* is a 2016 novel in which Sherman Abbott colors the lauded American Witch Brigade of World War II as double agents—'"

Nimue held up a finger and Merga stopped. Spandemager let out a little bleating sound as everyone watched Nimue, waiting for her to say something.

"Gowdie," she said aloud, knowing Merga and Spandemager would only get some of the story but needing to hear her ideas bounce off of others anyway. "Sherman said he couldn't write. Wayne agreed."

"*Yeah, when Sherman started. Thirty-five years ago.*"

Nimue chewed her lip. "I mean, authors can improve, but… he also said Rona was a genius."

"*Yeah…*" Gowdie's head almost flopped sideways as he studied his witch, waiting for answers.

"Rona sent an email to Wayne asking about the American Witch Brigade in World War II," she said, not sure he'd followed her conversation with the history professor well from the hallway. "And then when he asked her if that meant she was writing something in a new genre, she stopped emailing him entirely."

"Spandemager, you're going to have to fill me on what she's talking about," Merga said out loud.

The familiars were probably having a conversation of their own as Spandemager got up to speed.

"Sherman emailed Wayne all the time about history questions for his books." She started pacing. "What if… And this may seem crazy." She swirled on Merga. "Merga, can someone send an email as another person?"

"What do you mean?" Merga asked.

Nimue tapped her wrist crystal. "Well, you know how there's no way to hide who's sending a message on the witch network? The magic wouldn't allow that."

"Oh." Merga nodded slowly. "Oh, yeah,

sure, humans can totally lie about who they are online. They can have multiple emails, all with different names—"

"Could one person log into another person's existing email and send a message as them?"

"Well, sure, I guess. If they're a hacker and can crack the password. Or they share a computer with the password saved or something. Or they're just a really, really good guesser."

"That's it!' Nimue snapped her fingers. "Rona asked Wayne a question from her email, with her name on it. Because she usually asked questions *as* Sherman, from *his* email."

"That could definitely happen, especially if they share the same computer," Merga said, which hadn't been something to cross Nimue's mind at all. "Maybe she forgot to switch over to the other account and just started typing an email like usual."

"You're saying Rona Brynhild wrote Sherman Abbott's books?" Gowdie asked.

Nimue's jaw went slack. "Yes, I guess I

am." Was it possible? Both put out one or two books a year.

But she knew from Lola Jackson, indie author extraordinaire, that some writers could pump out at least three times as many books as that. The traditional publishing industry itself slowed the pace down.

"It fits," Nimue said. "The similar writing styles—noticed by multiple people. The shared email, Rona freaking out about being caught writing as Sherman from the wrong email..."

"*But they hate each other,*" Gowdie pointed out.

"But maybe he has something on her," Nimue said. "Maybe he forced her to ghost-write for him."

But what could he have used as blackmail?

And what was it that made her so dread the truth coming out that she'd done his bidding for decades, pumping out book after book after book in his name?

"If she was finally going to tell someone the truth, that might explain why he killed her."

Merga jumped in place but didn't say a word.

"Nimue, you're forgetting something impor-tant," Gowdie said.

Now it was Nimue's turn to look confused.

"If Rona's dead and you're right about the ghostwriting, who's going to write Sherman Abbott's next bestseller?"

CHAPTER TWENTY-TWO

"I don't know. Another ghostwriter?" Nimue suggested. She hadn't thought about that.

"But what if fans noticed the change in style? He could still risk being exposed. Not to mention the new writer brought in on the secret..."

"Maybe he wasn't thinking that far ahead." Nimue paused in front of the teleportation pad, having thanked Merga for her assistance and asking her to send a message if Sherman ever happened by. Merga claimed he hadn't been there to store any items, though, and she'd been there ever since she'd finished cleaning up the lobby, minus her lunch hour.

She tapped her wrist crystal and brought up a message to Zelena. *I'm looking for Sherman Abbott*, she wrote to her. *He gave Cary the slip. We need to talk to him.*

"How goes the investigation?" Linden asked, his voice going quiet at the last word, though his smile never faltered as he looked out over the lobby.

"I'm on it," she said, flicking her projection screen away. "I'm looking for Sherman Abbott."

"Abbott, huh…?" Linden's lips pursed.

"Wonder if he knows anything," Gowdie said. Dyer the chinchilla let out a little squeak as she scattered across the floor in front of them. *"Considering the tour he took Sherman on last night."*

That's right… Nimue thought back to him.

"I haven't seen him," Linden said. Dyer climbed up his leg and then skipped up his torso, settling on his shoulder.

"What about last night?" Nimue asked. "Ren told me he had you take Sherman on a tour." She frowned. "Doesn't seem like a good idea, taking a human around behind the scenes."

"Oh, nothing untoward happened, I can assure you. We just did a quick turn about the place, and I answered his questions about how we set up our conventions."

"And did he have a *lot* of questions?"

Linden chuckled and leaned slightly toward her. "Afraid they'll discover all of our deepest, darkest secrets?"

"Well, I'm afraid of *him* nosing around for any excuse to make a witch or warlock the villain in his next book. Well, I was, I guess."

"You *were*?"

Nimue let out a deep breath and focused on chinchilla Dyer twitching next to Linden's ear, her little nose in constant movement.

"I don't think he writes his own books."

Linden stiffened, his hand shaking slightly where he grasped it with the other. "Now that's a serious accusation. What makes you say that?"

Was it so serious? Nimue supposed.

Some authors were open about using other writers, but when they weren't… Fans didn't like to be deceived like that.

"Have you read any of his books?"

Linden blinked slowly. "One or two."

"And any of Rona Brynhild's?"

Linden was slow to respond. "I have. Hasn't everyone?"

Almost anyone who read, Nimue supposed.

She grew quieter. "I think Rona wrote Sherman's books for him."

Dyer let out a little chittering noise that Gowdie translated as a gasp.

"She doesn't talk in words much," he told Nimue.

Dyer buried her muzzle behind Linden's ear.

"What proof do you have?" Linden asked.

"It's not proof, per se…"

"Well, I'd keep that quiet, then." Linden noticed a man and a woman with attendee badges approaching and flashed his gleaming, white teeth. "Can I help you?"

"We're just wondering when the next

Rona Brynhild signing will be?" the woman asked.

Nimue flinched.

"Not until tomorrow, I'm afraid. She's indisposed." Linden didn't even stumble.

"Oh. That's too bad. Thank you…" The woman and the man stepped inside the teleportation pad, the light glowing black.

"Best to delay addressing the real circumstances as long as possible," Linden said, leaning toward Nimue again. "Keep the cauldron happier for longer."

Right.

"So you think Sherman killed Rona?" Linden asked, his voice as quiet as could be, but his expression so open, so amenable, Nimue almost didn't believe she'd heard the question. "To keep the fact that she's his ghostwriter quiet?"

"Maybe… Can you send a message if you see him? Maybe stall him?"

"Of course."

Nimue's perma-charm wrist crystal flashed red and she checked it to find a message from Cassie, asking if she had a minute to meet up in the office.

"Zelena's looking for him for me," she said, looking for a message from Zelena and finding none. Surely, Cary had explained the situation to her, though.

"Then you're sure to find the man responsible." Linden nodded and strolled closer to the entrance from the sidewalk out front as another group of guests walked inside the lobby.

Nimue stepped through the teleportation pad, the light flashing red and letting her through to the employees-only wing.

No one was in the hall as she approached her office, and she stepped inside, leaving the slight murmur of the convention conversations behind.

Cassie popped up from behind a stack of books that littered her desk. Nimue let out a little scream, and Gowdie leaped off and took to the air in flight.

"Didn't mean to startle you," Cassie said.

All of this sleuthing was making Nimue a nervous wreck. "You messaged for me?"

"Right, uh…" Cassie started picking up stacks of books by the handful, setting them aside in two towers that grew higher and higher. "It's actually about Comic Hero Con. The head of the Comic Enthusiast Society called, and I know you've got enough on your plate, but she wasn't taking *no* for an answer—"

Nimue felt her heart sink as she watched Cassie rearrange the books to make space on her desk, looking for something. Like they needed to worry about the next big convention, too. After what had happened here got out, who was to say the Comic Enthusiast Society wouldn't demand a refund for its deposit?

"Sorry about the mess," Nimue said. "I asked Merga to bring the books back here, and I suppose she didn't have time to shelve them again. But I didn't mean for her to pile them high on your desk—"

Nimue froze. Sensing the cold sensation tingling down her spine, Gowdie flapped over from where he'd settled on the nearby hat rack and landed between the two tower-high stacks of books. Laveau the green ferret popped out from behind one tower on the desk, settling in beside Gowdie.

"What is it?" Cassie asked, the paper in her hand forgotten as she followed Nimue's gaze back and forth to the two stacks. Nimue spotted her copy of *Jane Eyre* on top of one of them and let her fingers graze the worn, familiar surface. She frowned, noticing one of the pages had been bent inward at the corner. She smoothed the page out as best she could before turning her attention to the sheer number of books piled up on and around Cassie's desk.

"Those are way more books than we sent flying over the lobby," Nimue said.

Cassie's face blanched. "Yeah, there are..." She dropped the paper back to the space on the desk, scrambling through the remaining books left to be unsorted, some of which were stacked high from the ground to her waist. "There are countless copies of—"

"Rona Brynhild's books!" Nimue said just as Cassie did.

Gowdie and Laveau worked together, their little paws and taloned feet combining to pull out the nearest such book from a stack. It was a bit like Jenga, and Nimue worried they might send it all to the floor.

They opened the book up, but there was nothing special to be found within the first few pages.

Nimue grabbed another, one of Rona's earlier cozies, and flipped through it. There was nothing particularly identifying in this one, either. It looked brand new.

"A bookmark," said Cassie, having grabbed one from the stack beside her on the floor. She held it out, a crisp black piece of cardboard with lace-like graphic design flourishes. But Nimue already knew what it might say.

There was only one person missing a massive amount of Rona's books.

"Nicola's Nook Bookshop," Nimue read off the bookmark.

"What are all of her missing Rona Brynhild books doing here?" Gowdie asked.

Laveau tilted his head as if speaking to Gowdie.

"They were hovering with the rest of the books in the lobby," Nimue said, her brain scrambling to make sense of it.

She hadn't sent those books up into the

air. They'd just used the books decorating the office.

Cassie let out a little yelp as she riffled through the stack still on the ground, putting a single book of Rona's down on the table behind Laveau with shaky fingers.

Laveau sniffed it, then scrambled up Cassie's arm.

"*'Rona's blood is on it,'*" Gowdie translated for Nimue.

Frowning, Nimue took in the dark splatter, making the brightly colored, cheery murder depicted on the cover—she found that ironic for a moment—like something darker, straight out of one of Sherman Abbott's books.

"Do you think… Do you think it was intentional? This book being chosen?" Cassie asked.

It was a copy of Rona's latest. With hesitating fingers, Nimue steeled herself and reached forward, flipping through the pages. There was another Nicola's Nook Bookshop bookmark, but nothing else of note.

"I don't know if the person who

smashed the perma-charm crystal could see well enough around the corner to time it to make sure it was Rona's latest release that fell on her," Nimue said, stepping back.

"Then why add Rona's books to the ones hovering over the lobby at all?" Cassie stroked Laveau at her shoulder, biting her lip.

The phone rang—the one on Cassie's desk that pretty much only took calls from human clients—and Cassie took a deep breath before picking it up, smiling, and saying, "Witchy Expo Services Corporate Office. Cassie Cabot speaking."

Nimue paced in front of the desk. They'd discovered the location of Nicola's missing books—they'd been in front of her face, or over her head, really—all along. Someone had dragged Nicola's boxes of Rona's books to the lobby and sent them flying up to the ceiling one by one, pressing them against the item storage crystal.

Why? How? And was it all related to Rona's untimely death?

Cassie's conversation with the client grew soft and indistinct in her ear.

Well, no one had been manning the entryway to the convention or the item storage area in the hour or so before the incident. She'd established that much. That was why Nicola had been able to walk past the entryway without her badge.

Nicola's booth being right up front would account for how someone could have brought two boxes to the lobby. It wouldn't have taken long, especially without witnesses, just heading back and forth the one time. Well, one more time at least to bring the empty boxes back so the missing books wouldn't immediately be noticed.

Unless it was two people who'd grabbed a box each to begin with. That would have required just one trip there and back.

Less chance of anyone spotting them that way, especially in the early hours, shortly before Nicola had noticed the books had gone missing…

Nicola had suspected the Delgados, and there was that one extra book of Rona's mixed amidst Sherman's stack of books.

"But that seems pretty foolish," Gowdie said, having picked up on Nimue's train of

thought. *"Besides, though Virgil may have doled out extra hard scritches, I don't think they did it. They may have hated Rona, but they wouldn't have taken it out on Nicola. I believed them about that Bookseller's Code thing."*

So did I, Nimue thought back.

But the Delgados would have been the perfect suspects. No other group of two had had access at that moment and a dislike of Rona—

"Lola and Shawna," Nimue said aloud. There had been another group of two in the area at the time in question who'd disliked Rona.

"Yes, of course," said Cassie, though she wasn't paying attention to Nimue at all. She was finishing up her call. "Thank you." She hung up.

Nimue's eyes snapped up to meet hers. "What did the Comic Enthusiast Society need from me?"

Cassie shook her head and pulled the paper she'd found out from beneath the dirtied book of Rona's now covering it. She poked at the book as if it might up and bite her. "Just a word about maybe adding another dozen or so booths. She specifically wanted to rearrange some in 5F to make room for a thirty-by-thirty-foot booth. I told her we're too close to the con to make sweeping changes—"

"No, it's fine. Ren and I can manage." Nimue waved a hand dismissively. Then she frowned. "Where *is* Ren?"

Cassie shook her head. "I messaged you both, but he hasn't shown. I haven't seen him since I got back from lunch."

Nimue felt her stomach harden. She hadn't been able to track down Nicola or Sherman, and now Ren, who'd been very defensive on behalf of his late wife's best friend, wasn't responding to his assistant's calls? Ren, who clearly had wanted to be Head Warlock General Manager all on his own?

But right now, she had questions that needed answers.

"Can you find out if Lola Jackson and Shawna Higgins have any events right now?" Nimue asked, already bringing up her witch network projection to send a message to Ren.

Urgent. Get in touch with me.

Cassie tapped her wrist crystal and made some sweeps in the air with her hand. "Nothing that I can see." She cocked her head. "Those two authors?"

Nimue was already sending a note to Zelena. *I need to locate Lola Jackson and Shawna Higgins. Is someone on your team with them?*

To Nimue's surprise, Zelena messaged back within seconds. *Hotel room,* she said back. *Room 409. Gave Charity the slip this morning. What is with all of these authors running from security? Like I don't have enough to do today—*

Zelena was about to lose herself in a rant.

But yes, Lola and Shawna *had* been spotted without a security guard in the employees-only area of all places, not too long ago.

They'd claimed their escort had dropped them off and left, which had seemed suspect, but there'd been no other explanation for how they'd gotten the teleportation pad to bring them to the employees-only area.

Unless…

"I'm off to the Southern Hotel," Nimue told Cassie. "Hold down the fort here?"

Letting out a deep breath, Cassie collapsed back into her chair. Books towered every which direction around and in front of her and her green witch's hat shifted, looking slightly askew. "Considering everything else going on, I'll happily stick to fort duty," she said. The phone rang again and she hesitated, her eyes stuck for a moment on the stained book that must have hit Rona's head. Then she cleared her throat and answered the phone. "Witchy Expo Services Corporate Office. Cassie Cabot speaking."

Nimue would trust in the assistant in which both Ren and she had seen potential and go crack this case—but only if all of these dangling, suspicious threads would finally come together to make sense.

CHAPTER TWENTY-THREE

As Nimue had made her way to the Southern Hotel and then Room 409, she'd felt apart from the con-goers with whom she'd crossed paths. Their bright smiles, the loads of books cradled in arms or tucked in tote bags or rolling suitcases they dragged behind them—it all made the bookworm in her happy. But the mystery of what had happened to Rona—of all the secrets around the woman—ate at her, making it so she couldn't imagine another moment's peace in which she'd be able to read a book and take a sip of tea again.

"We'll figure it out." Gowdie rubbed his

scaly face against her cheek as they headed down the hallway of the fourth floor of the hotel. *"And you'll be back to enjoying the con in no time."*

Even that felt insensitive, considering the death of the author before the con had begun. Nimue considered that, and how the only way she'd be able to enjoy Rona Brynhild's books ever again—and Sherman Abbott's, if she were right—was if she viewed them through the lens of the metaphorical death of the author.

Rona Brynhild had written about a fluffy, funny human cast of friendly characters caught up in murders. She'd been a sour, unfriendly human caught up in the same.

She nodded at Charity McAllister, security witch posted outside of Room 409, as she approached. Her pink chimp familiar stood in echo of her, one hand over the other wrist in front of their abdomens, at the other edge of the door.

"Nimue." Charity nodded at her, and her familiar—Nimue thought his name was

Lucas—nodded at the same time. "Zelena said you might be by."

"Lola and Shawna still inside, then?"

Lucas saluted and Gowdie gave him an outstretched wing in salute back.

"Yes," Charity said. She was thin but very toned, wearing a sleek, brown track suit beneath her brown witch's hat. Her straw-colored hair was pulled back into a tight bun behind her head, her cheeks a bit ruddy in her tanned complexion. "They walked around a bit after their signing, then said they wanted to come back."

Nimue hesitated, her knuckles over the door to knock. She lowered her voice. "Zelena told me they gave you the slip earlier today?"

Charity's chin dipped down, her lips tight. "They told me they were going to the showroom floor. When I stepped through the portal right after them, they were gone already. Took me a bit to find them—Tituba led me to them at their signing."

Lucas the chimp let out a little series of squawks.

Gowdie nodded. "*He pointed out they never went to the showroom floor ahead of them. Not the first time.*"

Charity's jaw dropped, but she quickly recovered, doing her best to seem stoic again.

"What?" Nimue asked.

Lucas squawked again.

"*The teleportation pad lit up red when they stepped through in front of them,*" Gowdie translated.

"Why didn't you point this out earlier?" Charity snapped out of the corner of her tight mouth. "I didn't notice. I was too busy looking around for signs of anyone following us."

Lucas made his chimp noises again.

"*He thought she knew,*" Gowdie translated. "*He thought it was a secret part of the mission. Throwing any potential stalkers off the authors' scent. Lola had an employee badge in her purse. He noticed the lanyard dangling out of it and took a quick peek.*"

Nimue's eyes flicked to Charity's badge around her neck, but it was still there.

"Where did they get that?" she asked.

Charity looked down at Lucas out of the corner of her eye, a silent conversation passing between them.

"He doesn't know," Gowdie translated. *"He never saw them take it from anywhere. It was dangling out of her purse the moment they were assigned to them."*

Nimue frowned. "And has there been anything else weird going on? Any sign of a stalker?"

"No." Charity shook her head. "That, at least, I'm sure of."

Nimue rapped her knuckles against the door. There was a muffled sound on the other side of it, a pause, and then the door cracked open, the inside chain lock still in place.

"Yes?" Lola's eye blinked rapidly through the gap.

"May I speak with you and Miss Higgins?" Nimue asked, her tone tense.

Lola stumbled backward. "No, I… No, I don't think we should let you in."

Nimue's thoughts froze a moment as her mind caught up.

"It'll just be for a moment of your time—"

"Lawyer," said Lola quickly. "Not without a lawyer present."

She slammed the door.

A pinpricking sensation broke out across Nimue's skin.

"Did I hear that right?" Gowdie asked in her head. *"A lawyer?"*

Charity scoffed. "Probably because they stole an employee badge, apparently." She tapped the perma-charm crystal at her wrist and brought up a message.

"What are you doing?" Nimue asked.

"Reporting to Zelena."

Nimue put a hand on the security witch's arm and pulled out her wand from its holster. "Don't tell her about this yet."

Charity cocked her head. "Why not?"

"Unlock Charm." Nimue waved the wand at the handle and the door opened, the chain lock inside unfastening as if invisible hands were at play.

Inside, two women let out a little shriek in tandem.

"That's breaking and entering, boss," Charity said.

Nimue gave her a wink as she re-holstered her wand. "Just say the door was unlocked when I tried it. I don't have time for lawyers."

She stepped inside and shut the door behind her, Gowdie taking off and soaring across the hotel room to land on top of the flat-screen TV.

Even the hotel rooms were a mixture of forest brought inside and sleek, modern design. In the corner, the trunk of the giant tree whose roots were visible in the lobby took up some space, like a load-bearing joint at the wall.

"You can't just barge in here!" Lola cried. "We have rights!"

"I can when I suspect illegal activity," Nimue said, putting her hands on her hips. Cauldron Cove laws were different than the typical human city's. "Activity that impacts the running of Witchy Expo Services."

Shawna, seated on the foot of one of the full beds, let out a sob and Lola, who'd been standing by the nightstand between the two beds, rushed forward to offer her friend her shoulder again.

Lola glared up at Nimue. "You can't go throwing around wild accusations like that. You're not the police."

"In Cauldron Cove, Witchy ExS *is* the law," Nimue said. Gowdie let out a little deep, throaty chuckle, which Nimue knew to be him finding his witch amusing, but Shawna let out a little yelp.

"Zelena's security team is, anyway," Gowdie said.

So Nimue didn't have the same authority Zelena did. She *was* Zelena's boss now. That had to count for something.

"So start talking," Nimue said.

Shawna sobbed even harder, burying her face against Lola's shoulders. Lola patted her back.

Shawna cracked first. "We didn't mean —is she hurt badly?"

Nimue blinked hard. What was she admitting to? Her eyes scanned the room for a hammer, all thoughts of the complicated web she'd woven between Sherman and Rona in her head out the window.

Had the threatening letter to Shawna been a decoy, something to throw the scent off of Shawna and Lola?

"*You* killed Rona Brynhild?" It slipped out before Nimue could stop herself.

Only Zelena had performed an Origin Charm and hadn't picked up on the writer of the letter being in Cauldron Cove…

Shawna's eyes widened, a gasp choking in her throat and morphing into a sort of gurgle. "She's dead? She's *dead*? We saw her cancelled signing and the books were gone and we thought something must have gone wrong. Maybe we overloaded it—"

"Hush," said Lola, standing up and crossing the room to her purse. "Don't say anything. We need a lawyer." She pulled a phone out of her purse.

Nimue whipped out her wand, causing Shawna to cry out again, and Gowdie swooped down from atop the TV to snatch the phone out of Lola's hand before she could do more than tap it a few times.

"You-You can't do this!" Lola jumped up, trying to reach the phone, but Gowdie swooped out of her reach, settling on a bit of the giant tree trunk in the corner that branched off into a small bough, just out of Lola's reach.

"If it involves the safety of the guests at this convention, I can and I will," Nimue said, trying not to let her hand tremble too much as she pointed the wand at Lola. "Now *sit down*." She was doing her best grumpy Zelena impression.

It worked. Lola's back went ramrod-straight and she sat back down beside Shawna. Her eyes were glassy, but her jaw tight, as if she were determined not to let a single tear fall.

"There's a security guard right outside that door," Nimue said, jutting her head to indicate Charity and Lucas's direction. "Now, I can call her in here and have her help me take you into custody—"

Shawna let out another cry, and Lola reached slowly, ever so slowly, to grab a nearby box of tissues for her.

Shawna took the first three, far less careful not to make any sudden moves.

Nimue took a deep breath. "Where's the hammer?"

Lola did a double-take. *"Hammer?"*

"The one you used to smash the perma-charm!"

Shawna and Lola exchanged a look.

"You don't… You didn't use a hammer?" Nimue asked.

"What's a perma-charm?" Shawna asked. Her voice was rough, scratchy.

"The crystal," Nimue said. "By item storage? When you smashed it with a hammer, you made the books the crystal had caused to hover in the air fall down. That's how Rona died. Did you just mean to hurt her?"

"No!" Shawna cried. "We didn't intend to hurt her at all!"

"Not physically, anyway." Lola crossed her legs tightly, the tears escaping down her cheek. She didn't move to wipe them away. "Our lives are ruined," she said quietly. "I was… I was going to call my brother," she said. "I don't have a lawyer. I'm an indie author. My brother kept trying to get me to get a lawyer for filing copyright claims and all of that, but… And now I need one. I don't know what to do!"

This time, it was Shawna who wrapped her arms around Lola, the two dipping their heads together as small sobs wracked their chests.

"I have an agent," Shawna said. "But she's not even into my new works anymore. This is the perfect excuse for her to drop me —if… if we're only going to be writing from prison from now on."

Nimue's hand wavered, lowering the wand to her side but still clutching it.

She'd thought… maybe… they meant they'd only meant to scare or hurt Rona, not kill her.

But had they actually not had anything to do with the perma-charm crystal's destruction?

"You know that crystal, correct?" Nimue asked. "The one that sends items you touch to it floating overhead?"

"Yes," Lola admitted. Her lips wobbled. "We didn't know you could overload it like that or… You said a hammer?" She cocked her head.

"You *can't* overload it," Nimue said. "It's

made to withstand quite a bit of belongings. It's for item storage."

"Yeah, we remember that. Shawna went to Bookshop Con a few years back and remembered the floating item storage. That's how we..." She looked at Shawna, as if asking permission to continue.

Shawna sighed. "It was my idea. She just... Rona made me so mad last night. When we ran into that bookseller hosting her for the signing, she dropped—"

Lola tapped her leg to get her to stop speaking.

Nimue pursed her lips. "She dropped her badge. I know that, remember?"

"Oh, yes, well... We went to return them, but she wasn't at her booth."

Gowdie let out a little dragon growl, and both Lola and Shawna flinched.

Shawna continued. "So we... We..."

"We saw the boxes of Rona's books," said Lola.

Shawna dabbed at her eyes. "I thought, well, I thought they'd find them eventually. I'd noticed the hovering books and I liked...

I liked the touch. New to the con this year, right?" She offered Nimue a flittering smile.

"Well, it *was*." Her heart sunk.

"And I thought, what better place to hide them! But surely, they'll find them soon enough. You could see the flying books from the front of the showroom."

"We left the woman's own badge for her, then grabbed a box each," Lola said. "Shawna stored some bags during her last con and said she didn't *think* you had to be a witch to send items flying. Sure enough. Each time we tapped a book to the crystal, it went up to join the others. Took a couple of minutes at most. Piece of cake." She let out a deep breath.

"Then we brought the boxes back, folded the flaps again to make them seemed closed, and hightailed it out of there." Shawna started wailing again. "Oh, I knew it was stupid the second we walked away, but it was too late! I just never imagined… Never imagined anyone would get hurt, least of all *die*!"

Nimue's mind raced with what they were telling her. "So you two… just stole some of Nicola's Rona Brynhild books and sent them flying with the item storage crystal? That was it?"

Shawna's sobs grew quieter. She hiccupped. "I guess… I guess we did steal. But we didn't even mean it like that. That Rona just made me so angry, we thought it would ruin her morning, maybe make her rant in front of her fans so news about her sour attitude would get around more, but… We thought they'd figure it out."

"Then the convention started and *all of the hovering books were gone*." Lola swallowed.

"We thought… We thought maybe that was because they found Rona's books right away." Shawna grabbed another tissue and blew out her nose. "Right? But then… We saw Rona's signing was cancelled. Then her panel…"

"Everyone said she was *sick*. We thought maybe sick with anger over the whole thing," Lola added.

"But we… We started worrying. Rona so angry she'd skip a signing, well, she was probably demanding to know who had done that to her books."

"So we thought we'd snoop around." Lola rubbed the back of her head, her tears drying up as she cleared her throat.

"The employees-only area." Nimue thought back to their jittery behavior, and to Shawna's reaction to Nimue mentioning the History Charm. "You thought we used human security cameras!" Nimue was beginning to think they really did need to install those. She wondered if Ren and Zelena would agree.

"But you said you saw things—" Shawna started.

"We have witchy ways of seeing the past." Nimue brandished her wand higher. "And I can go back and see the two of you steal those books and send them all flying, so don't think you're in the clear there."

Lola grew tight-lipped and Shawna just dabbed at her eyes.

Nimue lowered her wand. "Your security guard said you gave her the slip. You *told me* she'd dropped you off in the employees-only area. But you stole an employee badge, didn't you?"

Before either could protest, Gowdie said, *"On it!"* in Nimue's head and soared to the table with Lola's purse. Putting her phone down gently on the table, he stuck his snout inside the open clasp, coming back out with a lanyard draped around his throat.

"That's—" Lola started, but Shawna hushed her.

Gowdie floated in front of Nimue, who took a look at the badge hanging off his neck.

No one had reported a missing badge, or Nimue might have put two and two together earlier.

Only now she knew why.

"It's Glinda's. She's off this week." And Witchy ExS staff tended to leave their badges in their lockers, considering they could fly right up to the second floor and didn't need to teleport there. It just made it easier to keep the place cleaned and locked down if staff didn't take their badges home with them and try teleporting into work from a pad at any hour of the day.

At least, it should have been easier.

Lola shrugged. "We didn't take it. That bookseller dropped it."

They'd left behind *her own* badge. Lola had even said "them" when Nimue had mentioned she knew they'd gotten a hold of Nicola's badge and had gone to return it. To return *them*.

"Nicola had this?" Nimue asked. She slipped it off Gowdie's neck and slid it over her own.

"If that's her name…" Lola started.

"It is." Shawna nodded. "I read her own badge when we gave her back hers. We knew that one couldn't have been hers, so we were going to turn it in, but…"

Lola frowned. "I saw it was an employee badge. I thought we might need it if there was footage of us messing with Rona's books."

It seemed like the authors had acted out their little prank in a moment of pure spontaneous revenge, but they'd regretted it pretty quickly. "I suppose once you sent the books flying, you didn't know how to get them back?" Nimue held up her wand.

"Anyone can send something hovering with the perma-charm, but only a witch or warlock can get it back."

"Unless… they have a hammer, apparently?" Lola asked.

"Sharp, that one," Gowdie said, taking his perch back up on top of the TV. *"She should write detective fiction."*

"You didn't hurt anybody," Nimue said. It was more a statement than a question.

Shawna let out a little gurgling gasp.

"I want you to be honest now—lay it all out on the table." Nimue brandished her wand again. "We have ways of extracting the truth." More or less. "Did you fake the threatening note, too?"

"No!" shrieked Shawna. Lola shook her head.

Nimue tapped a finger to her chin. *What do you think, Gowdie?* she thought to him.

Gowdie let out a little puff of smoke. The TV screen steamed. *"I believe them."*

So the killer is still out there, Nimue thought. *And maybe these two authors' little prank made it easier for them to ensure Rona got a really good old conk on the head, considering how many more books fell on her.*

"Don't tell them that, though," Gowdie said. Shawna and Lola both trembled just a bit, their eyes focused on Nimue's wand. *"I don't think they can handle a single word more."*

Sighing, Nimue holstered her wand. Shawna let out a visible breath and Lola slackened her posture.

"Stay in this room," Nimue said. She did her best to project Ren's sternness into her tone. "Get room service. Ask Charity outside the door if you need anything. But for your own safety—and until I figure out what really happened today—I need to know you're not going to keep sneaking around where you don't belong."

"We promise." Shawna held up a hand with crossed fingers.

Lola nodded slowly. "Are you… going to charge us?"

"That's up to Nicola," Nimue said, pursing her lips. "Since you stole from her —for a prank or not."

Lola let out a sigh. "That could wreck our careers, if fans find out."

"We could still go to jail..." Shawna whispered.

"Well, let's hope she's in a generous mood," Nimue said. And after Rona's death and the impending doom of her bookshop, maybe the lost books would be the last thing on her mind.

If only Nimue could pin the elusive bookseller down to find out.

Having updated Charity and Lucas about the situation, Nimue and Gowdie walked down the hall toward the elevator that would take them to the lobby.

"Now what?" Gowdie asked.

There were no messages from Zelena or anyone having located Sherman. Then again, she wasn't sure anyone had checked out his room.

Cassie, Nimue thought to the witch network. *Any sign of Ren?*

Ren hadn't responded to Nimue's message, either.

No, Cassie messaged back, almost immediately. *Should I walk the floor, looking for him?*

No, that's fine, Nimue sent back. *I was wondering, though, if you might be able to tell me Nicola Nash's and Sherman Abbott's room numbers at the hotel?*

"Does Witchy ExS keep records of that?" Gowdie asked in her mind. He was peering at her projection screen from her shoulder, following along with the message exchanges.

Almost as if in answer, Cassie wrote back, *That's Southern territory. You'd have to ask hotel staff.*

Nimue bit her lip, looking down the hallway. No other security besides Charity was posted, but she hadn't requested any for booksellers and Sherman had given his the slip.

Still, the hotel often booked guests together. Maybe Sherman's room, at least, was on this floor.

Sending Fidelity, Cassie wrote back. *He's on break, but he has access. He'll meet you on the fourth floor. Since it's an emergency and all.*

"Fid is Cassie's boyfriend," Gowdie explained. So the familiars had been gossiping. Nimue had picked up on some of that vibe anyway.

Nimue sent her thanks, then sent another message to Ren.

I'm seriously getting worried about you. We're supposed to be in this together. Hello?

After a few minutes more, Nimue was just about to check her witch network screen for messages when the elevator door opened and out stepped Fidelity.

Fidelity was alone, his Southern Hotel uniform crisply pleated. He carried his wand in one hand, a keycard with a perma-charm crystal attached to one side in another.

Good thing, because Nimue was all out of Unlock Charm for the day.

"Cassie told me you needed to get into some rooms?" he asked.

She nodded. "Con security purposes."

Fidelity's familiar lizard poked his head out of his warlock's suitcoat pocket. He looked kind of like a pocket square handkerchief on display. "They're understaffed," he said, as if he'd already heard it today. He led Nimue and Gowdie around the corner, out of sight of Charity outside of Lola and Shawna's door.

"Which room is most pressing?" Fidelity asked, pausing in front of Room 422.

"Whose is this?" Nimue asked instead.

"Abbott's," he explained.

She nodded at him. "Open it up, please."

Fidelity used the hotel's master keycard and the door opened. He was about to step in, but Nimue stopped him, pulling out her wand with one hand and blocking Fidelity from entering with another.

"Hello?" she called into the room, taking one careful step after another inside the room. "Mr. Abbott? Sherman?"

The room was dark, but the late afternoon light streaming in through the wide window with its curtains drawn back left no hidden crannies for a man to hide in.

"Room's been turned down," Fidelity said, his voice a hush. He tiptoed in behind Nimue, his wand also at the ready. "Why are we sneaking?"

Nimue put a hand to her lips as Gowdie flew inside, doing a sweep of the room.

"*All clear,*" he reported.

"Check the closet," Nimue told Fidelity, motioning to the one behind the room's door. "I'll check the bathroom."

He did as bidden, despite the slight, questioning tilt of his head, and Nimue found no one in the bathroom. She stepped outside, letting out a breath.

Gowdie and Fidelity's lizard were in discussion on top of the single bed in the room.

"*Rhutwine*," Gowdie said, giving Nimue the lizard's name. *"He's explaining everything to Fidelity."*

That explained the ashen brown color of Fidelity's face.

"You think Sherman Abbott—*the* Sherman Abbott—might be a murderer?" he asked.

"And a bad writer, too," added Gowdie. *"Don't forget that."*

Rhutwine let out a little rumble in his throat that might have passed for a laugh.

"I don't know," said Nimue, tossing her hands to either side of her. "But I'm running short on suspects, and the man hiding from Witchy ExS staff isn't doing himself any favors."

"They already looked for Sherman in his room," Fidelity said. "Not too long ago. Said he'd given his tail the slip?"

So Zelena *had* thought to look here. Of course, if Sherman didn't want to be found, he wouldn't have run right back to his room. "Yeah. It was supposed to be for his own protection. But if others are in danger *because* of him…"

She walked over to the dresser. Beside the table was a large rolling suitcase. Nimue remembered it from the day before, when early arrivals had checked in at the Bessa to get their badges.

"He didn't swing by to get his things," Nimue said. "Unless he didn't plan to leave?"

"He could be anywhere," Gowdie pointed out. *"Maybe he just wanted some fresh air again. Dodge the claustrophobic feeling of being watched."*

"Then he's either a fool or the culprit." Nimue took hold of the suitcase's zipper, which she noticed was only halfway zipped up. "He's in danger or he *is* the danger. He needs to be found."

She took the suitcase lid by both hands and flipped it open.

Inside were a bag of toiletries, clothes, and a small stack of books.

Gowdie flew over and landed on the suitcase's open lid.

"I'm not sure we have the authority to search people's belongings—" started Fidelity.

"It's a con security issue." She shuffled through the items, immediately drawn to the books.

"These are his," she said, flipping through the titles. *The Axis and the Witch Brigade. No Time to Fly.* "He brought his own books for some light reading?"

"That doesn't seem exactly out of character. Though Virgil did say he likes to bring extra books when signing." Gowdie jumped down and landed on the book about World War II. *"Didn't Merga say this one was going to be a streaming series? Maybe he needed a refresher if he's interviewed about the new series."*

"Right..." The last book at the bottom, stuffed under a pair of crisp, white, folded unmentionables, had a bright pink cover.

"That's Rona Brynhild's latest," said Fidelity, looking over her shoulder. She guessed he didn't have *that* much of an objection to rummaging through guests' belongings, then.

So it was. The same book that had been stuck between Sherman's books in the Delgados' booth. Which Virgil had insisted had come from Sherman himself, not the boxes of missing books. That made sense since she knew Lola and Shawna had been responsible for what had become of those. She doubted they'd have risked sticking just one such book amidst Sherman's pile—or even thought to.

Was this the book from the Delgados' booth, then? Or another copy?

Nimue opened the first page. It was signed.

"Did Rona sign any *before* the con started?" Fidelity wondered out loud.

Only this one was personalized.

To Sherman, the long, curling writing read. *With love, Rona.*

"'*With love*'?" Gowdie practically

shouted in her ear. "Love? *Between those two?*"

"It's just an expression," Nimue said aloud, flipping through the rest of the book. She found nothing else odd about it. And even she knew her excuse was weak.

Rona didn't seem the type to want to sign anything for Sherman—she hadn't even wanted to lay eyes on the man—let alone be forgetful enough of her hatred of him to sign, "With love."

Had Rona Brynhild been capable of loving *anyone*?

"Hey," said Fidelity, offering his hand out to take the book from her. "Look at that."

Nimue handed it over, eager to learn what he'd seen.

"It's an Advanced Readers' Copy," Fidelity said, turning the book over and tapping to the small band at the bottom of the spine. Sure enough, it said that this edition was not for sale. The band continued onto the back of the flap jacket. "But ARCs are usually paperbacks. Or e-books these days."

"Rona demanded hardcovers," Nimue

said, remembering Virgil's list of complaints against the author. "Said they looked better on her shelf."

"She couldn't just wait for the finalized version?" Fidelity offered, handing the book back.

Nimue shrugged. "Maybe she wanted the best format for her earliest readers?"

"Like her one-time writer's group member Sherman Abbott?" Gowdie suggested.

Like Sherman indeed…

Gowdie flapped down to the bottom of the suitcase and started sifting through the man's clothes, flinging them everywhere.

"What else are you looking for?" Nimue asked.

"I don't know. Anything else to explain what he's been hiding from us regarding his relationship with Rona."

"Proof she's his ghostwriter?" Nimue asked.

"Who's *whose* ghostwriter?" Fidelity asked, but Nimue didn't get a chance to explain.

Gowdie's talon clicked against something hard beneath a pale lilac dress shirt.

He shoved the shirt aside, revealing a hammer tucked away at the bottom of the suitcase.

Nimue gasped and went to grab it, but Gowdie's little jaw chomped at her hand.

It didn't hurt, but it startled her, and she pulled her hand away.

"Better leave it," he said. *"If we have to get human authorities involved, they'll probably want to do their fingerprinting thingy."*

Rhutwine let out a little gagging croak.

"All right, forensic fingerprint analysis, you hotshot human crime show enthusiast," Gowdie said.

Rhutwine let out a little happy croak, jumping up into Fidelity's waiting arms.

Human authorities?

Nimue's stomach sank and she could have sworn she felt the energy in the room suck right out of it. The cauldron below town was growing restless.

And that was *before* they made the big announcement that Bookshop Con had been the site of an author-on-author murder.

CHAPTER TWENTY-FIVE

Nimue holstered her wand and tapped the perma-charm crystal at her wrist. *Zelena,* she thought into the witch network messaging center. *Make finding Sherman Abbott a priority. I found a hammer amidst his things in his room. He has to be the one who killed Rona.*

She tapped the crystal again and put her hand at her side.

"But the motive," Gowdie said. *"If you're right about Rona being Sherman's ghostwriter, who's going to write his books from now on?"*

"Someone else. Himself. Or maybe he'll retire," Nimue rationalized. She tapped at the copy of *The Axis and the Witch Brigade.*

"Maybe this is why! Maybe whoever's making the streaming TV series is asking too many questions or Rona is sticking her nose in because she's jealous—"

"Wait," Fidelity said, interrupting. "So you think Rona Brynhild writes Sherman Abbott's books? But Rona's books are made into TV shows and movies all the time."

"Okay, so maybe jealousy isn't a factor…" Nimue chewed her lip.

She wasn't going to find Sherman just standing here, though. And she still had to wonder what had become of Nicola Nash… and Ren, for that matter.

Cassie, she thought at the witch network once more. *Any sign of Ren?*

No, she wrote back pretty quickly. *And I'm getting worried.*

Nimue, too.

There still wasn't a response from Zelena.

Nimue turned to Fidelity. "Do you know Nicola Nash's room number, too?"

"Cas said you might want to check on her as well." Fidelity shook his perma-charmed keycard. "Let's go."

They left Sherman's room and Nimue braced herself for another long walk, only to pull herself short as Fidelity stopped at the room next door. He knocked on it. "Miss Nash? Hospitality."

Nimue blinked. "But was Nicola next door to Rona Brynhild?" Her eyes fell on the door on the other side of Nicola's—the one that wasn't Sherman's. "And Wayne Gomez…"

"Room 425," Gowdie reminded her. Sure enough, that was here, too, right across from Nicola's room. If Rona's was really the one two doors down from Sherman's, it stood to reason that Wayne would have heard any number of them slamming their doors over and over again last night.

"She's not answering," Fidelity said. "I can either go back down and call her from the hotel phone or…" He held out his master key.

"Just a second," Nimue said. "You don't happen to have your History Charm still available for the day, do you?"

Rhutwine, having hitched a ride in Fidelity's pocket, popped out and stuck out his tongue.

"I don't know if I *ever* use that one," Fidelity said.

Nimue took a step back and gestured. "Do you mind showing me the hallway last night, then? At around 11:00 to start?"

If Ren was somewhere with Nicola as she suspected, neither one was likely in danger. And she had to assume if someone was knocking on the door and he was inside, Ren would have at least answered.

She could spare a moment more before checking inside Nicola's room.

"Sure thing." Fidelity took out his wand and waved it in the air. "Just hope I cast this right. History Charm."

He and Rhutwine shimmered into nothingness, Gowdie and even Nimue's own body becoming invisible to her eye. The hallway was empty at first, then a shimmery reflection of a stranger, an older woman, walked by from one end to the other, a bucket of ice in her hand.

The hallway emptied again and then

Nicola's door opened in the illusion's echo of the past, the woman, with dark bags under her eyes, looking right and then left. She stepped out, the door shutting behind her.

She walked to the door Nimue assumed to be Rona's and knocked.

Her mouth moved, but the History Charm didn't capture sound.

She waited.

She shuffled back toward her room.

Sherman's door opened, the man practically ready for bed, complete with a robe on. His expression was pinched.

His door slammed behind him as he made his way toward Nicola.

Nicola looked up and instead of indifference or even awkwardness, as Nimue expected to find written on the bookseller's expression, she saw…

A beaming smile, a warm glow to Nicola's cheeks. She looked up, her face softening.

Sherman stepped forward and took Nicola gently by the arms.

And then they kissed.

"Uh, what was that?" Gowdie's voice carried out over the illusion into Nimue's head.

"I, uh…" Nimue stuttered. She looked closer. Sherman didn't have his wedding ring on.

And why, of all people, did her mind jump to Ren? Would he be sad to know Nicola was taken?

Did that make *Nimue* happy to find out? But why?

"He's a bit old for her, isn't he?" Fidelity added from wherever he was observing the events. "Considering human lifespans?"

Maybe. Nicola had to be about Ren's age if she'd been Lydia's best friend, which didn't make it entirely inappropriate to be dating someone a couple of decades older, but…

What was it about this pompous, perhaps-pretend author that had gotten Nicola's attention?

When had they met? At a signing?

And what about Sherman's wedding ring? Was he a widower or… Was he cheating?

And did Nicola know that?

The two broke apart, Nicola's hands coming together at Sherman's chest. Her mouth moved, her eyes stuck on the ground. Sherman nodded and continued to hold her, grabbing her by the upper arms softly as only a lover might.

The door to Rona's room opened. It slammed behind her.

She shuffled out into the hall.

Her jaw dropped.

Her face reddened, her fists shaking at her side.

And she shouted, but rather than attack the couple standing beside her as Nimue subconsciously braced for the author to do, she went back into her own room, the door swinging shut again.

Sherman dropped Nicola like a sack of hot potatoes, his lips trembling as he spoke —was it "Rona" that passed his lips? Nimue thought perhaps it was. A sheen of sweat glistened on his brow in the overhead light. He knocked on Rona's door rapidly, then opened it without waiting for a reply and stepped right in.

Nicola stumbled backward, clutching

her own door handle. Her face grew slack as she stared at the door to Rona's room. Then she slipped inside, her own door slamming behind her.

Nimue wondered if the muffled voices Wayne had heard were carrying out into the hallway and beyond now as the illusion kept moving, but there was no movement.

"Should I fast-forward?" Fidelity asked.

"Sure," said Nimue.

Another ten minutes flew by as Fidelity adjusted the illusion, then Sherman burst out of Rona's room, the door slamming shut. He made his way to his room, his eyes practically bulging out of his skull as his fist shook at his side. He stepped inside, his door slamming behind him just as Rona's flung open again and swung shut behind her.

She knocked on Nicola's door, hard, her fist flying.

Nicola answered, and Rona brushed her aside to step inside.

The door shut again.

The hallway went silent, but for Wayne's door opening and the professor peeking out both ways, shaking his head. But there was nothing for him to see.

"Faster again?" Fidelity asked once Wayne had gone back inside his room.

"Yeah…"

A few minutes later, Rona came out of Nicola's room and stormed back to her own. Two more doors slamming.

Then Nicola came out of her room, wringing her hands. She knocked on Sherman's door, her mouth opening.

He didn't answer, and Nicola didn't grab for the handle.

She lay her forehead against the door and spoke some more, her fist plastered unmoving above her head against the door.

The door didn't budge.

Tears in her eyes, Nicola stepped back, then slipped inside her own room, taking care to pull the door quietly shut behind her.

"What time is this?" Nimue asked Fidelity.

"About 12:20," answered Fidelity. "How much further should I go?"

"Fast forward as far as eight this morning," Nimue instructed.

Fidelity did, a whole lot of nothing going on in the hallway for several more hours' worth of skipped time.

Then Nicola stepped out, her eyes puffy, but her makeup thick, and knocked on Rona's door.

Her mouth moved, but Rona never came to the door.

She took soft, slow steps toward the elevators but stopped at Sherman's door and looked at it.

She knocked on his and spoke again. She waited, intent, as if listening.

Under Sherman's door, something slid out into the hallway.

Nicola bent down to retrieve it.

"What's that?" Gowdie asked.

"A… badge?" Nimue tried to get a better look.

A badge with a lanyard. Witchy Expo Services. Employee badge. Nimue felt for the two badges swinging around her own neck. "That's Glinda's badge. The one Nicola must have dropped when she bumped into Lola and Shawna."

"The one they kept in order to get up to some mischief?" Gowdie asked.

"Why did he have a Witchy ExS employee badge?" Fidelity asked.

"I don't know," Nimue answered. She watched as Nicola took her own badge off of her neck and stacked the two in her hand together. She walked to the end of the hallway and stopped, looking back over her shoulder and biting her lip.

No sooner had she turned the corner than Rona's room opened, startling Nimue even without the benefit of sound.

Rona pounded down the hallway, her fists swinging.

But her eyes, too, looked puffy. She stopped in front of Sherman's door, opened her mouth, then shut it.

She'd either spoken a single syllable or changed her mind about saying anything entirely.

She stalked off down the hallway.

Moments later, Sherman's door opened.

He was dressed, patting his brow with a kerchief that he then tucked into the folio bag in his other hand, which Nimue had seen him with later. Large enough to hold books… and a hammer. He stared down the hallway, the way the women had gone. And then he took off in the same direction.

"What time was that?" Nimue checked.

"About 5:45," Fidelity replied. That allowed Sherman enough time to get outside to the park at the ridiculously early time of 6:15, as he'd said he had. Had he intended to get out early, before he could potentially bump into Rona? Only she'd left before him… Had he not heard? "Do you need to see anything else?"

"Check just another couple of hours," Nimue said. According to Wayne, he'd stayed in his room until nine. Sure enough, they watched time flow and Wayne eventually stepped out, heading to the elevators. At nine o'clock, exactly as Wayne had said. He'd never left his room between the time he'd stuck his head out until after the murder.

Not that he'd ever been much of a suspect in Nimue's eyes.

The illusion faded out, but the current

reality was little different. Only the sight of Fidelity and Rhutwine in front of her, the flap of Gowdie's wings in front of her eyes, brought her back to the current moment.

"Do you think Rona was mad at Nicola for swapping spit with her rival?" Gowdie asked.

Ever the elegant wordsmith, Gowdie.

"She seemed angrier at Sherman than Nicola to me," Nimue said. "I mean, wouldn't she know him better than she even knew Nicola? Ren said Nicola contacted Rona through her agent. It wasn't like they had a connection before this."

"But I can't see Rona caring much about that. The bookshop owner who was hosting her betrayed her. She got mad at Penny a decade ago just for suggesting her and Sherman's books were similar. Not knowing the bookshop owners well didn't stop her from slugging one!"

He wasn't wrong there. But Nimue still felt like she was on the right track. In that moment they'd witnessed, it had been *Sherman* who'd betrayed Rona. Not Nicola. Or not Nicola nearly as much as Sherman, anyway.

Rhutwine must have translated

Gowdie's words for Fidelity because he shrugged. "I don't know. Looked like a wife catching her husband cheating red-handed to me."

Nimue's jaw dropped. Fidelity wasn't as familiar with the people involved in this case, so it stood to reason he wouldn't have known how much the two authors hated one another.

"Sherman's secret wife…" Gowdie said.

The wedding ring, which slipped on and off his hand—mostly off, except for that time in the park.

"But…. But they didn't live together," Nimue said. As if that were the final word on a marriage. Her own parents sometimes took off in separate directions for different jobs and adventures and then came back together as soon as they could, happier than ever. And those two actually *loved* to be around one another.

If you were married to someone you could hardly stand to be around…

It stood to reason they might opt for separate living arrangements.

But then why stay married at all?

She couldn't imagine staying married to Gregory and moving back to Cauldron Cove without him. Meeting up on occasion, sure, it might have worked, but Greg had wanted someone who'd be with him. He wouldn't have been able to get married again if Nimue hadn't let him go.

Sherman had still been out there, playing the field, judging by his lingering glance at Mercy, and maybe he'd been dating Nicola…

"Maybe the man doesn't care about settling down with a single lover," Fidelity pointed out. "Not if he's married to the Queen of the Bestseller Lists, bringing home all of the bacon. Then again, his own books sell plenty—"

"But *she* might have written them!" Nimue gasped. "Of course he had to stay married to her if she wanted things that way. It was the only way she'd keep writing his books."

It hadn't been blackmail, then. Rona had written Sherman's books for him… because she'd loved him?

"And yet she also couldn't stand the man

enough to live with him? Humans are strange, I tell you." Gowdie nodded absentmindedly at his own comment.

"Was the rivalry an act?" Nimue posited. "So people wouldn't suspect Rona was Sherman's ghostwriter?"

Before either Gowdie or Fidelity could weigh in on that, though, the door behind Fidelity creaked open.

Inside, bleary-eyed and with messy, disheveled hair, stood Nicola Nash.

"You figured it out," she said softly, her voice croaking. "Sherman Abbott can't write a word to save his life. And he's been secretly married to Rona Brynhild for decades. Something he *failed* to mention to me during the past year of our romance."

CHAPTER TWENTY-SIX

"Nicola!" Nimue stepped forward, putting her foot in the door before the bookseller could change her mind and retreat inside once more. "I've been looking for you. Why aren't you at the con?"

Nicola let out a sour laugh and stepped back inside her room. "There's no point."

Nimue exchanged a look with Fidelity, who took a step back.

"I should probably get back to work, if you're done with me?" He winced and Rhutwine chittered.

"'*He's awkward around drama,*'" Gowdie translated.

"No, it's fine, you can go. Thanks for

your help." Nimue stepped inside Nicola's room and the woman didn't ask her to leave. The door shut behind her.

She looked around. There was no sign of Ren in this room.

Of course there wasn't. Nicola had been having an affair—unbeknownst to her, apparently—with Sherman Abbott.

Ren—Soren—had only ever been a friend. Like he'd said.

But then where *was* the warlock?

She quickly checked the witch network and didn't find a reply from him. Zelena had sent a message that they were doubling their efforts to find Sherman but hadn't had any luck yet.

Maybe Nicola knew where he'd be.

The morose bookshop owner took a deep breath and shuffled over to the stiff, plush chair beside her window. The blinds were pulled back, the view of the Bessa and Lake Salem behind it clear, and Nicola sat in the chair, looking out at it, ignoring Nimue entirely.

Gowdie flapped his wings and soared off his witch's shoulder, landing on a branch of the giant tree that snaked its way through so many of the hotel's rooms.

Nimue took a look around. There was an open suitcase atop a dresser, its contents emptied, perhaps placed in the drawers beneath it. There were also several boxes from which dangled bits and pieces Nimue was familiar with for booth display, like bookstands and business card holders.

The bed was ruffled and unmade.

"Hasn't housekeeping been by?" Nimue asked, sitting gently at the edge of the bed near Nicola.

"I sent them away." Nicola flicked her hand but didn't turn away from looking out the window.

"You've been here?" Nimue asked. "In your room? Most of the day?"

Nicola shrugged. "It's not like I have anywhere else to go."

"But your booth. It's right at the front of the convention."

"Yeah, and there's no star attraction anymore, is there? No reason for anyone to shop at Nicola's Nook." She stared down at her left hand, inspecting her manicure.

"You left the booth unattended."

"It doesn't matter. If people take the books, whatever. Saves me the trouble of having to discount or return it all. I'm broke." She sighed and met Nimue's eyes for the first time in a while. "Rona's signing was my last hope. And now she's… she's dead. And my personal life is over." Tears danced in her eyes as she hugged her legs to her, her heels just barely managing to fit on the small seat.

Nimue took a deep breath, not sure where to start. How to not upset the woman further. "Until just now, I had no idea… You and Sherman…"

She shrugged. "He wanted to keep it quiet. 'Keep my name out of the presses for the wrong reasons,' he said." She scoffed. "I should have known. The man wouldn't have cared about his name in the presses. He loves attention. And who was going to report on us anyway? 'Popular but Not Superstar Author Dates Unknown Bookshop Owner.' Real newsworthy there. I mean, maybe it'd get a blip if we got married like he kept promising me." She looked at her bare left hand. "But there was always some excuse why he wasn't ready. I know he couldn't have actually married me now. Not if he *was* married."

"Motive?" Gowdie questioned in Nimue's mind. *"Being widowed easier than being divorced, especially if that means keeping all of Rona's sweet bestseller royalties?"*

And then he would actually marry Nicola? Nimue thought back to him. *Judging by the way he was looking at Mercy, I'm not sure how serious he was about a single woman.*

"He barely looked at Mercy," Gowdie pointed out. *"I know human men can let their eyes wander a lot…"*

Nimue bit her lip. She still wasn't so sure she was wrong about this.

"When did you meet Sherman?" she asked Nicola aloud.

"My bookshop." She dabbed the back of her wrist against one eye. "A little over a year ago."

Nimue settled in, crossing her legs on the bed and giving Nicola her full attention.

Nicola gave her a look but sighed, seemingly resigned to get the story off her chest.

"He contacted my store to do a signing. I don't get a lot of big-name authors doing that, so I leaped at the chance."

"Why your store specifically?" Nimue asked.

Her shoulder bobbed. "He said he'd just moved to the area. Mine's the only indie bookstore in town—though there's about to be none left."

"Huntsville?" Nimue asked, trying to remember if that was where Lydia had done her study abroad.

Nicola shook her head. "I grew up there, but I moved out West after college. I'm in a tiny town in Oregon, outside of Portland."

"Wasn't Rona's cabin she hides away in outside of Portland?" Gowdie asked.

So her husband didn't stray far when living apart? Nimue thought back to him.

"Maybe they brainstormed 'Sherman''s books in person," Gowdie added.

Or maybe they still… got together as husband and wife? On occasion?

"If they could manage to spend more than two seconds with one another without screaming."

Nicola looked to the little dragon but didn't comment on the odd, rumbling noise that was his laughter.

"We had a fairly successful book launch. He asked me out on a date." Nicola tucked a piece of hair behind her ear, letting her legs fall back down to the ground. "I know he's a bit older, but I like that in a guy. And he was so… charming."

Nimue thought immediately of Ren, and how he didn't fit the bill at all. But then she wondered why that even mattered.

"So you dated. Not knowing he was married?"

"I found that out last night." She cocked her head. "I didn't know witches could look at the past like that."

"You saw that?"

"Through the peephole." She gestured toward the door. "But what did that matter? I *lived* it."

"So when Rona came out and found you two together…"

"She was livid. She shouted that he was a cheater. Sherman scrambled after her. I was in shock…" She sighed. "I talked to

Rona first. She was *my* guest, after all, even if Sherman helped me book her."

"He *did?*"

"He asked his agent for me—said they shared an agent. I doubt most agents bother listening to random booksellers' requests without an in like I had."

"They *used to* share an agent," said Nimue. "Rona got another agent about five years ago."

"Another lie," spat Nicola. "She was his *wife*. He probably just asked her. As a favor to me. And she had her agent contact me. Sherman knew my shop was on its last legs, and though he'd do another signing for me, I needed something bigger." She shook her head. "I never could have imagined it would lead to all of this."

"But if Sherman asked Rona himself… Rona acted as if she hadn't even known he'd be here!"

Nicola shrugged. "I don't know what to tell you. I knew Sherman was signing with the Delgados—after he snagged me Rona, I didn't care that he wasn't signing at my booth. I just wanted him here so we could sneak in a few romantic moments." She sniffled. "But I never told Rona about Sherman. I had no idea she had any opinion on the man until we arrived here yesterday."

"He didn't tell you not to mention him to her?" Nimue wondered.

"Well... He didn't want me talking about our relationship with anyone. So no, I wasn't about to discuss it with this author I hardly knew. Especially not after I saw how much she hated him. At that point, keeping her happy was most important. Without her signing, everything I'd sunk into this trip, the booth rental, the travel expenses, the extra stock, was going to put me in a hole I'd never recover from." She looked back outside the window.

"Well, at least we can definitely say she wouldn't have wanted Rona dead. Not before the signings."

Or ever, I hope, Nimue thought back.

"I, uh, wanted to ask you about something else." She shuffled the badges around her neck, showing her Glinda's badge they'd found in Lola's room. "I saw you had this this morning..."

Nicola's eyes widened. "I lost that! I figured I dropped it somewhere…"

"Yeah." Nimue cleared her throat and decided not to bring up Lola and Shawna. Not just yet. "Near the teleportation pad in the convention center lobby? But why did you have it in the first place? It looked like Sherman shoved it under his door at you…"

"Yeah." She scratched the back of her neck. "He told me to take it and meet him near the teleportation pad in the lobby before the convention opened."

"Why?" Nimue asked.

"I thought to talk about things. I knew Rona lived alone, so I thought maybe they'd separated. Maybe he'd explain it all and there was still a shot…" She shook her head. "I didn't know. I wanted to forgive him for lying to me…"

"Why did he give you that badge?"

"He told me to give it back to the Director of Guest Services if I saw him first. He had *something to do* before then."

"Linden?" Nimue cocked her head, fingering the badge. "Linden Varlett?"

She shrugged. "I didn't ask his name.

Sherman used it while on the behind-the-scenes tour and forgot to give it back."

It had to have been Linden. But why had Linden dug through Glinda's locker to grab her badge so Sherman could use it? True, they didn't have all-access guest badges since there was typically no need to bring anyone into the employees-only sections, but to swipe a badge from another employee who was gone for the week?

When, as long as Sherman was with Linden, he should have been able to access any place?

And then to forget to take the badge back…

Nimue would have to talk to Linden about that. And Ren, for allowing this behind-the-scenes excursion in the first place.

"I hoped the staff found it." Nicola offered a flittering smile.

Nimue stared down at Glinda's badge, and a strange feeling overcame her. During the History Charm illusion Merga had cast on the item storage alcove, there'd been a flash of red in the dark. Could it have been the teleportation pad, off in the background?

But red indicated travel to or from the employees-only lounge.

A place for Sherman to hide and retreat, away from prying eyes?

"But Lola had the badge by then," Gowdie pointed out. *"And before that, Sherman himself gave Nicola the badge to return. Hardly seems like it was part of his master plan."*

Blast, the dragon was right.

"Have you seen Sherman since this morning?"

Nicola stiffened. "Not when he promised to meet me, before the con. But he did show up about an hour ago, here, at my room."

Nimue jumped up. "We've been looking for him! He gave his security the slip!"

"Security?" Nicola's face grew ashen. "Is Sherman in danger, too?"

"Sherman *is* the danger!" Nimue paced around the room, thinking. "He killed Rona!"

Nicola let out a gasp. "He would never!"

Nimue froze. "But you said yourself.

They hated each other—and if they were married, she was standing in the way of him marrying you."

The bookseller drummed her fingers on the table beside her. "I'm sure he had no intention of ever marrying me."

Gowdie flew over and landed on the table in front of Nicola, looking up at his witch. *"Don't forget if she died—if he didn't smooth things over with her—he'd lose his cash cow. Both via her own royalties and royalties he'd earn for future Sherman Abbott thrillers."*

"But if she died before she divorced him, he'd inherit her fortune, as her spouse," Nimue pointed out.

"No." Nicola shook her head. "He laid it all out for me when he came by—to apologize for leading me on. Yes, they were married, almost thirty-five years."

"So almost as soon as he met her. After they argued in that class—" added Gowdie.

After she told him he was a terrible writer. He extolled her genius.

"And, what, he charmed her into becoming his wife?"

Apparently.

"I wonder if he always intended to have her write for him or if there was ever any love between them?"

She had to love him, Nimue pointed out. *Or why ghostwrite for him? Why not take the credit for herself? She could have even still used a pen name if she wanted to keep it separate from her cozies. Just without a face to put to the name.*

"He said he loved her—at first," Nicola explained. "But that love had died long ago. She belittled him constantly. He thought she could do better than write 'fluff,' but it was her idea in the first place to have him pose as the author of her more 'serious' works."

"It was?" *Why?* Nimue wondered.

Nicola held out a finger to Gowdie, who sniffed it and allowed her to scratch along his cheeks. "She thought they'd sell better with his male face attached to them. He always wanted to be a writer anyway. But over time… He took it too far. He admitted as much. Even criticizing the works she put out under her own name, but that was because he thought her works as Sherman Abbott deserved more accolades. She worked harder on them, he said." She took a deep breath. "But she wouldn't *get credit* if those books did well. She'd grown to resent him for it, for hogging the spotlight. They argued a lot, even amidst happier days, so they'd each agreed to having their own living spaces. Eventually, he just spent more and more time in his separate place. He'd told me he was new in town when he first contacted me, but he'd had a condo there for ages. He was just living there full-time now."

"But she kept writing—as Sherman *and* as Rona."

"It was what she loved to do," Nicola said. "And he loved all the attention. It brought in more money they split between them both, but…"

"But what?"

"He mentioned she'd written him out of her will, after the Super Chilling Award mess. Her husband he may have been on paper, but he was not to inherit a dime of her money as Rona Brynhild."

"So if she died, he'd only have the Sherman Abbott earnings," Nimue said. It hadn't seemed like Clint Moore the agent had even been aware they'd been one and the same, from the way Virgil had put it. It would have made just Rona splitting off to work with a new agent stranger, if he knew she was still his client under a different name. "And no more Rona to ghostwrite future books…"

"I don't think he'd get even the Abbott royalties." Nicola snorted. "Apparently, she told him there were instructions in her will for her lawyers to reveal the truth upon her death and pursue claims against him. He wasn't sure if her lawyers would even have a case, considering she'd willingly ghost-written, but he didn't want to find out…"

The more Nimue learned, the less it seemed likely Sherman would look forward to Rona's death.

"So if not to free himself to marry Nicola or to inherit Rona's money, why would he kill her?" Gowdie asked, flapping his wings as Nicola began to wring her hands. *"They just pushed each other one step too far? A crime of passion?"*

It took several smashes of that hammer,

Nimue pointed out to him. *He'd have to have held on to his rage for long enough to see her death through.* And he hadn't been seen at the scene of the crime. He couldn't have retreated to the employees-only lounge without that badge, either.

"He… He didn't know she was dead." Nicola's voice grew quiet. "I thought he'd been told. Ren told *me*… but he just thought she was sulking. She was supposed to meet him in the park early this morning so he could smooth things over, he said. He waited and waited and she never showed, but that was typical of her, he explained. He mentioned one of the other authors getting a death threat and con security overreacting…. But he wanted to check on Rona and then talk to me, and he didn't want security following him to either Rona's or my room. He'd knocked on her door first and she hadn't answered. I told him."

"He really didn't know?" Nimue's heart pounded wildly.

"He fell to the ground and sobbed. I tried to comfort him, but he brushed me away. He stumbled right out that door and then I knew… I knew he still loved her. At least part of him."

Gowdie cocked his head at Nicola. *"So either he's a great actor or…"*

"He didn't kill her," Nimue said aloud.

Nicola shook her head. "You're sure it wasn't an accident?"

"I'm sure," Nimue said softly.

Nicola swallowed and shook her head. "Poor Rona… Despite everything, I feel sorry for her. And even Sherman."

A thought struck Nimue. "But then… the hammer?"

That snapped Nicola out of her reverie. "Hammer…?"

"There was a hammer in Sherman's suitcase," Nimue explained.

"That… makes no sense," said Nicola. "I doubt he brought one along for the convention."

"He could have stolen it from somewhere around the con," Gowdie pointed out.

But we don't use hammers. We use magic, Nimue thought back to him. She pulled out her wand. *I'm sure there are some human tools somewhere in town, but if we ever actually need tools, it's far easier to…*

She stopped, staring down at her wand.

Willow had disguised her wand as a ruler. Wands *could* be transformed, but few witches or warlocks ever felt the need to.

But seeing the hammer smash the perma-charm crystal in that vision of the past didn't preclude a witch or warlock from having done it. She'd been so foolish to ever think such a thing! Not only were they capable of acquiring the tool from a town as near as Huntsville, their own wands could transform into human tools!

"What does a hammer have to do with anything?" Nicola asked.

"Did someone come by before? With con security?" Nimue asked.

"I guess…?" Nicola tapped her chin. "Not to my room, but to Sherman's. Not too long after Sherman was here. They knocked, and I wasn't sure if it was my door or the room next door at first, so I peeked out of the peephole to see if it was Sherman come back or Soren"—Nimue winced at the mention of her colleague—"but it was hotel staff."

"Fidelity?" Nimue asked. He'd mentioned Zelena having sent someone to search for Sherman in his room. "The young man I was with just outside this room?"

"Yeah…" Nicola said. "I remember him. And his lizard."

But surely, Fidelity couldn't have…?

"That young warlock is an open book," Gowdie assured her. *"And Rhutwine could never keep a secret the likes of framing someone for murder from me."* He shook his head. *"There are only a few familiars who are capable of…"* He went quiet, cocking his head.

"He wasn't alone," Nicola said. "It was hard for me to see who was with him, but he was talking to someone."

"A woman?" Nimue wondered.

Whose familiar's mind was slow, who could keep Gowdie from getting a good read on things?

A sloth.

"I don't think… Well, maybe? If she has a deep voice?" Nicola said, tapping a finger to her chin.

Zelena Varlett did. She had the strong, deep voice of an alto singer.

"Whoever was with that hotel employee was the one who went inside Sherman's room to check. Fidelity stood outside in the hall the whole time. I saw it."

"Told you it wasn't him," Gowdie said.

She rolled her eyes. She hadn't thought it for more than a second.

"But you didn't see exactly who came out of Sherman's room?" Nimue asked.

Nicola shook her head. "I heard the door shut and their voices carried down the hall. I didn't think much more about it and walked away from the peephole."

Could Zelena have framed Sherman by dropping the hammer amongst his things?

She knew Nimue was looking for a human suspect—with a hammer. She knew Nimue kept asking for the security team to find Sherman Abbott specifically.

He'd be the perfect patsy if it'd really been her to do the deed.

"Broomsticks!" Nimue shouted. She'd been alerting Zelena to her every move.

But *why*? Why kill Rona to begin with?

Beneath their feet, the very ground began to rumble.

"What's that?" Nicola gripped the table edge as if it would save her.

"I think… I think it's the cauldron. Something's wrong with the convention's energy."

"I don't understand."

But Nimue didn't have time to explain it.

She slapped at the crystal at her wrist to bring up the witch network. A message from Cassie blinked at her, so she opened it.

Cary checked in, said he lost sight of Wayne Gomez.

Nimue's stomach went fluttery.

Where's Zelena? she messaged back. Were other authors really in danger? *What's going on that may have caused the cauldron to bubble? Did something happen to Wayne?*

"Bubbling" was how her grandmother described it, the rumbling of the cauldron beneath the soil as it filled with the wrong kind of energy from the con-goers above.

Cassie wrote back. *She's not answering my messages.*

If only Nimue hadn't used her Communication Charm up for the day.

"What's going on?" Nicola asked.

"Stay here!" Nimue said. "And don't open the door for anyone until I get back."

"*Is* Sherman in danger?"

Was he? He was missing, too. Along with Wayne. And Ren.

Only Ren didn't fit the pattern of missing or endangered authors.

"I hope not," was all Nimue said before rushing to the door.

SEVEN

"*Nim, you saved your History Charm all day. Why not use it for this?*"

Gowdie flew ahead of Nimue down the hall, floating in a circle in front of Sherman's door.

That was the question. What to use it for?

Sherman had left Nicola's room not too long before. Could she use her History Charm and follow his path, see where he had gone? Could she stop herself from walking into something when she couldn't even see herself in the illusion? She'd never used a History Charm and moved much within it before.

Of course, Sherman wasn't her primary suspect anymore. But still, perhaps his path could lead Nimue to discover what had happened to Wayne and even Ren as well?

If Zelena was picking off people one by one, and this time, keeping the murders less showy…

No. She couldn't be murdering more people, could she?

Not if Ren was among the missing. *Soren…*

Nimue ran down the hall toward the elevators.

Gowdie was a little slow to follow her. *"What about Sherman's room? Aren't you going to see who went into that room to plant the hammer?"*

"Who else could it have been?" Nimue asked, pushing the button for the elevator to go down. "Zelena knows all about my investigation. And she hates me. She's trying to confuse me, throw me off the scent while she makes this entire convention crumble. I bet if we performed the History Charm outside of Lola and Shawna's room, we'd find her delivering the threatening letter, too. No wonder she pretended the Origin Charm hadn't worked on it!"

The door opened and she stepped inside. Gowdie flew in and settled on her shoulder as she jammed her wand against the first-floor button.

"Maybe it's better I touch base with Cary. We can use my History Charm to track where he lost Wayne. Sherman could be anywhere, maybe not even in immediate danger. At least we know Wayne wouldn't have intentionally given his guard the slip like Sherman. Something tells me if we find him, we'll find answers." She brought up her witch network connection to send Cary a message.

He, unlike most everyone right now, messaged back almost right away.

Bessa lobby, he wrote.

She brushed past a group of businesspeople listening to a man drone on about "the state of the industry" and "sales numbers" to step through the teleportation pad. The light flashed brown.

Her eyes scoured the convention center lobby, which was rather empty as the sun began its descent in the early evening. The showroom was just an hour or so from closing for the day. Humphrey was behind the concierge desk, and as she turned the corner, scouring for Cary, she found Merga still behind the item storage counter, swiping at her phone. There was nothing but empty racks behind her.

Nimue looked up. What there was left in item storage was back overhead.

"The crystal is fixed?"

Merga jumped as Nimue's voice echoed out over the empty space. She slid her phone on the table in front of her. "Yeah, Linden delivered it. Bernadette swung by with both crystals about twenty minutes ago." She tilted her chin slightly upward. "Didn't take long to get everything re-maining back up there. Most people are on their way out of the con for the day. Or—they were."

"Were?" Nimue looked around. Her grandmother was nowhere to be found. Had she really swung by and dropped off the replacement perma-charm crystal and gone on her merry way?

"Crystals," Gowdie pointed out, taking his favorite fluffy perch on Spandemager the llama's back whenever he was in his vicinity. *"She brought more than one. She wouldn't have stopped to make a new item storage crystal before she'd finished the one she'd been working on, for one thing."*

"But the other crystal she was working on..." Nimue said, more to Gowdie than Merga.

But Merga picked up what she'd been saying. "Yeah, the Book Scene Booth! It's a hit!"

Nimue blinked—hard. "It's... operational?" But they hadn't even tested it.

"Herne messaged me about it." Merga held up her wrist and the blinking perma-charm crystal affixed there. "I asked for some relief so I could give it a whirl, but the line is too long, anyway, he said. And right now Soren is—"

Nimue slammed her palms against the table and Merga, Spandemager, and Gowdie alike jolted.

"Soren's there?"

"So says Herne. A couple of guests went

first, but things went a little rocky, so now he's testing it."

Nimue spun on her heel, her boots echoing out across the floor as Gowdie soared above her and slid onto her shoulder. She practically bowled Morpheus down and noticed he was talking to Cary.

But she didn't have time to talk to Cary just yet. Not until she got Soren—Ren, whichever was there—to help her.

"Boss!" Morpheus cried, but she kept going, passing Nicola's empty booth.

Virgil was chatting with a customer in his own booth, leaning on one of his shelves. He held up a finger to the woman and walked to the edge of his booth as Nimue passed by. "Weren't you looking for Sherman?"

Nimue stopped, practically skidding to a halt on the brown carpet fixed in place just for Bookshop Con.

"Is he there?" Nimue asked. Gowdie flapped his wings behind her head. Morpheus and Cary hadn't followed her, so whatever they'd wanted mustn't have been that important.

"No." Virgil looked over his shoulder, as if he thought maybe he'd be proven wrong and the elusive author had snuck up behind him. "But he stopped by since you were last here, grabbed a couple of books from his stash—"

"So he did grab that book he'd had there. The ARC signed to him with love from his wife." Gowdie shook his head. *"Was that before or after he saw Nicola?"*

Probably before, she said. *He swung by after he gave Cary the slip, on his way back to the hotel. Then he tossed it inside his luggage before screwing up his courage to try to talk to Rona—and failing that, Nicola.*

"Thanks," Nimue said. "If he shows up, tell him to stay here. Or flag down one of the staff." She pointed at Morpheus and Cary, who were still in discussion at the con's badge checkpoint. "They can message me."

She didn't wait for his response, heading down past the rather empty aisle between booths and nearly screaming when the illusion of Kitt the Spy jumped out ahead of her.

"Hi! I'm Kitt the Spy! I go on adventures all around the world, and my parents have no clue! Would you like to learn more about my books?"

Nimue swatted it away and turned the corner, headed to where the buzz of conversation grew louder. A long line had formed along the curtains leading to Booth 3F. The area Soren, in his flight of fancy, had put aside for the Book Scene Booth.

"Esteemed guests, I'm afraid to say we won't have time to take any more participants today." Linden stood in front of the booth instead of Herne, his smile broad even when delivering bad news. "Please make your way to the rest of the showroom floor or head to the exit. The showroom will close in less than an hour. There's always tomorrow and another bright day at Witchy Expo Services presents: Bookshop Con!"

The crowd let out a series of sad moans as they shuffled and dispersed. The ground rumbled just slightly beneath them, causing a series of gasps in the crowd, and Nimue pushed herself through, tossing out "Excuse me!" over and over.

The cauldron was feeding on the crowd's disappointment.

"What's going on here?" she snapped as she pulled up beside Linden. She hadn't meant to be so rude to the unflappable man who always had a smile on his face, but she was anxious and lightheaded after a day of chasing after people who didn't want to be found, all while letting the *real* culprit loose to hurt others.

As Dyer the chinchilla climbed up her warlock's leg and torso to rest on his shoulder, Linden held both his hands out in front of him. "Now, I know what you're going to say—"

"I'm going to say this-this *event* is leading to bad vibes for the cauldron!" She hissed the last part, looking over her shoulder to see if any of the crowd was paying attention to her. But most of the curious looks sent her way were focused at the curtain behind her, trying to get a peek.

"Yes, now, but once the event is fully up and running—"

"*Why* is this up and running?" Nimue

tossed her hands up. "I didn't give approval—"

"It was *your* idea. So Soren and Herne told me."

Gowdie let out a little croak at Dyer, a conversation passing between them Nimue sensed had to do with how this event had been opened and what had happened before they'd arrived.

Dyer, trembling as rodents did, tucked her head behind Linden.

"It was my idea, but not without testing it! Not after… After…"

Linden clasped his hands together in front of his waist. "I thought we established that what went wrong with the item storage crystal wasn't connected to your hovering books idea."

Nimue frowned. Yeah, now she knew exactly what had *gone wrong*. "Have you seen Zelena?"

"Not since lunch." Linden cleared his throat. "She's stretched a bit thin today. Herne, too." He grinned.

How much did he know?

She pointed behind him. "Is Soren in there?"

"He's testing it, as you said he should."

She went to push past Linden, but he stopped her, clutching one arm. She twisted out of the grip of his left hand, his white glove catching on Gowdie's talon and peeling off. There was a scar there on his hand she'd never noticed before. Faint, but pale against his otherwise tanned skin. It was in the shape of—if she wasn't seeing things—a witch's hat.

"Or a triangle with an extra-long base?" Gowdie suggested, shaking his foot to get the glove to fall to the floor.

Doesn't Zelena have a scar on that same hand?

"The illusion is active," Linden said, interrupting her thoughts as Dyer scrambled down to pick up his glove. She scurried back up and held it out to him in her mouth. He didn't look at her as he moved to slip it back on. Something against his palm caught the light overhead before the glove was back in place. "If you step in there, the perma-charm won't be available to change to whatever book scene you seek. You'll step right into the scene at play."

"I'm not going in for *fun*," she said. "I just need to see Soren—"

She pushed his hand aside and drew back the curtain.

The wind sang, rustling across the endless expanse of dour moors in front of her like a wailing specter.

Gowdie's jaw dropped as the curtain moved back in place behind them.

Nimue spun around. Even the curtain was gone. It looked as if she'd stepped into an endless field, dipping and misty, going on far beyond the horizon.

"Jane!" cried a voice, deep and harrowing, joining in the winds.

"*Jane Eyre*," said Nimue softly, with reverence.

"*Check it out.*" Gowdie tapped his talon against her shoulder.

Against the shoulder of the plain, long-sleeved dress she wore, which reached down to her ankles, the hem covered in mud.

Gowdie let out a little sneeze.

She took a look at him. He was covered in fluffy dog fur, his little dragon face the only bit normal about him. Otherwise, it looked as if a large dog sat upon her puffy-sleeved shoulder.

"Pilot," she said.

"*I don't think I need to learn how to be one,*" he quipped. "*Since flying comes naturally for me.*"

"Pilot's—"

"*The dog, I know.*" Gowdie used his doggy hind leg to scratch his chest. "*I read all your favorite books with you, remember? A witch and her familiar—*"

"Are always together," Nimue finished for him. She gave his chin a little scratch and lifted her skirts. "Almost always."

"Jane," cried Mr. Rochester over the winds. Only his voice—was too familiar.

"Ren?" she cried out, taking a careful step forward down the craggy moor. Though she knew it was all an illusion, she could feel the uneven ground, the dip she took as she moved downward. Her grandmother had outdone herself with this perma-charm. "Soren?"

"Jane!" cried Mr. Rochester's spirit. "Lydia…" That name, he spoke quieter.

"Soren?" Nimue called. Her chest tugged tightly at the sound of her colleague's—her friend's—sadness.

"Nimue?" Her own name carried out over the endless grasses. Only this time, it seemed focused behind her.

She spun around and found the moors around her changed. Instead, she stood in front of a crackling fire in a dark room, the stone tiles below her feet, the stone hearth indicative of a mid-nineteenth century English home.

In a high-backed plush chair before the fire sat a man, dressed in a fine suit contemporary to the period in question, high-collared with a strip of purple silk tied in a knot at his Adam's apple. His blond hair wasn't sleeked, but there was some method to its frequent madness, swept over one ear.

At his feet, a rather sour-faced Balfour was curled up in fur rather like Gowdie's own Pilot-dog costume, a little-faced cat in the middle of an oversized dog frame.

"Nimue," Soren said softly, every bit Mr.

Rochester, down to the surly lips, the pompous way he looked down at her even when seated and gazing up. Nimue realized with a start that meant, despite the wavy hair, she was actually looking at *Ren*. "'Tell me now, fairy as you are. Can't you give me a charm, or a filter, or something of that sort, to make me a handsome man?'"

He'd quoted the book.

Nimue found her face flushing at his line. "Ren, you—"

Gowdie nudged her. *"Quote it back. You know you can."*

"I... 'It would be past the power of magic, sir. A loving eye is all the charm needed: to such, you are handsome enough. Or rather, your sternness has a power beyond beauty.'" She took a deep breath, letting the magic of living the moment, the awkward beginnings of a harrowed romance, slip out of her, returning her to the present. Though it galvanized her a little to remember that even nearing two hundred years ago, human authors like Charlotte Brontë had written of the world's magic in a story of love between humans. "What have

you been doing all day? We need to find Zelena." She took a step forward, but Balfour
hissed, drawing her to a halt.

Gowdie hissed back, and Nimue could
hear the flap of his wings even if she
couldn't see them behind the dog costume
illusion.

"She says to—watch out!" Gowdie
screamed in Nimue's head.

Nimue turned around as Gowdie did to
find—dressed like Mrs. Fairfax, the older
housekeeper in the book—Zelena Varlett
herself.

CHAPTER TWENTY-EIGHT

"Where's Wayne Gomez?" Nimue asked, whipping her wand out from its holster. She couldn't see it until she'd held it in her hands. "Did you take Sherman Abbott, too?"

Nimue shuffled backward, standing beside a hissing Balfour. "Ren, watch out," the Head Witch Co-General Manager said. "She killed Rona!"

Gowdie flew overhead with wings made invisible by the book scene illusion.

"Nimue…?" Ren asked. "Jane. Lydia…" His eyes were clouded, his gaze focused ahead of him.

Balfour hissed.

"He hasn't been himself—either of himselves —for hours," Gowdie translated for Balfour. *"First he was Befuddled Charmed, then stuck into a closet, then thrust into this book illusion."*

Zelena, carrying a tray with tea cups, as if no more than an innocent nineteenth-century housekeeper, slid the tray down on a table in front of Ren and started pouring from the pot. "Your tea, sir." She picked up a tea cup by its saucer and extended it with both hands toward Nimue. "And Miss Eyre."

Around her neck, at first not even noticeable because she seemed to be dressed up to resemble a wool shawl of some short, Messenger the sloth moved one arm slowly, slowly out, pointing a finger.

"I'm not taking—" Nimue started, but Ren grabbed for the tea and took it to his lips as Zelena went back to pour another cup.

"Don't!" Nimue called, snatching the tea right out of Ren's hand.

"Miss Eyre, why *really...*" Ren said. There was something in the way his lips upturned just slightly, as if he were amused.

"Nim, Zelena's eyes are clouded," Gowdie said, flapping and not yet spraying the Convention Security Manager with any fiery attack. *"Balfour doesn't know who got Ren befuddled like this, either."*

As if to agree, the cat let out a hiss, jumping up on Ren's lap.

"Pilot!" Ren snapped. "Down! Bad dog!"

Balfour sulked back to the stone hearth and paced in front of the fire.

Zelena, a wan smile on her face, held out another cup of tea to Ren, who took it and thanked her. Messenger's slow-moving arm extended out from the illusion of the shawl to point, point, point behind her.

Nimue brought the cup of tea she held to her nose. It smelled aromatic. Like lemon and black tea.

But it could have been anything. It could have been nothing. This was all an illusion and she didn't have time to be drinking tea.

She tossed her cup into the fire, which snapped as the glass smashed against the hearth.

Zelena let out a little cry. "Miss Eyre! Mr.

Rochester, I am so sorry I hired this woman. She's devoid of manners."

"I can see that." Ren shook his head just slightly and held back the hint of a snort. "But perhaps that's what we're missing at Thornfield Hall."

Nimue reached over to grab his cup of tea and threw that in the fire, too.

"*Miss Eyre!*" Zelena cried.

What was it that had triggered Ren's change into Soren earlier that day?

Emotions he didn't like to deal with. Nicola seeking solace in a friend's arms.

Nimue bent down and wrapped her arms around the stiff-backed Ren in his Mr. Rochester attire, leaning her cheek against the top of his head. Though she couldn't see it in the illusion, she could feel the brim of her wide witches' hat bend against his scalp.

"Wake up," she said softly. "Soren."

Balfour meowed pitifully, kneading her costume dog paws against the hearth.

"Scandalous!" Zelena said. She stepped backward, not taking her eyes off of the simple hug on display. "Improper!" Messenger's arm had stopped moving backward now and was slowly, ever so slowly, shaking up and down.

"Nim, I'm picking up on Messenger's thoughts—for once. She says—"

"Nimue?" Ren's—Soren's—hand went up to pat Nimue's arm. He stood, swirling around, his hair even messier than before as it draped over his eyes.

Balfour let out a little meow, rubbing against Soren's legs.

"It wasn't Zelena!" Gowdie shouted in Nimue's mind.

Nimue swept her wand out, but as she did, the fireplace and warm hearth faded away, replaced by a dreary alleyway. The moon shone overhead.

Nimue looked down and found her long dress had transformed. Now she was wearing a red dress that came down to her knees with sleeves that ended at her elbows and gave way to white gloves that went up most of her forearm. The dress hugged her curves in a way that was certainly not appropriate in the setting of *Jane Eyre*. On her head, she felt her witches hat, but when she looked into the reflection of a small glass window on a nearby door, she saw a red pillbox hat instead, complete with black veil that covered one eye. Her hair fell over her shoulders in voluptuous waves.

"Soren?" she cried out. "Gowdie?"

She spun around at the sound of a little hiss coming from behind a trash can. She almost screamed when a giant rat scuttled out, only she saw it had Gowdie's face.

"Well, at least you look nice," he said. *"Like a club singer from the 1930s."*

She held her arm out for him and he scuttled up. She tried not to wince at the sight of a giant rat climbing up her leg and torso.

"You have wings still," she pointed out.

Gowdie the costumed rat looked to the side of him. The air was struck with flapping noises. *"So I do. I guess I forgot that since I can't see them."*

"Grandma's perma-charm works well. *Too* well." Nimue bit her lip, clutching her wand in her hand tighter. A wand she could still see. "I'm… actually scared right now." She took a step down the long alleyway, her heels splashing through a small puddle of dirty water. "Where's Soren?"

Gowdie sniffed the air. *"I'm picking up on Balfour—just up ahead. Around the corner!"*

Nimue didn't know why she didn't just rush forth, running to her only ally in this place. But her feet moved slowly, careful to make as little noise as possible.

"What book is this?" Nimue asked.

Overhead, a set of sirens went off that echoed loudly for miles around them.

"Don't know," admitted Gowdie. *"But that can't be good! Run!"*

Nimue bolted forward, the siren warring with the thumping of her heart to block out all other noise.

"Ici! Vite!" a man with a gun strapped over his shoulder jumped out at the end of the aisle and waved her on.

"Sher… Sherman?" Nimue gasped.

As she neared, she saw his eyes were clouded over and he kept waving her toward him.

"Vite, vite!" said another man, also with a gun over his arm. They were both dirty, their clothes tattered. They didn't look at all

like soldiers. More like the scattered components of… a resistance.

"Wayne Gomez!" Gowdie said.

So it was. Both missing authors were here, alive—trapped in this illusion.

They were both speaking French in hushed, whispered tones, leading Nimue forward down the block.

Overhead, the engines of airplanes echoed out into the night.

"Where are we—?" started Nimue, but her question was silenced by an explosion that rocked the distance.

"Mettez-vous à couvert!" Sherman called, laying her flat against the ground.

Nimue's ears rang, her vision growing dizzy, but she didn't have a chance to catch her breath before Sherman was back on his feet, Wayne holding his hand out to her and pulling her up. They ran, around the corner, and down into a cellar.

Sherman turned and barred the door at the top of the stairs behind them, Wayne working quickly to drag crates up onto the upper steps, acting like some sort of buffer against intrusion.

In the dank cellar, a single overhead bulb swayed as the night sky shook. Dust trickled down from the ceiling, and a chorus of little gasps and cries directed Nimue's attention to the corner.

People huddled there between shelves stocked sloppily with threadbare sacks of flour and cans of food—a variety of men, women, and children. Beside them, Soren, dressed in dirty, mismatched clothes like Sherman and Wayne beside him, a gun dangling from his arm, spun around.

"Nimue!"

He had a giant rat at his feet, too. One with the grumpy face of cat poking out from it.

"Soren! What's going on?" Nimue sidled up next to him. "Who are these people?"

"Just illusions, I think," Soren said. "Part of the book. I… I've been trying to talk to them. They're all speaking French."

Sherman and Wayne conferred in French near the staircase, in harsh, sharp whispers.

"What book is this?" Nimue asked, louder this time. She didn't care if anyone heard her. She didn't need to play along.

No sooner had she thought that than another boom, louder this time, rang out overhead.

"I… I'm not sure," Soren admitted.

Sherman approached Nimue, slapping a dirty hand on her shoulder. She jumped and let out a little yelp.

"You," he said in accented English, "are you our contact? The blood moon flies…"

Nimue blinked rapidly at him. Sherman was inhabiting a character from the book, that much was clear.

And Nimue was, too. She looked down at her dress, at the crowd on the ground beside her. It seemed like she'd just stepped out of a nightclub while these people had been crawling under the streets for weeks. What was she supposed to be? A singer?

"The blood moon flies!" said Sherman, practically shaking her.

Nimue's jaw dropped as she scrambled to think of what to say. Her gaze traveled to Sherman's hand. And there she saw a mark that was entirely familiar. Not a faded scar as she'd seen it, but freshly carved and still red and raw, as if with a knife.

The triangle with the longer third edge. The symbolic witches' hat, or so she'd thought it when she'd seen it on…

"Linden!" she cried. She swirled around.

Balfour let out a loud yowl.

"She says she's been sensing Dyer," Gowdie said. *"That her thoughts are scattered, but—"*

In the darkest corner of the huddle, a figure stood up. No longer trembling, ignoring the woman at his feet—Zelena, Nimue realized—who was clutching up at his legs. Dirt smeared his smiling face. And the back of his left hand, too, like Sherman's, was red and raw with the carved symbol. He turned it around to show her his palm. A small perma-charm crystal was… embedded into his flesh. Nimue had never seen such a thing.

"Useful, a perma-charm crystal for the Befuddled Charm, don't you think?" he asked. "I've had it… Well, since World War II."

Dyer the chinchilla blended in perfectly as a rat that wove around his legs.

"I take it you've never read *The Axis and the Witch Brigade*?" Linden asked. "Because you're Zethica Gala, my dear, and you're about to be outed as a witch double agent. Though of course you're using a code name. One perilously close to outing you, should someone know your family history."

Nimue removed the glove covering her left hand and saw the witches' hat scar carved into her skin, too. She'd seen this scar on a woman's hand before…

"The French Resistance suspected us of working for the Axis Powers," Linden said.

Soren took shaky steps to stand beside Nimue, clutching the illusory rifle with both hands, facing Linden.

"Something which I thought no one knew… No one alive, anyway."

"*Traîtresse!*" Wayne cried out.

As the sky shook again with another boom, dust fell down from the floorboards above, obscuring Nimue's view as Wayne Gomez launched at her with a knife in hand.

CHAPTER TWENTY-NINE

G owdie let out a burst of fiery smoke, sending Wayne stumbling.

"Careful!" Nimue called. "He's innocent."

Her back jutted up against Soren's as Sherman let out a cry and shoved his rifle at the warlock, who held his own up to clash against it. The two gritted their teeth and pushed hard forward.

"You have a wand!" Nimue shouted. "You can't see it, but it's in your holster."

"You mean this wand?" Linden called out. Dyer the chinchilla rat scrambled up his legs and torso to rest on his shoulder, a black wand Nimue recognized as Soren's caught between her teeth like a carrot. "Of course I didn't befuddle him and leave him with his wand."

Befuddle, thought Nimue. She turned toward Wayne, her wand waving. "Undo Befuddle Charm!"

Wayne the resistance soldier blinked, the dagger he'd been holding dropping to the floor.

Linden scoffed. "You can only do that once without a perma-charm. Though I do wonder how you broke Soren out of it…"

Wayne stared at his arms, at his clothing, at Nimue, at the scene around him. "What is this? Where am I?" He made for a rather old soldier now that she saw him closer in the flickering light. Though there'd probably been people of all ages in the Resistance.

"Illusion," Nimue explained, whipping around and gesturing for him to hide behind her back. "This is a book."

If only she could use her Undo Charm again, she'd take care of Sherman—and Zelena, too. If Zelena wasn't on her husband's side.

But if she were, why was she currently Befuddled?

"The Axis and the Witch Brigade," Wayne said. Nimue detected a hint of reverence in his voice. "It's… It's exactly how I explained things to Sherman… No, that was Rona, actually. That one time she asked that historical question out of the blue. The theory some scholars had about the darker role the American Witch Brigade played. Pretending to spy for the Allies when actually—"

"Spying for the Axis Powers," Linden finished for him. "I know. I was there."

Nimue swallowed, the only other sound in the air the grunting coming from Sherman as he forced Soren backward against a wall, using the force of their rifles together.

"You… *You* killed Rona!" Nimue screamed. Sweat dotted her palm as she gripped her wand tightly, a strange, soft feeling coiling around her wrist. On her shoulder, Gowdie let out another threating puff of smoke.

Soren let out a grunt. "Ren… figured that out… I think."

Balfour let out a wild yowl and leaped at Sherman from behind, sinking her teeth into the man's shoulder.

He cried out and shifted backward, allowing Soren to push forward and knock Sherman's gun to the ground.

Then he took the butt of his gun—the gun that should have just been an illusion—and knocked it against the back of the man's head.

Illusion or not, the man slumped down to the floor without another word.

"No, actually, it was Zelena who was getting suspicious," said Linden. "Former spy that she is... A real firecracker of a spy, and a firecracker of a woman." He gazed down at his wife. Perhaps with genuine affection. Zelena... Zethica... Descendant of Gala Varlett. "And she reported her suspicions to Ren—not you, of course, since she doesn't like you—making it so I had to take both of them captive."

Nimue scrambled to think of the last time she'd seen either of them. Hours before. "But I've been messaging Zelena all day," she said.

"I know. Thank you for the updates on your investigations." Linden pointed to his wife's wrist, where, if not for the illusion, they might have seen her perma-charm witch network crystal. "I've been befuddling her into responding this afternoon and planning to make Sherman my patsy as your suspicions centered around the wrong target. More than once, I might add."

Nimue scowled. It wasn't her fault so many people had been up to suspicious activity.

"Though I'd pegged him for a good patsy from the start. That was why I gave him Glinda's badge during the tour and 'forgot' to take it back from him. I figured if anyone *snooping around* found him with that badge that allowed him access behind the scenes, well, that might explain some of the fallen 'killer''s movements."

"You planned to kill Sherman and Wayne, too," Nimue said. She didn't bother telling him that Sherman had parted with the badge early this morning.

"Eventually. Once I'd spun it to look as if Sherman had regretted his actions this morning and took out another old friend, too. Once Bernadette dropped off the perma-charm, I thought the Book Illusion Booth would be a *fun* way to get it done. Maybe have the authors attack one another while caught up in the illusion. Maybe take out *every other* problem I had along the way in another *tragic, freak* accident."

Nimue shuddered to think of what—or whom—he considered *problems*. "But the note to Lola Jackson and Shawna Higgins—"

"A distraction," Linden said. "To make you think someone was targeting authors. I knew all about Miss Higgins's brush with a stalker of sorts in years previous. She confided in me about her concerns." His eyes went a little too wide, so he almost seemed mad. "Everyone confides in the amiable Director of Guest Services about their concerns when at a convention."

A little croak echoed out over the air behind the rumbling overhead and Dyer let out a series of angry chittering noises, looking down toward Zelena.

"That was Messenger talking," Gowdie

said in Nimue's head. *"Slow lass… She said Zelena knew Linden had written that letter as soon as she cast the Origin Charm, but she didn't want to tell you. Not until she could find out herself what he was up to."*

Nimue clenched her jaw. *And of course, once she finally felt like turning him in, she went to Ren, not me. She may not be a killer, but she helped one get away with things for at least a couple of hours.*

Gowdie let out a little growl and a series of clucks and chitters answered back.

"They really had no idea until then," Gowdie translated. *"And they wanted… They wanted to be sure before they accused them. Zelena loves her husband."*

Accused them? Nimue asked.

Gowdie's eyes narrowed. *"Dyer, too, of course."*

Right. In the History Charm of the moment in question, even though it'd been dark, Nimue still hadn't seen *any* shadowy figure. Just the hammer coming down on the item storage perma-charm crystal. The hammer wielded by—

She gasped. "Dyer smashed the perma-charm crystal!"

Linden scratched under her chin and the skittish chinchilla-rat leaned into the pets, relaxing for the first time in ages. "Only on my command, of course. We've worked together as a team for nearing a century."

"In the Witch Brigade?" Nimue asked.

Soren shuffled closer to her, his hand awkwardly positioned on his rifle, which he kept pointed at Linden.

Linden lifted up his hand, showing off the mark. "Yes. I was young, then. Idealistic."

"And there's… something in this book of Sherman's you don't want out there? But the book has been published for years—"

"Yes, and it was finally fading into the background of Sherman Abbott's successes. And yet, the streaming series is renewing interest in this book."

"There wasn't a lot of proof," said Wayne quietly behind her, "but some of the Axis's movements… And knowing the Witch Brigade was in touch with them under the guise of spying. Historians have had to wonder if they were actually helping them."

"Not the entire Witch Brigade." Linden spat. "We're not so easy to paint with broad strokes like Sherman Abbott does in his books. Or should I say Rona Brynhild did in *her* books—which she wrote under Sherman's name."

Wayne gasped. "The emails! I should have known."

"What's he talking about?" Soren asked.

So he hadn't met up with Nicola since Sherman's confession.

Actually, if Rona had been killed long *before* Sherman's confession…

"Did you always know Rona ghostwrote Sherman's books?" Nimue asked. "I didn't find out until after… her murder." She grit out the last few words.

"I've known for a long time. A long time." Linden waved his wand, tapping something off to the side Nimue couldn't see—and the illusion fell away, the sounds of war and terror dying out.

Everyone was wearing the clothes they'd last been seen in.

Linden stood over Zelena's crumpled form, her eyes still glazed. Herne was there, befuddled, beside her. He must have blended in with the illusory citizens. His familiar piglet, Ten Ham, was curled up in his arms, shivering.

They were on top of a wide area of mats Soren had installed earlier in the day, behind a curtain. Beyond it, the sounds of the showroom floor were quiet, confined mostly to the limpid chatter and scuffling associated with the end of the day at the Bessa, the sun almost completely setting through the skylight overhead.

Nimue slammed her wrist, ready to tag her perma-charm crystal.

Only it wasn't there.

That furry feeling she'd had at her wrist.

"Dyer got that too," Linden said, nodding at his familiar. Her chinchilla tail flicked up and on it was a perma-charm crystal. "Don't want you calling for help before I have my say."

"And then what?" Nimue snapped. "You kill all of us?" She gestured at the group, even Zelena. "Not even you could take us all alone. And you didn't get my wand." She held it out in front of her.

"Nimue," Soren whispered in her ear. "I can cause a distraction. You charge—"

"Stop!" Linden shouted, lifting his own wand overhead. "Explosion Charm."

Nimue's stomach dropped to the floor.

"What's… What's he doing?" Wayne asked.

"Don't. Move," said Soren.

Linden waved his wand back and forth, the magic settling at its tip in a bright orange glow. The moment he stopped swinging the wand, an explosion would rock the entire area around him. Its radius would depend entirely on his intentions, but Nimue had no doubt he'd extend it at least as far as making sure all of the witnesses to his treachery evaporated with it.

"But you'll die, too," she said.

"So be it." Linden's eyes flashed wildly and Dyer started shaking a bit again. He pet her limply with his free hand. "I'm sorry, old girl. I know explosions are hard on you after what we went through, but… For the sake of the Brigade. Let's see this through."

"Wait!" Nimue said, her mind scrambling for solutions. She couldn't have a complete conversation with Gowdie in her mind without risking Dyer translating it for Linden and making him set off his explosion. And Gowdie was planted on her shoulder. He wouldn't be able to move without Linden or Dyer noticing. She expressed as much to Gowdie, who didn't reply to her, other than to growl a bit and sink his talon into her shoulder. "I don't want to die before I know. How did *you* know about Rona writing as Sherman? No one did. Not even their agent."

Linden's hand faltered just slightly. "I was… a fan of hers. At one time, she was my favorite author. Probably still is, even after I figured it out."

"You like Sherman's gritty spy mysteries?" Soren asked.

"No, not *those*. Rona's books. A light, happy world without witches and magic at all. Funny, cheery, and a few murders. I took to them, as a customer service worker. Always keep a smile on your face, a bright attitude. And wish you could strangle a few necks without dirtying the world." He laughed darkly.

Nimue wondered if he'd killed before Rona—perhaps in the war. If it had changed him. Or if he'd always had this dark side.

She didn't ask.

"She left her writing cave, so to speak, about five years ago," Linden said. "Just the once."

"The signing at Delgado Books!" Nimue said. Wayne let out a little grunt, like he knew what she might have been referring to. "But that was cancelled."

"Only *after* Rona showed up. I was there, you know. First in line." His hand lowered, the orange light like a firefly in the dim neon glow of the overhead light far above them. "I saw her smack that bookstore worker—"

"Owner, actually," Nimue said.

His brow narrowed at the interruption. "I helped the other man pull Rona off of her. Got a black eye myself to thank for it. That woman just loved hitting, didn't she?"

So yesterday hadn't even been the first time Rona had smacked Linden. She wondered if that had been one of the final straws or if he'd planned her murder the moment she'd been announced as a guest.

"But it was *what* had set the woman off that intrigued me," said Linden. "The comparison of her work to Sherman Abbott's."

"But Sherman and Rona publicly disliked one another," Nimue said. "Though they were actually married in secret."

"*What?*" said Wayne.

"Seems like you discovered quite a bit today," Soren said quietly.

"Were they?" Linden laughed. "I had no idea. But I *did* know they had the same agent—or they did at the time. I read the books side by side, started seeing the comparison, though Abbott's books were grittier. Magic was ever-present but *wrong*. Witches and warlocks were always the bad guys."

"*He's not exactly proving that theory wrong,*" Gowdie pointed out.

Dryer chittered in response, but Gowdie snorted.

"And then I read it. *The Axis and the Witch Brigade*. I'd heard the title before, had brushed it off as another one of Sherman Abbott's flights of fancy, but the truth of the book hit too close to home. And it was really my favorite author, Rona Brynhild, who'd written it."

Beneath their feet, the cauldron rumbled, the positive energy of much of the day not enough to outweigh the negative energy Linden was seeping into the floor beneath him.

"Nimue—" Soren whispered.

"I know," she said back. She spoke louder, addressing Linden. "But the book was already out there by then. What did you think might happen? Someone might track you down?"

"No one knew the real identities of the Witch Brigade," said Wayne, his voice shaky. He straightened up behind Nimue, trying to put on a brave face. "No one would have found you."

"Except by this." Linden held up his left hand, the faded scar. "It was carved in with a perma-charm knife." He nodded at Dyer, who twirled around, dropping Nimue's perma-charm wrist crystal as

Soren's wand in her mouth transformed into a knife.

"It was a wand that acted as a hammer, wasn't it?" Nimue asked.

"Yes. There's more strength, more magic in such things. I'm not sure a regular hammer could even destroy a perma-charm crystal. But after you came up with your theory, well, it was simply a matter of finding a human hammer lying around in maintenance, one that had probably never seen any use but someone had brought along anyway for backup when charms were overused, and planting it in Sherman's room."

"You went with Fidelity into Sherman's room?" Nimue guessed.

"I did. Told him Zelena's team was over-worked—not a lie—and that she had sent me to look for the man." He tapped his thigh. "Had the hammer tucked under my pants and the kid didn't notice. I guess witches and warlocks aren't made like they used to be."

Nimue could hardly fault Fidelity for not examining the bulge in Linden's leg. He wouldn't have been looking for the Director of Guest Services to be up to anything nefarious.

Linden and Zelena Varlett had worked for Witchy ExS for decades. Since…

"You came here after the war?" she asked. "To work for Witchy ExS?"

"We did." Linden looked down at his wife softly, then snapped his attention past Nimue, to Wayne. "Did you know, historian, that my wife was Zethica the lounge singer, spy working on behalf of the Witch Brigade?"

Nimue's breath caught, though she'd put as much together. Had Zelena been in on it all, then? Then why was she befuddled right now?

Maybe she didn't agree with Linden going so far? He was about to kill them both along with the rest of the witnesses he'd gathered here.

Wayne swallowed. "No. Like I said, they were just theories. No one knew the Witch Brigade's true identities. No one even had pictures of them."

"But you knew about this." Linden shook his hand out again.

"There were written accounts," said Wayne quickly. "A drawing. That was it."

"Well, that explains why you got one thing wrong. Zethica never betrayed the Allies. None of the other Brigade did." His eyes narrowed on Wayne. "Only I did. See, I agreed with their thinking that humans were better than witches. Witches have too much power. It's unnatural. I just couldn't help what I'd been born as. And then… Well, I'd never met a witch I'd liked before Zelena. I stopped leaking secrets toward the end because of her. Because I wanted a life with her. An Ally hero of the war whom *you* besmirched."

Wayne shook his head. "I never… I never told Sherman—Rona—much, just those weak theories. He—She—would have made the rest up."

"I gathered." Linden frowned. "But it was too close to home. And then to hear they were making one of those human television dramas out of it, to bring that blasphemed story to the screen, to do some digging, and look at your *drawings* and see what this scar truly means... No. Some things are best left to wallow in the past."

Gowdie grumbled softly but stopped himself from saying anything.

"And now..." Linden lifted his wand, which he'd kept moving, the light leaving a trail behind it like a sparkler. "With the authors' deaths—the real author, the sham author—and the historian who helped them, no one will ever know."

"I'm not the only one who's seen those notes! That drawing!" Wayne protested. "Please! I have a family—"

Soren hushed him as the ground kept rumbling.

Linden laughed. "I might have cared. Back when I thought I could get away with it, that Zelena and I could go on living as we had been. Happily. Here in Cauldron Cove." His smile was that of a madman now, his face orange in the light of his moving wand. "I planned to kill you three at the convention, make it look like accidents. A stalker. Something."

"But that would ruin us!" said Soren. "If

you care so much about Cauldron Cove, you shouldn't have wanted to ruin a convention—"

"I know that now. And with you two being so nosy and Bernadette *retiring*…" He scoffed. "There's nothing left for me to fight for. Let them make their little human Internet show. Show off the Witch Brigade as villains, tarnish my wife's noble history… We'll be gone. And so will you. So will all of Cauldron Cove!"

"Now!" shouted Gowdie into Nimue's ear, and he took to the air.

She didn't know what he was calling for exactly, but she snapped into action, waving her wand. "Summon Charm!" she shouted, aiming it at the wand in Linden's hand.

At the same time, Zelena jumped up from where she'd been crumpled on the ground, tackling Linden at the knees and wrestling with him, knocking the wand transformed into the magical knife out of Dyer's mouth.

But Nimue had to focus on what she was doing. She caught Linden's wand as it came to her, the light glowing. It was red hot in her hand, and she screamed, but she wouldn't let it go.

"I can't undo it!" she shouted. "I used Undo!"

Another witch or warlock would know what she meant.

Soren grabbed her own wand from her and waved it at the glowing wand in her hand. "Undo Explosion Charm!" he shouted.

The tip of the orange-glowing wand caught on fire.

And then sputtered to a halt.

Nimue breathed deeply, staring at it.

A series of meows and shrieks and squeals rang out in front of them and Nimue turned to see Gowdie dive-bombing Linden on the ground as Zelena wrestled him to pin him, Balfour hissing and howling and biting at the warlock's ankles. Even Messenger the sloth had jumped on top of Dyer, keeping her pinned down.

"How could you?" Zelena screamed. Linden wasn't fighting back now. "You murderer! You traitor! What do you mean, you were working for the Axis?"

Linden chortled, a dark, hollow sound. "When did you regain consciousness?"

Zelena nodded her head slightly to Balfour, who growled and bit harder on his ankle.

"She nipped me awake halfway through your mad plan spilling out." She sniffed. "I can't believe I... I ever trusted you. That I gave you the benefit of the doubt, tried to see why you'd written that threatening letter... I'm sorry."

She said that part not to her husband, but to the two co-managers approaching behind her.

"I'm sorry," she said again. "I thought I knew... I thought I knew the man I married."

Nimue swallowed and bent down to pick up her witch network crystal, where it had scattered several feet from Linden's head.

"We thought we knew him, too," she said, tapping it to bring up her messages. Cary had asked her if she'd seen him in the lobby and if she still needed to meet with him. He still couldn't find Wayne or even

Zelena, but Morpheus had seen the latter, looking like she'd seen a ghost as she'd made her way to the employees-only floor after lunch.

"If my grandmother had found out about you being in the Brigade, do you think she would have fired you?" Nimue asked, after she'd sent her emergency message for all of security to converge on the Book Scene Booth for backup.

Linden looked away. "If she believed in Rona Brynhild's lies."

"But you said yourself you really were a double agent," Soren said.

Nimue took him in, his soft face, the sadness hiding in those eyes behind his bangs.

She realized something. Something she'd want to tell him soon.

Maybe he'd be stronger after realizing it, too.

"I wanted a world without witches and warlocks once," Linden said. "At least... I thought I did. And they were the side that was working toward that. I was caught up in the propaganda.

"I never should have... I'm sorry," he

said to Zelena. "Just know that… My love for you was real. And in the years since the war, I've regretted my actions every day."

"And yet you're still a murderer." Zelena scoffed and leaned back, but she didn't stand up and free him.

"That I am…" he said softly. "That I am."

The curtains leading to the showroom floor burst open, and in stormed Cary, Morpheus, Merga, Humphrey, Tituba, and half a dozen security witches and warlocks. Even Florence and her med team trickled in, wands at the ready to help whoever might need help for whatever had gone down.

They immediately went to work on Herne and Sherman, lying still as they were. Ten Ham had roused, rubbing her snout against her warlock's cheek.

Nimue had called and they'd all come—because they were a team, and she was one of their leaders.

She gazed up at the giant tree that wove its way through Cauldron Cove, spiraling up and through the buildings that had been built all around it.

The ground was quiet now, the buried cauldron at rest.

She made a promise to it, then, in her heart.

They'd weed out the bad seeds and come together as a team. They'd make the conventions better than ever.

If the cauldron would only grant them the magic they'd need to get through the coming blowback.

CHAPTER THIRTY

"Auntie, you have to come! You have to come!"

Little five-year-old Oscar Jonesdochter was literally hanging off of his aunt, Tituba, outside of the Book Scene Booth on Sunday, the last day of Bookshop Con for the year.

"There's Alice and the Treasure Cat—"

"The Cheshire Cat?" suggested Tituba as she settled her nephew into her arms. He looked a lot like his father, who in turn looked a lot like his older sister, so he was a bit like the echo of Tituba, only with slightly shorter coiled hair.

"Yeah, the Chester Cat," he said. Tituba sent a wry grin over his head to Nimue.

"And the Mad Hatter and the White Rabbit and the Queen of Hearts—"

"That's a *lot* of characters in one book scene!" Nimue remarked.

Oscar turned around and his jaw dropped, reaching out for Gowdie on Nimue's shoulder.

"Dragon!" He knew the dragon familiar well, but he lit up every time he saw him. Gowdie let out a little puff of smoke and Oscar squealed. Tituba set him down and Gowdie took to the air, flying in circles overhead as Oscar chased him this way and that across the long, long line waiting for turns in the Book Scene Booth.

"You were right about this idea," said Tituba, crossing her arms and taking in the crowd. Sundays were usually among the least crowded days of a convention as people packed up early and tried to beat the traffic outside of Cauldron Cove to head home. Now, not only were few people leaving, the convention had sold out of tickets entirely.

They were operating at max capacity.

"The Comic Enthusiast Society wants

something similar for Comic Hero Con." Nimue scratched the back of her head, her chest flittering with a mixture of pride and dread. "But I don't know…"

"You do know." Tituba nudged her. "Your idea, Soren's implementation, and Bernadette's magic are putting Witchy Expo Services back on the map."

"I wasn't aware we'd ever gotten *off* the map," Nimue said. Conventions were her town's lifeblood. Figuratively and literally.

Tituba's brother, Atlantes, exited the booth with his wife and other two children, as well as his familiar, Sullie, a sleek and miniaturized neon violet Great Dane. He was the only one in his immediate family with a familiar, since warlocks didn't pass on the magic gene. The other two kids squealed and reached out to try to grab Gowdie, too, but he teased them by just barely swooping out of their reach.

"We might have been off the map after the huge scandal." Tituba stepped aside as a group of people tried to make their way down the aisle. Graves croaked from around her feet and leaped up into her open hand. "Well, don't walk around on the floor when there's a crowd," she said to him.

Witches were used to hearing half of conversations like that. Just like familiars were when listening to other familiars talk to their witches or warlocks.

Nimue wondered not for the first time what kinds of things Linden had thought to Dyer right in front of her nose. Maybe, as a former spy, he'd trained his familiar to keep quiet and not respond in thoughts other familiars could pick up on. It would explain why Dyer barely spoke, according to Gowdie—and why she was always so jittery.

Whatever they'd been up to in the war so long ago, it was sure to come out. The esteemed council of Witches and Warlocks of the Greater Midwest had come to collect Linden, after Ren and Nimue had reported his crimes.

Murder and espionage were beyond the scope of Witchy Expo Services's jurisdiction. Zelena's security force was the only law enforcement they had in town.

And even if she had been able to do anything about a criminal among them, Zelena had been in no state to arrest her own husband. She was already scheduling time off for her witness statements, as far back as their days in the Witch Brigade and anything else fishy she'd noticed about him over the years.

She really insisted she hadn't noticed much.

But she'd admitted, with her familiar being as slow as she was and Dyer as quiet as she was—Linden could have been up to *anything* and their familiars wouldn't have chatted about it.

Gowdie, Nimue called to her own familiar, happy not for the first time that they had such an easy relationship.

He did one last pirouette in the sky to delight the children and landed on her shoulder.

Nimue's perma-charm witch network crystal blinked with a message from Cassie to meet her and Ren in the office.

"Have fun at the con," she told Tituba. The catering witch was still keeping an eye on any catering situation that might arise, but with just hours left to go in the con, she'd taken to wandering around with her family. Nimue waved to Atlantes and his wife, Evelyn, who waved back before she slipped down an aisle between booths.

"Hi, Nimue!" said Virgil as she passed between the Delgados' booth and Nicola's Nook. Nicola's booth had been cleared out days before. She'd gone home early and had promised to keep Soren updated on her plans.

She was out of the bookstore game.

Done with authors entirely.

Broken-hearted but in no mood to comfort Sherman Abbott, no matter what he'd been through.

"Packing up?" Nimue asked, stepping over to his booth.

"Oh, just putting together some books for last-minute clearance." Penny smiled at Nimue as she gathered some books off a shelf, arranging them in a box marked "Half Off." It was mostly Sherman Abbott books.

"We're not sure we want to keep selling his stuff." Virgil winced. "I mean, her stuff. Though they're bound to go fast at this price. We've had a lot more requests for his books—his and Rona Brynhild's."

Penny *tsked*. "I still can't believe you were onto something, saying they wrote similarly…"

"Clint is beside himself." Virgil scratched his bearded cheek. "I reached out to him. We're talking again. He's had to deal with all of the blowback. Well, him and Rona's second agent. They teamed up for some press releases."

It was all coming out now, started by press releases from Rona's lawyers after news of her death and exacerbated when more and more women who had intimately known Sherman Abbott came forward. Then the Witches and Warlocks of the Greater Midwest's official statement. The ghostwriting, the secret marriage, the affairs, the murder—the book that gave away too much for a wicked warlock spy's tastes.

No wonder Sherman Abbott books were selling well, along with Rona Brynhild's. His stories had been proven right. Only the true details of that—how Linden insisted it'd been he, alone, on the Brigade who had been up to dastardly deeds—would likely never see the light of day.

Nimue sighed.

"There have already been movie offers," Penny said, heaving the box and letting her husband grab it from her to set up at the front of the table. "Clint said he might ask Virgil and me to meet with a few producers. Tell a firsthand account of what happened here at con." She looked up at Virgil and shrugged. "But Virgil told him we didn't notice a thing!"

"That's witches and warlocks for you," Virgil said, nodding appreciatively at Nimue. "We had no clue."

Nimue frowned. A movie about Rona Brynhild and Sherman Abbott, which no doubt would have to culminate in what had happened at Bookshop Con?

She'd imagined the news about an author's death would keep people away. Not draw even more people to the convention. Well, that, and the not-to-be-missed Book Scene Booth. Luckily, the human media didn't seem to know the role the booth had played in the capture of the criminal.

"Hold on, though," Nimue said. "But who would get money for such a film? Can agents *sell* the rights?"

"Well, Sherman would have a say, and he was Rona's husband. Apparently." Virgil chortled. "And she has no other family, so…"

"*Sherman* is selling the rights?" Nimue gasped.

"*I'd say I can't believe it, but I can believe it.*" Gowdie rustled his wings.

"And with book sales for both *his* and Rona's books soaring now with her death… I guess he won't have to worry about not writing another one." Penny wouldn't have known about Rona's will. Which made Sherman's desire to sell the rights to the sordid true story all the more understandable. Sort of. The bookseller turned her attention to a group that approached the discount box, letting out yelps of surprise as they pulled a Sherman Abbott mystery thriller out of it.

"These are signed?" the middle-aged man asked.

"Well… by Sherman Abbott," Penny said. "And we know—"

"He didn't actually write them." The man chuckled. "I'll take the whole box!"

Virgil lifted an eyebrow but waved a hand at Nimue as she stepped away.

"Big-time authors and their mystique," she heard him say. "Next time, we're only inviting indie authors."

Nimue made it to the lobby, which was still full of guests despite the convention being hours from closing, and was about to head for the teleportation pad. She tossed a look at Humphrey, along with Glinda, called in early from vacation since they were missing the head of the department, and almost ran into a person getting out of the pad in front of her.

"Excuse me!" Shawna Higgins said. Her face blanched when she saw whom she'd almost bumped into. Behind her, the pad flashed black and Lola Jackson stepped through as well. She froze.

"Coming from the hotel?" Nimue asked. "Not anywhere you shouldn't be?" She was teasing. Still, she sort of meant business.

"Yeah... Lola has one more signing." Shawna chewed her lip.

Lola adjusted her purse over her dress. Her attire was bright green today. "So... Is that bookshop owner pressing charges?"

Nimue had almost forgotten about that. "Over the stolen books?"

"We didn't mean to steal—" started Shawna.

Lola held out a hand to cut her off.

"No," Nimue said. "She never even asked about it. Too many other things on her mind. And she's going out of business anyway. We located the books and are shipping them back to her. Since Rona Brynhild books are selling like hotcakes lately, maybe she can recoup some of her losses with the sale of the last of the stock."

"Springy hotcakes," said Gowdie, flexing his talons on her shoulder.

She really needed to get the dragon some hotcakes to dance on.

Tomorrow. Tomorrow she was doing nothing but curling up at home and chatting with Willow after her classes—she'd been in touch, but her daughter insisted she wanted to know every last detail of what had happened, but Nimue had just been too busy to tell her. And after that, she was diving in to a good book.

Maybe not as literally as she had at the convention, but getting lost in the written word offered its own magic, too. To humans as well as witches and warlocks, as Bookshop Con could attest to.

"That's good," said Shawna, wringing her hands together.

"And the employee badge?" Lola asked.

"Returned to its owner. I know you didn't steal that, though you conveniently kept it a bit too long, in my opinion…"

Shawna chewed her lip.

Nimue leaned forward and whispered to the women. "Your secret is safe with me." She leaned back. "Now get out there and enjoy the end of Bookshop Con. Have you tried the Book Scene Booth yet?"

"It's been too crowded," said Lola, offering a flittering smile. "Though I admit I'm tempted."

Nimue stepped backward toward the teleportation pad. "Both of your books are huge hits when people choose a scene!" She winked at Lola. "Might be fun to see one of your book heroes sweep you off your feet."

The portal flashed red and Nimue stepped through, but not before Nimue heard the both of them laughing.

Nimue's boots echoed out over the empty hallway as she approached the Head Witch General Manager's office—her office. Hers and Cassie's and Ren's.

Cassie looked up from her desk and offered a wave. Laveau the ferret lifted his head and nodded as they passed.

"Other boss is in," Cassie reported.

"Good. We'll finally be crossing paths for once," Nimue said as she grabbed the door handle. It was often left open, but Ren must have wanted some peace and quiet. She let herself in.

The books that had been floating over the lobby were back on the bookshelves in the office, minus the Rona Brynhild ones they'd sent off to Nicola.

Nimue's eyes flitted over her copy of *Jane Eyre* and she felt her cheeks rising at the memory of Ren in his Mr. Rochester getup.

Gowdie chuckled and flew across the room, landing on the perch by her desk.

Ren was writing on a file below him, his perma-charm crystal at his wrist scanning as he wrote so whatever information he was working on would be uploaded to the proper place in the network.

Balfour was seated behind Ren, on the back of his chair. She opened one eye, sending a glare toward Gowdie, but she didn't appear to say anything to him before nodding back to sleep. Gowdie ruffled his wings, stretching them.

"You wanted to see me?" Nimue asked. She felt weird standing in front of his desk, like an employee summoned to meet the boss. Remembering herself, she shuffled over to her own desk and pulled the chair out, sitting down.

"Comic Hero Con wants a modified Book Scene Booth, too," he said.

"I know." Nimue folded her hands over the table. "I wonder if it's a good idea."

Ren lifted an eyebrow but didn't look up from the paper. "Why wouldn't it be?"

"Are you sure it's Ren I'm speaking to?"

Sighing, he put his pen down and folded his hands in echo of Nimue, turning his chair just slightly to meet her eye kitty-corner to him. "Obviously, the idea has paid out in spades. I was… wrong to dismiss it."

"Wow, that *is* something. Ren Southern admitting he was wrong?"

Gowdie snickered and Balfour let out a little growl.

"I wouldn't exactly call all of your ideas *right*, considering." He glanced at the books that had been flying over the lobby.

"It would have been fine, if not for Linden…" She chewed her lip. "But I'm sorry. I'm sorry I went ahead and did it without consulting you."

"Soren went ahead and implemented the Book Scene Booth without consulting you. I'm sorry for that, too."

Silence descended over the room.

"You know, I kept thinking you—as in you, Ren—would come back," she said. "During that confrontation with Linden. The spy novel. The Explosion Charm. It was all quite frightening."

"Balfour filled in the gaps," he said.

"And I remember a lot of it anyway…" He blinked hard, swallowing.

"Soren is stronger than he thinks. I wanted to tell him that. I think him staying with me through that ordeal proves it."

"I'll… I'll tell him that." Ren's face grew just a slight bit red.

That was what she'd wanted to tell Soren. That was *all* she'd wanted to tell him.

"You tell yourself that," Gowdie said.

Nimue waved a hand to dismiss him and his giggling. Balfour stared at her with one observant eye.

"So…" Nimue said after the silence had settled. "Ideas for how to tweak the booth?"

Ren cracked the smallest, smallest hint of a smile. "You tell me. You're the creative one."

"You are, too." Nimue pointed at him. "Soren's in there somewhere, and he's as bright and brilliant as you are, in his own way. But you know… I think you're creative, too."

"Oh?" Ren leaned back, steepling his fingers, his smile gone entirely.

"Yeah! I know it was you, not Soren,

under the Befuddlement Charm. You quoted *Jane Eyre*. You only read non-fiction books, my shiny gray shoe."

Ren cleared his throat. "Well, I have many of Soren's memories—"

Nimue crossed the room and took down her copy of *Jane Eyre*. She opened it to the page she'd noticed with the bent corner and put it on the table in front of him. "Why don't you take it home tonight? Finish it on your day off tomorrow?"

Ren flushed. "Why do you think I've read to this page?"

"Soren and I don't *bend pages*," she said. "We use bookmarks like civilized readers." She puffed out her chest, though she was only teasing him.

Ren closed the copy of *Jane Eyre* and slipped it to the side of his paperwork. But he didn't get up and put it back. He didn't deny it had been him who'd bent the page.

Chuckling, Nimue headed back to her desk, patting Gowdie on the head, and settled down to finish the day's tasks.

They had another big convention to

plan, and a number of smaller events before then.

Comic Hero Con had to blow Bookshop Con out of the water—though she could do without the murder this time.

If only that kind of mystery-novel-come-to-life were indeed truly behind her.

JOIN WITCHY EXPO SERVICES IN: IT'S A NERD! WITCH IS SLAIN!

Witchy Expo Services. We host your convention, expo, or trade show—with a dash of magic!

Nimue Toothaker, recently named co-Head Witch General Manager of Witchy Expo Services, is finally getting a handle on the job—and the dual-personality warlock with whom she shares it. While the fallout from the murder at her first convention as manager certainly led to plenty of publicity, she's not eager to repeat the dreadful experience for her largest con yet: Comic Hero Con, which brings in comic book fans and comic hero film buffs from around the world.

The highlight of the con? One of the biggest stars in *the* mega comic hero film franchise of the century. Unfortunately, his real-life persona is nothing like his on-screen one, and it's up to the Witchy Expo Services staff to make sure the neurotic celebrity shows for his advertised con appearances. To make matters worse, the head of the group that booked the Cauldron Cove Convention

Center for the con doesn't know what she wants—but she knows she isn't happy with Nimue and her staff's top-notch efforts.

Juggling two eccentric VIPs is just the start of Nimue's problems when a Cauldron Cove witch turns up dead on the showroom floor. Because of the town's magic, the convention must go on—and Nimue and her co-workers will have to table their grief until they can figure out if there's another murderer in the convention center. It'll take a heroic feat, but they have to beat the villain on the loose before it's too late.

A SPOOKY GAMES CLUB MYSTERY: CURSED WITCH, CUTE BROOMSTICK, SMALL TOWN MYSTERIES

Dahlia Poplar is a genuine witch, an unofficial gofer, and Luna Lane's only cursed resident.

With a werewolf best friend, a vampire ex-boyfriend, and a ghost for a hanger-on, Dahlia is far from the most unusual dweller of her sleepy small town, but she's the only one unable to leave. Dahlia has to perform at least one good deed per day—or she's one step closer to turning to stone.

Fortunately, the residents of Luna Lane have plenty of tasks for Dahlia to complete to avert the curse until Cable Woodward, fetching professor and nephew of her elderly neighbor, stops by for the semester on sabbatical. Attempting to help Cable's uncle work through the trauma of losing his wife, Dahlia uncovers the man's collection of board games, which leads to him reminiscing about the long-forgotten Luna Lane Games Club.

Dahlia reestablishes Games Club, only to find evidence of a number of horrible demises connected to the original group. While trying to uncover the truth about the deaths, Dahlia has to fight off her curse, protect her elderly neighbor from becoming the next victim, and most vexing of all, keep Cable from figuring out Luna Lane's supernatural secrets. Only with eerie board games like these, there may not be a loser — or even a winner—who survives.

Luna Lane's witches, werewolves, and vampires welcome you to the Spooky Games Club—in which even the winners could find themselves six feet under.

ABOUT THE AUTHOR

Amy McNulty is an editor and author of books that run the gamut from YA speculative fiction to contemporary romance. A lifelong fiction fanatic, she fangirls over books, anime, manga, comics, movies, games, and TV shows from her home state of Wisconsin. When not editing her clients' novels, she's busy fulfilling her dream by crafting fantastical worlds of her own.

Sign up for Amy's newsletter to receive news and exclusive information about her current and upcoming projects. Get a free YA romantic sci-fi novelette when you do!

Find her at amymcnulty.com and follow her on social media:

amazon.com / author / amymcnulty

bookbub.com / authors / amy-mcnulty

facebook.com / AmyMcNultyAuthor

twitter.com / mcnultyamy

instagram.com / mcnulty.amy

pinterest.com / authoramymc

ALEXANDRA'S RIDDLE
ELISA KEYSTON

Lose yourself in the magical forests and charming towns of the Pacific Northwest,

where picturesque Victorian homes hide mysteries spanning decades, faeries watch from the trees, and romance awaits... for those bold enough to seek it.

Cass is a drifter. When she inherits an old Queen Anne Victorian in rural Oregon from her great-aunt Alexandra, all she wants is to quickly offload the house and move on to bigger and better things. But the residents of the small town have other plans in mind. Her neighbors are anxious for her to help them thwart the plans of a land developer eager to raze Alexandra's property, while a mysterious girl in the woods needs Cass's help understanding her own confusing, possibly supernatural abilities.

And though little surprises Cass (thanks to her own magical powers of prediction), she never could have anticipated her newfound feelings for the handsome fourth-grade teacher at the local elementary school—feelings that she thought she'd buried long ago. Cass has sworn off love, but Matthew McCarthy is unlike anyone Cass has ever met.

If she isn't careful, he could learn her secret. Or worse—he just might thaw her frozen heart.

But falling in love could spell danger for both of them. Because it's not just the human residents of Riddle that have snared Cass in their web. Cass's presence has caught the attention of the fae that dwell in the woods. They know she has the Sight, and they don't want to let her go...

With its unique blend of small-town romance, cozy mystery, and light fantasy, the Northwest Magic series is sure to delight anyone who believes in faery gifts and happily-ever-afters.

Bianca Wallace is a work from home mom raising her teenage daughter as a single parent. She's determined to stand on her own two feet in Edenville, Texas after her bitter divorce. When the town's wedding of the year stars her friend as the bride, Bianca can't wait to celebrate the nuptials. Neither she nor the guests expect a corpse! When the police suspect the bride, Bianca's determined to prove her friend's innocence.

Lamar Sims, the new police detective in Edenville, is investigating the murder case. Bianca's "interference" is not helping, but she won't stop when her friend's freedom is on the line. He makes it clear he wants her to let the police do their job, so she has to find ways around him.

No one in Edenville is safe until the killer is behind bars. Bianca won't let Detective Sims dismiss her hunches. They may have to work together before another dead body shows up.

YA BOOKS BY AMY MCNULTY

The Never Veil Series:

Nobody's Goddess

Nobody's Lady

Nobody's Pawn

The Blood, Bloom, & Water Series:

Fangs & Fins

Salt & Venom

Iron & Aqua

Tears & Cruor

Vines & Florets

The Fall Far from the Tree Duology:

Fall Far from the Tree

Turn to Dust and Ashes

Ballad of the Beanstalk

Josie's Coat